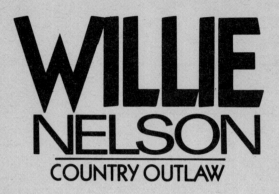

WILLIE NELSON
COUNTRY OUTLAW

BY LOLA SCOBEY

ZEBRA BOOKS
KENSINGTON PUBLISHING CORP.

ZEBRA BOOKS

are published by

KENSINGTON PUBLISHING CORP.
475 Park Avenue South
New York, N.Y. 10016

CONTENTS

You are about to begin reading the second biography of Willie Nelson. The first, Willie says, is written in his songs.

"I have done it *all*."
                    Willie Nelson

LIFE IS JUST A BOWL OF CHERRIES

Everybody was getting rich quick.

America was betting on America, and, in 1927, the speculative boom exploded wide open.

"The important thing is to know when to get aboard," preached Arthur Brisbane, earning $200,000 a year dishing out financial advice in the Hearst newspapers. *"Get aboard!"*

When he couldn't get in touch with his regular advisor, Groucho Marx took stock-market tips from an elevator operator in the Copley Plaza Hotel in New York.

A nurse made $30,000 by investing on tips she got from grateful patients.

A valet played the market and made a quarter of a million dollars.

When Wall Street's biggest operator, William C. Durant traveled to Europe, he would place transatlantic phone calls to Wall Street a dozen times a day at a cost of as much as $25,000 a week.

A. Atwater Kent, making millions by manufacturing radios, scolded his wife, "Mabel, you just aren't spending enough money!"

In a seven-month period, the stock of the Radio Corporation of America (RCA) rose over four hundred points. Buying on margin with a piddling $1,000 in cash, an investor could have picked up one hundred shares in May, sold out in September, and pocketed a cool $40,000.

In 1927, Ira Doyle Nelson, fourteen, and Myrle Greenhow, thirteen, soon to be wed, were just a couple of country kids in backwoods Arkansas, almost out of earshot of the roar of the roaring '20s. But country music itself was arising in a period of profits, power, bigness, riches, optimism, and success. Forces were afoot.

That same year an enterprising man named Peer was up on the high border between Tennessee and Virginia scouting out some of the world's most amazing hillbilly recording artists for the Victor Talking Machine Company. Another enterprising young man named Wills, had made himself a star fiddler on three different radio stations in Fort Worth, Texas, and was hatching plans. Ira Nelson, himself, had a gleam in his eye, and Myrle Greenhow had an itch in her soul.

Only Ira and Myrle would ever come together in body, but—like characters in a Dickens novel, living in the best of times and the worst of times—the destinies of Peer, Wills, Ira, and Myrle were intertwined; their legacies fated to meet in spirit in the form of a red-headed baby boy named Willie Hugh Nelson, as yet just an unsung melody in the great mind of God.

SPEAK OF THE DEVIL

Top Records—1928

"T for Texas"
Jimmie Rodgers

"Bury Me under the Weeping Willow"
The Carter Family

In the sticky heat of early August, 1927, Ralph Peer, age twenty-seven, traveled with a mobile record-making crew to the city of Bristol, which was split right down the middle by the Tennessee/Virginia border. Placing a front-page ad in the *Bristol Herald*, he invited local musicians to auditions that could lead to a contract with the Victor record label: MOUNTAIN SONGS RECORDED HERE BY VICTOR COMPANY, the headline announced.

Word spread like wild fire through the isolated Clinch Mountains, and overnight Peer was besieged by eager hillbilly musicians pouring out of the "hollers" in response to his ad.

For four hot muggy days, Peer and his crew recorded with their primitive equipment on the stuffy top floor of a three-story building on Bristol's Tennessee side. At least one highly promising trio showed up, but some of the other flotsam and jetsam, like a skinny young city detective from Asheville, who had been kicked out of his own band right before their recording session, didn't look so inspiring.

The trio called themselves The Carter Family. The man was named Rodgers—Jimmie Rodgers.

Nonetheless, Peer, endless repository of entrepreneurial enthusiasm (credited in 1923 with making the first commercial recording of a hillbilly performer), offered recording contracts to both acts.

In so doing, Peer unwittingly provided the first national arena for a battle of the bands that still rages today—that is, the neck-and-neck battle between God and the Devil, waged on the turf of country music, for the eternal souls of working-class America.

Singing in three-part harmony learned right at the foot of Jesus, The Carter Family stood, musically, for everything right, good, and true this side of heaven.

Jug-eared, tall, handsome A. P. Carter; his buxom, dark-eyed wife Sara; and their gentle, blue-eyed sister-in-law Maybelle, were marvelous musicians, honest and real, who sang songs learned in the rustic churches and schools deep in the Clinch Mountains. A. P., who had a soul-stirring way of coming in with his bass harmony when the spirit moved him or when the song needed a lift, had been raised in a fundamentalist home so strict they wouldn't even let the boy own a fiddle.

The Carters' music preached the soul-saving virtues

16

of home, hearth, decent living, and prudent dying. In later years, as their popularity soared, they earnestly promoted their shows as "morally good" entertainment.

For rural folks raised on turnip greens and the Ten Commandments, listening to The Carter Family's "Album of Old Family Melodies" was as edifying as going to Wednesday-night prayer meetings. And in answer to prayer (Ralph Peer's, no doubt), The Carter Family was a hit from record one.

Jimmie Rodgers, however, was a dark horse of a much different color. In the first place, the day before their recording session, the Jimmie Rodgers Entertainers kicked Jimmie Rodgers out of his own band and changed their name. When they showed up without Rodgers, Ralph Peer went right ahead and recorded them anyway.

Although badly shaken, Rodgers was not to be daunted. He couldn't be—he was semidesperate. Two years before meeting Peer, Rodgers had been told he was afflicted with tuberculosis. .

Tuberculosis was the young detective's second bad break. When he was just a tyke of four, his mother had died. Trailing along with his dad, a section boss for the Mobile and Ohio Railroad, the little boy had roamed railroad construction sites across the nation.

He'd met every breed of human being, spent nights around hobo campfires, witnessed the tragedy of train wrecks, listened to the Negro work gangs chant out a steady tempo as they pounded out the rails that were pulling America together. Black men had taught him to play guitar and banjo. At age fourteen, he had his last brush with school and started working full-time as

17

a railroad water boy.

Fourteen years later, when the hacking and coughing got too bad, and he suffered a nearly fatal pulmonary hemorrhage, he was forced to quit the tough railroad life. He fell back on music, landed a job as a blackface comedian on the medicine-show circuit, plucked a little ukulele in a Hawaiian band, crooned some Crosby tunes—nothing solid.

When he spotted Peer's ad in the paper, Rodgers was thirty years old, with a disease that was probably going to kill him, and with a young wife to support. He desperately needed to win Peer over.

Although already starting to lose his hair at thirty, Rodgers was graced with bright, boyish eyes and a wide, winning grin. Sauntering over from his cheap hotel, he climbed up the two flights of stairs to Peer's domain. Fast talking and grinning, he finally badgered the extremely reluctant Peer into recording one record on him. His pleas for a second record were cut short by a coughing fit.

Luckily, the first record sold just barely well enough to earn him a second recording session. This time Peer suggested they cut some of the songs Rodgers and his sister had been writing. In Camden, New Jersey, they recorded a Rodgers-penned blue yodel called "T for Texas (T for Tennessee)." Each three-line stanza of the song ended with a high-pitched, quavering yodel. The record was a smash.

Quickly becoming known as "The Singing Brakeman," Rodgers began releasing a string of captivating records glorifying the foot-loose, carefree life of the hobo; the fast-moving, lonesome world of the railroad man; the independent, rough-riding existence of the cowboy; the magnetic allure of the open road.

So there the country folks sat each night, the fields outside dark, the kerosene lantern turned high, the radio on. Thanks to Ralph Peer, Jimmie Rodgers was yodeling about living it up on the road to parts unknown, and The Carter Family was harmonizing about toughing it out on the road to heaven above.

Those radio waves carried the first nationwide signal of what, to this day, is an unresolved conflict for boys and girls raised all across the Southern Bible Belt, as that hellfire-and-damnation fundamentalist Protestant region is known. Namely, the kids who liked their chicken fried a little hotter, their grits sugared a little sweeter, kept getting the urge to get off the farm, to get out of the house—and keep going.

Home, Sunday school taught, was the spiritually safe, securely sanctified realm where Mamma, who realized what a friend we have in Jesus, darned socks, cooked for the sick and shut-ins, and listened to The Carter Family singing on the Philco. Home was where a person ought to be to guarantee the salvation of his immortal soul.

Hitchhiking out on the road somewhere—anywhere—with Jimmie, though, was where a person was dying to be. Where the Devil might pull over, swing open the door, and offer you a ride at any time. And, God save your holy spirit, you'd probably give up and get into his fiery chariot.

It was hard to be southern, country, and fundamentalist—your eternal soul raised on the un-moving Rock of Ages, while your profane feet itched to tap-dance to the song of the open road. It was hard to be good, even when you knew in your heart your sins would surely find you out. And it was especially hard for a farm kid to get the words out that could explain all those mixed-up feelings to the slick kids like the flappers and ragtimers—the ones who were so crazy about "Rhapsody in Blue" and Rudy Vallee. Had Bing Crosby ever taken another man's wife and paid the price in sin and misery?

The immortal battle between sin and salvation, between home and highway, that Ralph Peer put into motion in country music when he recorded Jimmie Rodgers and The Carter Family on the same day, is an unending celestial skirmish.

When Hank Thompson canonized cheap whiskey and loose women in "The Wild Side of Life," protesting he "didn't know God made honky-tonk angels," it was up to Kitty Wells to become queen of country music by poignantly informing him "It Wasn't God Who Make Honky-Tonk Angels."

Even in the 1960s, when the times had become hip and cool, a rural southerner couldn't escape his schizophrenic heritage. Gram Parsons, born in Waycross, Georgia, paved the way for the soon-coming explosive fusion between rock and country music. But despite his role as an innovator, Bud Scoppa of *Rolling Stone* revealed that Parson's "central theme" musically "has always been that of the innocent southern boy tossed between the staunch traditions and strict moral code he was born to, and the complex, ambiguous modern world."

And the man today credited with fulfilling Parson's legacy by opening the riches of country music to the long-haired, dope-smoking fans of rock and roll, sits uneasily at the peak of his country music stardom, still trying to redeem his footloose soul, still trying to resolve whether he's destined to save sinners or sin with the saved, whether life is the devilish headache of a "Bloody Mary Morning," or full God's "Amazing Grace."

WILL THE CIRCLE BE UNBROKEN?

"I was relieved when the Crash came. I was released. Being in business was something I detested. When I found that I could sell a song or a poem, I became me. I became alive. Other people didn't see it that way. They were throwing themselves out of windows."

> Yip Harburg, songwriter
> "Brother Can You Spare a Dime?"

Ira Doyle Nelson was barely shaving at age sixteen when he took a budding fifteen-year-old girl in marriage, and moved with his mamma and daddy one state west from Arkansas to Abbott, Texas.

That same year in Milwaukee, a millionaire businessman committed suicide and left a note willing his body to science, his soul to U.S. Treasury Secretary Andrew Mellon, and his sympathy to his creditors.

A popular joke told how two men jumped hand in hand from an upper story of the Ritz Hotel, because they had a joint bank account.

It was 1929. "I'm afraid," said steel magnate Charles M. Schwab. "Every man is afraid."

The Great Depression postponed 800,000 marriages that would have occurred sooner, if it had not been for hard times. But for Ira and his bride, Myrle, a couple of hillbilly kids isolated deep in the Ozarks but full of the hunger to love and start living, there was no holding back.

In 1929 Myrle Greenhow Nelson, a fetching girl with a streak of wildness behind her eyes and a restlessness under her feet, moved to Texas with a bunch of new relatives and a fancy new name. But, in months, Myrle also found herself in that most mundane of situations—she was pregnant.

Three years later, in 1932, the Depression hit rock bottom. Frantic businessmen scrambled for new ways to boost sagging sales. In Fort Worth, Texas, the Light Crust Flour Company decided to hire a local band named Aladdin's Laddies to broadcast for them over KFJZ Radio (and to work on the side as truck drivers and unloaders). The company changed the group's name to the Light Crust Doughboys.

The band was a terrific deal for the flour company, because it included a charismatic fiddle player named Bob Wills, born Jim Robert Wills and dirt poor in Turkey, Texas, in 1906. A staff fiddler on three radio stations at the time the Doughboys came into being, Wills's magnetic personality outshone even his sparkling old-time fiddle playing.

The Doughboys were a swinging, jazz-influenced band who dished up a rhythmically infectious music just made for dancing. Their sound was a potpourri of hot licks—blues, Cajun, country, jazz, and pop.

Broadcasting two thousand, three thousand miles west of the closed-in southeastern mountains and Ralph Peer's recording equipment, the Doughboys were sending out music made for people who lived in flat, dusty, sunburned country where you could squint your eyes, peer off in any direction, and hardly see any other folks at all; music for people buffeted on all sides by gritty, howling winds, rather than wrapped in snug, Appalachian hills.

It was music for families thinly spread across miles of prairie who needed to get together and socialize with their neighbors. And, out west, most everybody's neighbors loved to dance—the French Arcadians, the Mexicans, the Germans, the Czechs, the Poles, the Blacks—even the Christians liked to dance, to swing. Seemed like the wide-open spaces had somehow gotten a hold on some of the "saved" out in those parts.

The Doughboys called their cowboy-orchestra music "western swing," and they played it to go with the body-hugging two-step, not the chaste square dance of the southeast; to go with drinking, with "lettin' go."

Ira Nelson was a pretty fair fiddle player and guitar player himself, but unless you were one of the best, or had your own radio show, a country musician was lucky to make seventy-five cents or a dollar a night.

Decca, Victor, Bluebird, Vocalion, all the nation's record companies sold only a scarcely mentionable six million records in 1932. Before the Crash in 1927, when Ralph Peer was so eagerly signing up new recording artists, record lovers had snapped up a whopping one hundred and four million records.

One artist who sold right on through the Crash, into the worst days of the Depression when people had precious few pennies to spend, was Peer's discovery, the amazing Jimmie Rodgers. In the six years since his first recording session, Rodgers had sold an incredible five million records all by himself.

Idolized as a rambling renegade and blue-yodeling hobo hero, afflicted with the "romantic" disease of poets and artists, Rodgers possessed a mystique that was engulfing him even in his own lifetime. Crowds swarmed around the frail figure, often outfitted in a cowboy suit or brakeman's uniform, reaching out just to touch the clothes hanging loose on his deteriorating body. Jimmie Rodgers, symbol of America's mania for moving on, was country music's first genuine solo singing star.

Musically, he never failed to be a leader, an innovator. His records ranged freely over all kinds of songs and featured offbeat musical instruments and arrangements. Equally liberal in the men who made up his friends, Rodgers counted among his pals everybody from celebrities like Will Rogers to simple bums.

But he was dying. In order to pay medical bills, he had been forced to sell "Blue Yodeler's Paradise," the $50,000 mansion he'd built in Kerrville, Texas, for his wife.

In 1932, when the Light Crust Doughboys debuted on KFJZ, Jimmie Rodgers and The Carter Family recorded together for the first time. Rodgers was so weak, it was all he could do to just sing. Maybelle Carter had to play guitar for him, imitating his style exactly, so record listeners would think it was Jimmie playing.

Meanwhile, tapping her foot to the radio in Abbott, Texas, listening to records of the Doughboys and Jimmie Rodgers, Myrle Nelson was now eighteen and pregnant again. She and Ira had been married three years, and had a sweet little two-year-old daughter named Bobbie Lee.

Ira took any paying jobs he could get to make ends meet. Sometimes there was cotton-picking in the area, and Ira was a whiz at tinkering with cranky farm equipment that its owners, deeply in debt, desperately needed to keep running.

Of course, even rich guys were scrambling. Jack Dempsey, former heavyweight champion of the world, got so strapped for cash, at the age of thirty-six he got himself in shape enough to fight fifty-six exhibition bouts. Babe Ruth tried to supplement his chronic big spending by opening a clothing store on Broadway, but lost his shirt after five months. Hit songwriter Frank Loesser's parents lost all their money, and he got a job screwing tops on bottles of insecticide.

Sadly, Jimmie Rodgers' problems were far more than financial. But he didn't give up, till the end. Rising from his bed for one last recording session, he sang, retreating in exhaustion to a cot between takes. Two days after that session, Jimmie Rodgers died in the Taft Hotel in downtown Manhattan. The year was 1933.

The nation, in the final throes of a twenty-four-year-old battle between religiosity and reality, hung up between the home and the speak-easy, and desperate for a drink, breathed a sigh of relief and repealed Prohibition. The year was 1933.

Guided by his own strong vision of what a band ought to be, Bob Wills, his banjo-strumming brother Johnny Lee, and Tommy Duncan, the singer who reminded you of old Bing himself, left the Light Crust Doughboys. Wills formed a new band with his brother and Duncan and named it the Playboys. The year was 1933.

A. P. Carter, having established The Carter Family across the nation, separated from his wife Sara, proving that the highway to heaven is a rocky road. The year was 1933.

Jimmie Rodgers, king of the road, was dead; the drinks were on the house; Bob Wills was fixing to take Texas to the honky-tonk; and A. P. and Sara had let the devil come between them.

On April 30, at 1:40 A.M., Myrle Nelson gave birth to a red-headed baby boy. She and Ira named him Willie Hugh. The year was 1933.

FAMILY BIBLE

1934 — Gene Autry moves to Hollywood
1935 — Elvis Presley, Jerry Lee Lewis born
1936 — Glen Campbell, Roger Miller, Kris
        Kristofferson born
1938 — Roy Acuff joins the Grand Ole Opry
1939 — Bob Wills has number-one record,
        "San Antonio Rose"

Myrle could start walking east along Farm Road 1242, stroll into downtown Abbott, saunter along a few minutes, leave downtown Abbott, keep going straight across the railroad tracks, cut out across a field, turn herself around, and see the whole little town just sitting there on the pancake-flat land like some solitary set in a cheap western movie.

During aimless afternoons Myrle might stand in the broiling sun at the end of the main street, right on the railroad tracks — turn and look off to her left, turn and look off to her right, and watch the tracks curving off into the distance, the telegraph poles shrinking smaller and smaller as far as her eye could see.

Heading back to the house, kicking her shoes along in the dust down the center of town, she would pass the new barbershop on the left, dry goods on the right, post office on the left, gas station on the right, cash grocery on the left, then the main intersection: Methodist Church to the left front, Baptist Church to the right front, Church of Christ on the right behind. Walk a few more blocks past some board-sided houses, past cotton fields stretching straight out to jam into the horizon, past a dusty road or two. So be it—Abbott, Texas.

It was more than Myrle Nelson, age nineteen, and the mother of two, could stand.

Despite the hard times that had plagued Ozark mountain people all during the 1920s, when she and Ira had moved from Marion County, Arkansas, to Texas in 1929, they had cut spiffy figures. Posing for a photographer around that time, Ira, though short for a man, stood tall and slim beside Myrle, sporting a good-looking leather jacket and tie, a Stetson, and cowboy boots.

Round-faced, chubby-cheeked Myrle, hair in a frizzy perm, appeared more fancy—dark suit with satiny trim, flouncy blouse, flowery hat, and perky shoes with cut-out toes. Ira looked as if he would turn the girls' heads at a honky-tonk down in Waco. Myrle looked as if she would turn the men's heads at a speakeasy up in Fort Worth.

When Myrle and Ira and the rest of the Nelson clan moved to central Texas, they all promptly joined the Abbott Methodist Church. From the turn of the century, back in the archaically conservative Ozarks, the Nelsons, as a group, had been active churchgoers. It was simply one of those things you married into.

But outspoken Myrle had a cocklebur in her soul. She just felt an urge to be free and alive and "out there," that the finer folks of Abbott, gossiping in their parlors, drinking coffee in their overstuffed chairs with the starched, crocheted doilies pinned to the arms, doubtless found hard to understand.

When Willie Hugh was two, and Bobbie Lee was five, Myrle left Abbott to look for a job and didn't come back.

"When the kids were young," Myrle told her home-town newspaper forty-five years later, "I left them with their daddy's folks, because I knew they'd take them to church and Sunday school. I wanted them to stay right there in Abbott, Texas, until they finished high school, rather than be out on the road with me. I wanted them to stay out of my kind of life—the restaurants and the bars."

Within the year, Myrle was a divorcee—a "grass widow," as polite folks called it then. Well, maybe she'd been married seven years, and maybe she had a couple of kids, but Myrle Greenhow Nelson, at twenty-two, was still a girl who knew how to put her best foot forward.

Restless and self-assured, Myrle set out to find herself a sizable chunk of life. She joined a be-wildered, demoralized, wandering multitude set loose by the Great Depression. Although Americans have al-ways been foot-loose, the Depression created a new kind of wanderer—hungry, discouraged nomads seek-ing escape from intolerable economic and mental pressures at home.

During the early part of the century, a single,

traveling woman looking for work would have been conspicuous and suspect. In 1935, Myrle was just one of hundreds of thousands.

Jobs were mind-bendingly hard to come by. In Birmingham, Alabama, the city advertised for seven-hundred-fifty men to dig a public canal. Over 12,000 hopefuls applied. By 1932 the average hourly manu-facturing wage was down to fifty-five cents an hour, and in the world of restaurants and bars where Myrle sought her fortune, there was no set wage. Twenty-one-year-old Ernest Tubb, later to be one of Myrle's two-year-old son's greatest heroes, was playing guitar and singing in Texas-oil-field honky-tonks for $1.25 a night.

Nonetheless, Myrle somehow made her way for about a year. Then she turned around and headed back to Abbott—still young, still restless, but now mortally scared. Doctors said she had cancer and was going to die.

Terror-stricken and morose, she came back to Ab-bott wanting to teach little Willie a song to remember her by after her death: "I'll Be Gone When You Read This Last Letter From Me."

When doctors proved able to cut out the cancer, Myrle promptly turned her back on Abbott and hit the road again, lining up for jobs as a waitress or dancer in clubs and cafés all over Texas. When a sec-ond marriage hit the rocks, she moved to Seminole, Oklahoma. Working her way through the steamy night life of cowhands and oil roustabouts, she even-tually ended up in the Pacific Northwest.

Good-natured Ira, a skilled mechanic, sometime farmhand, and musician was only twenty-four, and eager to start life over again.

One afternoon, working on a gravel haul in Abbott, Ira spotted a couple of good-looking girls walking along the road. Braking the big gravel truck, he pulled up alongside them, and offered the girls a ride. The short, cute one with black hair didn't much like the idea of taking a ride from a strange man, but her girl friend, all eager-eyed, talked her into climbing up into the cab next to Ira.

Soon after, Ira married cute, lively, dark-haired Lorraine.

Lorraine's own daddy was dead, and she felt sorry for little Willie and Bobbie, growing up without a mamma, so, at first, the newlyweds set up housekeeping in Abbott. But soon Lorraine and Ira had two boys of their own, Doyle and Charles. One day Ira loaded up his new family in a pickup truck and they started moving around—Amarillo, Levelland, Houston, Cleburne. They ended up in Fort Worth where Ira landed a job as an auto mechanic.

As their parents pursued new lives and loves, Willie and Bobbie were taken in by Ira's parents, Mama and Daddy Nelson, a warm, religious, down-to-earth rural couple in their 50s.

For Willie's grandparents, both big-boned, heavy-set, friendly people with thirty-five years of hard work behind them, and their three grown kids finally raised, the 1930s were tough times to be taking on two new little children. Some seventy percent of the citizens of Texas in those days lived on farms or in small communities like Abbott, dependent on farming. The double whammy of the Depression and the dust-bowl drought had nearly devastated their lives.

But, in their own way, the Nelsons were a rather exceptional pair; and, if nothing else, they possessed two very important qualities: spunk and love—love for each other and love for God. When Christians held fast to God's unchanging hands, as the Nelsons had for years, life was often dead hard, but not complicated. Heaven was above and hell was below. Right was right and wrong was wrong. Religion was pure and undefiled. It gave you the strength to carry on.

So, without hesitation, Mama and Daddy Nelson welcomed Bobbie and Willie into their modest home filled with warmth, old-fashioned faith, laughter, music, and affection.

In some ways, the older couple may have felt a special closeness to Ira's two tykes. Bobbie, a quiet little girl with a mass of thick brown hair, was nearing first grade and already possessed many of the traits she would carry through high-school days. She spoke in a light, singsong country accent, head cocked to the left, shyly smiling a straight, demure little smile. Mama Nelson had a lovely, quiet manner herself, and in later years, neighbors would comment on the similarity between grandmother and granddaughter.

Willie, with his big, round, brown eyes and thick shock of bright, red hair, had a wide grin that looked like the smile on a "have a nice day" button. His ears kind of stuck out like his daddy's, and he could win you over in a cowpoke minute. Willie was named after his granddad, William Alfred Nelson.

William Alfred Nelson had only made it through second grade, but he was a smart man, immensely friendly and cheerful. Although dressed in the rough coveralls and work shirt of a farmer, he was a beautiful and eloquent letter writer, a man always looking for ways to better himself and rise above his limited education.

He had married Nancy Elizabeth Smothers on a cold day in the winter of 1900 in Marion County, Arkansas. The hard-working teen-agers had spent the early years of their marriage homesteading forty acres of hilly, backwoods land in neighboring Searcy County, right on the north edge of the Ozarks.

Culturally and geographically, this remote world of narrow creek valleys and rocky ridges, still clinging to customs from a prior century, was very much like the Clinch Mountains of Virginia where the members of The Carter Family grew up. Rigidly fundamentalist in religion, the Ozarks were populated by grim-faced mountaineers who attended strict, hell-fearing churches of the Baptist, Methodist, or Church of Christ conviction.

Despite the natural beauty of the sweet-smelling azaleas and hearty red oaks growing in profusion, the soil was agriculturally depleted, and life consisted of just getting by. The dominant money-making crop was "shoetop cotton," so named because farmers had to stoop to pick the scant lint from scrubby plants growing on the barren mountain sides.

In the years from 1920 to 1940, the area lost all its cotton gins but one, and the economic prospects became even more dire. In 1929, with their three children (Clara, Rosa, and Ira) grown, William and Nancy and their clan moved to Abbott, to the cotton-farming country north of Waco, to find better fortunes. Unfortunately, those were desperate days to be heading for Texas.

A one-time breaker of horses, Nelson took up black-smithing in Abbott. But old-fashioned forge-and-hammer blacksmiths were a dime a dozen then, and competition was stiff. The Nelsons were poor, even poorer than their neighbors.

Willie's grandparents' house, close to downtown and just across a dirt alley from the local ecumenical "tabernacle," had no electricity; its walls were papered with cardboard and newsprint to keep out the cold northers that rolled in from west Texas. The couple raised their own pigs and chickens for food, and had a cow for milk.

Despite the poverty, all those in the newly formed little Nelson household had their dreams. Mama and Daddy Nelson wanted mail-order music degrees. Little Willie wanted to be a cowboy singing star, and Bobbie, well, Bobbie was so sweet and quiet everybody just wanted her to have whatever she wanted.

Willie and Bobbie were fascinated to watch Mama and Daddy Nelson hard at work each night over their mail-order music correspondence courses. The aging farm couple wanted to learn how to teach music, and aware that the Lord helps those who help themselves, applied themselves diligently.

Just four years old at the time, Willie still remembers seeing his grandparents getting their lessons ready to mail back to school the next day. "They used to sit up all night," he marvels, "studying their music under a kerosene lamp. They were both tickled to death when they finally got their degrees."

An avid and creative student, Mama Nelson soon developed her own theory of music. "Music," she announced to the household, "is anything that is pleasing to the ear."

To get a jump on the book learning, Mama Nelson also decided to start practicing her teaching ability on six-year-old Bobbie. Every night after supper, under the kerosene lamp, Mama Nelson instructed first-grader Bobbie in piano. The little girl proved to a surprisingly apt pupil.

"My grandmother told me how to read music," Bobbie recently told writer Joan Ackerman-Blount. "My first piano book was a Methodist hymnal. She said, 'These are the lines and the spaces up here, and these are the lines and the spaces down here.' It made sense to me right away."

Throughout the Ozark valleys, hymns had always been the most popular songs, and Mama Nelson's lessons concentrated on music appropriate to be a devoted, Methodist household. The first complete song Bobbie learned to play was "Jesus, Lover of My Soul."

Not to neglect "Little Red," as the family nicknamed Willie, Mama Nelson started coaching him in "expression"—short poems that children were taught to recite in a convincingly theatrical manner. After due training, she decided Willie, still just four, was ready for his first public appearance.

Having selected an all-day gospel singing and dinner as the grounds for bright-eyed Willie's debut, his proud grandma got her red-headed protégé all dressed up in a spanking white sailor suit.

As the all-day event wore on, Willie, wiggling impatiently on a hard church pew while chorus after chorus of gospel hymns rolled over his head, started fidgeting and picking his nose.

Just as a stream of blood started gushing down his tiny upper lip, Willie was summoned to the front. Frantic, he stumbled up to the podium, half his face buried in a small, cupped hand hopelessly trying to protect his new, white sailor suit from disaster. Miserably he mumbled:

> "What are you looking at me for?
> I ain't got nothing to say.
> If you don't like the looks of me,
> You can look some other way."

By the time he finished, his suit was a mess, and Willie, veteran of his first performance, was a four-year-old wreck. "I think everybody was glad when I sat down," he sighs. "I know I was."

But under the encouragement of Daddy Nelson, who kept pushing his two grandchildren to step out and make something of themselves, life on stage (sanctified, not secular, of course), quickly improved.

Willie's house was a short block down from the main intersection of Abbott, dotted with Protestant churches on three of four corners. ("The Catholics were across town; we never talked to them," he grins.)

On Sunday mornings at the trim, white Methodist Church right up the street, Daddy Nelson puffed up with loving pride as Little Red would come stand beside him and enthusiastically pipe out hymns in a high, thin voice. ("I don't ever remember having stage fright," Willie says.)

On special days, the big, jovial blacksmith, his preschool grandson trotting alongside, would go over to the county courthouse and meet up with Christians from all over the area in the high-ceilinged courtroom for an all-day gospel sing-along. As the saints burst forth with soul-stirring rounds of four-part harmony, Willie would march manfully to the front with his granddad and lead favorites from the Stamps Quartet hymn books.

Eventually Daddy Nelson even convinced retiring Bobbie to come along and play piano for the all-day gospel sings. "You might be able to make yourself a living doing this someday," he cajoled her.

But Willie's music world was rapidly expanding beyond gospel-singing conventions. By the time Willie entered school, he had discovered Saturday had it all over Sunday as the greatest day on the face of the earth.

Saturday meant cowboy serials—crisp, hot popcorn with salt; munching away in the dark, eyes big and round as the end of a rifle barrel; cheering on Gene and Roy and Ray Whitley as they chased runaway stages, saved the Melody Ranch from certain destruction, serenaded the girls, and blasted the bad guys to kingdom come.

Ol' Gene Autry was keen—he could sit on a horse and sing at the same time. Cocksure Willie was confident he could do that, too. "The Last Round-up," "Tumbling Tumbleweeds," all the cowboy songs— Willie learned them and practiced them around the house. It was an important step in being a real cowboy. "Those were my heroes when I was growing up," Willie admits fondly, "and I think every little kid I knew thought the greatest thing in the world would be to be in the movies."

'Course, if you were gonna be a cowboy and get

yourself in the movies, Willie knew you sure did need a guitar. The Sears and Roebuck catalog had some sharp ones any boy would be proud to own—like the Gene Autry Round-up beauty, or the Melody Ranch model.

One day, in a perceptive gesture designed to warm the cockles of a cowboy's heart, Daddy Nelson went out and bought Willie a Stella guitar, thumbpick, and chord book. Soon, at night, while Mama Nelson and Bobbie practiced piano, Daddy Nelson started showing Willie a few chords on the guitar.

Daddy Nelson wanted to help Willie become a really good guitar player. Maybe, he thought, Little Red and Bobbie could make themselves a living someday playing together at tent revivals. But in 1939, when Willie was six, the little family, growing ever closer, was suddenly dealt a crushing blow. Daddy Nelson died.

The Nelson clan was stricken, and bewildered Willie, for the second time in his brief six years, had lost the central male figure in his life.

Mama Nelson was full of her own sorrow, but with a huge, comforting lap for a grieving little boy to cuddle up in, she quickly became the primary adult—and the only reliably stable one—in Willie's precarious world.

It was not that Willie and Bobbie and Mama Nelson were all alone. The geographically extended Nelson clan was an ever-present and sociable moving feast. Aunts Clara and Rosa, Ira's sisters, were always dropping in and out. The whole family would get together for picnic reunions down in Waco to swim and eat watermelon on hot days. Ira and Lorraine would come visit and bring half brother Doyle, jauntily dressed up in a little soldier suit, to play with Bobbie and Willie.

But to Willie—abandoned by his parents, robbed by the death of his granddaddy—now, more than ever, Mama Nelson was the emotional rock. It was on this rock that Willie built the basic, formative attitudes of his life. If Willie could not forever believe every word of the family Bible on which Mama Nelson stood, he could always believe in Mama Nelson's life and in her love.

Willie's first important song, "Family Bible," portrays life under Mama Nelson's guiding hand; a touching family photo album complied by Willie's daughter for his forty-seventh birthday is dedicated to Mama Nelson; and the intensely personal gospel album, "Family Bible" was recorded by Willie and Bobbie as a tribute to Mama Nelson.

But those were the loving thoughts of the future. In 1939, God had taken Daddy Nelson to his heavenly reward, and it was just Mama Nelson and Bobbie and Willie who had to go back home to what seemed a very empty house, and pick up the pieces, pick up the tempo, and keep going on.

TEXAS IN MY SOUL

December 7, 1941 — Pearl Harbor
1943 — Ernest Tubb joins the Grand Ole Opry
1943 — Frank Sinatra joins "Your Hit Parade"

After Daddy Nelson died, Willie, age seven, started writing cheating songs.

When Willie was seven, however, the infidelities of love were a taboo subject, off-limits even for adult country songwriters. Nice people, you see, didn't discuss such things in public.

It wasn't until six years later that a song called "One Has My Name, the Other Has My Heart" would admit to the world that the war in Europe had pulled a lot of bewildered boys away from their sweethearts down on the farm and into the fickle arms of sweet city women.

Of course, at age seven, Willie had never yet met a sweet city woman, and even now he's still baffled over how those love triangles originated in his as-yet-untantalized mind. "Maybe I got it from soap operas on the radio," he muses.

Willie has always possessed a depressingly effective

gift for writing about the unfair, perplexing side of life. "That was what was so strange," he puzzles. "I always seemed able to write about the sad side of everything. It was always easy for me."

However obvious the reasons for his empathy for sadness to the outside observer, in Willie's own mind, they were buried deep. He recalls his school days after Daddy Nelson died as happy times, filled with music, sports, movies, and the radio.

A likable, outgoing kid, Willie was quiet-spoken, but hardly shy. Wearing striped union overalls, sometimes rolled up to his skinny knees, Willie seemed to be everywhere, all over town.

His taste in movies now encompassed the deliciously nasty snarled-lip gangsters like Humphrey Bogart, James Cagney, and George Raft. On sultry afternoons when they weren't in the cool, dark movie house, Willie and his pals liked to skinny-dip in the cattle ponds around Abbott.

"Everybody later said we were poor," Willie remembers, "but I didn't notice it. We had plenty to eat, and clothes to wear, and went to school. I rode my bike, played sports, and played hookey."

Still, it took all three Nelsons' bringing in money to make ends meet. Willie, who the present Abbott mayor remembers as "a little freckle-faced boy who was real ambitious," worked odd jobs after school, trimming trees, chopping cotton, and running errands around the railroad tracks.

Mama Nelson, her big solid body wrapped in a cotton print apron, worked in the school cafeteria during the day. After school she taught music to kids sent over to the house by their culturally conscientious parents. As soon as she had mastered Mama Nelson's lessons, Bobbie started teaching piano after school, too.

When they could scrape up a little spending money, Mama Nelson and Bobbie bought sheet music of the latest popular songs on the radio—"Pennies from Heaven," "Night and Day," "Stardust," "Moonlight in Vermont," and other pop hits by crooners like Bing Crosby and Frank Sinatra.

Since Mama Nelson had not the faintest idea about playing a guitar, Willie was on his own with his except for the chord book. Gradually, he taught himself to play "by putting my fingers on those black dots in the book," he laughs.

"He could pick up things just like that," Bobbie marvels in her soft, singsong voice. "His ear is so fantastic, *he* doesn't even know how good he is."

Despite Bobbie's big-sisterly pride, it would take the rest of the United States nearly forty years to see what Bobbie saw in her little brother back in those days. Then, the state of Texas was filled with buckets of boys seemingly just like Willie Nelson—back-yard baseball players, front-room guitar players, crazy about music and sports.

In fact, the whole, vast sprawling, optimistic state of Texas, then and now, had and has two great loves—sports and music, not necessarily in that order.

Football, baseball, basketball—all of which Willie loved—were as American as apple pie. But the music of Texas was about as ethnically mixed as an immigration desk at Ellis Island. Even in tiny, rural Abbott, black field hands, Mexican wetbacks, east European storekeepers, and farmers with Scottish and English

43

surnames, rubbed shoulders daily. Each of these groups cherished their own music, and in a state that thrived on music, a kid breathed it all in just as he breathed in the dry, exhilarating air.

The first genuine, raw-soul blues Willie ever heard was out in the field picking cotton with black farm hands.

"I used to work in the fields a lot, pick cotton alongside of niggers," as Willie puts it, "and there would be a whole field full of niggers singing the blues.

"One would sing a line at this end of the field, another one at that end. I realized they knew more about music, soul, feeling than I did. I felt inferior. Plus," he ruefully admits, "they could pick more cotton."

After searing, back-aching days in the cotton fields, nights lazy with outdoor smells followed when, Willie would lounge around on the front porch and listen to the Christians sing. The tabernacle was right across the alley, and it was available to churchgoers of all persuasions. One night the local Booster Band might be blaring out "Revive Us Again" for a foot-stomping revival, and the next week the Campbellites might be holding a gospel meeting and pleading (a cappella, of course) "O, Why Not Tonight?"

"Sometimes I'd go over there, and sometimes I'd just sit on the porch and listen," Willie explains. "So, you see, a lot of times I went to church without going."

However, there're two sides of every alley, and for a while a crowd of Mexican migrant workers lived across the street.

"They were cotton pickers and fruit pickers who

traveled around in big trucks," Bobbie remembers. "On weekends they'd come in and have a big party." Intrigued, Bobbie and Willie would sit on the porch and "watch 'em play music and dance and drink. We picked up on Latin music that way," Bobbie smiles.

Willie's school days were war days, and along with the war came a great burgeoning of country music on the radio. Boys and girls from the farms were suddenly spread out all over America and homesick to hear their kind of music. During the '40s over six-hundred stations programed some country music during the week, and big, powerful radio stations boosted their reputations with enormously popular live country shows that boomed out to eager rural ears wherever they might be. WSM's "Grand Ole Opry" out of Nashville, the WLS "Barn Dance" out of Chicago, and KWKH's "Louisiana Hayride" out of Shreveport were three of the biggest and best.

It was hearing Ernest Tubb on the "Grand Ole Opry" that gave Willie the idea he wanted to be a singer.

Tubb, the "Texas Troubadour" who once walked twelve miles as a boy to hear Jimmie Rodgers on the radio, was one of the first country bandleaders to develop the honky-tonk style. When he left Texas to join the Opry in 1932, he brought on stage an exciting fusion of the traditional southeastern string bands and the more open, swinging southwestern style of music. He also brought two significant innovations in musical instruments: the electric guitar and the steel guitar.

Recognized as a musical ground-breaker, Tubb had a voice once described by a British music critic as sounding like that of "an owl with emphysema." Once

45

he moved to Nashville a standing joke was that "ol' Ernie Tubb is successful because beer drinkers who listen to him figure they can sing better—drunk or sober."

This phased Tubb, who knew he was a star, nary an iota. "I don't care whether I hit the right note or not," he dismissed his critics. "I'm not looking for perfection of delivery—thousands of singers have that. I'm looking for individuality. I phrase the way I want to; I sing the way I feel like singing at the moment."

That distinctive voice hit the mark with budding musician, Willie. By the time he'd heard Ernest Tubb sing "Walking the Floor Over You" a couple of times, Willie, at age nine, was ready to hit the road with a band.

It was up to Mama Nelson to rein him in. "My grandmother said it was O.K. for me to go into the music business," he explains, "but she told me, 'Don't ever go out on the road.' She was afraid of all the horrible things that were supposed to happen to young people. My first job was six and a half miles away," Willie grins, "and she wouldn't let me go. She thought that was 'on the road.' "

Around that time, Willie had pretty much had it with cotton chopping. Not only did he detest it, but the owner of the cotton fields where he worked, observing his technique, acidly informed him that it was obvious he was never going to amount to anything.

("I'd take him out in the field," his dad once admitted, "and he'd pick good for a few minutes—till he got enough cotton in his bag to make a pillow. Then he'd lay down and go to sleep until time for lunch.")

Fortunately for his future, Willie's cotton-picking days were numbered.

Bobbie was already living up to Daddy Nelson's hopes by playing on the road in circumstances circumspect enough to check her grandmother's fears. During summer revival season, she would accompany a singing minister and his wife to their far-flung tent campaigns.

So, by the time Willie was about eleven, Mama Nelson had softened her views a bit, and consented to let Willie play his first professional date. He went with a local Bohemian polka band to a town six miles west of Abbott called, appropriately, West.

"I used to yodel," Willie reveals of these early performances. "I had a voice that sounded like a girl's."

Willie figured he'd "made it" when he played West. "I'd been making two dollars a day choppin' cotton, and I went out one night and made eight dollars playin' music. From that day on, I had it made. That was the turning point. That was it. No more cotton choppin' for me."

But jobs were pretty spotty for a sixth-grade musician, and most nights Willie ended up listening to the radio. Hardly any radio stations played country music full time. Many only played country records an hour a day—on the 6 A.M. farm show, or at noon. The rest of the day they played pop hits the soldier boys requested, or city jazz, or western swing, or black blues.

Saturday nights, "the radio would have the "Grand Ole Opry" coming in on one station, and "Ernie's Record Shop" on the other, playing Ella Mae Morse and Freddie Slack," Willie vividly remembers.

By the time the United States declared war on

Japan, The Carter Family had become huge national country stars thanks to radio station XERA, a gigantic outlaw station camped right over the Mexican border, surging across the Rio Grande with 150,000 watts of radio power that blanketed the southwest and reached as far north as Canada.

XERA was a folksy shrewd rabbit-in-a-hat grab bag of musical merchandising designed to reach country listeners' pockets through a solicitation of their souls. "Friends, order yoreself a bee-yo-tee-ful eight-by-ten glossy photograph of our dear and precious Savior," Willie would heard the announcer exhort. ". . . Thank you Sister Cora Mae for our inspirin' hymn of the day. . . . *Jeezuus!* What an inspiration. . . . Yes, that's 1,000—yes, 1,000—baby chicks, sex not guaranteed . . . and now here's a little tune from Cowboy Slim Rhinehart, goes something like this. . . ."

Most nights as Willie twisted the knob across the dial, he would hear "Harbor Lights," "Don't Sit under the Apple Tree," or melancholy favorites of the boys in uniform like "Coming In on a Wing and a Prayer," or "When My Blue Moon Turns to Gold Again"—pop hits like Bobbie played on the piano.

Willie also liked to hang out at the house and listen to records by a big, new star named Frank Sinatra. Sinatra was singing with the top big-city swing bands of the day, and when Willie heard Sinatra, he knew he was hearing a voice as distinctive in its own arena as Ernest Tubb's was in his. "I'd get to thinking, boy, he sure does that nice," Willie says. "Then I'd start hearing my songs that way. So, I just started singing 'em like that."

Willie was still writing songs, but self-conscious about putting his feelings down on paper for all the world to see, he'd first work out the tunes on his guitar, then write the words down and hide them in a secret place around the house. But often, unable to resist some possible praise from Mama Nelson, who was herself writing gospel songs, he'd "leave 'em lying around; see if somebody'd pick 'em up and comment on 'em," he smiles.

When he was ten, Willie's mother, Myrle, married a third time and finally found happiness. A couple of years after her marriage, Myrle, now Mrs. Ken Harvey, came all the way from her new home up in Oregon down to Texas to visit. Looking forward to seeing his mother, Willie made a little present in her honor.

It was a small homemade booklet tied with string. The cover was cut from a brown paper sack with Scotch tape folded over the edges. Inside, some pecked out on a typewriter, some in pencil, were fifteen song lyrics. Written on the cover in a boyish scrawl were the prophetic words: "Songs by Willie Nelson."

ALL MY BASES LOADED

1946—RCA begins regular recording in Nashville
1948—Bob Wills hits with "Bubbles in My Beer"
1949—Hank Williams joins the Grand Ole Opry

Although three years younger than his sister, it was Willie, the hyperactive kid with the winning ways, always promoting this and selling that, who gradually took the lead in the brother/sister relationship.

"I was her little brother for a while," Willie said of Bobbie in 1975. "Now I'm her big brother."

Their deeply shared instincts about music, the values instilled in them by Mama Nelson, the sense of being two kids adrift together in a constantly changing stream of adults, have bonded Willie and Bobbie together in a way only they can fully appreciate.

Since the '60s Bobbie has played piano in the Willie Nelson Family band, earning her the unusual distinction of being the only female musician playing the road in a well-known country band. "Willie and me, we think so much alike," Bobbie says today in her soft country drawl; "time apart from him, I always miss him."

Sunday mornings while they were growing up, Willie sang hymns in church and Bobbie played piano accompaniment. Every Friday, they performed together in the school assembly.

Both Bobbie and Willie were very popular at Abbott High. Bobbie, locally acclaimed as a pianist, was asked to play at virtually every school function, and won quite a following. As a grade-school girl, and in high school, Bobbie always conveyed the image of a delicate, sensitive young lady. Wearing a striped sunsuit, her hair a thick mass of Shirley Temple curls, or in high school, with her hair parted down the middle and demurely twisted up, Bobbie had a charming way.

She married a local farm boy during her junior year, but still graduated from Abbott High. She was elected class favorite both her sophomore and junior years, was secretary of the junior class, and landed a role in the junior play. She also played on the girls' basketball team, and was a dutiful member of the Future Homemakers of America.

Willie's eighth-grade school photo shows him all polished up in a white shirt, dark suit, and tie—Sunday church clothes, no doubt. And even that early in his "career," it's the eyes that have it—miles deep, dark, round, and friendly, but just a hint perplexed, or detached. In eighth grade, Willie Nelson, country outlaw, was a member of the Boy Scouts.

His first year in high school, Willie's classmates elected him "class king." A formal oval photo in that year's annual shows Lord Willie Hugh from the House of Nelson escorting the charming, evening-gowned, ninth-grader, Lady Ramona.

His freshman year at Abbott High also formalized Willie's totally fanatic infatuation with sports. As a freshman he signed up for softball, baseball, and track. The following year he added basketball, volleyball, and football. Being short and skinny didn't deter left halfback Willie one bit.

Although Willie pursued sports full tilt all during high school, the year Bobbie got married, she and Willie were pulled into music on as fairly regular, semiprofessional basis. Bobbie was madly in love with her tall, good-looking husband, Bud Fletcher—a farm boy with dreams of being a bandleader like Bob Wills. They formed a little band with Bud, Bobbie, Willie; and Glen Ellison, the local football coach, was on trombone. Often Ira Nelson, who lived nearby, played fiddle or guitar.

Bud booked all the dates, and they'd hit the honky-tonks thirty miles south in Waco, or, mostly, go over to West and play the Nite Owl, a beer-drinking joint owned by a big, robust woman named Margie Lundy. "Yeah, Willie used to play in here," Margie relishes remembering. "He was just a kid. Why, he was playing here when his voice changed."

"Bobbie was the only one who was any good," Willie declares. "We never played the same place twice. Usually we played on percentage, and I remember one night we cleared eighty-one cents each."

The band made Bobbie and Willie somewhat of local celebrities around Abbott High. The band played regularly at radio station KHBR in Hillsboro, about ten miles north; and sometimes their classmates would come up to the station and watch them play live on the air, and go tell all the other kids about it.

A photo snapped around the microphone at KHBR shows Willie, expectantly peering sideways toward the camera, wearing a brightly printed short-sleeved shirt and strumming a big electric guitar. Bobbie, legs demurely crossed, sits on the bench of an upright piano wearing a smart plaid dress with white collar and short cuffs. Tall, slim, tan, movie-star handsome Bud, holding a fiddle under his chin, is dressed up in a white shirt and tie. A girl singer stands at the microphone, and five more musicians, including an upright bass player and Ira Nelson on guitar, round out what must have been a constantly expanding and contracting group.

"When I found myself singing over the radio," Willie says, "I didn't think life got much better than that."

Mama Nelson, however, viewed all these developments with a somewhat baleful eye. Mainly, she dreaded seeing all her predictions about life on the road come true. Bobbie, so carefully and closely raised, was already having problems in her own mind.

"I experienced guilt from it," Bobbie says of her new night life; "until then I'd never been inside a place where they served alcoholic beverages."

Although music gave Willie and Bobbie a certain status, at the same time it made them somewhat morally suspect. Waco, Texas—just thirty miles down the highway—was then, and is now, one of the biggest, most firmly clinched buckles on the heaven-bound, fundamentalist, Protestant Bible Belt that stretched east to west across the South. The creed: no drinking, no smoking, no dancing, no taking of the Lord's name in vain, no Coca-Colas. The body is the temple of the spirit, and the temple is to remain undefiled.

To the rural-poor, but middle-class moral Texas Christians of those days, musicians were, for the most part, a sorry, shiftless, seedy, loose-living lot. Certainly not the type that careful parents would want their daughters to know—even remotely.

Bobbie escaped some of this stigma, because of her ladylike demeanor, because she played the piano (obviously an instrument of the classical persuasion), and because she played frequently in church. Using your talents for God was above criticism.

Willie, however, did not confine his talents—or his demeanor—to the side of sanctity.

Actually, Mama Nelson had felt Willie slipping from her efforts to keep him on the straight and narrow ever since he had entered his teens. "Ever since I was young, I was going out drinking beer with the guys," Willie admits. "My grandmother had a lot of objections to the way I was running around."

Also, Willie had picked up a little more than Latin music from those Mexican wetbacks across the street. He'd noticed them smoking something that wasn't tobacco, something with a sweet, haylike smell. He hadn't tried it yet, but he was interested.

When Willie was about thirteen, the ever-enterprising schoolboy and his ambitious brother-in-law, living more modestly than they had planned on eighty-one-cent-a-night bookings, decided to take up promoting on the side.

Shortly after starting Bud's band, they got the fantastic chance to book Bob Wills, King of Western Swing, into nearby Whitney, Texas.

54

They rented an outside dance pavilion close to Whitney Lake and hauled a piano over from a beer joint on the highway. A fine-sized crowd showed up—1,200 to 1,500 people. Jack Lloyd had by then replaced Tommy Duncan as Wills's lead singer, and he did "I Don't See Me in Your Eyes Anymore," destined years later to be a hit by Charlie Rich.

To Willie's heart-thumping joy, he was able to finagle his way into getting up on stage and singing a song with Bob and the band. It was an awfully big moment.

"Everybody I knew when I was a kid was a Bob Wills fan," flatly declares Willie. "I didn't know anybody who didn't like Bob Wills's music."

"In fact," Willie recalls, "western swing was just about the only kind of music you could hear in the state of Texas. Until Hank Williams came along, it was just Bob Wills. He was *it*."

In 1934, Wills had moved his band from Texas to Tulsa, Oklahoma, changed its name from The Playboys to The Texas Playboys, and joined the staff of KVOO, a 50,000-watt station that boomed the music of The Texas Playboys across millions of square miles of southwestern prairie. The popularity of the band jumped explosively, and they became so busy playing live shows, Wills had to pull his brother Johnny Lee out of the band to head up a second band just to play all the bookings he was having to turn down.

Wills played a hot fiddle, but, first and foremost, he was a bandleader, one of the most magnetic bandleaders in the history of popular music. His famous "Aaaaaaah-ha!" and "Take it away, Leon" became musical punch lines as eagerly awaited by audiences as his legendary hits like "San Antonio Rose" and "Bubbles in My Beer."

Novelist J. R. Goddard told Robert Shelton about his memories of Bob Wills: "Imagine a Saturday night at a dance hall in Norman or Muskogee, Oklahoma. There might be 1,200 people jammed in the hall, some of whom drove one-hundred-fifty miles for the dance. Some were hard-shell Baptists, oil workers, and mule farmers. Most of Bob Wills's fans were poor working class. They were just coming out of the Depression, out of the worst sort of rural isolation, just beginning to get electricity in their homes.

"Wills dressed conservatively in a starched white shirt, but maybe he wore a hundred-dollar pair of boots or a hundred-dollar cowboy hat. He had bought a big bus to take his band around, a bus with a big longhorn steer head on the front. The people had never seen anything quite like that. He was sort of a folk hero, but a reachable hero who gave these people something to live up to and look up to. His old theme went something like, 'Howdy everybody from near and far/You want to know just who we are?/We're The Texas Playboys from the Lone Star.'

"Those dances had incessant music. You could hear the feet of the dancers stomping on the old wooden floor. Up near the bandstand were fifty or sixty people standing, hollering, trying to give Wills cigars. They had a strong need to get in contact with him."

Although Bob Wills's music dominated Texas, Oklahoma, and California—the southwest—ironically, to this very day, Bob Wills is known only in a limited way outside those states.

"If he'd done the national tours and international

tours—all the *right* things," Willie defended his hero in *Country Music Magazine*, "—then a lot of other people would have been aware of how good he was; but he's known well enough in the country—western swing area as being a bandleaders' bandleader, that it doesn't matter if the rest of the people knew about him or not. He was that great."

Wills's career had an incalculable influence on Willie's ideas of what it meant to have your own band, to be a band*leader*.

"When Bob went to the Grand Ole Opry for the first time," Willie wrote of an incident that deeply impressed him, "first of all, they didn't want him to use drums, so he refused to appear. They finally conceded that he could use his drums. Then, he went on stage, and he had his cigar in his mouth. So, then they wanted him to not smoke his cigar on stage. And he refused again. Consequently, that was the first and only time Bob Wills ever played on the Grand Ole Opry, so far as I know. He had to have his drums and his cigar."

Fine example for a kid who later grew up to be called an "outlaw."

One time Myrle came home to find her two teen-age children playing in a band, and let it be known she was most upset to discover that her plans for their Christian upbringing were not being carried out.

But what was Mama Nelson, now an old lady in her sixties, to do about a teen-age boy who was into drinking and running around? She'd have to take on the whole family to do away with a band that included two grandchildren, her grandson-in-law, her own son, and the high-school football coach. Believing discretion the better part of valor, Mama Nelson pretty much kept her views to herself.

At least Willie was still in school. And, really, she knew she didn't have to worry much about Willie straying far from the hallowed halls of Abbott High for the time being. Despite his fooling around with Bud's band, everybody could see the boy was almost totally dedicated to sports.

Willie's freshman and sophomore mania for sports—any sports—persisted on into his junior and senior years.

"More than music, I was hung up on sports," Willie says of his high-school days. Now, when Willie got into something, he got *really* into it. Trying to hit all the bases, he lettered in four sports in school—basketball, track, baseball, and football. One day he was wanting to be a professional football player, the next day a professional baseball player.

With the same nonstop stamina that has characterized him all his life, Willie was determined not only to play every sport the school offered, but also to participate in all the other extracurricular activities, plus be in his brother-in-law's band and play over at the Nite Owl in West.

In addition to the four sports he won letters in, Willie played softball four years, played volleyball three years, was King of his freshman class, played a role in the junior play, was on the newspaper staff his junior and senior years, was on the annual staff his senior year, and was songleader for the Future Farmers of America for three years.

When he graduated in 1951, he had a "B" average. Willie didn't make "A's," his teachers say, because he was making money playing music every night—and kept falling asleep in class.

But by graduation day, he was sure of one thing. Sports was it. He was going to be a professional baseball player. And as the slogan of the Abbott High School Panthers prophetically preached: "A quitter never wins, and a winner never quits."

BORN-AGAIN SCUFFLERS

1951 — Pop artist Tony Bennett hits with Hank
Williams' "Cold, Cold Heart"
1953 — Hank Williams dies
1954 — Bill Haley changes the name of his
band from "Saddles Pals" to "Comets"

"I have no negative memories about growing up,"
Willie once told *Newsweek* magazine. "It was being
grown-up that started to be a problem."

Throughout high school, Willie's ambitions constantly shifted — first to be a professional baseball
player, then to be a professional football player.
"Although he was small," recalled friend Crash
Stewart, "some college scouts thought he had possibil-
ities, because Willie had lots of determination, was
very quick, had lots of stamina, and did not know
what the word 'quit' meant."

Encouraged by the scouts' reports, Willie, after
graduation, headed to Weatherford Junior College,
west of Fort Worth, to try to land a baseball scholarship. But even during the critical baseball tryouts,

Willie never gave up playing in bands.

Consequently, the "B" average student who kept falling asleep in class, now watched his college scholarship deteriorate daily, as each morning the alarm clock clattered, and he headed for practice, body aching for sleep, and head splitting with a hangover.

"It's hard to be playing clubs and stayin' out till three or four in the morning, and still stay in shape to play sports," Willie sighs. Today still an avid jogger and parking-lot basketball player, college-prospect Willie never seemed to make a clear-cut choice between music and sports; music just won out by sheer physical harassment. He never even registered at Weatherford Junior College.

His dreams for a sports career extinguished, just another high-school graduate with no real training for any solid job, Willie joined the air force about 1951. It was not a wise decision. In the early '50s, with the Korean War an international short fuse, the U.S. Air Force was geared up for world-wide action. Willie, an independent teen-ager, mostly used to doing exactly what he wanted to do, hadn't even begun to reckon with the strict discipline and regimentation he would have to kowtow to in the air force.

"Military life didn't exactly agree with me," Willie says. "My back started bothering me a real lot around then." After eight months, he was discharged for medical reasons.

His military career ditched, Willie, still in his teens, was more frustrated than ever about what on earth he was going to do with his life. Naturally, he had started playing in bands again, but that was hardly what you'd call a career decision.

One day, out tooling around Waco, Willie pulled into the Lone Oak Drive-in, and "there she came," he says, "with that long black hair." Destiny had presented itself to Willie Hugh Nelson in the bewitching form of Miss Martha Matthews, sixteen-year-old high-school student and carhop.

"I think we went together three or four weeks," Willie says.

On October 27, 1952, Willie and Martha Jewel Matthews ran off to Cleburne, Texas and got married. Martha was vibrant at sixteen, a beautiful, outgoing, vivacious girl—and a full-blooded Cherokee Indian.

They eloped to elude Martha's socially outraged and absolutely furious parents. Martha's father, a plumber, and his wife completely disapproved of their only child—and she was certainly a mere child—marrying a no-account musician. Without success, they tried to get the marriage annulled.

Hotfooting it back from Cleburne, Willie and his teen-age bride moved in with well-worn Mama Nelson in Abbott. "I was an only child and had never washed a dish," Martha declares. "Mama Nelson taught me everything."

After disentangling himself from the air force, Willie had started playing again with Bud and Bobbie's band. "Willie was into music before we got married," Martha says, "but he wasn't all that great. Nobody thought he was great; he was just another musician."

When Willie and Martha married, every little town in Texas had a guy—maybe a guy like Bud—who wanted to be a star; if nothing else, in the eyes of his neighbors. Like Buck Bonham in *Honeysuckle Rose*, they roamed Texas by the hundreds in their dilapidated buses crammed with ill-paid band buddies.

Playing a week here, a couple of nights someplace else — or, most likely, a different bar in a different town every night of the week — competing for coveted spots on the morning farm shows, the noontime live radio shows, they made up an elusive but highly active migration from normal life, rolling back and forth across Texas, Oklahoma, California — bands on the run in hot pursuit of the passion of their souls: music.

Now that Willie's career seemed headed toward music by default, he was no exception.

Stalemated with the family band, Willie started kicking around, looking for some real action. In 1953, the year "I Love Lucy" debuted on television, Willie drove down to San Antonio to look around. Compared to Abbott, or even Waco, the metropolis of San Antonio, a bustling, loose town with a spicy night life nearly as Mexican as American, sounded eminently promising to Willie. He'd heard the city was full of bars, crammed with cowboys who liked to "dance, scream, yell, and drink beer."

On that trip he met a rowdy, truck-driving drifter named Johnny Bush, who had recently moved to San Antonio when he'd landed a job at a place called the Texas Star Inn and had now started playing in all the joints around the area. Bush had ambitions to be a singer, but was learning to play drums, because as he'd gotten it, "drummers work full-time."

After running into Bush, Willie moved Martha to San Antonio so he could play guitar in Bush's new band, the Mission City Playboys.

Arriving in San Antonio and needing more income

than a musician could make, now that he was married, Willie also landed his first job as a disc jockey at KBOP in Pleasanton, thirty miles south of San Antonio.

Being totally inexperienced, he was given the traditional low-man-on-the-totem-pole's slot as morning jock, opening the station at the crack of dawn each day. The station itself was located four miles outside Pleasanton on Parker's ranch, so Willie and Martha set up housekeeping in Pleasanton.

Willie figured being a disc jockey was the perfect day job for a musician. "I always like to disc-jockey, 'cause you'd get to play music all day long," Willie says, "have earphones, and the whole bit."

At night, he drove the thirty miles up to San Antonio to play with Johnny Bush.

In San Antonio, Willie now joined the musical sea on which thousands of country pickers floated and bobbed, deep-diving nightly into the bars and honky-tonks of Texas. It was an impetuous, bawdy, nomadic, neon world; powered by high horsepowers of musical macho; fueled on booze, women, and the simple joy of music.

Its inhabitants would play for a few bucks, for drinks, for nothing—just let them get up on stage and show how they could pick. Many had day jobs, virtually all had troubles with the wife because they wouldn't stay home nights.

Out of a regular gig (most bands didn't hang together long), pickers would jump at the chance to sit in with any band, in any bar. On the town night after night, a guitar player might pick with ten or twelve different bunches of musicians in one month.

Few had the faintest idea about anything called the music "business"—they just lived and breathed music.

Nights Willie didn't play guitar with the Mission City Playboys, he'd sit in with popular local groups like Adolph Hofner's swing band, the Pearl Wranglers. Bush also occasionally sat in with the Wranglers. (Hofner recalls that Bush, with his spine-tingling operatic voice, sang a beautiful rendition of "Stardust.") Eventually, Bush also landed a part-time job at KBOP.

The Nelson/Bush duo was a "Butch Cassidy and the Sundance Kid" close and crazy relationship. High-spirited, drawing on a bottomless pit of young-buck energy, the pair hit gigs, as Bush puts it, "at joints all over the state from West Hell and back."

Mostly they hung out around Forth Worth, Waco, Houston, and San Antonio, constantly starting up bands, breaking up bands, playing in each other's latest band, playing in anybody's band.

Still holding down his job at the station, Willie, who Mrs. Parker remembers as being "hard-working," soon became one of KBOP's top D.J.'s, and ran a very popular show. Usually he rapped and played records, but sometimes he'd pick guitar and sing on the air live.

Of course, as a disc jockey he was making next to nothing, and most of that money went to Martha who, by March of 1953, found herself pregnant at seventeen.

On gigs, he made less than nothing. Willie and Johnny would land a date in Houston, but wouldn't have the cash to get there. They would hock their guitars to get the gas money, drive to Houston, then lean on some friendly local musicians for a couple of guitars to play the gig. Collecting their pay (ten dollars was a top night), they would buy a few drinks, maybe slip a tip to a waitress or two, drive back to San Antonio, and get their guitars out of hock. End of money.

One penniless afternoon, Willie and Bush were trying to hitchhike to West Texas to make a gig, but having no luck catching a ride. The highway they were thumbing ran alongside a railroad track, and when a freight train going their way pulled into a station up ahead, Willie got the bright idea they could hop the freight.

As they were running up to the train, it started pulling slowly out of the station, so they quickly threw their luggage and guitar cases up on the flat car. As they dashed alongside getting ready to jump on, the train suddenly picked up speed, and steamed off into the distance carrying the heart of their worldly belongings off to parts unknown.

One dark, early morning Willie ran out of gas on the way to KBOP and had to abandon his car and hitch on in to work. Several hours later, Bush headed out from San Antonio to take over Willie's shift. He passed Willie's empty car on the road, and treated himself to a broad chuckle. A mile or so on down the road Bush's own car sputtered and coasted to a halt—out of gas. Climbing out of his car, Bush glumly hitchhiked to the station himself.

Mornings at KBOP, at the miserably early hour of 5:30 A.M. when he signed on the air, Willie was fighting his old schooldays-and-scholarship nemesis—sleep.

Bleary-eyed from playing till just a few hours before

time to go on the air, he would flip the switch open and force his mouth into a snappy intro like: "Good morning! This is your old cotton-pickin', snuff-dippin', tobaccer-chewin', stump-jumpin', gravy-soppin', coffee-pot-dodgin', dumplin'-eatin', frog-giggin', hillbilly from Hill County."

On nights when he played till three or four A.M., then foggily drove the thirty miles to Pleasanton, Willie didn't make it to bed at all. "The hours weren't so easy," Willie sighs. "Opening up in the mornings can get to be a drag. Or at least it was to me, 'cause I was always playing at night."

At first, he only missed opening up a couple of times. But over a period of months, he showed up late more and more frequently, leaving the Parkers with empty air space to greet the early-rising farmers. Finally, Dr. Parker had to get after him. "If you're late again," he warned, "you're fired."

The chance of losing his job was just one of Willie's many problems. Since moving outside family bands, Willie had discovered some country musicians didn't like the odd, back-phrasing way of singing he'd developed listening to Frank Sinatra, Ernest Tubb, and the black blues singers on the radio.

Bush, with his technically perfect voice, superiorly advised Willie to forget singing and "stick to that gi-tar." A band called Dave and Frog Isabell always dodged letting Willie sing. "When Willie wanted to sing, they would pull him off and tell him they needed him on guitar," Crash Stewart remembered.

Even his own dad couldn't hack Willie's sense of rhythm. "He wanted me to join his band," Ira, a traditional country fiddle player, told a Dallas

67

reporter. "I said, 'Willie, you've got to get yourself another boy'—I was never able to pick with him till a couple of years ago. He was always singing out of time, seemed to me. I couldn't get with it."

At that point in the interview Lorraine chimed in: "I didn't like it," she volunteered about Willie's singing. "I thought it was funny the way he talked all the way through his songs."

A friend told Ira that someday Willie was going to be famous, but Ira replied, "Naw, he'll never make it."

In those days, his dad recalled, Willie was "doing the same thing he's doing now, only he was starving to death." When Willie started trying to support his family off music, Ira didn't think he had a prayer of a chance. "I advised him against it—I said, 'go get a regular job, son.'"

If all that wasn't enough, things were starting to slide downhill at home. On November 11, 1953, a lovely black-haired dark-skinned, and obviously Indian little girl was born to Martha and Willie. They named her De Lana, a Biblical name.

Mrs. Parker remembers Lana as a bright, precocious baby. "By six or seven months, she could talk," Mrs. Parker marvels; "she could say words."

Still just a high-spirited vivacious teen-ager, Martha was now stuck at home with the baby. With Willie running around every night in honky-tonks and bars, stress quickly developed in Martha's hot-tempered, Cherokee-blooded mind.

Being Indian, Martha didn't cotton much to drinking, and Willie, as he recalls, was not an effective drunk. In fact, since his sports career had faded, he'd been abusing his body badly—too much drinking and carousing, too many nights without sleep. "I started playing music more, and not taking care of myself," Willie admits.

Faced with a new mouth to feed, still earning next to nothing, absent from home nightly, Willie ran into a raging storm every day at noon when he got off work at the station.

Martha's outbursts only kept Willie remote and quiet, and away from home even more. But he got to thinking that, maybe, being a father and now twenty-one years old, he ought to get into something more substantial.

Although Willie had a lot of respect for Dr. Parker, who kept encouraging him to keep on writing songs when he already had suitcases full of tunes he couldn't sell, nonetheless, one morning Willie simply didn't show up for work at KBOP. "We didn't hear from him for two or three years," Mrs. Parker exclaims. "He even left his third-class radio license, that you've got to have to work on the air."

Apparently, Willie had decided to go to college and get started in a profession. On March 9, 1954, two months after school officially opened, Willie enrolled under the G.I. Bill at Waco University. At a conservative Baptist college where the lifestyle was akin to a twenty-four-hour chapel service, Willie's scholastic days, from the beginning, were lived out on borrowed time.

His records show he registered for a wide variety of courses, no major listed. Willie says he planned to major in business administration, but, in fact, concedes he devoted his days to "majoring in dominoes."

Not to neglect his responsibility as family wage earner, however, Willie took up selling books, door to door. If folks ordered a set of encyclopedias, they got a Bible free. "We didn't try to sell the Bibles," Willie says. "We assumed people needed them."

Willie would walk up to the front door, knock, and "I'd tell 'em that I was new on the job, and in order for them to be sure they knew exactly what we were saying, and that I wasn't misinterpreting anything in any way, the company asked me to read this.

"I'd read them the pitch, and when they'd say, 'Well, we can't afford it,' I'd say, 'Well, let me see what the company says about that.' On the back of the thing they had some rebuttals. I did it right from the pitch sheet."

Either he was pretty good at it, or the customers sensed some sincerity in the young man's eyes, because the first night out he sold three sets of books. "When I was in the encyclopedia business," he later explained, "I learned that whatever you want to sell, first you've got to sell yourself."

(Thirty years later, stressing the importance of his Fourth of July picnics to his career, Willie explained, "I needed to get around, to sell myself. It's a game you gotta play in this business.")

He even worked his way up to manager of the Waco branch of the book company, but that didn't last. "I was selling to young couples who had to borrow ten dollars to make the down payment," Willie says; enough said.

During his college interlude, Willie also pursued research in the then rather esoteric field of surfing. There were only two main drawbacks to this project:

no surfboard and no waves in Waco.

The obvious solution was to construct a surfboard which could then be pulled around in glassy-smooth, fresh-water Waco Lake.

After building the board, Willie and a cohort planted Willie, the homemade surfing device, and a speedboat in the lake. The accomplice revved up the motor and Willie, pulled along behind, was soon "surfing" at full speed. Unfortunately, at that point the motor quit. Willie's body, still skimming along at maximum velocity, went flying forward and under the boat. At that point, the motor revived, the boat lunged forward, and the surfboard smashed into Willie's head.

Aghast, his friend, a part-time employee at a local funeral parlor, loaded the unconscious Willie in the car and sped off to the funeral parlor. Willie woke up on a slab.

His friend was in the process of sewing up the gash on his head with mortician's thread, an operation which Willie describes as "a funny feeling, but a pretty good job." Not perfect, however. Willie still has a slight scar from "surfing" to this day.

Willie only made it partway through his second semester; he withdrew from school early, "before," as he puts it, "I really got interested in education." He withdrew on July 10, 1954, over a month before the summer session was over.

His second radio job, Willie told *Picking Up the Tempo*, in 1975, was at KVAN radio in Vancouver, Washington. Myrle Nelson Harvey was living up there with her third husband, and Willie says he hitchhiked up there to see her one time, and "stayed for a while."

This mention of a job in Vancouver is the first in a series of tortuous puzzles as to what, exactly, Willie really did for the next twenty years. Although it is clear he stayed in Texas till the end of the '50s, then spent about twelve years in Nashville, the precise details of his multitudinous wanderings are extremely difficult to pin down. Especially since Willie himself—and others present at the time—often come up with conflicting information.

For example, based on what Willie told *Picking Up the Tempo*, he would have been in Vancouver in 1954—the same year he was enrolled in Baylor, and also the year he says he took a job in Fort Worth. Maybe he hitchhiked up to Vancouver by himself for a brief spell, perhaps to escape from marital problems. At any rate, Willie told his discographer that he was in Vancouver in 1958. Martha says Susie was born there—that was about 1956, because Lana and Susie are two years apart in age. His discographer finally pinned down that Willie released a record in Vancouver in the fall of 1957. The only problem with all that, is that all involved say Willie was in Vancouver only about a year.

About ten years after he moved to Nashville, the house on Willie's farm in Ridgetop burned down. This has been reported as happening in 1969, 1971, and 1972. Willie, who enjoys a picturesque anecdote, says it was around Christmas, or on Christmas Eve. But the song he has been quoted as saying he wrote the night before the fire, was cleared for radio performance on December 8, 1970.

In a hard-driving life as long and complex as Willie's—spanning nearly fifty years, three marriages, dozens of bands, five major music centers, song-writing, records (two or three times as many as you'd expect from any one major artist), and movies—it's just hard for any one person to recall it all totally accurately. This leaves the researcher to do his level best, to establish dates that are publicly substantiated, to compare reports from reliable sources, and to tell the story in a way that has as few questions as possible. In the main, and in the spirit, this is the way it happened. For errors of detail, an apology is hereby offered.

According to Willie and his longtime drummer, Paul English, Willie and Martha moved to Fort Worth in 1954.

Ira and Lorraine were already living in Fort Worth where Ira was an auto mechanic and the family were members of the Metropolitan Baptist Church. Willie and Martha also joined Metropolitan Baptist, and Willie landed a job at KCNC radio, working a split shift.

He would sign on at six A.M., sign off at 7:45, then go back on the air at noon with a live three-hour show called "The Western Express." Most of the show was the call-in type. "That was the only country music on the station at that time, and the show I took over was a show that had been done by a lot of other pretty popular disc jockeys around the area," Willie told Fort Worth D.J., Lew Staples. "We'd have people call in, ask questions, and we'd shoot the breeze over the air; find out what was bothering people."

The first half-hour, though, was a live program featuring Willie picking guitar and singing with a band. One afternoon, they were about to go on the air, and the drummer hadn't shown up. Another band member, Oliver English, got the bright idea to call up his brother to come fill in. The only drawback to Oliver's brainstorm was the fact that his brother, a former Salvation Army trumpet player, had never played drums in his life.

"They taught me to hold the sticks and told me just to keep the rhythm," Paul English recounts, savoring a story he has told many times with relish. "When did you become a drummer?" one reporter asked him. "I didn't," he smiled and answered; "I just play 'em."

About this time, Willie discovered a western ballad released in the early '50s by Arthur "Guitar Boogie" Smith, a deeply religious singer and songwriter. The song was called "Red-Headed Stranger."

"The song, 'Red-Headed Stranger' came out, and I would play it every day," Willie once explained. "At 1:00 in the afternoon when the mothers wanted to give the kids a nap, I would say, 'O.K., you kids, I'm going to play you some music, and then you can go to sleep for Mom.'

"And I'd play 'Red-Headed Stranger' and some of the novelty tunes Tex Ritter had out, and some kiddie songs. I got a lot of requests and a lot of response from 'Red-Headed Stranger.' I loved the song, and I sang it to my kids at night."

Soon after Willie met Paul English, they put together a band and started playing nights on the edge of Fort Worth along a miles-long strip of bar fights called Jacksboro Highway.

Jacksboro Highway . . . Paul English . . . Fort Worth . . . they were everything Mama Nelson had dreaded, and probably more than she had ever imagined.

Fort Worth in the middle '50s was a gangster-ridden midwestern city, reminiscent of Chicago during prohibition days.

Hoods like Tincey Eggleston, Cecil Green, and Herb "The Cat" Noble (who survived repeated murder attempts before a mailbox bomb ended his criminal career) ruled the turf around Fort Worth. Just a few miles straight west of the sophisticated Dallas, country cousin Fort Worth had grown up as a rough-and-tumble cowboy town, end of the trail for cattle drivers herding their thundering stock to the railroad at the enormous Fort Worth Stockyards, its fenced pens at one time covering dozens and dozens of city blocks. By the '50s Fort Worth had become end of the trail for a herd of gamblers, pimps, thieves, and racketeers, their rules spelled out in blood, guns, and Mafia-type contracts.

Paul English was a known hoodlum of that period, a time he has spoken of openly, matter-of-factly, and with some pride.

When the underworld got too bold to stay underground, the now-defunct *Fort Worth Press* would periodically publish an exposé under the eye-catching headline, "The Ten Most Unwanted Men in Fort Worth." "I always made the list," English told Countrystyle News Service.

At about the same time Willie was trying to hang on to his college baseball scholarship, English, age seventeen, was serving nine months on the Ellis County prison farm in Texas. As he told Pete Axthelm in 1978, he was bitter about his sentence because, "I committed some burglaries in my time, but not the one they got me for." He was also openly displeased that three of those months were spent in solitary. According to Axthelm, "After Paul emerged, he remained a frequently arrested local character in various Texas cities."

By his 20s, Paul had drifted into a wide-ranging assortment of legal, semilegal, and apparently illegal activities. An intense, yet soft-spoken man, he was an odd combination of artistic inclination and criminal bent — a skilled leather worker, a used-car salesman, a hood, and a sometimes horn blower.

At the time Willie met Paul, he was running a used-car lot, which he told Countrystyle was actually a front for his less respectable activities, which sometimes netted him in the neighborhood of $3,000 weekly.

"I was a character and I still am," he admitted to Countrystyle in 1978. "The other characters started hanging around Willie because I was there. And like everybody else, they liked Willie, and he liked them." Used-car dealers, low-level gangsters, small-time promoters, and owners of rough Dallas/Fort Worth nightspots became Willie's frequent associates.

But most important, Willie liked Paul, and Paul liked Willie. Nearly ten years before Paul adopted his official "devil" look, he was already a striking character. Gaunt and menacing, with a slick continental style, Paul fancied satin brocade dinner jackets, typical for lounge bands at the time, expensive jewelry on his scarred hands, and his sinister black Mephistophelian beard.

"That guy looks like hell," laughs the recording engineer on the "Red-Headed Stranger" album, "but he's such a good-natured, lovable guy. Stern: you don't push him around—he's not a, ha-ha, good-natured pushover. He's strong-willed, a good business-man, very intelligent, likable. If you ever tool around with him, he's hard to deal with, but he's a swell guy."

In the early days, it was more a case of Paul adopting Willie, than Willie consenting to take on Paul. Willie was just a midlevel musician and disc jockey with precious little going for him. But Paul volunteered to play in Willie's band, and at times, manage his financial affairs, virtually for free. The day the drummer didn't show, marked the birth of a brother-close, still ongoing friendship between Willie and Paul English.

At that time, the Sunset and Vine of redneck entertainment in Fort Worth was the notorious five-mile strip of road called the Jacksboro Highway.

Today, you can stand on a rise outside the city, look several miles down Jacksboro Highway into the skyline of Fort Worth, and see nothing but a winding line of seedy, dingy, lackadaisical beer joints, many abandoned, most over the hill.

But in the '50s Jacksboro Highway had the trumped-up attraction of a hooker—not much to look at by day, but full of bawdy allure at night. Under its fluorescent, neon make-up, Jacksboro Highway was the height of redneck glamour, with enough of a come-on to make grown men fight.

"There was this one joint called the S&S Club where we played a lot," Paul says. The fights there were so rough, the owner had to string chicken wire across the stage to shield the band. (This protection was not offered until the musicians threatened to organize and boycott the place.)

"It was too dangerous," Willie says. "You're standing up there playing, and somebody hits you in the back of the head with a beer bottle. Maybe not intending to—maybe he's throwing it at his wife."

"It was about our favorite joint, I guess," Paul laughs.

Then there was the County Dump, Paul describes as, "right next to the real dump, down the end of an old dirt road; didn't even have a phone.

"They hired us to cover up the noise of this big dice game they were runnin' in the back room. We played there nine months, and saw two killings; had at least one good fight every night."

The County Dump paid twenty-four dollars a week, for six nights of playing, leading to Willie's definition of a successful musician: anybody who could play music and eat, too.

Just one of thousands of struggling singers and guitar players picking in hundreds of obscure honky-tonks, Willie could hardly hope to be making good money; but, even the biggest, most famous country stars were having serious money problems at the time.

In 1954, the same year Willie moved to Fort Worth, a man in Memphis named Sam Phillips started calling the music he was recording on his Sun Records label, "rockabilly." A sharecropper's son named Carl Perkins put on his blue suede shoes, a former student at the Waxahatchie Bible Institute in Texas named Jerry Lee Lewis showed up with his "pumping piano," an ex-appliance salesman named Johnny Cash immortalized the "bop" set in "Ballad of a Teen-age Queen," and Elvis Presley checked into "Heartbreak Hotel." Bill Haley changed the name of his band from the

Saddle Pals to the Comets, the kids of America started rocking around the clock, and country music was suddenly as uncool and unhip as the moonlight over Vermont.

Country record sales dropped sickeningly, country radio stations switched by batches to rock and roll, and huge country stars found themselves out of work. The careers of Ernest Tubb, Roy Acuff, and Lefty Frizzell faded. The only singers making any money were slick young stars like Marty Robbins with his "White Sport Coat and a Pink Carnation" or Sonny James who understood "Young Love" and could sell to teens.

For Willie, just twenty-one, and getting a hard time from fellow country pickers over his odd singing and what seemed to them, weird sense of timing, it would have been the smart moment to abandon country music and move on over to rock and roll. But Willie simply didn't *feel* his music rockabilly style—with a heavy beat and twitching hips. Although he grew up on a blend of jazz, blues, smooth pop, and country, Willie still felt mostly country. "Country music was the easiest for me to play," he says of his early days, "and the one I liked best."

Although he held fast to his musical heritage, in Fort Worth Willie left behind forever another mainstay of his raising—organized religion.

All the Nelson family members in Fort Worth, reminiscent of the days when they had moved from Arkansas to Abbott and all joined the Methodist Church, had joined the Metropolitan Baptist Church, located in an area of modest, working-class homes.

Willie and Ira were both serious enough about their

79

religion to be teaching Sunday school.

One Sunday morning after Willie had started play-ing on the Jacksboro Highway with Paul, the preacher approached Willie with a stern pronouncement: "You can't be teaching Sunday school and singing in them honky-tonks, too," he pompously declared. Taken aback by the man's officious religiosity, Willie suggested the preacher — and his supporters — were taking a dogmatically one-sided view of things.

"I tried to explain to them," Willie says, "that the plumber was in there putting in the commode; he was getting his money and nobody was bitching — same with the electrician stringing the lights. But the guy who was up there singin' his ass off, couldn't sing in beer joints and churches, too."

Willie also pointed out that he was seeing several of the same faces in the honky-tonks on Saturday night that he was meeting in church the following morning. But his arguments fell on deaf ears — the church leaders demanded that Willie make a choice.

The way Willie viewed it, his choice was whether to hang in at Metropolitan and try to change the congregation over to what he believed was a more honest way of thinking, or to just move on to some other place where people thought as he did. Bitter over the fact that the preacher seemed to take whatever position the big contributors in the congregation told him to take, Willie decided to leave. He quit teaching Sunday school, and Ira did, too.

Willie rarely darkened the door of a church again. From that day on, he preferred to conduct whatever religious ministry he felt called you to practice in places where people thought as he did — honky-tonks and bars.

Off leading her own life, Bobbie was having problems with music and religion, too. Her husband Bud had died a young, untimely death, and although she later remarried, Bobbie was pretty much on her own raising three young sons. With the help of Mama Nelson, who moved in with her, Bobbie managed to hold down jobs playing piano in restaurants, cocktail lounges, and piano bars.

Plagued by guilt brought on by her religious upbringing, she entered business college to try to find a more respectable job. But, ironically, business school led her into a job demonstrating organs.

"When I was raising my boys, I worked for the Hammond organ people," Bobbie told *Esquire*. "I worked ever' fair, ever' stock show. I was on this little carousel, had a microphone strapped to me. I'd be turning around, talking, turning around and smiling. Shoot, it was the nearest I could get to performing, demonstrating the organs."

Finally, she told writer Jack Hurst, she just decided a real musician "couldn't quit."

"We finally thought," she explained for herself and for Willie, " 'I believe I'll just go on and be bad — I believe I was happier being bad than I was when I was trying to be good.' "

Or, as Paul English says smiling satanically, "We was just born scufflers, I guess."

CRAZY

1956 — Elvis records in Nashville
1957 — Porter Wagoner joins the Grand
       Ole Opry
1958 — Kingston Trio wins Grammy for
       best country performance with
       "Tom Dooley"
1959 — Buddy Holly dies in a plane crash.
       Waylon Jennings, who gave up his
       plane seat, lives.

An old ex-scuffler herself, Willie's mother, Myrle, had been prevailing on Willie and Martha for some time to move up to Vancouver, Washington and live near her.

Around 1956, they packed up Lana and their meager belongings and moved to Portland, just across the bridge from Vancouver. Willie went to work at KVAN radio where he ran his own country radio show from ten A.M. till two in the afternoon.

Willie, who radiated a low-key, friendly, and sincere personality on the air, had a natural knack as a disc jockey, and his show was second only to Arthur Godfrey's in the Vancouver area.

It wasn't long until his selling instincts came into play, and Willie got to thinking that his popular program was the ideal vehicle, not just for country music in general, but for Willie Nelson music specifically. In the fall of 1957, in the little station studio where they cut radio commercials, Willie recorded his first record.

The "A" side of the initial release on Willie Nelson Records was a tune written by W. Nelson, sung by W. Nelson, and produced by W. Nelson. W. Nelson was twenty-four.

The record was a big hit with Willie's radio audience. "I hammered it pretty hard," he grins, "telling folks that for one dollar I would send them the record plus an autographed picture of myself. And, by golly, I pressed 3,000 of 'em, and sold every doggone one."

Right out of the box, Willie hit on a combination he would often use in his later recording career. The "A" side, "No Place for Me," is a melancholy country blues song written by Willie. It is an adult statement of the deeply repressed feelings of a little boy who, years ago, found he could somehow always write about the sad side of life. "Your love is as cold as the north wind that blows/ and the river that runs to the sea. . . . There's no place for me," the song mournfully goes.

The back side, however, is an upbeat pop tune called "Lumberjack," written by Leon Payne. Decades later Willie would break his career open singing pop tunes penned by other writers.

Willie was having a small measure of professional

success with his songwriting around this time. Actually, his first taste of professional writing had come back in 1949. When Willie was a sophomore, he had written a song with Steve Pulliam called "Pullamo," and it had been published by Sophisticate Music.

Around 1956 he teamed up with a well-known Texas songwriter named Jack Rhodes, who had penned hits for Sonny James and Hank Snow, and they co-wrote "Too Young To Settle Down." That was published by the substantial California publisher, Central Songs.

As luck would have it, while Willie was living in Vancouver, one of the hottest writers in America came though town: Mae Boren Axton who had co-written "Heartbreak Hotel" for Elvis Presley.

"I was in Washington," Mae Axton remembers, "and this skinny little D.J. ran up to me and said, 'Mrs. Axton, I'm Willie Nelson, and I play every one of the songs you write.' He said he wanted to be a songwriter, and asked if I'd listen to one he had on tape.

"I told him I was trying to catch a plane, but I'd listen to one. He played it, and I told him to leave the recorder on. I told him to quit that radio station and start writing songs."

Apparently, Willie decided to take Mae Axton's advice. Around 1958, he moved back down to Fort Worth for a while, then on down to one of his old kicking-around centers, Houston. He had hustled and hitchhicked and bummed beds around Houston dozens of times before, but now there was some promising activity developing in the oil town in the person of one Harold W. "Pappy" Daily.

Daily, a native of Yoakum, Texas, was one of the most colorful and successful executives in country music after World War II. In the early '50s, he started a record company in Houston called Starday, and scored hits with Arlie Duff's "Y'all Come" and George Jones's "Why Baby Why."

At the time Willie hit Houston, Pappy Daily was regrouping and had started a new label called D Records. With his Vancouver record and stacks of unpublished songs, Willie was able to work some deals writing and recording for Daily.

Willie and Martha, living east of Houston in Pasadena, now had three really cute kids, all with Martha's dark skin and Willie's big round eyes. Susie was two years younger than Lana, and had been born in Vancouver; and son Billie was three years younger than Susie.

Hurting for money as always, now with five mouths to feed, Willie landed a day job as a disc jockey, started teaching at Paul Buskirk's School of Guitar on the side, and played with bands seven nights a week.

Unlike Bobbie, Willie had never learned to read music, and he was just barely able to hold on to his guitar-teaching job. Scrambling to teach himself what key a song was in, or whether it was a waltz or a foxtrot, Willie just narrowly managed to stay one lesson ahead of his pupils.

The one bright spot was that he had started writing some songs that he thought were pretty decent. "I didn't come up with anything I thought was worth anything till I was twenty to twenty-five years old," he once told Robert W. Morgan.

"I was singing around different clubs and getting

requests for them—I was a local hero," he laughed. "But I knew local was about all I was going to get with those songs, so I had to come up with something better. I graded it—out of a possible ten, I got three. I'm pretty critical of my own songs."

In Houston, Willie's songwriting was starting to mature. One night driving from his house to play at the Esquire Club, he started a song when the idea "the night life ain't a good life, but it's my life" popped into his head. Willie's always found that his songwriting juices get rolling when he's moving in a car, and he put together half the song on the drive to the club, and the other half on the way back. It was, of course, "Night Life."

As always, the night life was raising havoc at home. With the head of the house in honky-tonks seven nights a week and working days, with a new baby in the house and never enough money to pay bills, Willie and Martha found themselves constantly flaring up in bitter, disheartening fights.

Searching for a way to relieve the pressure, knowing he would never give up playing in bands, dearly loving his two girls and little boy, Willie knew he simply had to come up with more money. Already working nearly every hour of the day and night, he resorted to hawking his songs for outright sale.

Selling a song means that whoever buys the song gets to put his own name on it as writer, in place of the real author's, and to collect all the money the song ever earns. Although heavily frowned on in the music industry today, selling songs was a common, if stupid, practice of the '50s and '60s.

Willie started out offering a once-in-a-lifetime deal:

three songs for ten dollars each—"Night Life," Crazy," and "Mr. Record Man." Luckily, the businessman to whom he made this proposition was both insightful and honest. He told Willie the songs were worth more than that, and simply loaned him fifty dollars.

Willie, however, who once described his financial acumen as somewhere next to that of Bob Wills's (who died penniless), either failed to grasp the point or was soon badly in need of money again. He sold "Night Life" to his boss Paul Buskirk and a friend for what it had cost to make a cheap recording of it.

"People get hungry, and instead of rippin' open a 7-11 store," Willie explained, "if they can sell their songs for a hundred bucks, they'll do that."

Selling his songs for a pittance, working three jobs, and constantly harassed at home, Willie was still not earning any recognition to speak of, as a musician. Freddie Powers, today a Vegas singer, who worked with Willie back then, was recently asked in awesome tones if all and sundry were aware of Willie's coming greatness at the time. "Naw," Powers replied. "Willie was just another guitar player."

Overworked, underpaid, and unrecognized, Willie found wild-eyed desperation setting in. He had always been a sensitive, moody, mercurial type, who tried to work out his feelings in songs, but still had to fight to keep a firm grip on himself.

Unless he was living up to his own self-imposed expectations, Willie was a man who could generate misery even in the midst of the most stunning success. "If you think negative, negative things will happen," Willie spoke from experience in later years. "I'm just so much of an extremist," he admitted. "I could go either way real quick. I could start thinking negative right now, and by showtime, I couldn't even go on."

Willie was also impatient and hot-tempered—"natural Nelson" his stepmother calls it. "It's in the Nelson blood," she says knowingly. "All the children have it; even Bobbie; even the grandchildren."

If Willie walked up to a door and wanted it open quick, he would bash it open with a boot, too impatient to fumble around with a key. He didn't like little obstacles; he didn't like to disappoint himself by failing to meet his own high standards; he didn't want to *wait*.

As the '50s neared an end, he found himself a married man with three kids to support, perilously near thirty, and after almost ten years still just an itinerant musician, puny local recording artist, minor songwriter, ex-salesman, ex-saddle maker, ex-plumber, or ex-any of the other fly-by-night jobs he'd held over the years.

He was mad at himself, depressed, confused. He even resorted to having his name paged in airports, just to keep his ego alive.

In 1959, Pappy Daily agreed to release a couple of singles by Willie on the D label, and they painted vivid testimonials to the state of mind he was in. "The Storm Has Just Begun" was backed by "Man with the Blues"; and "What a Way To Live" flipped over to "Misery Mansion."

Frustrated, angry, Willie didn't know what to do. Everything he tried seemed to move sideways or down—not up. His life had been repeating itself over and over in a vicious cycle since Abbott days. It hadn't really been fair to Martha—seemed as though every time the rent came due, they had to pick up and move. He knew he'd gone as far as he could go in Texas, and people kept telling him that Nashville, Tennessee was where all the money and action had moved in the country-music business. But he dreaded even thinking about moving to another strange town without a dime.

Finally, he admitted he was at the end of his rope. He only had two choices. He had to go really professional with his music, make some money, get into the big time; or he had to forget the music business forever, forget writing songs, shape up, and get a nine-to-five job. Maybe he'd become a lawyer, as he'd considered when the thing at Baylor didn't work out.

He went out and sold a song he'd always liked to sing to Lana, Susie, and Billy to lull them to sleep at night; a song he'd written about his days growing up with Mama and Daddy Nelson. Willie sold "Family Bible" for fifty dollars.

He returned home with the cash, only to have his wife and oldest daughter burst into tears.

"I cried and cried, because it was my favorite song," Lana once said. "Daddy said, 'Don't worry, I'll write more songs for you and make plenty of money.' "

On the price of his birthright, Willie prepared to go to Nashville. Carrying a "Texas credit card"—a gas-siphoning hose—he headed out of Houston in a '41 Buick. Days later, rolling into Nashville, the car promptly died.

"I wasn't really looking to set the town on fire," Willie says. "I was looking to sneak into town, make a contact, and sneak out."

A LAND THAT IS FAIRER THAN DAY

1959—Jim Reeves releases his biggest pop/country hit, "He'll Have To Go"

1959—Ray Price, defender of traditional country, releases "Heartaches by the Number"

Willie Nelson, in his old clunker, was one of hundreds. Day after day, they descended on the big little hillbilly town local citizens preferred to refer to as "The Athens of the South": families in wheezy old rattletraps who figured little Johnny could sing as good as ol' Ernest Tubb; dusty, red-necked farm boys with songs penciled on lined notebook paper and stuffed in a guitar case, slick pop songwriters who sensed that something big was breaking down south.

For the brightest, most cunning, and above all, most talented, the payoff would be head-spinning. For Nashville, in the '60s, it was the best and most intoxicating of times. The worst of times, thank God, and thank a cryptic, lanky guitar player named Chet Atkins, were over and done with.

Years later, journalists, caught up in the tap dance and media blitz called the "outlaw movement," would pit Willie Nelson against Chet Atkins: Willie, the lone-riding outsider, creator of unslick, down-to-earth music, versus Chet Atkins, well-connected insider, all violin strings and uptown Nashville sound.

In truth, Atkins had been far more of a musical maverick when he arrived in Nashville in the early '50s, than Willie was when he arrived in the early '60s. A desperately shy, introverted Appalachian-raised guitar player, Atkins had been fired from job after job with country bands and radio stations who didn't like his radical, "too modern" way of playing guitar.

He first made it to Nashville playing guitar on the Grand Ole Opry with Red Foley, only to find that then, and thereafter, the three-ring Opry with its Martha White "hot rize" and "Goo-Goo, it's good" atmosphere was a disaster for his relatively quiet, sophisticated picking.

"I was trying to play nice things," Chet remembers, "and they were selling popcorn in the aisles, babies were crying, and women were nursing babies at their breasts, and somebody would be out in front of you on stage talking about going fishing." He pauses and grins slightly. "That's what makes the show so great, you know."

Mere months after his debut, an edict came thundering down from the Opry's parent company in New York: Chet Atkins was to be banished from country music's greatest show. Crushed and humiliated, the depressed young guitarist retreated out of Nashville into a second round of doomed jobs, finally finding himself right back at the radio station near home where he had started six years ago.

Much to his amazement, several years earlier he had

been signed to an RCA recording contract, but as record after record after record bombed, he became increasingly despondent and withdrawn.

Nervous and pale-skinned with fidgety fingers that picked ugly sores in his perpetualy morose face, Atkins concluded, at age twenty-three, that he was washed up, a failure. It was over.

Providentially, The Carter Family, who had admired his picking from afar, selected that moment to give him a call. He quickly hit the road with Mother Maybelle and her three attractive daughters, Helen, Anita, and June. On the heels of their success, Fred Rose, the legendary mentor of Hank Williams, urged him to give Nashville another try.

Arriving the second time around, Atkins was elated to find himself quickly accepted by fellow musicians as one of the best of the so-called "Nashville cats." In 1951, he recorded his first hit, "Galloping Guitars."

In the early '50s RCA built their own recording studio in Nashville, and turned its management over to Atkins. On top of constantly hassling with sanctimonious members of the Methodist Radio and Film Commission, who rented the other half of the dinky studio, Atkins found himself forever at odds with the reactionary, dogmatic views of his recording engineers. Devotees of the old string-band sound, they refused to mike drums, let the singer get close to the microphone, or try any innovations. "It seemed like we did the same things over and over on every record," Chet says. "I felt like I could make better records, if given the chance."

Ever since moving to Nashville, Chet had been bickering with an assortment of conservative forces in town, including Opry manager, Jim Denny, who continually tried to get him kicked off the Opry, and Fred's son, Wesley Rose, partner of Roy Acuff and publisher of Hank Williams, who seemed to think country music peaked out with "The Great Speckled Bird."

Call it destiny, call it dollars, call it survival, if you will.

Around 1954, rockabilly hit, and hit hard. Country record sales dropped like barflies, attendance sagged at the Opry, television stations canceled their oldest country shows. Nashville panicked — and stayed panicked for four years.

Nashville's country record labels frantically tried cutting black music, but it didn't ring true. Through-the-nose, twangy, country singers tried to sing rock and roll, but they couldn't sing it — they were too square. Atkins started cutting rock groups, adding his own guitar, but that didn't mix right either.

Then Chet got an idea: Don Gibson.

Gibson had been on MGM, Columbia, and RCA and never made any hits for anybody. The first time around, RCA dropped him almost before they got him signed up. But Chet wanted to sign him. Everybody in the Nashville music industry, including his own boss, thought Chet had checked out and gone to the hop.

But Chet *knew*.

First and foremost, he knew Gibson could write songs. Second, he'd heard a Gibson demonstration tape that appealed to him — it had a bass drum on it.

Gibson's manager, unfortunately, was Wesley Rose, overwhelmingly powerful in Nashville at the time, and

Chet started out cutting the session Wesley's way: fiddles, steel, corny, dull.

As the dreary hours plodded on, normally soft-spoken Chet finally got fed up. "O.K., Wesley," he announced, "we've done it your way. Now let's try it my way." Chet's way included an echo unit and a bass drum.

In that one afternoon Atkins recorded a two-sided smash—"I Can't Stop Loving You" backed with "Oh, Lonesome Me." Gibson's record soared to the top of the country charts and crossed over to the pop charts. The Nashville sound was launched.

Actually, Atkins, like Willie, was a musician strongly influenced by jazz. They are both admirers of French guitar player Django Reinhardt, famous for his work in the '30s with the quintet of the Hot Club of France. Even before moving to Nashville Chet had been enamored, not with the big bands, but with the little jazz groups where each player improvised—Artie Shaw, the Gramercy Five, the Benny Goodman Trio.

Striking a deal with a club owner in Nashville's seedy, downtown neon strip called Printer's Alley, Chet and a bunch of musician friends started jamming every Sunday night. It was a stunning ensemble of Music Row's first string studio players—Floyd Cramer, Boots Randolph, Hank Garland, Bob Moore, Buddy Harmon—all just sitting in and picking.

"We were all just musicians—we didn't consider ourselves country, just musicians," Chet explains, in sentiments later echoed by Willie, Waylon, and other independent-minded types. "Boys like Buddy and Bob were playing jazz. Floyd was playing rinky-tink Dixieland-type piano. And we were all playing country music to make a living."

"That was the number-one team," Chet adds. "If you couldn't get them, you couldn't make a great record. Everybody else was old-fashioned musicians playing old-fashioned two-beat."

Working daily in the studio, Chet realized that rock and roll, aimed exclusively at teen-agers, had left two groups of music lovers without much music to listen to: country fans and the pop fans of smooth, mainstream artists like Frank Sinatra, Perry Como, and Dean Martin. (In reality, the old pop departments of major labels had been even harder hit than country by the onslaught of rock and roll.)

The town-and-country "countrypolitan" sound Atkins developed in the studio, with artists like Jim Reeves, the Browns, Eddy Arnold, and Don Gibson, was designed to hit all the bases: young people, country listeners, and longtime pop fans. It was a stunningly successful recipe.

Hit after hit developed under Atkins' regime at RCA, rising to the top of the charts and paving the way in the mid-'60s, for a whole new generation of country/pop performers: Roger Miller, Bobby Bare, Bill Anderson, Buck Owens, and Glen Campbell.

There is no question that the Nashville sound drew country music away from its hard country, fiddle-strong rural roots. But whatever the harangues and hard feelings over the negative effect the Nashville sound had on pure country music, there can be no debating that it was the savior of the Nashville music industry economically. To a country music rapidly losing its audience in the mid-'50s, hits that crossed to the pop charts meant economic preservation. The

Nashville sound was commercial, it sold records, it made *big money*.

Specifically, it made Willie Hugh Nelson big money. If the smooth pop legacy of the Nashville sound drove Willie back home to Texas in the early '70s to search for a rawer, more earthy, more basic music; in the early '60s, it put into Willie's pockets the first real bucks he had ever seen off his music. Why? Because Willie Nelson, whether he recognized it or not, was a genius, but not entirely country, songwriter.

Songwriting really began to emerge as a professional business in Nashville in the early '60s. Along with sacks of pop dollars came the businessmen, and a steady stream of hopeful writers from all over the country—and some of these boys and (a few) girls, were very, very good. Harlan Howard, Hank Cochran, Wayne Walker, Bill Anderson, Mel Tillis, formed a new breed of writers who crowded into Tootsie's Orchid Lounge across from the Opry every Saturday night to psych each other out with their latest, greatest tunes.

" '59, '60, '61, for a songwriter was kind of a magic time," says Howard, author of "Busted," "Pick Me Up on Your Way Down," "I Fall to Pieces," "I've Got a Tiger by the Tail," and dozens more. "The town was much more open. A tremendous group, including myself, hit town all within about a year of each other.

"There was Roger Miller, Bill Anderson, Hank Cochran, Willie, myself, Dallas Frazier, Doodles Owen. Loudermilk had just been here a little while. Wayne Walker, Mel Tillis . . .

"I've never seen that many prolific, productive

writers come here all at once. All of us got a lot of records and made a lot of money. Hell, I got as high as a dozen records in a week.

"There were two main studios then," Howard remembers. "We used to run back and forth from one place to the other because we were getting songs cut at the same time in different studios.

"There was something magic about the early '60s. It'll never be that wide open again."

SOMETIMES IT'S HEAVEN,
SOMETIMES IT'S HELL
(Sometimes I Don't Even Know)

1961 — Jimmie Rodgers honored as one of first in-
         ductees into Country Music Hall of Fame
1962 — Loretta Lynn's first hit, "Success"
1963 — Charlie Pride moves to Nashville
1963 — Johnny Cash records "Ring of Fire"

Two weeks after Willie left Houston, Martha, Lana, Susie, and Billie arrived at the dingy, soot-covered bus station in downtown Nashville. Willie moved them all into a small green trailer out at Dunn's Trailer Court, on the working-class side of town — east Nashville.

Located between a used-car lot and a veterans' cemetery on one of east Nashville's main drags, Dunn's consisted of twenty or thirty trailers lined up behind a drab house with big, heavy stone pillars. In the middle of the court, on a concrete pavilion, was a pay phone, since most of the residents couldn't afford their own phones. Out front was a sign, immortalized by Roger Miller in a line from "King of the Road":

In the ebb and flow of writers pouring into town, Willie was just one more unknown face. But this time Willie was determined to spend all his time breaking in—not tied up all day selling encyclopedias or fixing somebody's plumbing. It was common scuttlebutt that if a singer was going to make it, it was mandatory to hang out at Tootsie's Orchid Lounge downtown, get drunk, get drunk with the right people, get noticed, get a record deal, form a band, hit the road, and then, naturally, become a star.

Willie started hanging out at Tootsie's in earnest, and Martha took a job.

The only job she could land was mixing drinks at the Hitching Post, a bar downtown on Broadway, across the street from Tootsie's and a couple of blocks from the Grand Ole Opry House. Pretty soon she was managing the Hitching Post, and filling in next door at the Wagon Wheel, as well.

When Martha worked, Willie would stay home and take care of the kids. When Martha didn't work, Willie would carouse all night, and try to get something going.

After several months of bringing home the paycheck, Martha's Indian temper started rising from a slow steam to a steady boil. For eight years she'd been putting up with this kind of life; now she'd picked up and moved halfway across the country with three little kids, and what did she get? More shabby treatment. A husband who was letting her support the family, while he hung out in bars for hours on end and came home drunk as a goose. It made her Cherokee temper hotter than Sitting Bull's the first time he spotted Custer.

One night shortly after they arrived in Nashville, Willie dragged in drunk and passed out on the bed. Martha saw warpaint red. She crammed every stitch of Willie's clothes in a suitcase, loaded it and the kids in the car, and drove off in a fury. Running into Wayne Walker downtown at Tootsie's, she told him the whole sorry story and announced, "I'm not going back for four days."

Four days later, she righteously pulled up at the trailer, and discovered Willie still sitting inside in his drawers. Virtually nude and without a phone, Willie had hesitated to knock on the doors of his new neighbors and explain his predicament. So, he had just sat there for four days: Shotgun Willie in his underwear.

"It was a miserable time," Willie says of his first few months in Nashville. "My wife was making a few dollars as a bartender, and I was hanging around Tootsie's or the Printer's Alley bars, bringing home nothing. But maybe all the pain and drinking was what I needed."

Into serious boozing, he also got into some serious writing. Maybe it was partly to fulfill his promise to Lana to write more songs for her and make a lot of money. "When you write for money because you are hungry and have a family to support," Willie once explained, "there is reason enough to get up and work hard all day." And as Lana once said of her dad, "He always made sure that we knew he loved us more than anything."

Hanging out at Tootsie's definitely was the right strategy, because in that smoky bar, located just across an alley from the back door of the Opry House, Willie was meeting the gang of topnotch writers who were becoming his running buddies: Hank Cochran, Harland Howard, Roger Miller, Wayne Walker, Mel Tillis. ("Bless 'em," said Tootsie Bess, the hefty, no-nonsense, but big-hearted proprietress of the bar, "they were the first of my funky ones.")

One of the leaders of the pack was Cochran, a heavyset, jovial man with a zany, wild streak that earned him a reputation as an eccentric, even among his fellow eccentrics. Cochran, who wrote for a California-based company called Pamper Music, had transferred to Nashville during the country music industry's annual Disc Jockey Convention in October of 1959. (One boozy night Cochran offered "Little Willie," as he called him, a lift home, and when they arrived at Dunn's, he exclaimed, to their mutual surprise, that the very same green trailer Willie lived in, was the second place he had rented after moving to Nashville.)

It was during a "guitar pulling" in the smoke-polluted back room of Tootsie's, that Cochran had first happened to hear "Little Willie" pick a few tunes. A tremendously gifted songwriter himself, Cochran couldn't believe what he was hearing. The future author of "Make the World Go Away," and "She's Got You," Cochran, at the time, was making fifty dollars a week from Pamper, and was in line for another fifty dollar raise. But he quickly hotfooted over to Pamper's Nashville office, and begged them to use his fifty dollar raise to sign up Willie Nelson instead.

Thanks to Hank, Willie was suddenly a professional songwriter, pulling in fifty dollars a week from a major publishing house owned by two giants in the business—singer Ray Price and booking agent Hal Smith.

But fifty dollars a week was still next to nothing with five mouths to feed. The trailer cost twenty dollars a week, and in the winter, the heating bill was forty dollars a week. "I don't know how I lived on fifty dollars a week," Willie once mused, then perked up, "Oh, yes, I do. I didn't pay my oil bill!"

Luckily, Pappy Dailey was still pumping away down in Houston, and one of Pappy's artists, Claude Gray, recorded Willie's song, "Family Bible." Charlie Dick, Patsy Cline's husband, remembers that Willie was so excited, he ran four blocks in the snow over to Tootsie's just to show him a copy of the record. "He'd gone out and bought it to show me, even though he probably couldn't afford it," Charlie says.

"Family Bible" was a top-ten record of 1960, which normally would have eased Willie's financial woes considerably. There was just one hitch—he had sold the song in Houston to get enough money to drive to Nashville. Willie didn't even get his name on the record, much less earn any royalties—his name doesn't appear as author of "Family Bible" to this day.

Martha was impressed, but less than mollified. Now that Willie had something going reputation-wise, he seemed to run amok more than ever. Actually, getting drunk and staying crazy for days on end is a basic custom of aspiring, on-the-rise singers and writers in Nashville. Partly, it's raw, unused energy; partly, it's mind-bending frustration, and partly, it's a virtually mandatory macho tribal rite where points are earned by hell-raisers who can drink the most and stay up the longest. It was not from fantasy that in these years Willie wrote a song called, "I Gotta Get Drunk (and I sure do regret it.)"

Lying in wait as Willie stumbled in soused night after night, Martha would let the steam build up for days. One snowy winter night, he bumbled into the trailer and blearily undressed, whereupon Martha whipped out a butcher knife and chased him (again in his underwear) out into the cemetery next door. Pursued by yells and threats (and the knife), Willie skipped and grimaced across the snow in his bare feet, dodging behind tombstones for protection.

"He's the shy type," offers Martha, a consistently charming and friendly woman now that she's married to a man who treats her right. "I'm always the one who raised the Cain. He'd rather just stay away or walk away."

Perhaps to make Martha happy, Willie moved the family to a new little house, out in the country about thirty miles outside Nashville, near the offices of Pamper Music. They found out about it from Tompall and the Glaser Brothers, who had just moved out.

"To me," Martha says, "it was a beautiful home."

In the daytime, Willie drove over to Pamper Music to hang around with Hank Cochran. About that time Willie had been trying to think of something to write for Billy "The Traveling Texan" Walker, who had recorded one of his songs a couple of years earlier. Walker had just moved from the Ozark Jubilee to the Grand Ole Opry and was planning to record in Nashville.

The drive to Pamper Music took about fifteen minutes, and on the way in one day, Willie got to mulling over a phrase he'd heard people use a couple of times. By the time he pulled in at the office, he had written "Funny How Time Slips Away."

"That's the only time I've written a song consciously for somebody else to sing," Willie once revealed. However, it was the second gigantic musical standard he had written in a car—"Night Life" was the first. This made it eminently appropriate that he wrote "Hello Walls" in a garage.

"There was a small garage outside the publishing company—it was a residence that had been turned into a publishing company," he explains. "Hank Cochran and I would sit out there and write songs in that garage.

"There was a door, and a window, and a guitar, and that was about it. We were out there this one particular day, and I started writing this song—I started talking to the walls," he laughs.

"Hank got a phone call. When he was leaving I said, 'Hey, I've got this idea for a song, and I want you to help me write it.' "

Cochran was only gone about ten minutes. By the time he got back, Willie had already scribbled the whole song on the back of a scrap of cardboard. "So he missed out on half of 'Hello Walls,' " Willie adds wryly, "fortunately."

One veteran Nashville journalist recalls nights when Cochran, "one of those crazy, blind-running songwriters," would call her on the phone down in Alabama at four A.M. yelling, "Listen to this, he's been reading my mail!", and zealously play her a new Willie Nelson song over the telephone.

Now employed by Pamper Music as a songplugger

as well as writer, Cochran had one of his first promotion successes when he played Willie's "Crazy" for a new girl singer whose records were getting a lot of pop airplay—Patsy Cline. She recorded "Crazy" almost immediately.

Then one day Martha was working the bar at the Hitching Post, when Faron Young, one of the slickest recording and television stars of the time (he'd even starred in a movie with Zsa Zsa Gabor) came in for a drink. A promoter walked up to Faron and Martha overheard him say, "There's this guy over at Tootsie's and he's got one hell of a song. Really plays good guitar, too."

"Well, hell, who is it?" Faron demanded.

"Willie Nelson," the man replied to Martha's astonished delight.

"Before that, Faron would never listen to Willie's songs," Martha says. "Faron was always so . . . I put him down to his face one time," she laughs, "but he still likes me."

Willie was over at Tootsie's, and Faron walked across the street, came in, and sat down. Hank Cochran introduced them.

"In my own way, I sang 'Hello Walls' for him," Willie says. "Even though it sounded totally different from Faron's hit version, it was one of the best performances I ever staged," he adds with conviction.

Although "Crazy" was recorded first, "Hello Walls" was released first. It jumped to number one, and ended up the third biggest record of 1961.

That year, mere months—not lengthy years—after hitting town, Willie Nelson had the incredible distinction of being a brand-new songwriter with three top-ten smashes: "Hello Walls" by Faron Young, "Funny How Time Slips Away," by Billy Walker, and "Crazy" by Patsy Cline. Right after that, Willie co-wrote a takeoff on "Hello Walls" called "Hello Fool" that was a big hit for disc jockey Ralph Emery.

"Hank Cochran and Willie and I were supplying most of the songs that Patsy Cline was doing before she died," says Harlan Howard. "We couldn't write songs for Patsy where she was married or had kids, because she was selling to a young girl's market. If you wanted a Patsy Cline record, you'd better write something that would be played on the pop stations."

Willie was quickly recognized as a writer that had that pop twist in his songs when "Hello Walls" and "Crazy" both crossed over to the pop charts. For Willie, that meant really big Nashville-sound batches of money rolling in.

To add to Nashville's growing awe over this short, red-headed writer from Texas, Willie's elegantly simple songs began to be snapped up by a rainbow of the top performers in the country. Soon, he was getting cuts by rhythm-and-blues and jazz artists, as well as country and pop singers.

When Chet Atkins was asked what he thought made Willie stand out as a songwriter and singer, he immediately replied, "I think it's his intelligence—his intelligence about communicating a lyric to people. I said this before he was known," Chet notes. "I always admired him, because he was so damned bright. You know, you read his lyrics, and you can tell it in the way he puts together a song. It borders on genius—the simplicity and feeling that he can get into a lyric. It's like he's talking to you."

By 1961 Willie's dirt-poor days were over forever. "I had a taste of success when I sold some songs," Willie once said, "and so many people started to record them that after a while there was no real hand-to-mouth struggling." But Willie had no experience to prepare him for the sudden money rolling in. "I could pay the bills, but I didn't know how to handle the money," he confesses. "It didn't take long to go through the first royalty check."

On top of songwriting, Willie had also started raking in top dollars on the road, playing bass for his song publisher, one of the hottest singers in the business—Ray Price. Shortly before "Hello Walls" hit, Willie had replaced a guy named Donny Young—now known as Johnny Paycheck—when he quit as Price's front man. Willie admits he didn't know how to play bass when he landed Paycheck's job. He just figured that if he could play guitar, he could play bass, too.

Ray Price, born and reared in Texas, was a masterful singer whose style vibrated musically on a wavelength between Bob Wills and Hank Williams. He had gotten his start in Texas with Wills, but one night when Hank Williams heard him do a guest spot on the Opry, he was so taken with the young singer, he demanded the Opry hire the kid as a regular.

At the time, Hank Williams was a giant on the Opry, and he and Price became Nashville roommates. But, sadly, as Price's career rose, Williams' career and life started to deteriorate.

When Hank was fired from the Opry, it looked as if his great band, the Drifting Cowboys would have to split up. Rather than let that happen, Price started using them on his shows.

On New Year's day, 1953, Price and the Drifting Cowboys had a show booked just forty miles from Canton, Ohio, where Hank was performing with another band. After their holiday shows, the two singers planned to get together and celebrate. It would be like old times.

"There I was, on my show with Hank's band," Price recalls with a shudder, "when somebody got up and announced that Hank Williams was dead. We did our show. It was the hardest thing I ever did."

Price recorded with the Drifting Cowboys for about a year afterward, but his records increasingly sounded like carbon copies of Hank. Never one to stay in a rut for long, Price formed a new band and named it the Cherokee Cowboys.

The Cherokee Cowboys proved to be an illustrious group. In addition to Willie, at one time or another it included Roger Miller, Johnny Bush, Darrell McCall, Buddy Emmons, and Johnny Paycheck. With the various versions of this band, Price began developing his distinctive "Ray Price sound."

During the rockabilly craze, Price had been one of the few aggressively staunch holdouts against the Chet Atkins solution—poppish countrypolitan music. Continuing to cut hard-country records, in 1954 he put out the smash "Release Me" and in 1956, with "Crazy Arms," knocked "Heartbreak Hotel" off the number-one spot on the country charts.

"In 1956, I took the music of the day, rhythm-and-blues and country music, and made some changes by new chord progressions; I raised the bass, lowered the steel, and got started," explains Price, who has been a paramount influence on Willie and dozens of other important country musicians. When he formed the Cherokee Cowboys, Price was idolized by traditionalists alarmed at the bastardization of hard-country music under the onslaught of rock and roll.

But Price, like a slew of other Texas musicians, Willie amongst them, is a pragmatic and unpredictable man. In 1957, he conceded a few points to the ever-more-lucrative pop/country market. "In 1957 I recorded the first big sound," he claims. "I used the Nashville Symphony and the Anita Kerr Singers, and recorded a faith album. That was the start of the big sound."

In 1958 Price cut Bill Anderson's first hit as a songwriter, "City Lights," and in 1959, he recorded Harlan Howard's first hit, "Heartaches by the Number." That same year he was voted "Favorite Male Vocalist." Price was an enormous star, when Willie joined his band.

After "Hello Walls" hit so big, Willie thought seriously about putting together his own band. Shrewd Faron Young, however, who knew a good thing when he saw it, had other ideas. "No, you stay in town, and be a songwriter," he urged Willie, "and let me record the songs." Willie who, even if he didn't have his own band, was fronting regularly for Price, just laughed. "Me not sing?" Willie says. "Just stay and write songs for him? 'Course, I'm a big ham. I like to get on stage and show off and sing, so that wasn't enough for me."

Now that Willie had tasted the kind of success that was possible in Nashville, nothing short of the total realization of his dreams was ever going to be enough for the man who was his own harshest critic.

Next, Willie was going to make himself a star.

Biff Collie, a top California D.J. and friend of Willie's at the time, recalls that "the producers and hot singers" in Nashville really admired Willie's unusual singing style; and the fact that Willie sang his own "demos" (demonstration tapes of songs for record producers to listen to and select songs for their recording artists) helped Willie a lot in getting his songs recorded.

In 1961, fired by success, Willie recorded dozens and dozens of demos for Pamper Music. He and Hank Cochran would rent a studio in Nashville, hire some of the town's top session musicians, and go to it. Once, they cut twenty-seven songs in three days.

Although many journalists have claimed that people in Nashville told Willie he was a great songwriter, but no singer, Chet Atkins retorts, "Aw, that's bull. Everybody thought he was a great singer. I did. I never knew anybody who thought he couldn't sing."

Although Willie's voice had been disliked by some local musicians out in Texas, who judged voices by what they were used to hearing; in Nashville, among the professionals, there is a constant search for the new star who is unique and different. "He was a great interpreter of lyrics," Atkins says. "That's all selling records is about—communicating that mood. It took me quite a few years when I was a kid to learn that. I thought you had to have a trained voice and all that. That isn't true."

Nonetheless, despite having demos on desks all over town, Willie didn't land his first recording contract in Nashville. Actually, once Willie got hot as a writer, Music Row executives found the new talk-of-the-town whisked out from under their noses almost before they could have typed up a contract.

Old "Hanktum," as Hank Cochran was known, came through again. In 1961, Joe Allison, who had just created a new country division for California-based Liberty Records, offered Cochran a recording contract. Amazingly selfless, the forthright Cochran spoke his heart, and told Allison he believed Willie was so talented, they should sign Willie first. Convinced, Allison signed Willie, and brought him out to Hollywood to record.

(Soon after, Liberty also signed Cochran who had a hit with "Sally Was a Good Ole Girl.")

Willie's start as a recording artist duplicated his almost unbelievably quick success as a songwriter. Although his first single, "The Part Where I Cry" didn't make the charts, the "B" side of his second single was a song called "Willingly," written by—of course—Hank Cochran. On March 17, 1962, "Willingly" hit the top ten on the charts.

"Willingly," however, was not by Willie unaided. Both sides of the record were duets recorded with an attractive, vivacious California singer named Shirley Collie.

Willie first met Shirley when he was on the road in California with Ray Price and was invited home to dinner by Shirley and her husband, Biff Collie. Collie, one of country music's most distinguished and successful D.J.'s, was working with KFOX radio in Long Beach. A Texan, and, in fact, the first country disc jockey in Houston, Collie met Shirley when he was manager and master of ceremonies for the famous Phillip Morris Country Music Show which toured thirty-seven states in 1957-58.

Shirley, a captivating and extremely talented singer and songwriter, had gotten her start on the nationally known "Rush Creek Follies," a live radio show similar to the "Grand Ole Opry," broadcast over KMBC in Kansas City. Next she moved up, as a yodeler and singer, to the "Ozark Jubilee."

Shirley had already been an artist on ABC Paramount Records when she met Collie on the Phillip Morris Show. They soon married and moved to California where, through Shirley's talent and Collie's friendship with Joe Allison, she landed a contract with Liberty Records.

Allison recorded four duets with Shirley and Willie, and Shirley came off the far better singer—she singing along easily and naturally, Willie straining to match his rare voice to hers. The somewhat uneven match perhaps suggested, even at the time, that the duo had other than a totally musical basis.

With the momentum of "Willingly," Willie's singing career kept moving up. On May 26, 1962, twenty-nine years to the day after Jimmie Rodgers died and left his legacy to country music, "Touch Me" became Willie's first solo record to hit the charts. It went to number seven and stayed on the charts thirteen weeks. Willie was also the same age as Jimmie Rodgers when he recorded his first hit: twenty-nine.

Building on the success of the singles, Liberty released Willie's first album, "And Then I Wrote," later that year. All twelve songs were written by Willie. It's an admirable album, simply and cleanly produced, and its finest instrument is Willie's voice which emerges sounding virtually the same as it does today.

"And Then I Wrote" was released to a shower of acclaim and optimistic forecasts. Charlie Williams, a well-known disc jockey who had hosted the Western Express show in Fort Worth before Willie took it over, wrote these enthusiastic liner notes that confirm Chet Atkins' claims about Willie's quick acceptance:

A vastly talented young man named Willie Nelson wrote these lyrics, and right now he's learning how you feel when you win.

With his songs being recorded as fast as he writes them, with his own records being played all over the country, he is, as they say in his native Texas, "hotter'n a depot stove."

I had heard of Willie Nelson before he ever made a record himself. In fact, everyone in the music business was talking about the new young songwriter who had come out of left field and knocked the old pros out of the best selling charts with hits like "Hello Walls," "Crazy," and "Funny How Time Slips Away." I had also heard he sang with a style and feeling you wouldn't believe, so when his first Liberty session was scheduled in Hollywood, I wrangled an invitation.

I went into the studio expecting to find the usual nervous rookie at the microphone. But there was Willie, perched on a high stool, a cigarette in one hand, and his chin in the other, calmly recording his own songs as if he'd been doing it all his life!

There's a certain intangible excitement that runs through the engineers, the musicians, and the spectators when a record session is really "coming off." By the time Willie had finished the last song about the wandering love who vows he's back forever and is asked, "How long is forever—this time?", Willie was the only calm person present.

On a different issue of that same album the liner notes continue this hyperabundant praise:

It is rare that a truly great songwriter is also an exciting vocalist—Johnny Mercer, Hoagy Carmichael, and a handful of others. Now, with pride, Liberty Records presents the latest member of that select group. His name is Willie Nelson.

As Willie's name lit up the national charts, a bit of hanky-panky took place back home in Houston. A song called "Nite Life" (note spelling) was released on R_X Records ("Prescription for Happy Times"). The artists listed were Paul Buskirk and His Little Men featuring Hugh Nelson.

Hugh Nelson? The record is a very jazzy, bluesy, martini-with-an-olive version of "Night Life" featuring a saxophone and Willie—singing with all the biting feeling built up during his tough days in Houston.

According to Dr. Thomas S. Johnson, Willie's official discographer and the current authority on Willie Nelson records, "Nite Life" was a "promotional record." The R_X on the label looked like the familiar symbol found on prescriptions. A note was enclosed reading something like, "Congratulations and many thanks. Your purchase of this record benefits a non-profit organization for cardiac research. . . ." It's signed, "Mary J. Hill, Ladies' Guild." The "nonprofit organization" and "ladies' guild," benefiting by the purchase, are not specified.

There was also a multitude of legitimate efforts to climb on the Willie Nelson bandwagon. Bowled over by Willie's stunning songs, giant stars began cutting Willie's tunes right and left. Over the next ten years his songs were recorded by a list of artists that read like the *Who's Who* of *all* music: Elvis Presley, Kris Kristofferson, Linda Ronstadt, Perry Como, Frank Sinatra, Leon Russell, Ray Charles, Lawrence Welk, Roy Orbison, Doris Day, Andy Williams, Aretha Franklin, Al Green, Bing Crosby, Eydie Gorme, Little Anthony and the Imperials. "Funny How Time Slips Away" alone has been recorded by more than eighty artists.

Even Ray Price got in on the Willie craze. In 1963, when Willie got his Texas buddy Johnny Bush a job with Price as drummer, Price recorded "Night Life" and started using it as his theme song. On the record, he introduced the song with a little intro/apology along the lines: "This was written for me by a boy down in Texas. It's not like what we usually do, but I think you'll like it."

In fact, what Price "usually" did, kept expanding and expanding. Continuing to experiment with violins (not fiddles, mind you) the Ray Price "big sound" culminated in 1963 with a recording of Hank Cochran's "Make the World Go Away." That record, Price advised, proved his theory that "one shouldn't ignore the symphony audiences that want to hear country music."

Although it's true that Willie never much liked the glittery, rhinestone-studded "Nudie look" (named after the Hollywood designer of the eye-blinding stage attire), it's apparently not true that he never wore gaudy outfits.

In the August, 1963, *Music City News*, a reporter somewhat overwhelmed by Price and his stage wear, described the outfits as "exquisitely tailored western costumes—in white, turquoise, shell pink, or shocking black—featuring an Indian chief's multihued headdress comprised of thousands of rhinestones on the back of the coat with a cascade of feathers outlined down the trouser legs. A heavy silver belt buckle with diamond initials add to the glitter along with boots that have toes and heels of sterling silver."

As for the band, which included Willie and Johnny Bush, the "uniforms worn by the Cherokee Cowboys are colored to match those of 'the chief' and all feature a thunderbird motif fashioned in rhinestones."

Meanwhile, Willie still had his own Cherokee to deal with at home. "It never occurred to me," says daughter Lana, "that people's parents were supposed to get along. After we moved to Nashville, Daddy was on the road a lot. Mom just couldn't handle it."

"Willie would be gone six weeks at a time," Martha exclaims. "Sometimes I would go with him, but I didn't like what I saw when I went.

"I'm not the kind of person that could share him with anybody," Martha says. "If somebody could do that one time, I could never trust them again. I would always look at them early in the morning and think, 'I wish I could get even with you.' "

Martha did her dead level best to even all unbalanced scores. One time she threw a fork at Willie that stuck in his ribs "with a strange humming sound," he recalls. Another time she dumped a plate of hot potatoes and gravy over his head at a sit-down dinner with friends. Still another time, she threw a shot glass at Willie; it sailed across the bar, smashed against a wall, and the pieces bounced back and cut open the face of a friend.

"I guess I do the things other people just want to do," Martha admits. "Willie laughs now, and talks about how damn' mean I was."

Her getting even reached its highest level of success the night she tied Willie up in a sheet. Although widely reported that she tediously sewed Willie up in the sheet ("Willie has gone along with it to the reporters," she notes), hair-tempered Martha could scarcely have bottled up her fury for that long. Instead, when Willie staggered in shellacked and fell across the bed, Martha "undid the bottom sheet, folded it over, and tied him with the girls' jump rope. The kids were asleep," she says, "and I put them in the car and started the car." She then marched into the bedroom with the broom, and proceeded to wham it down, again and again, on Willie's trussed-up carcass.

"I woke up in a straitjacket getting pounded like a short-order steak," Willie grimaces.

By the time Martha worked the frustration out of her system, Willie's nose was broken and bleeding. Scared of the potential fallout, Martha took off in the car with the kids and stayed gone a week.

"By the time I got loose," Willie says, "she'd lit out

117

in the car with the kids, her clothes, and my clothes. There was no way I could follow her naked, and that was kind of the end of it."

As would always be true in his recording career, the songs Willie was recording at the time were radically true to his life. Every one of the twelve songs on Willie's first album tell of broken relationships, lonely houses, lovers wounded and done wrong—every single song. "Wake Me When It's Over (when the need for you is gone)," "Touch Me (and you'll know how you feel with the blues)," "Three Days (that I'll always dream of you)," "Where My House Lives (this house that used to be my home)," are just starters.

In one song he even seems to be coming out and asking for a divorce ("If you can't undo the wrong, undo the right").

"I felt it could have worked out, if he was not a musician," Martha has decided. "That's just a musician for you—that's just a man. When something's thrown in your face . . . there's not one musician I've seen that hasn't been with somebody on the side."

Hurt, angry, feeling used and helpless, except when she evened the score in a fight, Martha was desolate. "One day I just sat down and cried," she says. "He started making good money with Ray Price and was collecting royalties off his songs. I had a Cadillac, new furniture, and a nice home. I had always thought that if we had money, it would solve all the problems."

There was certainly plenty of money—a fortune to a couple who had scraped along in crummy apartments and junky cars for ten years. At points in the '60s, Willie was earning $70,000 a year and up—sometimes in the six-figure range—on his songwriting alone. But

118

for Willie, as for Martha, the money didn't help. Willie was now distraught over the rapid bottoming out of what had appeared to be a sure-fire, up-and-coming record career.

His second Liberty album, "Here's Willie Nelson," had again been released with much fanfare—this time heaped on by Willie's boyhood hero, Bob Wills. "I have had the pleasure of being an entertainer for nearly thirty-five years," Wills wrote in the liner notes. "During this time I've seen a lot of new talent appear on the music scene. But hardly ever have I seen the likes of Willie Nelson. Here is a young man who is not only a talented writer of songs, but also a vocalist with a unique style. What's more—and this is probably a very natural thing—Willie's style is just right for his material."

But for reasons hard to pin down, Willie's recording career took a stomach-churning nosedive. Maybe it was because he only wrote four of the twelve songs on "Here's Willie Nelson." Maybe it was because a bunch of strings and syrupy production was tacked on to the second album by Willie's new record producer. Most likely, it was because Liberty Records was on the verge of going out of business.

At any rate, not one of the eight singles Willie released in 1963 and 1964 made it to the top twenty of the charts. Most didn't chart at all.

A second duet with Shirley Collie, "You Dream About Me" was a loser. The follow-up didn't chart. "Half a Man" (which excited a lot of talk along Nashville's Music Row) rose to a sluggish number twenty-five in April, 1963. Another single bombed, then "You Took My Happy Away" in January of 1964

119

fizzled out after a three-week spurt to number thirty-three. Three more duds in a row, and Liberty Records was out of business, and Willie was out of a recording contract.

Meanwhile, on the road, Willie was still fronting for another singer—not fulfilling his dreams of becoming a big star and heading up his own band.

"All of a sudden I had a lot of money," Willie says of the early '60s, "but it wasn't worth anything because of what I was going through.

"So I started throwing it away with both hands. I was playing bass with Ray Price, making thirty dollars a day, and I was flying to all the jobs, renting penthouses and suites, buying everybody dinner—while Ray was riding on the bus with the rest of the guys."

Willie once, in the midst of playing the big-wad, high-roller, became so despondent, he attempted what must surely be one of the world's most bizarre suicide attempts. He simply lay down in the four-lane downtown street outside Tootsie's and waited to be run over. Martha and some friends dragged him to safety.

Many years later in Nashville, Willie and Faron Young found themselves on the same stage together. "Sixty years ago," Faron joked, pointing to Willie, "this guy wore a crew cut and didn't have a beard. He walked into Tootsie's Orchid Lounge, and sang me a song he had just written.

"That song," Faron laughed, " 'Hello Walls,' sold three million copies. We both got rich, didn't we, Willie?"

"*You* got rich," Willie replied; "I got drunk."

In May of 1963, Willie wrote a very touching letter,

apparently while on the road, to "my dearest children."

Here he is again, he writes, their "big, fat ugly daddy," who misses them very much. Everywhere he looks, he says, he sees little boys playing ball or little girls dressed up in pretty dresses, and it makes him think of his own kids at home.

As the three grow older, Willie counsels, they will come to realize that life does not always work out exactly the way you want, even things you want "more than anything in the world." They won't understand, and will think life has played a "dirty trick" on them. But they must always remember what their daddy tells them: life does not come from getting everything you want, but from "understanding and accepting all," and having faith that everything happens for the best. Write soon, he urges, and signs, "All the love in the world, Daddy."

In October of 1963, Willie and Martha decided to call it quits. "Neither of us had anybody else; we just sat down one day," Martha says. "It really hurt me, especially because of the kids. They have always been very devoted to Willie."

"I tried being like other people," Willie sighs. "I tried to work and come home and watch TV. That just wasn't me."

Ego-bruised and mad, Martha packed up the kids and moved to Las Vegas, then Los Angeles, finally back to Waco. For two years she refused to let Willie see the kids, Lana says, "to get back at Daddy."

"For two years we bickered back and forth," Martha says, "and then I realized I was just hurting the kids."

Martha readily admits that the kids adored their

121

daddy, and that Willie has "always been a good father." Gradually, she let the children start visiting Willie on weekends, and when Lana was twelve, she went to live with Willie and his second wife.

Lana, Martha says, is "Willie made over." A dark, attractive woman of twenty-seven, with her mother's flowing black hair, Lana once told a newspaper, "My father is a music lover first. I guess I understood it better than my mother did. When you're the daughter, you don't feel like you come second; nothing ever stood between us, because there was no rivalry.

"When he is with us," Lana said, "he gives us his undivided attention."

"Willie is real quiet-spoken with the kids," Martha adds. "He never really gets mad at them; just tells them not to make the same mistake again. Anything they ever wanted, even when we didn't have money, if he possibly could get it, he would."

Martha says she and Willie are "best of friends" now. Even Willie and her current husband are friends, and "that doesn't happen very often," she points out.

"A lot of times my husband and kids will go see him when he comes to Waco," she continues, "and the first thing he will say is, 'Where's your mamma?'

"I can't say there's no feeling left," Martha admits, "and Willie says, 'I'll always think about you.' " Then she laughs. "But he adds, 'Well, I don't dwell on it every day.' "

By the time his divorce was final, Willie was earning six hundred dollars a week in songwriter advances alone. (" 'Funny How Time Slips Away' paid a lot of alimony," he notes.) In 1962 Faron Young hit again

122

with Willie's "Three Days" and in 1963 Roy Orbison recorded Willie's emotional Christmas song, "Pretty Paper." After the divorce, really big royalty checks started rolling in. "He told me," Crash Stewart wrote, "that of all the things he missed, the one he missed most was that Martha wasn't there to share the success for which they both struggled."

Although not struggling financially, Willie was struggling in every other way, and mainly with himself. Willie became his own worst enemy. In his own mind, all the positives became null and void in the face of what he viewed as the overwhelming negatives. "I went through thirty negative years," Willie confesses, "wallowing in all kinds of misery and pain and self-pity, and guilt and all of that shit."

Looking back from the perch of his superstardom today, Willie declares that if the success he so longed for as a singer had come when "I was seventeen or twenty or even thirty, I'd probably have thrown it all away."

Why? "My thinking wasn't right," he realizes. "I was too extreme in a lot of things."

MY OWN PECULIAR WAY

1964—High-school diploma in hand, Dolly Parton moves to Nashville to find fame and fortune.

1964—Johnny Cash bridges folk and country, recording Dylan's "It Ain't Me, Babe"

1964—Tex Ritter elected to Country Music Hall of Fame

His marriage bitterly ended, banned from seeing the kids he adored, face to face with the humiliation of eight singles failing in a row, his career strangled with the collapse of Liberty Records, Willie, age thirty-one, disgusted with the music business and feeling excessively sorry for himself, decided to retire and become a farmer.

His old Tootsie's drinking pal, Mel Tillis, was hotter than a pistol singing hits like "Walk On By." Longtime buddy Roger Miller carried off an incredible five Grammy's that year for "Dang Me." Willie Nelson was retiring.

"I went to the country and vowed not to return," Willie told *Rolling Stone*. "Everything was goin' wrong, and I just said, fuck it all, I'll never write again, never sing again, don't wanta see anybody, don't call me. I stayed out in the country a year and didn't go anywhere. I didn't work any dates. I let my beard grow."

In early 1964, after Willie lost his contract with Liberty, Chet Atkins, who had had his eye on Willie for some time ("I think Willie had more admirers than anybody who ever came to town here," Chet says), approached Willie and asked him to come with RCA. It was an offer from the top producer heading up the top label in town, and Willie said yes.

But in one of his more baffling moves, like the time he was working at KBOP and just never showed up again, Willie, without a further word to Atkins, went over and signed with Monument Records instead.

Monument Records, a local Nashville label, owned by songwriter and record producer Fred Foster, had enjoyed a string of national pop hits with Roy Orbison in the '50s. In 1964, the year Willie signed with Monument, Orbison released Willie's Christmas tune, "Pretty Paper," and Willie co-wrote a song with Foster called "To Make a Long Story Short (She's Gone)."

During the entire time he was on Monument, however, they only released one single record on Willie, "I Never Cared for You" (backed with "You Left Me"), which Chet recalls as a "kind of weird record that wasn't a hit."

Meanwhile, Willie holed up out on his new farm at Ridgetop. Perhaps the most solid indication of his financial status at the time was the fact that he could buy himself a farm and just up and "retire."

This year of relative musical inactivity on the farm

marked the real gelling of the Willie Nelson "family"—that shifting band of blood relatives, in-laws, Texas buddies, Nashville pals, musicians, musicians' families, roadies, general admirers, groupies, and whoever else—into a psychologically cohesive tribe ready to tramp loyally over the face of America wherever Willie, the wandering gypsy, and his wandering destiny might lead.

As the mailbox on the farm at Ridgetop read: "Willie Nelson and Many Others."

Likely the "family" is rooted in the emotional life of a sensitive boy and his delicate sister, who realized that, when facts came down to facts, there was security in numbers. Growing up in a constantly changing, roving clan of parents, stepparents, grandparents, half brothers, cousins, aunts, and in-laws, Willie became used to being part of a large extended family, held together more by felt familial ties than a solid sense of place. Deep down an outgoing man who genuinely enjoys people, Willie simply extended this boyhood world right on into his musical career.

The "family," which today numbers over a hundred strong, all financially dependent on the fortunes of Willie Nelson, first began to view itself as a unit during the early days on Willie's just purchased acreage in Ridgetop.

Tiny Ridgetop is just a couple of curves of grocery stores and gas stations on two-lane Tennessee Highway 41. It winds outside the outskirts of rural east Nashville, past several isolated country-music roadhouses, through gently rising, heavily wooded hills that conceal dozens of truck farms tucked down in the hollows under a profusion of lush greenery. The road begins a steep rise, climbing out of the Cumberland Basin, and there it is, up on the ridge—Ridgetop. Back in the '30s it was a resort with big wide-porched, white-board hotels where hot Nashvillians retreated from the muggy, coal-polluted city air down in the basin up to the cool breezes on the edge of the ridge.

Housekeeping with Willie at Ridgetop was his new wife, Shirley Collie Nelson, his singing partner on "Willingly."

One day in California, where Shirley was appearing on Joe Allison's television show, she left a note at home: "I have gone to the dress shop, and I may be a little late." She was so late, in fact, she hasn't made it back yet.

"Hey, Willie," wrote Biff Collie in 1978, "remember when my old dad introduced himself to you at a club in Bandera back in 1962 by saying, 'I don't know whether to slug you or congratulate you?'

"And you answered, 'Whatever you think's fair.'"

Fair or foul, Shirley erratically ran off with Willie, and Collie (now happily remarried to the true love of his life), with the dignity befitting a member of the Disc Jockey Hall of Fame, continued to program Willie Nelson records.

Although Willie once attributed his Ridgetop retirement to marital bliss with the good-looking Shirley ("for eight years it was great, so great I quit the road"), actually he had mostly just given up, because he was fed up.

Demoralized and embarrassed by his failures on Liberty, shortly followed by another bomb on Monument, Willie, seemingly, just decided to succumb to fate. He convinced himself that the whole music world was convinced that Willie Nelson, although brilliantly talented, was incapable of motivating the public to go out and buy a record.

"There was no incentive to go out and work, because I felt they had put me in a slot," Willie told the *Los Angeles Times*, "He's ahead of his time, so what can we do for him? Nothing. He'll just have to wait till his time comes."

So, he took up family and farming with a vengeance.

It wasn't long till Willie had moved the whole Nelson clan out from Texas to live at Ridgetop—Bobbie and her sons, Ira and Lorraine (now affectionately nicknamed Pop and Mom Nelson), half brothers Doyle and Charles and their families. Later, even Lana, Susie, and Billy moved in.

"We wanted to stay together," Mom Nelson explains. "Willie wanted us to be there, and we wanted to be with him. We've always been a very close family."

"We all lived in Tennessee on a road with our houses about a mile and a half apart," she remembers fondly. "Pop and I lived in a tent down by a pond. It was just fine; we had all our furniture and everything in there."

Mom and Pop worked as truck farmers, taking their produce into town to sell. "I loved Tennessee," she sighs, today still an attractive black-haired woman living in a modern Willie-owned Austin apartment house. "You know, they have all those canyons there," she twinkles, referring to the gentle valleys of the Tennessee hills.

Although songwriting royalties were funding the

Ridgetop venture ("I was successful as a songwriter and could have lived on my farm in comfort," Willie once noted), Willie, a chronic workaholic who must constantly generate a staggering multitude of projects in order to feel normally active, was doggedly adopting the life of a farmer.

When longtime Nashville music journalist Red O'Donnell referred to him as a "songwriting farmer," Willie conceded, "I'll buy that, if you'll rephrase it and make it come out a 'farming songwriter.'

"Farming is my business, and songwriting is my hobby," earnest "Old McWillie" explained. "I can make a good living working the farm, and it would bug me if I thought I had to make it writing. The pressure would get me. Yet, it is nice to have a hobby that is financially profitable."

It's especially nice to have a hobby that's financially profitable when your farming is going, shall we say, hog wild.

Former Future Farmers of America songleader Willie's first professional agricultural venture was hog raising. Back in high school, Willie had raised pigs for the FFA, although only one pig at a time to enter in shows.

Now, he figured, if he could win a prize with one hog, he could make a killing with hundreds. "Raised some hogs," Willie says stonily. "I fed 'em that high-priced feed. All they could eat of it. I had some fat hogs.

"Feed prices kept going up, and hog prices kept going down. I lost about $5,000 in three months there—on one load of hogs."

Well, hoggone.

Apparently Willie was eating as majestically as his pigs. He had ballooned from a skinny kid to one hundred-eighty or so, pretty hefty for a man of 5' 9". Having sprouted a short beard that mainly looked as if he hadn't shaved for a week, he would wear old denim farm overalls, like his granddaddy used to wear, white cotton T-shirts, an old dress hat, and cowboy boots.

Ridgetop marked a hard-nosed attempt to recapture his self-respect by returning to his rural roots; and in fact, a 1964 photo of Willie on the farm next to the hog trough looks eerily like an uncanny duplicate of a photo taken of Daddy Nelson right before he moved to Texas in 1929.

Over the next six years, the Ridgetop farm (which Willie still owns) developed into an impressive farming enterprise.

In late '65, he purchased a neighboring farm in the valley below his place, and spent most of November building a pen for one hundred head of cattle he wanted to move over to the new property. The problem, he told *Music City News*, was that the new farm was ringed by hills and hollows, and he hadn't figured how to move the cows "without driving them over a cliff." There was no road between the two farms, and he couldn't get a bulldozer to cut one. "If anyone had a good solution," the paper reported, "Willie is interested."

The farm, which eventually expanded to four hundred acres, was run by a wise old local farmhand, George "Tinker" Hughes, and his wife, Ruby. A lanky, rough-hewed, jack-of-all-trades, Tinker was pictured in a farm journal at the time, squinting into the camera and showing the USA how to "roll one."

Tinker and Willie were growing two hundred acres of oats, clover, fesque, and Lespidiza grass for grazing a couple of hundred head of black Angus. In addition to twenty-five brood sows, they had eight hundred Duroc and Poland China hogs, several hundred white leghorn chickens, and some milk cows. They even raised two government-allotted acres of tobacco.

As befits a Texan, Willie owned nine horses — three Tennessee Walkers (expensive preference of the blue-grass show-horse set), two palominos, two ponies for the kids, and Willie's own favorite, a six-year-old quarter horse aptly named "Preacher."

Ridgetop might be subject to being dismissed as a hobby farm for a gentleman farmer/songwriter, but in fact, Willie still loves the land and is an avid out-doorsman. (He's certainly genuine country, too. He and Bobbie both still talk in a soft Texas drawl, using 'em for "them" and ever' for "every.")

At least once a year, Willie set out on a major big-game hunt. In 1966, he trekked off to the Tetons to stalk deer, elk, and bear in Wyoming. Never one to let his pleasures interfere with his pleasures, Willie had a show scheduled in Denver the night before the hunting trip, so he just lugged his gear to the show, then flew from Denver to meet up with two friends, a sheriff and club owner from Dallas. The trio had bought an old bus, and outfitted it with bunks. Pushing their "RV" as far up in the mountains as it would go, they then set off on horses through the forest up to timberline, where they hunted and camped for two weeks.

Willie also liked to make the fourteen-day trail ride from San Antonio to Bandera, Texas. Bandera, about forty miles west of San Antonio toward Kerrville (where Jimmie Rodgers built his "Blue Yodeler's Paradise"), looks like a town straight out of a Saturday cowboy matinee. Surrounded by rustic resorts and dude ranches, Bandera sits in the midst of stunning prairies, dotted with low bushes and gnarled mesquite, where an orangy, pulsating sun settles down over gentle rolling mounds that lope toward the horizon for miles.

For two weeks each year, hundreds of riders would trot along the trail on horses, moseying through the mesquite and around the armadillos, just like the trail hands who scouted out the West. Eating out of tin plates and drinking strong, hot coffee in tin cups, Willie was in his element.

Back at Ridgetop, the hog fiasco behind him, Willie took up calf-roping—in a manner that befits his intellectual bent as a heavy reader and thinker. ("Willie's very, very intelligent," says Martha. "He can talk to you a little bit on any subject. He's very book-minded and always read a lot. He always wanted to learn a little more.") First, Willie proceeded in a systematic, academic manner to read every book he could dig up on the subject of calf-roping.

Then he built a full-fledged, regulation rodeo chute on the farm and commenced obstinately and optimistically, to practice. "Working the horse, refining the technique of lassooing, cutting down the time, each time, until today he could probably compete with the best in the rodeo circuit," claimed an onlooker at the time.

Willie is an acute observer who can pick up on the most insignificant passing phrase for a song. It was calf-roping that led him to one of his most popular records on RCA. One Texas afternoon, he was practicing with a friend, who was priming him with a few pointers. Every time he made a successful catch, the coach yelled out, "That's one in a row!" "One in a Row," released in 1966, made the top twenty on the charts.

Farm life had its sporting moments, as well. In fact, the incident of Ray Price's rooster is passing into the annals of legend.

Price, also a Texas farmboy, was living in an affluent tiny suburb of Nashville where he was secreting some fighting roosters. Needing a more discreet place to exercise his top bird, Price asked Willie if he could keep one of his best cocks at Ridgetop.

Willie said sure, but warned Price that Shirley was already raising hens. Price assured Willie the cock would keep his claws off the hens, actually Shirley's pets, each with its own specially selected name.

A couple of mornings after the rooster arrived, Willie woke up to find one of the hens dead.

He phoned Price: "Ray, you'd better come get your rooster, because he's killed one of Shirley's hens."

Contrite, Price promised to come get the rooster and bring Shirley another hen. "I'll be right out," he promised.

Three weeks later, during which time Price's face was yet to be seen, Willie woke up and found another hen murdered. "So Shirley is really pissed off," Willie tells the tale, "and she went to get the shotgun to shoot the rooster. I knew that if she got out there with a shotgun, she was liable to kill the horses and cows, chickens, and everything else as mad as she was. So, I got the gun, and I shot the rooster."

Willie gave the dead fowl to the housekeeper, who promptly took it home and fried up a tasty chicken dinner.

"Then I called Ray," Willie says. "Eye-bugging irate, Price yelled that the housekeeper had just downed a $1,000 chicken feast. Willie retorted that no fighting rooster in the world was worth one good laying hen.

"He wouldn't speak to me for a year," Willie grins. "He said that killing that rooster would cost me thousands of dollars, because he would never record one of my songs again. And he didn't," he admits, "till just recently."

Between hogs pigging out on high-priced feed, roosters fouling up the works for his songs, and for obvious career reasons, Willie returned to the world of music in late 1964.

On November 24, 1964, Willie made a mental truce with the powers that be, and joined the Grand Ole Opry. Four nights later, clean-shaven, hair slicked back in a modest Porter Wagoner-type pompadour, wearing a crisp white shirt, dark suit, and tie, Willie made his first appearance as an official member of the greatest traditional country music show on earth.

ONCE MORE WITH FEELING

"Willie, you know, turned me down the first time," Chet Atkins says, "and a lot of people would have said, go to hell. 'Cause he went to Monument. But I didn't," Chet laughs. "I *thought* about it. But I still knew he was so damned great."

Although the failures on Liberty and Monument loomed large in Willie's mind, they scarcely made a dent in the opinions of executives on Music Row. It was nothing for a guy to be on a label or two before he made it—look at Don Gibson. If people thought about Willie's days on Liberty at all, they recalled that the boy had earned two top-ten records.

Observing that Willie's Monument record flopped, Chet thought, "Well, he'll probably come over right now." Which he did.

Far from being put off by Willie's unusual bluesy vocal style, that voice was precisely what captivated Chet. "He's such a very, very different song stylist," Atkins says, "I think everybody knew—or I did anyway—he was going to be tremendously big sometime. He's not like anybody in the world."

A complex, contradictory man, Willie has an intriguing make-up as a human being as well as musician. About the only publication covering country music in the '60s was the *Music City News*, owned by Faron Young, and a writer for the paper around the time Willie signed with RCA, was captivated by Willie's charisma and extraordinary mental combustion system.

"If you stood all the Willie Nelsons side by side and counted them, you'd still find that you had just 'One in a Row,' " the journalist enthused, "because this is one of the most unique personalities in show business today.

"There is only one Willie Nelson. Extremely talented in many areas . . . most of all a real human being—this is Willie Nelson. He's vibrant, bubbling with compassion for others, but stern and determined.

"Willie Nelson will not allow a second of time to get away from him without living it to the fullest extent. He loves life so much that he wants to take advantage of every minute of it.

"He's a quiet man, very soft-spoken with a feather-light step, but filled with energy. This remarkable restraint which he employs probably marks his success as much as any one factor in his life.

"Willie Nelson might have been a great jazz guitarist had he chosen to do that. . . . He might have been a fine educator, because he has a natural magnetism that draws people to him and makes for excellent leadership. . . . He could have been a great scientist, because of his lust for discovery of new ideas, but whatever Willie Nelson decides to do, he's going to do it best.

"It's this kind of daring that sets Willie Nelson apart

from all others. It is this quest for the undone that allows Nelson to create unusual poetry and set it to music that is totally different from anything heard before."

Whew! And this is thirteen years before Willie, to Burt Reynolds' slightly green-eyed astonishment, mesmerized Jane Fonda and Candice Bergen.

Even in 1965, though, Willie seemed poised on a whole new beginning as a singer that could nab him fame and fortune at any moment. He was on RCA, the biggest, most powerful, most respected and successful label in country music. They were going to promote him, to push him—they promised. Willie was going to get out, go for it again; things *were* going to work.

"In the future I'll be performing more," Willie told writer Red O'Donnell in his best polite-and-upcoming-young-man style in March of 1965. "I am going out on the road with package shows. I'll be recording my own material, so that means I'll have to accelerate my hobby (of songwriting)." He even added, "I recorded some tunes in German (phonetically), so perhaps my traveling will include trips overseas."

To get mentally prepared for the big push, to shake off the negative mental spiral of the preceding twelve years, Willie had started experimenting with thought control through the study of karate. In fact, Willie and Shirley both took up Kung Fu karate. Karate was described in interviews with Willie as "seventy-five percent mental and twenty-five percent physical."

One magazine story pictures Willie decked out in a Japanese-style kimono with a big wide sash, and reveals that Willie "is able to break two-inch boards or bricks with the side of his open hand without pain."

As Willie remarked, "This is a good thing to know, if you're attacked by a board or brick."

In the early months of 1965, with his mental attitude karated into a positive configuration, with one of the best producers in the nation at the control board, Willie went into the studio and cut his first RCA album. Chet, who always had a special affinity for singer/songwriters, wanted to showcase Willie as an artist who could sing his own songs with unparalleled feeling. Like the first Liberty album, all twelve songs they recorded were penned by Willie. The album was called "Country Willie—His Own Songs."

Even before his first single was released on RCA, journalists were continually hailing Willie as a "success." Obviously, this was because of his enormous credibility as a songwriter.

Although about half the songs on "Country Willie—His own Songs" had been written years earlier ("Night Life," "Funny How Time Slips Away," etc.), Willie was still writing new songs, but at a leisurely, erratic pace. Willie has never been one of those writers who gets mental constipation if he doesn't plop forth a song every day or two.

"I work at my 'hobby' when I feel it. I don't push it," Willie said at the time his first RCA album was recorded. "I stay up until three A.M. nearly every morning, reading and leaving my mind open for ideas. The ideas will come, if you wait for them. I am patient," this normally intensely impatient man claimed. "If I go two or three weeks without putting something down on paper, I don't worry too much.

I'm sure an idea will come along.

"It's like when a well goes dry," he explained. "You just have to wait until it fills. I'd rather write one good song a month, or even three or four a year, than one a week which would only be accepted as passable or fair."

In 1975, asked why he didn't turn his quick wit and facility for language into turning out lucrative novelty songs, Willie replied, "I can't. . . . I like to make myself believe that my songs will still be around five hundred years from now, and I wouldn't want the people to find songs like that among 'em."

A distaste for novelty, however, did not prevent Willie from plowing into intense, bizarre situations, rarely dealt with in country songs. He once explained how he came to write a startling song called, "I Just Can't Let You Say Good-bye," which pictures a scorned husband indenting his thick fingernails in the pale flesh of his wife's throat, rather than let her leave him one more time. "Please don't scream, please don't cry, I just can't let you say good-bye," menacingly begs the crazed lover.

"I'd been to bed," Willie nonchalantly said, "and I got up about three or four in the morning and started readin' the paper.

"There was a story where some guy killed his old lady, and I thought, well, that would be a far-out thing to do. To write this song where you're killing this chick. So I started there.

" 'I had not planned on seeing you' was the start," he explains, "and I brought it up to where she was really pissin' him off; she was sayin' bad things to him, so he was tryin' to shut her up and started chokin' her."

139

"I Just Can't Let You Say Good-bye" was exactly the kind of odd, off-the-wall song Chet Atkins loved to find for his artists. "It was different," Chet says with enthusiasm, "and I would always try something different, no matter what it was."

During his seclusion at Ridgetop, Willie had apparently been giving a lot of thought to his erratic recording career, and to why, possibly, some of his Liberty records hadn't hit. During their first recording sessions, Willie went to Chet and explained that he wanted to record with just his own guitar.

That moment marked the beginning of a suppressed undercurrent of communications problems that laced through Willie's RCA career. Thinking Willie meant he wanted himself as the only guitar player on the record, and not considering Willie's playing equal to the studio guitarists of the day, Chet suggested, "Don't do that; let's use two other guitars—let's use you, and Grady (Martin), and myself." They cut "I Just Can't Let You Say Good-bye."

"We made a great record," Chet says, "but, you know, I've thought about it since, and probably what he meant was just his guitar playing the solos, like he's doing now. It was a communications problem, if that's what he meant, but I've never asked him."

Outside the studio, Willie kept practicing his old encyclopedia maxim that the best way to sell your product is to sell yourself. In addition to playing the Grand Ole Opry every week, he was a regular on Ernest Tubb's popular syndicated television show. "Little Willie," as he was known in Nashville circles and introduced by Tubb, would always sing the sacred hymn of the day.

Writer Mel Shestack recalls seeing him on the Tubb show one year around Christmas, standing under a papier-mâché arbor, dressed in a Perry Como sweater and pleated slacks, singing a Christmas hymn with that curiously flat, expressionless look a television camera always seems to pull out of him.

He did make it over to Europe on package shows, as Hal Smith had promised, and he played all over the United States opening on the shows of big stars, like the Johnny Wright–Kitty Wells Family Show. He was also one of the few country artists of those days able to book in Vegas, where he played the Golden Nugget.

Oddly, the main thing that stands out about Willie's professional moves around Nashville in the '60s is their passive, play-it-by-the-rules conformity. All the public signs indicate that he conducted himself conventionally, doing all the expected things, taking the lead from the establishment.

It was only out on the road in Texas with his band that his individuality began to emerge, that he began to feel a direction for himself, to sense there were winds of change blowing in the hustings that music executives, closeted in their offices, weren't feeling at all.

In fact, Willie himself credits Kris Kristofferson, Mickey Newberry, and Tom T. Hall—not the so-called "outlaws"—for taking the steps that broke the set ways of making music in Nashville. Nashville, to Willie, eventually became a place of "elements I couldn't combat." Unable to combat them, he left—to Texas. But Kristofferson stuck—and fought.

"It takes a lot of nerve and guts to do what people like Kristofferson have done," he freely admits of a man he today considers one of his best friends. "Kristofferson's got to be recognized as one of the first to really break open both fields (pop and country) without following what Nashville put down as the rules of the game. Kris made his own rules, did it his own way. That's why I admire and respect Kris and anyone else who does it the way it should be done regardless of the people who say it should be done another way."

Certainly, there were no out-of-line changes in Willie's "image" in the '60s. His look gradually altered over the years as current fashion changed.

Chet Atkins remembers Willie as a "real handsome dresser" who "always had that beautiful red hair." Photos of Willie with businessmen in the mid-'60s show him wearing expensive-looking suits sporting a silk handkerchief in the breast pocket.

While he was holed up on the farm, Willie had even taken up smoking a pipe. "Wearing a beard is like smoking a pipe," he laughed at the time. "By the time a man realizes it doesn't make him look any more dignified, he begins to enjoy it."

For casual attire he favored leisure suits, a turtle-neck and sports coat, or more dubious casual items like a synthetic, furry zip-up jacket.

His early days of performing in a western-cut suit or mock cowboy outfit with yards of long white fake fringe were behind him, but in the mid-'60s traveling with the Kitty Wells Show, he'd sometimes turn up in fringed buckskins and beaded moccasins.

With the emergence of the Beatles and hippies on the national scene, Willie donned lapelless, English-cut suits, and on one album cover, even costumed himself in a hideous mustardy yellow Nehru jacket.

Although he briefly experimented with a debonair mustache and beard that made him look something like Mitch Miller's cousin, for most of the sixties he was clean-shaven, showing off shiny, round cherubic cheeks like his mother Myrle's, and those forever-big, brown eyes.

His hair was impeccably combed straight back in a plastic-perfect pompadour style now favored by many gospel artists, or neatly parted on the side and waved back in the front. Whatever the style, nary a strand of hair strayed from its Bryl-creem appointed place.

In the mid-'60s, when the "Buck Owens long-length" became the newest trend in Nashville male hairdos, he started letting his hair grow slightly longer. By the end of the '60s, he had a shaggy, Beatles-type cut that just brushed the top of his collar, covered a bit of his ears, and flopped down on his forehead.

Frequently wearing flashy sunglasses, and noticeable, expensive jewelry, Willie kept step image-wise with the "new breed," the hip guys, the Glen Campbells, Roger Millers, and Buck Owenses, whose audiences were crossover, not country.

"Willie Nelson looked very 'cool' in his white Levi's, sneakers, and orange shirt in RCA's parking lot a few days ago," wrote gossip columnist Audrey Winters. "Told me that his personal manager, Crash Stewart, has some network appearances lined up for him this fall. His song 'Good Times' has been recorded by Jack Jones, and Don Gibson recorded 'Half a Man.' "

ON THE ROAD AGAIN

"(In the '60s, if you had enough records and enough hits, you could make a fine living. You didn't have to leave town, you didn't have to sing in honky-tonks. You could be home every night with your wife and kids. Come to Music Row and pitch your songs and so forth. Just live a nice, normal life."

Harlan Howard
Songwriter's Hall of Fame

With his RCA career launched, Willie took action on the ambition he'd nursed ever since "Hello Walls" hit in 1961. He put together his own band, and named them "The Record Men" after the back side of his first Liberty single, "Mr. Record Man."

For Willie Nelson, putting together a band was a vastly more portentous step than for most country singers. For a lot of singers, a band was first, an ego boost, and second, a convenience. Rather than use unpredictable pickup musicians, you had a regular group of guys who knew all your songs down to the letter. If your band was really good, they learned to play your songs so they sounded just like your records — an exact imitation of the way the studio musicians played them on the recording session.

But for Willie, starting his own band went far beyond convenience — with a significance for his future that even Willie himself didn't fully grasp for several years.

The elusive genius of Willie Nelson lay in his total uniqueness and startling difference — in the "weird" voice and "funny" sense of timing fellow musicians often found it hard to relate to.

It was only by playing this uniqueness up to the absolute hilt that Willie would ever become a star.

To a certain extent, this was impossible under the way Nashville made music in those days. It was very difficult to walk into a studio with studio musicians, no matter how great — musicians so popular they had already played on two other sessions with two other artists by the time they got to your session — and walk out with a sound that was radically different.

Although not many road bands have the technical proficiency to play in a studio; creatively it was far, far more effective for a great stylist like Willie — or Waylon Jennings — to go into the studio with their own bands who were intuitive to, and *sympatico* with, their style — who, in fact, had played a creative role in the development of that style.

If you could put that special feeling of a man and his band on record, you would have a genuinely different record; perhaps a superstar-caliber record.

It took Willie years to figure this out, and years more to figure out what to do about it — how to record effectively himself and his band (who were rough-edged players for studio work) on a record. When he finally did figure it out after ten years of struggling, the result was self-evident: the "Red-Headed Stranger" album, his breakthrough.

Doubtless, Willie initially expected that the band would quickly become a big money-maker as his RCA records hit the charts and his price as a performer went up. But that financial plan, like his recording career, did not materialize for nearly ten more years.

Frequently Willie supported the band, including salaries and road expenses, out of his own pocket—continually replenished with the ever-faithful songwriting royalties. Burning with a chronic case of performing fever, Willie relished the band, thrived on life on the road. The band was something Willie wanted to do, was determined to do—was compelled to do. He wanted to run his own band his own way—like Bob Wills. Even if he had to pay for it himself.

Signing on with a still obscure boss, the band agreed to work for one hundred dollars a week (compared to the thirty dollars a day Willie had pulled down a couple of years earlier with Price)—providing they cleared that. Salaries stayed on that uncertain basis for nearly a decade. "We didn't really turn the corner as a band until about 1975," Paul once revealed.

Paul English and Bee Spears, still playing with Willie now, were both early members of The Record Men. Paul and his wife moved to Nashville from Texas, and at first, Paul just booked and managed the group, sometimes even drove the bus. His wife, Carlene, handled the bookkeeping.

Johnny Bush signed on as drummer after quitting the job Willie had landed him with Ray Price. After Willie paid for the session that got Bush started on his own recording career, he also urged Bush to open the shows so he could sing more and get more audience exposure, which Bush did until 1969.

Paul took up his old Fort Worth post as drummer about the time Bee Spears signed on to replace a bass player who was going into the army. Jimmy Day, a zany former Cherokee Cowboy, who wore his hair greased back Fonzie-style, and who is simultaneously described by acquaintances as a "magnificent maestro" and "crazy as a bedbug," played steel.

At various points, Buddy White from San Antonio played guitar, David Zentner played bass, and Wade Ray, a fellow performer with Willie on the Ernest Tubb TV show and a virtuoso violinist, played fiddle.

As roadie, Willie hired a roustabout from San Antonio named Larry Trader who, like Bush and Day, had been working for Ray Price. Trader, who liked to joke that he held the B.A. degree ("Back Alley, I mean"), quit Price and asked Willie for a job. "I don't know why I did it," he says, "I guess it was just meant to be." He still works for Willie today.

Until about 1967, Nashville had a crazy set of liquor laws that held drinking down to a few die-hard night-spots. Consequently, there were virtually no places around Music City for a musician to play and make any decent sort of living. You could play the Opry (if you were lucky enough) for minimum union scale, and that was about it.

Willie was booked by J. Hal Smith (also his song publisher) who represented Ray Price and Ernest

Tubb; Smith had promised Willie spots on some of the lucrative package shows as an opening act for bigger stars. Willie also knew he could land some work back in his home state of Texas.

Most of his Texas dates were booked by Crash Stewart, a San Antonio promoter who had gotten his start booking Hank Williams. About the time Willie formed The Record Men, he and Stewart started a booking agency called Alamo Productions.

"Willie and I were partners for five years," Stewart wrote before his recent untimely death, "and my first agreement with Willie was that I had to get four hundred dollars a night for Willie and the band on a weeknight, five hundred dollars on a Friday or Sunday, and six hundred dollars on a Saturday night.

"Our first engagement was at the VFW Hall in Alice, which we had to promote ourselves. We came out O.K. on the date, and never looked back."

After that, nearly every week, Willie and the boys, first driving an old station wagon, later in a rattletrap road bus, set out on a two-thousand-mile round trip to the honky-tonks of Texas and back.

If Music Row was ruled by record executives, the southwestern country bars were ruled by the queens of the honky-tonks—waitresses. "They were our first critics and our best ones," Willie says fondly. In a rowdy bar it's obvious in minutes if the crowd goes for an act or not, and the waitresses bequeathed favors on bands that could please the patrons—and pull up their tips. "If I had a turkey of an act, it would hurt their audience and cut their tips," Willie explains, "and if my performance was good, they'd be very grateful for it."

148

This gratitude could extend to intimate levels. "I think every singer in every band had a following of waitresses," Willie reveals. "Before we even heard the word 'groupies,' we all had our favorite waitresses."

The realms of the honky-tonk queens were populated by rednecks, as they came to be called in the '60s. Rowdy subjects, rednecks demanded their rights of citizenship—music to cry in their beer by, to snuggle up to their woman by, or to kick some ornery cuss in the ass by.

"Fights—oh, sure there were always fights," Willie once said, elucidating on how he came by the quick-getaway nickname "Fast Eddie." "The boys will join in, if they can," he added cheerfully. "Texans love a fight. They'll come running for miles around just to watch, if you tell them there's gonna be a fight."

Paul recalled to the *Waco Tribune* that one of the worst fights the band ever played background for was a private party in Dallas for the Dallas Cowboys. "They kept fighting till they had literally leveled the place," he said. "Funny thing is, the band saw the two guys who started it sneak away—they weren't even members of the Cowboys. By then, no one was left standing."

Willie remembers well the night at a "skull orchard," as the fist-prone bars were known, when he stepped out the back door to sign an autograph, was grabbed by unknown assailants, socked in the head, and wound up silently slugging it out in the dark for thirty minutes until another rowdy stumbled out the back door and broke things up.

That was in Phoenix where, rolling through town on a thirty-day tour in 1965, he met a singer Bobby

Bare and Don Bowman were raving about in Nashville: Waylon Jennings.

Waylon was making top dollar in Phoenix as leader of the house band at JD's, the hottest club in the state. He had built up a strong following in Arizona, the way Willie was doing in Texas. "We were instant friends," Willie says.

Waylon, who had just been signed to an RCA recording contract by Chet Atkins, asked Willie what he thought about his moving to Nashville.

"I told him to stay where the fuck he was," Willie says. "Don't move anywhere, stay. He had a good deal where he was," Willie explains. "Why quit something that's good and go to something you're not sure of?"

"Fortunately," Willie adds, "he didn't listen."

Waylon moved to Nashville, and Willie moved on . . . and on . . . night after night, day after day, night after day . . . always on the road . . . setting up, playing a show, breaking down, getting in the bus, driving all night, driving all day, dragging out of the bus, setting up, playing a show, breaking down, getting in the bus, popping a few pills . . .

Lefty Frizzell, a huge star at the time (and one of Willie's heroes), told a magazine, "I have been on the road so much lately that the other day, when I had a couple of days off, I had just climbed into bed and fallen asleep when the wife walked in and turned on the light.

"I sat up in bed and was halfway through my theme song, before I realized where I was," he wearily chuckled.

For The Record Men, if two or three were gathered together in your name, you played. Don Bowman remembers a series of shows he and Willie did in Texas to promote the candidacy of former state Senator Ralph Yarborough.

"You talk about hot," comedian Bowman laughs, "hot we were not. I remember we played some auditorium in Austin. You know: FREE CONCERT: WILLIE NELSON.

"The only people that showed up was me and Willie and Paul and Senator Yarborough, and a couple of other dudes we had to call to come down and open up the building. We were not exactly overrun!

"But we had the nicest hotel suites in town," he adds, "and we just stayed stoned for eighteen days. Wasn't no reason to straighten up. We got paid for that first gig, and the check bounced, bigger 'n hell. But God, did we have a lot of fun!"

Still short on business acumen, Willie, at one point, convinced Crash Stewart to put his half brother, Doyle, on the road promoting Willie Nelson. "Willie put Doyle on one hundred-ten dollars a day salary and gave him a new Lincoln." Stewart sighed. "Doyle's job was to tour the country and promote Willie Nelson. Doyle got as far as Fort Worth and wrecked the Lincoln. I convinced Willie that you could do more promoting and book more dates and save more money by using the telephone," he stoically concluded.

Around 1965 Paul decided to do his part by upgrading the band's image. "About 1965 or so I had the same beard I have now," Paul told a Waco newspaper. "We were walking down the street one day, and Willie saw this cape in the window. He said, 'Paul, I don't want to hurt your feelings, but did you know you look like a devil?' " Intrigued, Paul bought

151

the cape to round out his look.

"I wore it a couple of days while we were in California, and then I left it at the hotel," he continued. "After the show that night a couple of ladies came up and said they missed it.

"We'd play Panther Hall in Fort Worth, two—three times a year, and there would be a dozen girls waiting for my autograph after we finished a set, and that never happened before. So, I went into this devil-looking thing."

The full-blown devil look embraces a sinister black shirt; black pants; wicked swirling cape; red patent-leather cowboy boots, needle-sharp toes crowned with silver tips; and black gambler's hat stabbed with pins, buttons, and medallions. Plus, of course, Paul's black, rapier-pointed goatee, complemented by lengthy black sideburns that maliciously curve into sharp points. The devil, indeed.

"And you know," Paul marveled, "all of the time I wore it—even in the toughest honky-tonks, I never had any trouble. I guess the guys said to themselves, 'If he's wearing that, he must really be able to play. Nobody can look like that in a place like this, and play bad.' "

A lot of the "places like this" were old halls Paul and Willie had known during Fort Worth days—the Sportatorium and the Longhorn Ballroom in Dallas; Panther Hall in Fort Worth—each a legendary institution with a tall tale of its own. They also worked a big Houston club named Shelley's for three hundred dollars a night. Today it's called Gilley's.

To citizens of Texas, the Longhorn Ballroom is what the White House is to citizens of another country—the United States. In the 1940s, a notorious real-estate promoter named O. L. ("thanks for helping me make another million") Nelms built a monstrous, mind-boggling farmers' market down on Industrial Boulevard. Apparently, like Willie, "ahead of its time," the soon-floundering farmers' market was hastily converted by Nelms into a "million-item store." Living quarters intended for farmers were converted into bars, and the warehouse into a gigantic ballroom.

With more fast-footed finagling, Nelms established Bob Wills in the dance-hall business. Adding an awesome cowboy statue and gigantic set of steer horns to the front of the building, Nelms opened the Bob Wills Ranchhouse, featuring the Silver Dollar Bar, biggest in the world at the time. Opening on to the dance floor were stables where Bob kept his champion quarter horse, Pumpkin.

Through the '50s Bob and the Playboys packed 'em into the Ranchhouse by the thousands, but the dance hall ran into IRS problems and was taken over by a man named Dewey Grooms. In 1962, Grooms opened the Dewey Grooms Longhorn Ranch with a couple of partners. One was a man named Jack Ruby.

Every Saturday night during the '60s, bands like Willie's would start off the night playing the Big D Jamboree at the Sportatorium down the street from the Longhorn, then break down, move over to the Longhorn, and start their set all over again.

The Sportatorium is a humongous gray metal building, headquarters for country-music shows and wrestling matches, at the dead end of Industrial Boulevard—the road that demarcates the first place you can buy liquor in Dallas coming north from Bible-bone-dry Waco.

Willie first played the Sportatorium back in 1956 with an unknown country singer named Roger Miller. Eight years later in 1964 Gene McCoslin discovered Willie playing there again—also again with Roger Miller, who by that time, unlike Willie, had become a star.

McCoslin, manager of KNOK radio in Dallas, drove over to the Sportatorium to check out Miller, who was riding high on the charts with "Dang Me."

Arriving early, he was leaning on a post near the back of the building when Willie ambled on stage by himself, with just a guitar, and opened the show with an hour of songs.

"Well, he knocked me right out," McCoslin told writer Jay Milner. "I forgot all about Roger Miller and everybody else. When I got a chance, I introduced myself to Willie, and told him, tried to tell him, how hard his songs hit me."

The next time Willie came through Dallas with a band, McCoslin quit his job to go on the road with Willie and The Record Men, riding their ancient fresh-air-conditioned bus back and forth across the southwest.

"I wasn't into music, understand," says hyperbolic promoter McCoslin, "I was a super salesman! But Willie Nelson turned me around. He had on a brown suit and a clip-on tie, ferkrissakes! What was I doing being impressed by a little man in a brown suit and clip-on tie?"

It was also out in Texas that Willie was discovered by a second fellow Texan.

About as far as daylight from dark was "Gino Mc-

Coslin (who, according to writer Larry King once owned such a rowdy club in Dallas that lawmen showed up at the club every night with police dogs and cameras to photograph the customers) from the football czar of Texas, Darrell Royal.

In the state and nation of Texas, Darrell Royal, even though now retired, is The Man—and a man with a fine sense of football, a fine sense of music, and a fine sense of his friends.

"A character?" he was once asked to define. "Well, I'd have to say a character is someone who isn't boring. At my age, now that I'm on the downhill side, I don't want to be around boring people. There's just no time for it."

Royal started listening to country music in the '30s as a boy, when he would buy a one-dollar seat in an Oklahoma City theater balcony to see Jimmie Rodgers. In 1957, he moved to Austin with his wife, Edith, to coach the University of Texas Longhorns; this was "the first time I heard outstanding country music," he says.

Rising to athletic director of the fourth largest university in the nation, and legendary in football circles as inventor of the famous wishbone formation, Royal became an almost mythological hero in the sports-crazed state of Texas as his teams took win after win after win.

As his fame spread nationally, country-music stars, who got wind of the fact that he was a big country fan, started inviting Royal backstage during shows. Artists like Buck Owens started sending him tickets to concerts in advance, and playing sixth or seventh billing on those concerts would be a guy in a white shirt, suit, and tie—named Willie Nelson.

To psych up his players, Royal used to seclude the Longhorn football team in a motel on Friday nights before a game. The Record Men happened to be playing one of those motels around 1967, and Willie left a note in Royal's box, inviting him to a poker game in Willie's room. "I had heard him play before," Royal comments, "but wasn't really a fan."

Wanting to be friendly, Royal sauntered down to Willie's room; they played a few hands of poker, and when he left, Willie gave him a copy of his album, "The Party's Over."

At first the only song Royal liked on the album was the title tune, but "Then one night I was at home by myself," he says, "and I listened to the album all the way through. It was contagious and infectious, and I really got to listening to the lyrics."

That night Royal became a confirmed Willie fan.

"Willie never has been commercial," Royal offers, "but once you listen to what he's really saying, you realize he's a poet."

As the football season progressed, Royal started mentioning Willie in his frequent sports-page interviews. Some reporter would ask, "How you gonna spend the night before the big game, Darrell?", and Royal would reply, "Oh, I'll be sitting around listening to Willie."

It was an invaluable boost from high and influential places to a little-known musician playing Texas joints, like the rotgut, redneck Broken Spoke in Austin, or Big G's in Round Rock, or the Melody Ranch in Waco, or some even less distinguished establishment.

In Fort Worth Willie was a big favorite at Panther

Hall, a futuristic octagonal dance hall that resembles a giant spaceship that has docked in honky-tonk heaven.

"Hell," says Paul, "we were selling out Panther Hall when we couldn't sell 5,000 records in the whole United States." Willie and The Record Men set an attendance record at Panther Hall in 1965, and, in 1966 cut a live album there—"Country Music Concert, Willie Nelson." It was one of the best albums he released on RCA. Like the others, it didn't sell.

After a couple of years spent with RCA and on the road in Texas, Willie was beginning to realize his records lacked something his live show had. "Willie always knew people'd listen to his music, if they could hear him the way he really was," Paul claims. "His fans'd come up and tell him they wouldn't buy his records, but they sure did like his singing."

But what was that different ingredient, and how could he capture it on a record? Willie knew his live shows had a certain jazzy flavor, not typical of country (or pop) music at the time. He kept thinking about changing the name of the band, and considered The Progressive Hillbillies or The Progressive Jazzbillies.

"The word 'progressive' was on my mind way back then," he told *Guitar Player Magazine*, "and I associated it with the kind of music I had in mind."

Not sure whether he was doing right or wrong, Willie continued to experiment. Writer Al Reinart recalls that "whenever Nelson found an audience, he challenged it. Playing Panther Hall, he would softly drawl a monologue about how, as one songwriter relating to another, he could appreciate a good tune from a fellow, no matter how different he or his music seemed. Then he would do a Beatles medley." And Willie would study what kind of response he got.

Although The Record Men were playing all over the nation, anywhere they could pick up a booking, even ranging as far afield as Canada (where they pulled in crowds of twenty-five, if lucky), Texas, Oklahoma, California, and Georgia had been consistently good states for the band. In the late '60s, Willie decided to hone in even tighter on the southwest and central Texas.

Around 1967, he started playing John T. Floore's Country Store, "the biggest store in the smallest town in the largest state." Strategically situated in Helotes, on the highway to Bandera, Floore's Country Store was a conglomeration of honky-tonk par excellence, outdoor beer garden, homemade bread and tamale eatery, and enormous indoor bar.

This potpourri of redneck riches was the domain of one man—John T. Floore, "six foot five" and "a helluva man," as Willie later immortalized him in song.

Aging, eccentric, philandering Floore took to the thin, short-haired musician in a suit and tie, and Willie befriended Floore, a beleaguered old man, bedeviled by business problems and bad health, and helped him, over the years, to turn his bar into a local legend as the favorite hangout of Willie Nelson.

Digging ever deeper into Texas, Willie even went back and played his boyhood stomping ground, the Nite Owl at West.

At about the same time, Willie, still the promoter he had been at fourteen, started putting together his own package shows.

Crash Stewart and Ray Price had been organizing a Texas tour for Price, when the singer got a substantial offer to tour up north. Price reluctantly told Stewart he had to go for the best deal, whereupon Willie quickly jumped in, proposing: "Let me take Price's place."

Stewart said O.K., but explained to Willie that he simply didn't even begin to have the drawing power Price had. Willie then came up with the idea of hiring another big star to replace Price, adding some medium-level acts, and calling the whole thing The Willie Nelson Show.

The artistic Willie hired to replace Price was Marty Robbins. One of the filler acts was Charley Pride.

Actually, that was the second time Pride's name had surfaced. The first time was when Stewart, Willie, and Gene McCoslin were promoting some shows around Texas and "looking for some people that would draw some people," Willie says. "Charley Pride's name came up, and I vetoed it right off."

At the time Lester Maddox had been elected governor of Georgia, freedom buses were aflame across the South, and the U.S. Congress was reluctantly edging into Johnson's civil rights program.

"I said," Willie laughs, " 'you know, we can't go south with a colored guy on our shows.' Anyway, I listened to some records of Charley's later on and decided we might ought to use him, because he sang real good."

When he was hired on The Willie Nelson Show, Pride had released "Snakes Crawl at Night," but was, as Paul matter-of-factly puts it, "just a skinny nigger from Dallas who'd cut one single."

"The first night I had me following Charley Pride, and they were still yelling for him after I got on stage," the proprietor of the show recalls," so, the next night I decided I'd let somebody else follow him."

The troupe moved on to arch-conservative Dallas. The promoters, stars, crew, "even Charley," Willie says, "didn't know how the people were going to react.

"He handled the crowd great." Willie grins. "He had them in the palm of his hand within ten seconds after he walked on stage."

Later, Willie took Pride still further south, way down into Louisiana. "Charley couldn't even get in the motel," Paul declares. "Had to sleep in Willie's room. Charley's manager wanted to pull out, but Willie said he'd smooth everything.

"That night, Charley's backstage, and Willie comes out to introduce him, gives him this giant build-up, lied for ten minutes about what a big star he was. Then he brings Charley out real quick and gives him a big kiss—kisses him smack on the mouth!

"I think them folks were so hot to lynch ol' Willie for puttin' em on," Paul devilishly grins, "that they clean forgot Charley was black."

By the end of the tour, Charley Pride was the biggest star on The Willie Nelson Show.

By the late '60s, Willie and The Record Men had built a loyal following in the southwest among old Webb Pierce/Ernest Tubb traditional country fans, but were still scraping along at the prices and places a so-so recording artist could command, still playing the crummy honky-tonks, dance halls, beer joints, and bars.

But it was an atmosphere where Willie thrived. "I

have yet to play an audience," he once said, "even back when I started out and there were very few people there, where I couldn't find at least one person in the audience who was enjoying what I was doing. That made it all worthwhile for me that evening."

The boys in the band, however, were getting plain sick and tired of driving back and forth from Tennessee to Texas all the time in a bouncing old road bus. Most of them were from Texas anyway, and they convinced Willie he should let them all move to San Antonio, then just fly out to the first date of each tour, ride around with them on the bus, and then fly home.

Soon, Willie was returning to Nashville alone.

It was an exhilarating but disheartening period; tough stuff made only for those afflicted, gifted ones who have music and movement in their blood so bad they're hopeless doing anything else.

"Will's paid his dues," once wrote a twenty-year veteran of life on the road with Willie. "He's run up and down the highways eating cold pizzas, mayonnaise and onion sandwiches, and drinking hot beer. He knows what it's all about."

NASHVILLE WAS THE TOUGHEST

1965 — Roger Miller sweeps the Grammys with six
awards, a feat not equaled before or since
1967 — Glen Campbell smashes to the top of the
pop charts with Nashville song, "Gentle
on My Mind"
1968 — Bob Wills elected to the Country Music
Hall of Fame
1968 — Top Records: "Stand By Your Man"
(Tammy Wynette) and "Folsum Prison
Blues" (Johnny Cash)
1969 — Bob Dylan records in Nashville
1969 — Merle Haggard hits with "Okie from
Muskogee"

In 1965, a brilliantly rising army captain, on the
way to assignment as an English teacher at West
Point, suddenly veered off one hundred-eighty degrees
in every direction, moved to Nashville, took a job as a
janitor at CBS studios for fifty-eight dollars a week,
and started wandering around Music Row looking for
Willie Nelson.

Kris Kristofferson, while winning four awards from

Atlantic Magazine for fiction writing, and spending two years at Oxford College in England on a Rhodes Scholarship, had been listening to Willie Nelson.

Here, in Nelson, the acutely talented Kristofferson realized, was a country songwriter whose songs had an unusual depth and density, who seemed capable of painting whole murals of feeling in song poems shrewdly crafted and passionately stated, in deceivingly simple everyday words.

He wanted to meet this Willie Nelson.

Kristofferson, the same age as Roger Miller and Glen Campbell—all of them just three years younger than Willie—had been virtually disowned with his decision to become a country songwriter, by his career-military family and by his distraught, furious wife who made coming home "like going to Alcatraz."

Now that he'd gone and done it, Kristofferson wanted to spend his time with the best. Kris wanted to look Willie Nelson up, hang out with him some, pick his brain.

Willie, however, when he wasn't on the road with the band or recording in the studio, was pretty much holed up out at Ridgetop. Sure, he knew some of the new boys, eventually met Kris, really liked his stuff—Waylon was around, too. But he didn't hang out with the music crowd anymore the way he used to do at Tootsie's with Mel, and Hank, and Harlan.

"I laid back and stayed out of it, and lived up on the farm," Willie told *Picking Up the Tempo*. "I went into town once or twice a year, whenever I had to record.

"I stayed out of politics, the local politics there, and didn't get involved in any of the organizations," (like the Country Music Association, newly formed to pro- mote country music) "because I am not organiza- tionally inclined. I don't . . . I can't be organized that easily.

"They already had their plans set in Nashville," he added, "the way they wanted things to be, and I didn't fit in them too well."

Ironically, the middle '60s, when Willie somewhat turned his back on Nashville and headed southwest with The Record Men, marked the beginning of a new songwriting surge in Nashville.

The early '60s had been a time exhilarating, open- ended days for writers like Willie, Cochran, Anderson, Howard, and Walker, but in the middle '60s Nashville became the tantalizing, creative incubator for a new breed of writers, more hip, more literate, more philosophical — country writers who knew the music of Dylan, Joplin, Morrison, the Jefferson Airplane, the Stones.

Their horizons Woodstock-wide-open, the second generation of country writers sat on Music Row and put a very different world of words to the simple melodies of country music.

Kris Kristofferson, foremost among them, Billy Swan, Donny Fritts, Guy Clark, Billy Joe Shaver, Son- ny Throckmorton, Mickey Newberry, Shel Silverstein, and Tom T. Hall all swelled the ranks of the new league.

"All the action and excitement started around the mid-'60s," Bobby Bare told *Country Music Magazine*, "and really heated up in the late '60s. There was *lots* of action then. Everything was changing, and you could feel it changing, and you knew that you were part of it, and that it was relevant. About '69 or '70, it was *steaming*."

Kris Kristofferson and his hero, Johnny Cash, would take maximum advantage of this new trend, become its finest practitioners, exploit it to the fullest.

Willie would not. The songwriter who had attracted Chet Atkins because of his "intelligence," because he was "so damned bright," would not.

Caught up with his growing audience in Texas, immersed in the hard-tonking country joints and bars, Willie stayed — Willie.

Willie, the man Biff Collie calls "the original country jazz singer"; the man who emulated Floyd Tillman and Bob Wills, not Bob Dylan, as his heroes; the man who once explained he never liked rock and roll much, because he couldn't hear the lyrics; the man who was getting as many songs cut by pop and blues singers outside Nashville as he was by country singers inside Nashville; that man just stayed Willie Nelson — for some reason unable, or unwilling, to latch on, commercially, to the world of Kristofferson and Cash.

It would take Willie seven long years and an alliance with Waylon Jennings to finally hook into the country-rock-folk fusion pioneered in those Nashville days.

But at the time Willie had much more in common musically with a California singer and songwriter deep into western swing, Bob Wills, Lefty Frizzell, and hard country music. His name was Merle Haggard.

Willie won the title Entertainer of the Year partially by capitalizing on the label, "outlaw." Merle Haggard (California 65959) spent seven years being outlawed by the cops and FBI for armed robbery, petty theft, bogus checkwriting, automobile theft, burglary, and jail breaking. He spent two years in San Quentin, where he became acquainted with Johnny Cash—from the audience. The year Willie formed The Record Men, Haggard, an ex-con, had his first hit and began developing into one of country music's finest songwriters and stylists.

Johnny became "the man in black," Kris became a movie star, and Willie became an outlaw. Haggard, however, never crossed media lines. As Patrick Carr once noted, "then there's Haggard, who is a world unto himself and acts that way, and that's about it."

In his own unhappy world, Willie, during the seven years from 1965 to 1972, was consistently denied the relief that total failure brings.

You'll find them around Music Row by the dozens—boys whose careers have the terminal blahs. Tap-dancing for years on the fringes of the real action, too-wide smiles permanently in place, hair slicked back, or newly long, or just frizzed; maybe a big diamond ring to suggest they are making some money somewhere—perpetually convinced that the new producer, the new label, the new booking agency, the new manager, the new "look" is going to do it. This time it's really gonna happen.

It made Willie puke to think he might ever drift into that category.

Willie released dozens of singles on RCA, but only fifteen made the charts and the chart positions are not so much a dismal picture of total disaster as they are simply boring—number forty-three, number forty-eight, number nineteen (bright spot with "One in a

Row"), number twenty-four (semibright spot with "The Party's Over"), number twenty-one (semibright spot with "Blackjack County Chain"), number fifty, number twenty-two (semibright spot with "Little Things," inspired by Shirley), number forty-four, number thirty-six, number thirteen (bright spot with out and out swing/pop "Bring Me Sunshine"), number thirty-six, number forty-two, number sixty-eight, number twenty-eight, number sixty-two, number seventy-three. End of RCA career.

What had gone wrong?

Chet Atkins, his producer for half of his RCA career, says Willie was "probably too different for the average country public.

"We used to have meetings with Willie and Lucky Moeller (his agent) all the time," says Chet, "trying to decide how we could spread his sales out of Texas where he always sold records and did well in personal appearances. But we couldn't seem to spread them anywhere else."

There was certainly no lack of choices for ways to please the average country public at the time. In fact, there were at least four distinctive sounds Willie could have plugged into to power his success.

Consider: the pop-sound-with-country-and-California-herbal-essence. In this marvelously money-making club one found Glen Campbell ("Gentle on My Mind," "By the Time I Get to Phoenix"), Bobby Goldsboro ("Honey"), Roger Miller ("King of the Road," "God Didn't Make Little Green Apples"), Buck Owens ("I've Got a Tiger By the Tail"). Ol' Roger, who Willie had known forever, was sweeping the Grammys right off their rear ends and becoming a living, if nutty, legend in his own time.

Consider: the original-Nashville sound, in mink. Taking command of pop and country charts in this contingent were Eddy Arnold ("Make the World Go Away"), David Houston ("Almost Persuaded"), Ray Price ("For the Good Times"), and Lynn Anderson ("Rose Garden"). Willie's old boss, Price, had had the good sense to take off his Nudie suit, put on a tuxedo, and get into that one.

Consider: the keep-it-uncool-and-country sound. Buying bigger buses than they had ever imagined possible off these record sales were Red Sovine ("Giddy-up Go"), Jack Green ("There Goes My Everything"), Tammy Wynette ("Stand By Your Man," "D-I-V-O-R-C-E"), Merle Haggard ("Okie from Muskogee"), and Charley Pride ("Kiss an Angel Good Morning"). Charley Pride, you recall, was the black boy who had been kissed by his boss on the Willie Nelson Show.

Consider: the bad-boys-with-good-guts sound. That's what Johnny Cash and Waylon were doing. You know Waylon—the guy Willie had told to stay in Phoenix.

The parallels between what Cash was pulling off in the '60s, and the route Willie would forge for himself in the '70s, are intriguing.

Cash, who served in the air force and sold appliances before landing his first rockabilly hit in the '50s, hit with "In the Jailhouse Now" in 1962, "Ring of Fire" in 1963, "Jackson" (with his wife, June Carter) in 1967, and broke totally wide open in 1968 with "Folsum Prison Blues."

A bevy of legends collected around Cash, at one time notorious as a pill popper and for antics like shortening all the furniture in a hotel room a couple of inches with a chain saw. With "Folsum Prison Blues," the public invented a prison record for Cash (who had been in a local jail one night in his life), and he became an "outlaw" whether he liked it or not.

At that point, in a brilliantly managed career, Cash pulled off an incredible coup. At one and the same time he became the personification of country music to respectable middle America (primarily via the Johnny Cash Show), and, simultaneously, a folk hero to the hippie, protest-minded fans of Bob Dylan who, in 1969, journeyed to Nashville under Cash's blessing and recorded "Nashville Skyline."

At the time, however, Willie was not publicly embraced as a member of the Cash set, either by music or life style.

Well, if Willie didn't slide naturally into any available category, why not start a whole new category: the Willie Nelson category? After all, Chet had signed him up, because he was "so damned different."

The magic road to becoming your own musical category is called record promotion. Through record promotion, it is often possible to break (as actually happened) an eighty-year-old grandmother, a trio of nonexistent chipmunks, or a singing dog.

As Willie had learned in his encyclopedia days, selling is the name of the game.

In the music business, there are very few "natural" hits—records the public just grabs from the minute they are first heard on the radio.

Dozens of huge record labels are continually releasing hundreds of records, month after month. There are not enough hours in the day for all those records to be played on the radio. In fact, there are so many records, disc jockeys who decide which records to play on the air don't even have time to listen to them all.

Therefore, it is almost impossible for a record to become a hit unless it is anointed—by the record company. The record company says, "We are going to make this record a 'priority' record. We are going to spend thousands of dollars, maybe even hundreds of thousands of dollars to get this record to the attention of the disc jockeys and to make them want to play it.

"When disc jockeys start playing it," the record company continues, "we are going to spend thousands more dollars to bring it to the attention of the public. And if we stay on top of the disc jockeys, and make sure they keep playing it, then, if the public hears the record enough, they will probably start liking it. It will be a hit. Because we picked it to be a hit." Course 101 in Record Promotion.

Now . . . who is the key person at the record company who says *this record*, out of all the other records, is a priority record, and we will spend thousands on it? (Oh, by the way, "the other records—we won't spend anything on them.")

During the '60s in Nashville, this authority came from the national headquarters of record labels, most of them located in New York or Los Angeles. Chet Atkins could sign any artist he wanted, and he could cut a record on that artist, but it was New York who decided which records got the promotion.

"I didn't have any promotion," Willie told *Picking Up the Tempo*. "There was no money being spent promotion-wise on Willie Nelson. I just didn't feel like the promotional department of RCA was behind me, and in fact, I knew they weren't, and they admit they weren't.

"I felt like I was working for a giant computer in New York," Willie revealed. "Everything had to be cleared through New York. Well, I knew once the computer got it, it was going to say, 'Willie Who?' "

Once an artist has been around awhile and not had any hits, he tends to get pigeonholed—as a loser. So, the record company just sits there and waits for his contract to run out. (How could a new artist have any hits in the first place, if no promotion dollars were spent on his records? Course 102: Catch 22 in Record Promotion.)

What can the artist do? Nothing much. Just cut the best possible records he can and hope he'll have a "natural" hit, or hope the executive who doesn't believe in him in New York will get fired, and a new one who does will get hired.

"When I went with (RCA), I felt it was the greatest record company in the world," Willie said sadly, "but unless there is someone in high places that has some definite, direct interest in an artist, he's not any better off on RCA than he is on any other label."

Trumpet player Danny Davis, who produced a few sides on Willie at RCA agrees. "Chet and the Nashville office always believed he was a giant," Davis insists. "I remember we had an RCA meeting, and Chet and I agreed on trying to get the company to do an in-store sales-display campaign on 'The Contemporary Song Poets of Today,' " Davis says. "One of the ones we had in mind was Willie Nelson.

"We could never convince the top brass at RCA about Willie," Davis concedes, "and maybe he was just that much ahead of his time."

Ahead of his time? It has been asserted 1,437,658,909 times that Willie was ahead of his time.

So, was he? No—and yes.

Would there ever come a day when there would be dozens of artists doing what Willie Nelson was doing, and he would rise from among the like-minded and become the best? No.

Today there's no other artist in America doing what Willie Nelson is doing. He's different. And he always has a way of being different today, that's different from the way he was different yesterday.

To get to where he is now (i.e., in the movies), Willie changed the way he sounded for most of his ten years in Nashville to the way Waylon Jennings sounded ("Shotgun Willie" album); then he changed back to the way he sounded in Nashville ("Phases and Stages" album, 1974/"Yesterday's Wine" album, 1971); then back to Shotgun Willie ("Waylon and Willie" album). Then he changed to being Little Red from Abbott ("Stardust" album); then to a guitar teacher in Houston with Paul Buskirk ("Somewhere over the Rainbow" album). 'Course all the changes are genuine Willie.

Ahead of his time? No, he's *all* his times.

Now, if you mean (by being ahead of his time) that he wanted to be Entertainer of the Year years before there were a sufficient quantity of people who liked him enough to make him a superstar, then: yes. His ambition was ahead of his audience.

In order for Willie to be a superstar (not just a minor recording artist) you had to have millions of people who really got into listening intently to the words of his songs, and who really liked his oddly great voice. That was destined to be the college students of the late '60s and early '70s, who, if they could like (their parents thought) Janis Joplin's singing and Kris Kristofferson's singing, they could like anybody's singing, and who were in the habit of listening closely to rock lyrics.

It's certainly true that the college students of 1972 were not college students in 1962 when Willie was having eight bombs in a row on Liberty Records. They were in grade school then, and too young to put "Honk, if you love Willie" bumper stickers on the backs of their cars.

So, in terms of having the right audiences to make him a legendary superstar, Willie had started struggling too early.

Not that, operating in the dark about this important point, RCA didn't try in a thousand different ways to make Willie appealing to the average country public.

The sound on Willie's first Liberty album, and on many of his RCA albums definitely was the Nashville sound—basic, simple, tasty, a musical "hook," an elegant bit of guitar playing, a few Floyd Cramer licks on the piano, some sweet voices, some uptown strings. In other words, just like everybody else. Or, more precisely, just like most of the stars having the big hits.

The first RCA album was intended to emphasize Willie as a songwriter, "Country Willie—His Own Songs." The second album was designed to take some songs everybody knew and showcase Willie as a vocal stylist. It was titled "Country Favorites—Willie Nelson Style."

On the second album Willie sounds much as he does now, but, admittedly, Atkins smoothed him out a bit. The "Night Life" on the first RCA album is not as bluesy and gutsy as the "Night Life" he cut in Houston five years earlier. His vocal style is the same, the feeling is milder.

Starting with the third album, Felton Jarvis, as much as Chet Atkins, was Willie's record producer. No mere second-string assistant, though, Jarvis was also Elvis Presley's producer.

In the late '50s Atkins had given up producing Elvis and turned him over to Jarvis, because Elvis was so headstrong in the studio. Chet had his own ideas, but the more easygoing Jarvis had a way of just giving an artist his head in the studio, and letting the artist do what he wanted.

As Willie's Texas crowds grew and grew, and his records continued to stalemate at midchart positions, he began developing the idea that he was simply not capturing on record the live excitement of his band.

"The music I played on a bandstand was better than the music I played in the studio," Willie insists. "For one thing, I'd be using my own band, and we'd have a better feel for it. It just felt more comfortable."

Although he wasn't sure recording with his own band was the answer, he knew how uncomfortable he felt when he walked into a studio with six or seven musicians he hardly knew, and as he later remembered it, "They pointed a finger at me and said, 'Sing, Shorty.' "

When Willie broke attendance records in Fort Worth in 1965, Jarvis let Willie record a live album with his own band at Panther Hall. Without question, it is one of the best albums released during his RCA career. But it didn't burn up any cash registers. (Of course, maybe this was because it wasn't promoted—the vicious cycle in the whole why-Willie-didn't-make-it issue.)

It wasn't until the fourth album that Willie broke the top twenty with "One in a Row" which went to number nineteen on October 1, 1966. Only once while on RCA, would Willie surpass this moderate success—at the end of 1968 when "Bring Me Sunshine" went up to number thirteen.

In 1967, Chet tried promoting the notion that Willie was from Texas, and they cut "Texas in My Soul"—ten songs, every one of them about Texas. Again, no big thrills.

In 1969, they tried to stir up some interest in the idea that Willie was just plain different, a remarkable oddity. They cut, "My Own Peculiar Way." Nothing charted off that.

The most intriguing album in Willie's whole RCA career is "Both Sides Now," recorded in 1970. With Jarvis producing, they picked up on Cash's heavy bass sound, and cut an LP that in many ways anticipates "Shotgun Willie." And contrary to reports that RCA never let Willie record in the studio with his band, this album includes several band members—Willie on guitar, Jimmy Day on steel and bass, David Zentner on bass and guitar, and "Billy" English on drums.

"Both Sides Now" is an exciting taste of what was to come, including Willie's first recording of "Bloody-Mary Morning" stirred in with pop hits of the day ("Everybody's Talkin' "), a honky-tonk Ray Price hit ("Crazy Arms"), and even a marvelous version of the classic Roy Acuff identity piece, "Wabash Cannonball." "Both Sides Now" hit all the bases, but the single, "Once More With Feeling," only hit number forty-two on the charts.

In 1971, RCA even anticipated the coming "family" image, and put out an album called "Willie Nelson and Family," displaying a photo of the whole gang on the front. But very uneven, this album clearly shows the searching, vasillating nature of Willie's career on RCA.

The public was silent. No matter what approach they tried, the records flopped. There was almost no feedback to go by, except their own creative instincts. And as any music person will tell you, nobody, but nobody, *knows* what makes a hit.

Do you put Willie's voice way out front because it's unique? Or because it's (to some) so irritatingly different, do you try to smooth it into the music? Do you try to ride the coattails of the Nashville sound? or the Johnny Cash sound? or the Glen Campbell sound? or try something totally off the wall?

It's evident, in hindsight, that there was a communications breakdown while Willie was recording on RCA—and it appears that most of it was Willie's fault. He just didn't have the nerve to speak up and demand what he wanted.

Chet Atkins had the impression they were doing what Willie wanted. "He recorded with whatever musicians he wanted to use when he was with me," Atkins comments. "We'd talk it over. I remember one time we used Wade Ray on fiddle. We did a kind of a Texas kind of—not what he does now, but a swing kind of album. 'Columbus Stockade Blues' and some things like that with hot fiddle on it. It was a good experiment, but it didn't sell."

You might say Willie was simply psyched out during his RCA career. He was intimidated by the brilliance of the studio musicians; he was too much of a conformist to speak his mind; and he wasn't entirely convinced anything was wrong with the records, anyway—maybe it was just lack of promotion.

"At the time I thought all my records were great," Willie admits, "but nobody was sure how to record me."

Part of the reason they didn't use Willie's guitar on his records was sheer intimidation on Willie's part.

"I think I could have sold a lot more records earlier, if I'd recorded with my guitar and band from the beginning," Willie told Jack Hurst of the *Chicago Tribune* in 1979. "I didn't volunteer to play my guitar, because Grady Martin and Chet Atkins were sitting there, and I automatically assumed they'd do a better job than I would. If I'd picked up my guitar and started playing, and let them join in with it, the way my band does on stage, I think I could've gotten a different feel to my records then," Willie says, answering the question Chet Atkins has never asked him.

And Willie admits he was too timid to speak his mind. "I felt like I knew what I was doing even back then," he says, "but most of the times when I was recording, I would go along with what I was told, even though I didn't agree with it particularly."

Jack Hurst, who writes from one of the most balanced perspectives in country music, pushed Willie pretty hard on how much his lack of success was the fault of overbearing record producers in Nashville who have been repeatedly and wrongly accused, in publications like *The New York Times,* of telling Willie he couldn't sing and of burying him in "syrupy" strings, against his will.

In reality, the Nashville producers recognized Willie was a unique stylist and experimented with all kinds of production on him, nearly always with Willie's tacit approval. "I thought each album I did was good at the time," he reiterated to Hurst.

But now, he says with the hindsight of later years, he thinks maybe some of the RCA albums weren't produced well enough to sell. "I've listened to some of 'em recently, and I tend to think that may be the case," he told Hurst. But, he added, his early disappointments were probably as much his own fault as Nashville's.

"I stood back and let it happen the other way," Willie concedes, "so it's as much my fault as it was theirs.

"I just think it was the times that were not right," he concludes.

Chet Atkins, meanwhile, still believes in Willie and is still waiting—for Willie to give him his gun back. One time he loaned Willie a .38 automatic, and has never seen it since. He laughs the long slow chuckle of experience, then opines, "I figured it was timing. Just like Waylon. You sit around and think, when in the hell is he gonna make it? Because he's the greatest thing in the business, he's gotta make it.

"I remember talking to Johnny Cash about Willie," he recollects, "saying, you know, I hope time doesn't run out on him, because he's getting older.

"I guess the pop people kind of discovered him first," Chet muses, "the college kids and the in-crowd.

But," he concludes, his voice brightening with conviction, "I think what did it first was his attire.

"I don't think he would have ever made it, if he'd kept that banker's look he had."

FIRE ON THE MOUNTAIN

What, Willie was once asked, makes you mad? "I get mad at my own inadequacies," he replied.

All Willie could see by the end of the '60s was that he simply wasn't pulling things off. A lot of his buddies had their acts together and were making it big. It was his fault. He came down on himself hard.

Morose, drunk, crazy, and depressed, Willie Nelson just didn't care for himself very much.

Things weren't going well with Shirley, either.

It had started so great; it had really been fun out on the farm. When he'd come in from Texas to record, Shirley would ride with him to the studio, and they'd sit there and smooch and neck between songs.

But now his and Martha's kids were living with them a lot, and Shirley's career wasn't going anywhere much, and Willie was out in Texas constantly, goodtiming with a band that hadn't really made it off the ground.

"Acting is like singing," Willie once explained. "And let's face it, it doesn't take much acting for me to play a hell-raising country singer who loves honky-tonks, tequila, and women, in that order."

"What about women on the road?" *Penthouse* magazine once asked Willie.

"How much time we got?" Willie shot back.

When she married Willie, a close friend says, Shirley was "dear, sweet, and very straight." But that far-gone streak that led her to run off with Willie had blossomed under her new mate's wild and earthy life style. Shirley was into some drinking, carousing, partying on her own.

Act Two, Marriage Two.

During the time she was married to Willie, Shirley had a destiny of her own to deal with.

"Shirley was a great singer," Crash Stewart observed, "and later became an outstanding songwriter. She was the inspiration for many of Willie's songs. One was 'Little Things' which was written while Willie, Shirley, Bush, and myself were in New York doing the 'Tonight Show' with Johnny Carson."

There was a lot of talk around Nashville about the Shirley and Willie team. They played Ralph Emery's show on Saturday afternoons, singing in tandem, or with Shirley singing and Willie playing guitar behind her. "She sang well; she had lots of energy," recalls a TV watcher at the time.

When they worked the Captain's Table, a posh, silver-serviced nightspot on Printer's Alley, the elite of the Nashville music industry—the insiders and the Willie cult people—would turn out in full force.

"Watching them work together I could see right away that Shirley was a genius in her own right. However," Stewart noted, "sometimes two geniuses find it hard to live together."

Willie had worked himself around to an almost

totally negative state of mind. Once, when Willie came home drunk, Shirley who had had it to the max (and who knew a little karate herself), pushed Willie through a glass door.

"My marriage was shot to hell," Willie recalls without pleasure. "I was workin' on my second divorce and drinking a lot, and I wrecked four cars in 1969. A lot of bad luck was going down."

"Willie had a party one weekend that lasted about two weeks," Ruth Cook, who was on the scene at the time, recalls. "At some point he and Hank (Cochran) came to, long enough to start reminiscing about the bad ol' days, the succession of Mrs. Nelsons and Mrs. Cochrans, and the quirks of a deity that had let all those bad things happen to them."

Deciding that life had totally bottomed out and absolutely nothing worse could happen, Willie and Hank woozily penned the woebegone song, "What Can You Do to Me Now?"

Several cold December days later, Willie was out on the town at a night club in Nashville. He was paged for a phone call, and when he answered a voice frantically yelled over the phone, "Your house is on fire, it's burning down!"

Possibly nonchalant due to booze, Willie was momentarily silent, then replied, "Well, then, pull the car in the garage."

On second thought, however, he got considerably discomposed. Out at the house was a prime stash of Columbian marijuana, and there were probably firemen all over the place.

Screeching out the winding road to Ridgetop, he jumped out of the car and dashed into the blazing house. "By the time I got there it was burning real good," Willie remembers, then confesses, "I wasn't being brave running in there to get my dope—I was trying to keep the firemen from finding it and turning it over to the police."

As he later realized, the mad dash was far more therapeutic than risky. "When I saw that house burning," he says, "I knew I was going to need to get high."

"It's the only time I've ever seen him rattled," Waylon says.

What can you do to me now? As he stood miserably surveying his house, its flaming timbers cracking and falling onto its foundation in a charred mess, he suddenly realized: inside the house were the only tape copies of hundreds of unpublished songs he had demoed over the past ten years—going up in smoke.

YE WHO ARE WEARY, COME HOME

"I had some friends down in Bandera," Willie says, "who were managing a dude ranch, the Lost Valley Ranch, so I called them and asked them if they had any houses on the ranch available for rent."

Leaving the shambles at Ridgetop for the insurance company to deal with, Willie moved himself and the whole band to Bandera in the dead of winter. "We rented five houses down there in Bandera," he says, "stayed down there for almost a year. Had a heck of a good time."

Bandera, population nine hundred-twenty-nine, is a beautiful place in which to reclaim your soul. Achingly picturesque, it floats somewhere out there on the shimmering horizon where, as evening comes, the sun sinks down on cascades of gently rolling hillocks dotted with dark-green bushes and stubby little trees, growing out of blankets of red, yellow, blue, and white wild flowers.

The Lost Valley Ranch was closed, deserted at the time, and the quiet little clapboard cottages all had friendly wooden front porches that were perfect for sitting on, gazing out toward the horizon, and picking your guitar ever' now and then.

Even now, ten years later, Bandera is—simply the West. Bleached chunky white stone buildings line the main street; a wide board sidewalk rolls down that thoroughfare, fronting stores and Arkie Blue's Silver Dollar Saloon. PEDDLERS AND SOLICITORS ORDINANCE ENFORCED sternly warns a sign leading into town. What do they do? String them up? Maybe.

The vintage Texaco station at the main intersection still announces itself with one of those round "chief" signs with the big red star on it. The owner hunts when he isn't tending his pumps, and the walls inside are lined with stuffed heads of deer, boar, and bobcat, all complacently guarding the entrance to the ladies' room.

Willie moved into the ranch foreman's old place. Some of the band set up in the wrangler's house. They settled in.

The mending took time. It was hard for Willie to erase the searing image of his blazing home, that sickening pit-of-the-stomach feeling of all those songs—gone.

He didn't really feel like keeping to a schedule or working, but it would help to keep the guys busy, make a little money. They could pick down the road at John T. Floore's Country Store. Keep it laid back, home folks, no pressure, just good times.

"If you drive your man to drink, drive him here—we need the business," jokes one of the multitude of droll, yellowing, tattered signs nailed up all over the rafters in Floore's big, dark inside dance hall, crammed with battered wood tables and chairs. "Don't stare at the help—it could happen to you," another fading sign wisecracks.

Right inside the entrance is a massive wooden bar, running the whole width of the place. Here you can buy fresh, homemade bread for eighty cents a loaf or plates piled high with dozens of steaming homemade tamales wrapped in cornhusks. "You look like Helen Black, but I look worse in white," a sign joshes.

Carefully winding their way through the stuffy, dark interior, balancing plates full of food, patrons emerge into eyeball-searing sun blazing down on a patio/dance floor ringed with wooden picnic tables. Patrons eat breakfast, lunch, or supper, indoors or out; shoot pool; dance; listen to the jukebox; play with one of the big dogs sniffing folks' plates, or just plain visit.

All this homey hoopla was presided over by Willie's cantankerous, colorful old pal John T. Floore, who locals claimed "spent more money on his women than his bands."

Well, the paycheck wasn't all that big a deal with Willie. Floore's was like going home, a place he could relax, kick back, and play—where the boys could keep their chops up. He started hanging out and playing at Floore's pretty regular.

Every Friday and Saturday night there'd be a big dance headlined by big country stars on tour in Texas. Every Sunday afternoon, in the spring and summer, there would be a free dance outside on the patio. Willie and the band might draw one hundred-twenty-five—nothing for Floore's.

One night he came in to play and the cashier stopped him at the door. "Hey, who are you?" she asked. "Well, I'm Willie Nelson," he replied. "Well,

186

I'm Eula—so what?" she retorted.

Just home folks, nothing big, no pressure.

"Willie would always come down after playing and sit down and have a beer with everyone," remembers Joe Alguseva, the current owner. "That's one thing about Willie—he always had time for everybody. Why, after the show he'd come sit down and talk and have a beer, and I'd finally have to ask him to leave. He'd talk all night, if you'd let him."

Sometimes he'd go up to Austin and visit around. Al Reinart, a Texas writer, remembers meeting Willie for the first time one March, at a mutual friend's house. As he told *Texas Monthly*, "I found this quiet little man perched on the back of an armchair, his feet on the cushion, strumming an apparently prehistoric guitar. He was wearing gabardine slacks, a tacky yellow Robert Hall's shirt, and seemed terribly shy.

"I'd been told he was a 'famous country songwriter' which didn't impress me—I was a graduate student then, very young and superior—but I liked him from the moment he shook hands and smiled at me: it's what everybody first responds to in Willie, that tremendously embracing smile.

"His hair was still pretty short in those days; no beard yet, either, and his face was plain bad luck and lumps. He looked to be the quintessential cedar-chopper, except, I noticed, for the tiny gold ring piercing his left ear."

But many of Willie's days were more solitary, spent in Bandera, sitting under the trees, reviewing things in his mind, trying to shift it all into a pattern, into some answers.

He kept trying to pull together a more positive perspective on his life, the ten years kicking around Texas, the first marriage gone wrong, the ten years in Nashville, the second marriage going sour. He leaned on techniques he had learned in his experiments in thought control. "I used to have a lot of nightmares that woke me up at night," he says. "I told myself I wasn't going back to that, and the dreams stopped, power of the will."

Willie had been reading the writings of Edgar Cayce, and Cayce's son, Hugh. They were works that emphasized positive thought, and theories of reincarnation—doubtless a comforting concept to one beginning to believe he was going to have to find happiness in some other world.

Willie was also intrigued by the writings of Kahlil Gibran, a far-eastern philosopher, who wrote in a cryptic, parabolic, and poetic style.

Gibran deeply hated any form of orthodoxy that bound man by law or convention, rather than freeing him to follow the call of genuine feeling and emotion. Gibran believed that the beauty found in fleeting moments on earth is actually derived from eternal experiences of the soul, and he urged his readers and followers to discover the miracles in nature and everyday living.

All of the revelations he brought, Gibran believed, were gifts given by God to the Poet, who, like the Prophet, with whom the Poet is one in nature, is the highest form of mankind.

The poet, Gibran believed, could sin only by denying his own inner being. The Poet is set free—like Jesus, a poet and prophet—only by death. Death, through the process of reincarnation, marks the return of the individual soul to all-encompassing God.

Life on this earth, Gibran taught, is but a quest, an eternal searching for and returning to God. This quest itself is the reason for life; thus, to realize a dream is to lose it.

To Willie, trying to make sense out of an erratic life of successes, failures, and temporal pleasures, still frustrated in his own great dream, the eastern mystic's ideas had power.

Gibran was also particularly eloquent on human relationships, especially those between men and women. He championed equality of the sexes, and believed in unions based on true love, not social convention and obligation.

Around 1969 Willie had met a young woman named Connie Jean Koepke. She was tall, blonde, beautiful, and a Willie Nelson fan.

His marriage with Shirley was careening out of control. "Both drifted into smashing up cars, drinking, drugs, and infidelity until the marriage simply died of neglect," wrote *People* magazine. At some point in 1971, they were divorced.

Connie, a working girl of twenty-five or so, had started coming to Willie's dances. "She would call me at my finance company office," wrote Crash Stewart in the *San Antonio Express*, "which was doubling as a booking office, and get Willie's schedule every week.

"After about three months, Connie had made friends with me and the band, but had never met Willie. One night Connie was at a club and one of the band members told her he thought it was about time she met Willie."

"I never even liked country music," Connie told a newspaper, "but he had a song called 'I Never Cared for You,' and I liked it."

That night in Cut 'n Shoot, Texas, "When Willie came out to sing," Connie told *People*, "he looked down and smiled. It wasn't a flirty look; just a warm, neat feeling. Before the night was over, he asked for my phone number, and the next time he came through Houston, he called. I went to the show, and that was it."

Willie remembers the moment of meeting as one of high-charged, romantic intensity. "It was a classic eye-contact thing, lightning across a crowded room," he recalls vividly. "I turned to my steel-guitar player, and said, 'Get that tall, good-lookin' blonde for me.' Like any good, obedient steel player, he came up after the show and said, 'Here she is.' "

"She's a beautiful woman," a smitten Willie says of Connie, who has the lovely, classic eyes and big, wide smile of an all-American model. Years later, when Willie met Candice Bergen, the actress considered one of the most beautiful women in America, Willie just kept exclaiming how much Candice resembled his wife, Connie.

Willie and Connie married on Willie's birthday, April 30, 1972 in Las Vegas at the home of Steve Wynn, owner of the Golden Nugget. Wynn and his wife were best man and matron of honor.

Under the influence of his reading and retrospection, his new romance, and the soothing atmosphere of Bandera, Willie, surrounded by supportive family and friends, was writing some of his finest songs. They were songs full of memories and values, like "Me and

Paul," the rakish ode to his long-faithful friend; and they would appear on an album Willie still considers one of his finest: "Yesterday's Wine."

Working out his feelings in music, he let himself flow under the healing hands of time.

While Willie was rebuilding his inner spirit, the insurance company had been rebuilding his house at Ridgetop. After about a year, refreshed and renewed, he decided it was time to return to the mainstream, to get back to Nashville.

YESTERDAY'S WINE

1970 — Flying Burrito Brothers release "Sleepless Nights"
1971 — Top Record: Kristofferson's "Help Me Make It Through the Night"
1972 — Top Record: "Happiest Girl in the Whole USA"

Heedless of the adage that you can't put new wine into old wineskins, Willie returned to Nashville full of hopes and optimism. He had a new house, a new booking agent, and Connie; and The Record Men were back on the road.

Willie released two radically different albums in 1971. The first expresses his anguish and despair over the fire and ten years uncertainly spent. The second reflects the new peace and resignation he found in Bandera.

In the aftermath of disaster, Willie was very conscious of the comfort and loyalty of "the family." The cover of "Willie Nelson and Family," his first 1971 album pictures the whole clan standing in the wintry outdoors, grouped in a semicircle around a big, smoky, blazing campfire: Willie and Connie, Paul and Carlene, Bobbie (in a bulky tiger-striped fur coat) and about twenty others, including a dog.

But musically, the album is an unremitting series of some of the most soulful "downer" songs in modern music. The theme is set by "What Can You Do to Me Now," the song Willie and Hank Cochran wrote in their crazed condition right before the fire. That's followed by Kristofferson's doleful "Sunday Morning Coming Down," Hank Williams' soul-breaking, "I'm So Lonesome I Could Cry," the melancholy classic, "Fire and Rain," and Merle Haggard's love-crossed, "Today I Started Loving You Again." The only hopeful note is an upbeat version of a gospel song Willie wrote in the early '60s, "Kneel at the Feet of Jesus."

Ironically, Dr. Johnson, Willie's discographer, feels that the chaotic time between 1969 and 1971 was probably Willie's strongest period as a vocalist. He cites the gut-wrenching "I'm So Lonesome I Could Cry," and "Truth #1," the "B" side of "Laying My Burdens Down," a Willie-penned gospel song which made number sixty-eight on the charts in 1970. He also mentions several cuts on the fine "Both Sides Now" album, somewhat of a predecessor to the later "Shotgun Willie" album on Atlantic.

"He had control of his voice, was trying new songs, and doing really fine improvisations of old standards," Dr. Johnson says.

The single off "Willie Nelson and Family," "I'm a Memory," went to number twenty-eight, the most successful record he had released in over two years.

All of this boded well for the album he was about to release, "Yesterday's Wine."

On a Saturday morning in 1971, when Willie was in Texas, Felton Jarvis called and announced they were recording an album starting Monday morning.

"Oh really?" Willie replied.

"Yes, really," Felton retorted firmly. "You had better get busy."

"So I stayed up all night and wrote several songs," Willie said; "then I went back over some of my old scribblings I had stored in a closet and came up with the rest of the songs."

During the recording session Willie was photographed, head encased in headphones, feet encased in tennis shoes. The photo caption reads: "Willie Nelson—a genius at work—a true genius."

The album was a masterpiece, the finest he had ever done.

"Yesterday's Wine" is a summation and questioning of Willie's entire life to that point. The imagery in which he chose to express himself was that of his boyhood days: the great doctrines of sin and salvation, guilt and redemption found in the Bible, and learned at the feet of Mama and Daddy Nelson.

But now, nearly forty, Willie saw those great Biblical precepts through eyes colored by his reading of Cayce and Gibran, as just one ethical moment in the continually recycling flow of the universe.

"Yesterday's Wine" reflects the nightmares that crowded his brain during the long, dark nights in remote Bandera; the remorse of another marriage gone crazy, gone bad; the guilt of three children, shuttled back and forth across America; the money misspent; the cars wrecked; the plaguing need for freedom and independence that made it so hard to be like other people; the endless recordings, the expression of his life and art, unsold and unappreciated.

Allegorically depicting a man's life from birth to death, it asks the great philosophical questions in song: Why am I here? Why must I suffer? What does life mean? What has value? Will I emerge triumphant in spirit?

It is the work of a poet looking at his life, through a glass, darkly.

Exquisitely produced, with a variety of country, jazz, and blues licks that foreshadow Willie's later successful records, "Yesterday's Wine" is sheer autobiographical poetry.

The beginning, spoken by members of the band in curiously flat tones, has the feeling of a Gibran parable. There is great confusion on earth. Perfect Man, a voice says, has already come to earth and his voice has been heard. Now, the voice of Imperfect Man must be heard.

"A typical man" (Willie), and a Taurus, must be reborn and assume this task. He must confront life with strength, combined with wisdom and love.

"Where's the Show?", the first music on the album, is an aching plea to be told where, in the great theater of life, is the role for this Imperfect Man. Is there even a part at all? ("I am born, can you use me?")

This segues into an even stronger plea, begging God for a chance, a fair audition, to be allowed to play a part and fulfill his potential. ("What would you have me to do Lord?/Should I sing them a song? . . . Please, Lord, let me be a man.")

"In God's Eyes" upholds the spiritual truth that man should live by the spirit and not by men's rules;

that although man looks on the outside, God looks on the heart. ("Never think evil thoughts of anyone/It's just as wrong to think as to say/For a thought is but a word that's unspoken/In God's eyes he sees it this way.")

"Family Bible," a fable of childhood, asserts the need to hold on to basic values, represented by the family, and the simple lessons of goodness learned in youth. ("Now, this old world of ours is filled with trouble/This old world would, oh so better be/If we found more Bibles on the table/And mothers singing, 'Rock of ages, cleft for me.' ")

Imperfect Man's agony and puzzlement over a child's blindness, "It's Not for Me To Understand," preaches sheer acceptance. Mere man cannot understand the mysterious all-knowing ways of an all-seeing God. "You, too, are blind without my eyes," God majestically replies.

Although God may comprehend his master plan, for a mere man "These Are Difficult Times."

"Lord, please give me a sign," the tortured man pleads. But instead of a sign, he is given a thought, "Remember the Good Times." Emphasize the positive, put away the negative. ("Remember the good times/They're smaller in number and easier to recall/Don't spend too much time on the bad times/Their staggering number will be heavy as lead on your mind.")

Side one ends with "Remember the Good Times": perhaps the answer Willie found in Bandera.

Side two begins as Imperfect Man falls in love. The first two, highly sophisticated songs, are among those Willie considers his best songwriting efforts. Perhaps they are his farewell to Shirley.

The man offers his love a "Summer of Roses." "So I bring to you all my possessions," he says, "and would that you'd share them with me." None of his possessions, however, are man-made gifts, but are gifts of nature: a "springtime of robins," a "summer of roses," and an "autumn of dry leaves" to soften the "winter of snow."

Winter signifies the end of the relationship. Reflective as a gray "December Day," the man searches back over the relationship. ("And as my memories race back to love's eager beginning . . . the ending won't go away.")

But "miracles appear in the strangest of places" and his old love appears in a bar, where the man and a friend are thinking and drinking "Yesterday's Wine." The three, "aging with time, like yesterday's wine," ponder the days of their lives.

With "Me and Paul" Imperfect Man affirms that while love is fleeting, friendship endures and prevails. Written about the mutual ups and downs of Willie and Paul English, this song reflects the ever-growing "us against them" sentiments of Willie and the family, and would later add fuel to the outlaw movement.

"Goin' Home" is a metaphor for death. As his body lies in its coffin at the funeral, "a mixture of teardrops and flowers," Imperfect Man's soul appeals to Jesus to continue with him on this new journey. His soul, however, admits that Imperfect Man was unable to confine himself within the simple, but stern boundaries set out in the family Bible. And the simple folk at home can't understand. ("Crying and talking for hours/about how wild I was/ and if I'd listened to

197

them/I wouldn't be there.")

The album ends not on a note of certainty, but still filled with doubt—doubt about the ability of imperfect man to follow the path of perfect man, Jesus Christ, to spiritual peace.

Willie's last days in Nashville were, indeed, "yesterday's wine." And "goin' home," Willie had discovered nothing had changed.

What can you do to me now? What they—Nashville or New York or indifference or pigeonholes—did to him now was to ignore "Yesterday's Wine," the best work he had ever done.

The album following "Yesterday's Wine," released in March of 1962, has the painfully descriptive title, "The Words Don't Fit the Picture."

His last album on RCA, however, released in July, 1972, was more self-assertive: "The Willie Way." If he couldn't turn his career in Nashville around, he could at least live on his own terms in one of his favorite places. Willie decided to go back to Texas—for good.

"The only bad Willie Nelson record I ever heard," says longtime observer of the Nashville scene, Bill Littleton, "was his last single on RCA, 'Mountain Dew.' It sounded like he was depressed, his creativity had dissipated. Actually, it was boring."

In August of 1972, when he was thirty-nine, Willie, Connie, and their baby daughter Paula Carlene moved to Austin, Texas.

The band, now consisting of Paul, Bee, Bobbie on piano, Jody Payne on guitar, and Mickey Raphael on harmonica, had moved up to touring in a big $20,000 camper. Jack Fletcher, Bobby's son, sometimes drove,

198

but, according to Paul, he was still "manager, accountant, part-time driver, everything." "Willie didn't get a real personal manager until 1973. It was tough. . . ."

As leader of the band, Willie had decided to follow the example of Bob Wills, who made it big playing just Texas, Oklahoma, and a few other southwestern states. He decided to reign in his territory.

"I left Nashville because of the performing," Willie explains. "I just decided I was going to have to go back to Texas where I had some sort of a base to work with. I know everybody there. I know every club, and know all the bartenders and waitresses by their first names.

"In the beginning, I tried to work too big an area—the whole world." He laughs. "The area I picked was a good area, because there were a lot of fans down there, and I could pay the bills while I was getting my little plan together."

My little plan?

Just before moving to Austin, Willie had attended the Dripping Springs Reunion, a financially disastrous three-day event, held just outside Austin and staged by a couple of promoters out of Dallas. Dripping Springs was based on the idea that you could stage one massive country extravaganza; book all the hot, new country acts and promote to college kids; book all the old-time country acts and promote to their parents; and sit back and rake in the admissions.

When the mud finally dried up after the cold, rainy, too-early-in-the-spring circus, one promoter had committed suicide, one had borrowed $30,000 to pay off Loretta Lynn's fee, and a lot of local people had gotten burned.

But to Willie, a short-haired guy observing the scene in a golf cap and big sunglasses, Dripping Springs was a revelation. Because, to everybody's amazement, the theory worked.

Not only did the old farmboy fans show up to see Loretta and Tex Ritter and Charlie Rich, but so did a bunch of young longhairs who wanted to see Waylon, Kris, and Tom T. Hall.

Although there were some tension between the two groups, and there were some overeager security men on horses who like to hassle longhairs; for most of the audience, the festival was simply one of the greatest country-music shows they had ever seen.

Willie remembers, "Somebody would look around and see his daughter over here, and a kid would see his dad over there, drinking beer."

Although Loretta left in a fit (once she got her lumbering bus unstuck from the gluelike mud) exclaiming she would never play out in the middle of a cow pasture again, Willie was beginning to have fond thoughts of what could be pulled off in a cow pasture.

"I knew I had to find some other way to reach people," Willie says.

What if you had a big concert featuring some of the hip names in country, and made the longhairs feel *totally welcome?* Could it be a whole new audience for Willie Nelson? An audience without pigeonholes and preconceptions?

Willie realized Bob Dylan, Joan Baez, and Buffy St. Marie had been recording in Nashville. He had noticed the growing interest of college kids in bluegrass. He had heard some of the experimental country-rock albums by groups like the Flying Burrito Brothers and the Grateful Dead.

While he was thinking, Willie let his hair grow longer, let his beard reemerge. The white shirts, ties, and polyester slacks were packed away. He started looking, a lot of his old buddies thought, "like something the cat dragged in."

Pop Nelson got alarmed, afraid that his boy was messing up bad. "The band all had uniforms then," he said, "and I got concerned when Willie decided to start wearing jeans and lettin' his hair grow. I was against it. He was only making eight hundred dollars for a personal appearance then—or five or three or whatever he could get. I thought he was gonna lose that."

But the move to Texas represented a whole new positive attitude for Willie. "I think there's a big freedom in Texas," Willie says, "that gives a person a right to move around and think and do what he wants to do. And I was taught this way: anybody could do whatever they fucking wanted to do. And that confidence, shit, if you got that going for you, you can do almost anything.

"The bottom line for me," Willie explained to Robert Hilburn in 1980, "is positive and negative. I began to change my life so I could emphasize the positive things."

He resolved not to keep making the same mistakes over and over. "You learn from mistakes," he says, "some of which I didn't make just once, but time and time again. You finally get to the point where you say, 'Hey, wait a minute, what am I doing?' "

Willie's RCA contract was up for renewal, but apparently each side had decided the other was a mistake they didn't want to make twice. Jerry Bradley had been hired as administrative head of RCA in Nashville, and Chet says, one day "I looked up and Willie wasn't on the label."

Enter Jerry Wexler, former vice president of Atlantic Records and a legendary talent finder in the rhythm-and-blues field. "I first actually met Willie Nelson in about late 1971," Wexler once said, "but I had known of him for a long time, of coure.

"I went to a party in Nashville after some banquet or other; all these big country stars were there, passing a guitar around, all of them playing a couple of songs. Then Willie got up, ice-cold unknown, and took over.

"In that setting it was the most remarkable thing I'd ever seen.

"I walked up to him afterward," Wexler said, "and I said, 'Willie, I've been looking forward to meeting you for a long time.'

"He looked back at me with that great and wonderful smile of his, and he said, 'Hey, have I been lookin' for *you* for a long time!' "

MINSTREL MAN

If Willie's voice has an eccentric character, then his guitar is the perfect old coot of a sidekick for it. "I figure this guitar and me will probably quit workin' about the same time," Willie once predicted.

Willie's guitar is as famous as any of the people standing on stage around it—picked clear through with a four- or five-inch hole (getting bigger), and autographed with the signatures of soulmates like Waylon, Leon Russell, Kris and Rita, Roger Miller, and Ray Charles.

Its breed is about as clear as a mongrel dog's; the guitar started out a Baldwin. "I busted it; it couldn't be fixed, and the company went out of business," Willie says, "so I had a friend (famous steel guitar innovator Shot Jackson) take the guts and put them into the Martin classical guitar I'm playing now."

The autographs are there, because when Willie bought the Martin about seventeen years ago, Leon Russell told him autographs make guitars more valuable. The hole is there because classical guitars are not made to be used with a pick. "It looks kind of soulful," Willie notes, "but it's just a hole."

The pickup off the old Baldwin, however, is in a class by itself. "All the guitar players ask me, 'Where do you get that sound on your guitar,' " Willie reveals. "But it comes out of that Baldwin pickup. It's a fantastic pickup."

Over the years, the guitar has taken on a dignity as rakish as that of its owner.

"That guitar," Willie's infamous roadie "Poodie" once explained, "is the first thing off the stage, and the last thing on. 'Cause that's our living."

The boss, Poodie continued, "won't let us do a fret job on it, even though the frets are wore down all concave, but we have built it up from the inside with plastic wood, so the hole won't just take over.

"He throws sawdust off that thing when he plays," Poodie said. "He used to carry it around by the neck. He'd get drunk, go off, and leave it in a truck stop in Sheboygan. We'd have to go back. It'd be lying there," Poodie paused, "but that was before it got famous."

Equally famous, or "notorious" as recording engineer Phil York puts it, is Willie's guitar amplifier. "I think he got it at Goodwill Industries, I swear," York laughs, shaking his head.

"I think it's a Bendix or a Philco—really odd," he adds with relish. "It's an aluminum amplifier, beat all to hell, made about 1951. It's got its own awful sound, and it's just great."

The hodgepodge old amp, which Willie says is also a Baldwin, has fallen apart innumerable times, and is glued together, braced with an angle iron, patched with new parts. Naturally, he refuses to use anything else—except one just like it. He's got three. "The one I like best, I've had so long it's wired up direct," he says; "there's no fuse or switch-on. When you plug it in, it's wide open."

Willie always used to play electric guitars. He had a Fender Telecaster, a Fender Stratocaster, even an Epiphone. "I got hung up on those Epiphone necks," he told *Guitar Player,* "and was real pissed off when they quit making them."

Now he plays the amplified acoustic, because "you can use an acoustical guitar in a motel room, partying."

He likes the thick neck of the classical acoustical, because "it keeps me from trying to get too funny and too clever. With the strings that far apart and the neck that wide," he modestly explains, "I have to keep it pretty basic, or I'll make too many mistakes."

Willie credits his hot licks to all the guitarists he liked over the years: Hank "Sugarfoot" Garland, Eldon Shamblin (who played for Bob Wills), jazz guitarist George Barnes, Johnny Smith, Segovia, Montoya. "I'd sit down and try to duplicate their runs," he says, "and what would happen, I'd make mistakes and turn those into hot licks."

Willie also mentions three Nashville session guitarists who used to play on his RCA records: Chet Atkins, Bucky Meadows, and Grady Martin (who now plays with Willie's band). But he says he's probably more of a Django Reinhardt fan than anything else.

Reinhardt, a gypsy who began playing professionally at fourteen, lost two fingers on his left hand in a tragic fire. His musical genius became evident when he developed a new, unorthodox method of fingering the strings. His group, The Hot Club of France, was internationally famous, and Willie's "Somewhere over the Rainbow" album is a tribute to Reinhardt.

Although Willie's granddaddy started him out with a thumb pick, "I got away from that in a little while," he told *Guitar Player*. "I began to hear other players like Eldon Shamblin who didn't use a thumb pick—he had a straight pick. And that was more what I wanted to play, the blues and jazz and western swing.

"Chet Atkins' style," he compares, "was the thumb pick, and the old black blues, but I was more into jazz."

Willie's picking has a good dose of blues in it (B. B. King is his favorite blues guitarist), and also a dash of Mexican blues ("Maybe I am half-Mexican," he once joked) which shows up as a kind of faint, upbeat embellishment, hinting at a flamenco trill.

What distinguishes Willie as both a guitarist and vocalist, is that he *improvises*. Jazz, the blues—they're music that takes flight with the feeling. Willie's making it up a lot of times as he goes along, creating it right there on the spot. Spontaneous and intense, with a twinkle in his eye, he picks and sings a whirlwind wrought by the moment's pleasure.

Willie's voice: you either love it or hate it.

To believers, it's "a rich, uniquely metallic voice that carries centuries of longing," or "not powerful, but exceedingly soothing."

"While he exerts firm vocal control," one reviewer noted with wonder, "he never seems to know precisely where the voice will land. That uncertainty, and the strength underlying it, make the voice particularly compelling."

On the other hand, the New York-hip *Soho News*

reviewer yawned, "Personally, I think he's the world's largest sleeping pill, but this country crooner's got his fans. . . ." Producers who turn out slick, sophisticated, technically perfect records will grimace and tell you Willie's phrasing is "interesting," but his voice is awful (not to mention off-key).

Like his guitar playing, Willie's voice takes you unawares.

"Will has a style of singing that is back-phrasing," says Waylon. "To this day I can't do it. As far as playing guitar, I have a straightforward approach, and rush the beat; that's my style. If I try to imitate Willie on stage," he laughs, "they think the boy is losing his voice and his mind at the same time."

In 1978, George Jones saw the handwriting that had been on the wall about ten years, and did an album of duets with progressive country singers like Linda Ronstadt, Emmylou Harris—and Willie.

After the first run-through of "I Gotta Get Drunk," it was obvious that George was uptight and holding back on his vocals.

Willie tried to put him at ease, remarking, "You know something, George? I wrote that song for you back in the '50s, but I didn't have the nerve to pitch it to you."

"Hell, Willie," Jones replied, "I tried to find you once, because I wanted to cut 'Crazy,' but I couldn't find you."

However, after a couple more tries, it was obvious George was still having bad trouble singing along with Willie. They moved on to the song "Half a Man," but George kept stumbling around Willie's voice.

"How the *hell* does Waylon sing with you?" he finally

blurted out. "I'm used to singing on the note. I could do two lines during one of your pauses." Willie laughed.

Willie's back-phrasing style is based on 1930s' black blues and jazz singers, and the 1940s' pop singers influenced by them.

Sitting by the radio as a boy back in Abbott, Willie was listening to an exceedingly odd bunch of musical bedfellows: Frank Sinatra; Tommy Duncan, lead singer for Bob Wills; Ernest Tubb; and the off-beat talent, Floyd Tillman.

Sinatra and Duncan are somewhat similar in style. Duncan, like many of the singers with western swing bands, borrowed heavily from the big-band crooners, as Doug Green writes in *Country Roots*, the western-swing vocal style was "a deep-pitched, sun-warmed, semicrooning style, a combination of Jimmie Rodgers and Bing Crosby."

Tommy Duncan, Willie explains, was a "phrasing" singer. "In my own mind," he adds, "Tommy was more blues than he was country."

Willie frequently credits Frank Sinatra's influence. "Actually what I'm doing when I sing isn't all that hard," Willie has claimed. "It was just that nobody in country music in those days was doing it. Sinatra's been phrasing for years. A lot of pop singers have. Ella Mae Morse, Freddie Slack, and some of the others I used to listen to when I was comin' up."

On the other hand, Ernest Tubb is about as country as they come—in the southwest. He doesn't sing in the high, harsh, whining sound of the southeastern, Appalachian-born vocalists, but he's country. And his career is interwoven with that of fellow Texan, Floyd Tillman. Tillman, little remembered until Willie started talking about him, has one of the more fascinating stories in country music. A writer credited with inventing the "cheating song," Tillman has a winding, waving, slurred vocal style unmatched except perhaps in Bob Dylan (who says he was influenced by Hank Thompson, and likely heard Tillman, also).

"Ernest Tubb was my favorite singer when I was a kid," says Harlan Howard, whose songs are usually big blues as well as country hits, "I liked Ernest's songs, but then he stopped writing, and all of a sudden Floyd Tillman was writing them. Like 'Slipping Around.' Floyd was putting them out on Columbia, and Ernest was doing them on Decca.

"Floyd Tillman," he says with satisfaction, "had this weird, crazy style of singing, but I love it to this day."

As one writer described, Tillman "swooped down on the notes with a tormented, pleading Texas drawl, toying with his melody's natural flow, and phrasing with the smoky back-room inflections of a jazz singer."

Growing up listening to all these jazz- and blues-based artists, Willie became his own peculiar amalgamation of them all. "Actually," Willie once joked, "I sang 'til I ran out of breath, and I noticed that it sounded pretty good."

In reality, Willie doesn't sing off-meter in the least. As Crash Stewart once defended, "If the pickers would just sing the song as it is supposed to be, Willie will be there at the proper time."

The actual sound of Willie's voice isn't "pretty." In fact, he credits his so-called "high slightly nasal baritone" to sinuses.

"I used to swim in them old cattle ponds around Texas when I was growing up. I got a real bad sinus problem." Asked if this was the source of his "unique, haunting, reedy, singing timbre," he grinned. "I owe it all to the ol' water hole."

Like the rest of Willie, his voice possesses incredible endurance. "I've heard him sing four- or five-hour sets," Jerry Wexler once marveled, "and still bend every note where he wanted it."

Willie credits a new-found strength in his voice to a physical fitness regime he adopted several years ago of jogging five or ten miles a day. He says cutting down on drinking and smoking helps his voice, and jogging strengthens his lungs.

On albums like "One for the Road" with Leon Russell, where song after song is an old battle ax written by somebody else, his singing, though occasionally flashing into true feeling, often descends to a perfunctory, listless level.

But Willie's voice and songs he writes himself, or feels on a deep emotional level, share a riveting compatible authenticity.

The greatest quality of Willie's singing is his ability to bring out a meaning in a song that you'd normally never realize was there. He bunches up his words in creative ways and crowds their meanings together in new, startling packages.

He acts out the song, feels and interprets the part for you, the listener. "Acting," he once said, "isn't much different from what I've been doing all my life. There's words on a piece of paper. You try to make them mean something."

With an uncommon triumvirate of talent he steps to the stage—his guitar, his voice, his songs: Willie Nelson, the "compleat minstrel" of his own music.

LET ME TALK TO YOU

"Who was it," Willie once asked, "who said there's only two songs, 'The Star-Spangled Banner' and the blues?"

Writers write eloquently about Willie's songs, but Willie, speaking about his songs, speaks simply. He says they are not "too heavy," they are easy to remember, they are true pictures of his life telling the way "I think and believe," and these days, they are more positive than they used to be.

It's all very to the point — just like his songs. Easy to understand, yet saying more than it seems to say.

In the early '70s, during his days at Bandera and for two or three years afterward, Willie entered a songwriting period as fertile as the torrential crop of songs he produced in the late '50s and early '60s.

The songs of the early days were fixated on loss of love. They described desperately sad situations, but offered no second act, no resolution, no moving ahead, no what next.

The protagonists of the early songs were passive victims of love.

In the '70s, though, after the emotional catharsis

and questioning that he went through following the burning of the Ridgetop house, his songs took a positive and active note—in Willie's own peculiar way.

You can study and listen and read and think and ponder Willie Nelson's songs, and at the end of puzzling over thirty years' worth of songs, you realize that, in the final analysis, he offers one message: life is movement.

You just have to keep on keeping on.

It's a message that's real and natural—check the reference point: Willie. Willie's life has been movement from the day he turned nine wanting to go "on the road." His heritage has been movement since the day his mother left home. His career has been movement because he never really gave up. As a sign in the Willie Nelson and Family General Store in Nashville reads: MAN NEVER FAILS, HE ONLY QUITS TRYING.

He even writes songs better when he's literally, physically moving.

"Night Life" and "Funny How Time Slips Away" were thought up while Willie was driving to work. He and Connie sketched out the whole "Red-Headed Stranger" album on an all-night drive from Colorado to Texas. If he's needing to write songs for an album, he'll sometimes drive himself from town to town on a tour.

Being on the road in a car or bus also puts him out where he can watch. Like great writers in all mediums, Willie is an intense, acute observer. He doesn't talk much—he looks, listens, evaluates. "I always get the feeling around him," Chet Flippo says, "that he's sizing me up: am I a potential song or just another disciple?"

212

The most microscopic experience—acutely observed—can lead Willie into a great song. One time Pop Nelson gave a few coins to an old beggar sitting on a curb at Christmas time in Fort Worth. Willie immediately went home and wrote the Roy Orbison hit, "Pretty Paper."

"Good-Hearted Woman" (written before Willie was an "outlaw," while he still lived in Nashville) got started during a pause in a poker game in Fort Worth—Room fifty-eight of the Fort Worther Motel, to be exact. Waylon and Willie were both in the game, and "one of the fellas admitted he was running around two-timing his wife," as Willie tells it. "Another player remarked he was lucky he'd married a good-hearted woman, or he'd be in divorce court." When the game paused for beer and sandwiches, Willie picked up his guitar, and started to pick out a tune. Waylon had hooked on to the chance remark, too, and they finished the song one morning over breakfast at Waylon's house while Jessi served orange juice.

When an idea strikes, Willie moves fast. "When I get an idea, I have to write it that minute," he says, "but I go for months without writing anything."

Usually the idea surfaces first, but sometimes a wordless tune floats through his head. "I often catch myself using gospel melodies that are similar to those I heard growing up," he admits. "They're like pop standards. And there are just books and books of them."

When he's writing on purpose which, he underlines, "*isn't* the way I like to do it," Willie sits down at the piano and hunts for a chord he's never heard before. "Whatever sound that chord brings to mind, then I start at that point and try to come up with a melody. It's like a guy opening a phone book, and the first name you come to, you go from there."

However haphazard his technique may be, the content of Willie's songs springs from one source only. "I write what I feel, definitely what I feel," he emphasizes. "I've thrown away a lot of songs, because they didn't express exactly how I feel."

"I write how I feel about other people's experiences," Willie adds. In 1967 he wrote a song called "Jimmy's Road."

"There was this young kid who was playing bass with us named Jimmy Hardmen," Paul once explained, "real young, seventeen or so, awful nice kid. Hell, he hadn't even been in a fist fight.

"Well, he got drafted then, right? And they give him a rifle and expect him to go off shootin' people just 'cause they told him to. Stupidest thing. Freaked the poor kid out. He ended up in a mental hospital.

"So," Paul said, "Willie wrote this song about it called 'Jimmy's Road.' I suppose, if you wanted, you could call it a protest song, but we didn't think of it like that. Willie hasn't ever been interested in politics much. It was just a sad song about a dumb war, and what it did to a friend of ours."

Even out of context, the truth in Willie's songs shines through. A famous Houston attorney was representing a construction worker who had been maimed in a job-related accident. At the trial, the lawyer recited "Half a Man"—"if I only had one arm to hold you . . ." and soon had the jury in tears.

Willie writes like people talk (if they would think before they speak). His songs often begin with teasers that irresistibly pull you into the song/conversation. "Well, hello there, my it's been a long, long time. . ." Who can resist eavesdropping on the rest of that little chat? "Three days that I dread to see arrive ... ." Wow, what's gonna happen? "Stop here . . . across the street, to your right. . . ." So, where are we going? "Hello, walls. . . ." Hello *what?* Try stopping with that one.

"Sometimes I get on kicks and only write about one thing," Willie jokes. "I got on house songs for a long time. Every song I would write would be about a house. 'Hello Walls' was one of 'em. You're probably not familiar with the rest of 'em — 'Hello Roof,' 'Hello Car' . . ."

The three writers who most influenced Willie, he says, are Hoagy Carmichael, Johnny Mercer, and Floyd Tillman. He also admires Roger Miller and Cindy Walker, too.

Carmichael, Mercer, and Miller are so well known they are celebrities. But Floyd Tillman and Cindy Walker are unfairly obscure.

As well as being an uncommon singer, Tillman was a matchless, ground-breaking songwriter. In the '30s his string band arrangements anticipated the big band sound of the '40s, and with his first hit, "It Makes No Difference Now," he launched a string of songs with dirge tempos and dejected lost-love lyrics that earned him a reputation as the creator of the cheating song. (Willie style, Tillman sold "It Makes No Difference Now" to his friend, and later Louisiana governor, Jimmie Davis for three hundred dollars. He estimates it has earned $60,000 in royalties.)

Plumbing the depths of crushed hearts, forgotten

vows, and parted lovers, Tillman was so effective, the story is told, that one Houstonian after hearing a particularly sentimental rendition of "It Makes No Difference Now," walked out of a Texas nightspot, put a pistol to his head, and ended it all.

The universality of Tillman's work was an eye-opening example for Willie; and, like those of his protégé, Tillman's songs have been recorded by a wide range of singers—Bing Crosby, Ray Charles, The Supremes, Perry Como, Tennessee Ernie Ford, Vic Damone; the list goes on and on.

Cindy Walker, a co-writer with Webb Pierce and Bob Wills, is surely one of the most underrated writers in country music. The granddaughter of the man who wrote "Hold to God's Unchanging Hand," broke into the music business as a singer and writer in Hollywood. But a woman in a man's world, where songs get cut by hanging out and drinking in bars with the boys, Walker eventually moved back to her home state, Texas, and submitted most of her songs by mail.

Her hits include "You Don't Know Me" (Eddy Arnold), "This Is It" (Jim Reeves), "China Doll," "Bubbles in My Beer" (the western swing classic), and "In the Misty Moonlight."

Being influenced by writers, each a distinct individualist in his own right, helped shove Willie's writing onto an ambiguous fence between pop, country, and blues. To make this point, Willie compares "Crazy Arms," a basic three-chord country song, with "Stardust," which, he says, "has a lot of different chords."

"My songs," he explained to Jack Hurst, "lie somewhere in between. I guess my whole career did that for a long time. It wasn't this, it wasn't that."

Lyrically, though, Willie's songs hold a steady course. Without flinching, they lay out a mesmerizing autobiographical saga of Willie's emotional life. And in exposing himself, he exposes us all.

Life, as Willie forces those who listen closely to hear, is often out of our hands. Life is frequently (a) in the hands of God, or (b) in the hands of other people. The ways of the all-seeing, all-knowing God are beyond our comprehension. The ways of other people, we, ultimately, can't control.

We should not fight genuine facts—the true unchangeables of life. We should not get stalemated, banging our heads against the brick wall of forces beyond our control.

Instead, we should control our own actions. This is the source of hope. We must face facts, filter them through our values, analyze them to the best of our intelligence, and then have the courage to act, to make a move.

In every case, doing something is better than doing nothing. Move on. Keep going. Don't give up.

It is, in Willie's own peculiar way, a calming, positive response to life. Truth (Face facts.). Movement (Take action.). Endurance (Don't give up.). It's the only way to save your sanity and your soul.

In different days Willie had an ace-in-the-hole philosophical alternative: get drunk. But he doesn't resort to that so much anymore.

"Songs I'm writing now are less hopeless," he told *Rolling Stone's* Chet Flippo. "I started thinking positive somewhere along the way. Started writing songs that, whether it sounded like it or not, had a happy ending. You might have to *look* for it.

"Even though the story I'm trying to tell might not necessarily be a happy story to some people. Like 'Walkin'.'

" 'After carefully considering the whole situation, here I stand with my back to the wall/I found that walking is better than running away, and crawling ain't no good at all/If guilt is the question, then truth is the answer/And I've been lying to thee all along/There ain't nothing worth saving except one another/Before you wake up, I'll be gone'—to *me*, that is a happy song.

"This person has resolved himself to the fact that this is the way things are and this is what ought to be done about it. Rather than sitting somewhere in a beer joint listening to the jukebox and crying. I used to do that, too."

Willie used to do a lot of that in the '50s in Texas and in early '60s in Nashville, when he was in a songwriting period of awesome creativity: "Night Life," "Crazy," "Funny How Time Slips Away," "Half a Man," "Hello Walls," "Undo the Right," "One Day at a Time," "My Own Peculiar Way," "Healing Hands of Time."

Virtually every song Willie released on his early albums deals with lost love. During his wanderings across Texas and his start in Nashville, he seemed obsessed with loss of love.

Every single song on his first Liberty album solemnizes this gloomy theme. Curiously, it's always the woman who has "left us all alone the way she planned," who's "gone now," who's "found someone new." Willie is the martyr who has "lost everything he could lose," who's been made "half a man," whose life

218

has turned to "darkness on the face of the earth," and who pleads "don't wake me 'til it's over when I won't love you anymore." Grim stuff.

Well, it was Don Meredith who once described Willie's songs as "music to slit your wrists by."

This posture of passive victimization continued on into the middle '60s. Willie, the one who could only numbly manage "one day at a time," the fool, the "only one who would let her act this way," the continual victim of women beyond his control, women he desperately loved who kept walking out on him.

It's almost impossible not to see the parallel with a little two-year-old boy in Abbott, Texas. Although Willie once said he never missed living with his mother and father because he never knew what it was like, the fact is, his parents didn't just go away once and stay away. They'd keep coming back—and leaving again.

Willie's early songs express an enormous emotional insecurity. They also reflect a primary love relationship—his marriage—that was a constant battle, a continual fight, with winners and losers declared daily.

Love to Willie means, foremost, loneliness. His characters are always desperately, maddeningly lonely. His songs are the lament of a man who never leaves one marriage until he has another in the offing, who keeps himself surrounded with people, so that loneliness (as distinguished from being alone, which Willie often enjoys) can never set in hard.

Willie equates love with pain, being rejected, being found wanting, being abandoned, losing, not being good enough ("crazy for thinking my love could hold you"), being diminished, being made "half a man." Even the potentially positive side of life—the future, two willing arms, capacity for love—is twisted into nothing but tortures.

It would be hard to portray a more negative picture of love, or to describe a deeper need, never filled.

Dr. Thomas Johnson, who has studied Willie's music intently, points out that Willie is never able to come right out and say, "I love you," in a song.

"He can never write a love song to another person," Dr. Johnson feels. "He just can't come right out and say, 'I love you.' " Willie's best effort at a straight-out love song, Dr. Johnson notes, is "My Own Peculiar Way."

"But even here," he says, "it's hidden behind an adult, ironic mask. 'I love you,' the lover admits, but retreats—only 'in my own peculiar way.' 'London,' " he adds, "is a beautiful lullaby, a love song for a child, but it's written to a city."

"My Own Peculiar Way" was written after Willie married Shirley, and was living with her at Ridgetop. They must have been very happy for a while, and in 1966 Willie also wrote "Home Is Where You're Happy" ("Home is where you're happy, just any house will do/And I'll feel at home as long as I'm with you"). But around the time of his break-up with Shirley, they together penned the poignant "Little Things," a sad litany of trivial news that at one time, in the past, would have been important to an ex-husband or wife.

Considering the negative picture of love Willie paints in his songs, the retreat from verbal commitment in his love songs is not surprising. Love is simply too big a potential risk; love is just impending disaster.

It was years later, after finding happiness with Connie, that Willie became enamored of Leon Russell's unapologetic love song, "A Song for You."

Very few songs of the '60s suggest what love's victim is supposed to do about all this agony.

The rejected lover in "Funny How Time Slips Away" mildly threatens that "in time you're gonna pay." However, it seems to be Willie who keeps paying and paying and paying.

Rather than *do* anything, he just begs to pass into oblivion (usually described as sleep) or to be given the ability to simply quit caring. When he's "gotta get drunk" to blank out the pain, he sure does dread it.

The only solution seems to be suggested in the 1965 song, "Healing Hands of Time": "Soon they'll let me sleep again, those healing hands of time."

"I went through thirty negative years," Willie once said of his life through the end of the '60s. "Wallowing in all kinds of misery and pain and self-pity and guilt and all of that shit.

"And out of it came the knowledge that everybody wallows in that same ol' shit—guilt and self-pity—and I just happened to write about it. I guess a lotta people who can't write songs, instead of writing songs, they'll get drunk and kick out a window."

Of course, Willie's taken that route, too.

Then, in the fading years of the '60s when his house burned, Willie reached a turning point. Things had just gone too wrong, too long. "Listen," he once told Burt Reynolds, "there's an age you get to, when crying in your beer isn't nearly as funny as it was when you were maybe in college."

He started pondering back over the whole sorry mess, looking for some answers.

During this time he wrote some of the finest, most

pensive songs of his career. Dealing with loss of love, hopes, and dreams; it was contemplative, probing poetry about the meaning of life, to the extent it has meaning. The culmination of this period was the beautiful and reflective "Yesterday's Wine."

Although philosophically healing, his answers were eastern, mystical, and essentially still passive — expressing resignation to the fact that we often can't understand life, and acceptance of the facts we can't change.

In 1970, though, that cycle began to turn. That was the year he wrote "Blood-Mary Morning," one of the first and best of his aggressive, blatantly American songs that commands: look, get out and assert yourself, say to hell with it, and kick up some hell of your own.

Although "baby left without warning," his new hero is "flying down to Houston, with forgetting her the nature of my flight." No longer moping around an empty house, just begging to go to sleep, this new jilted lover finds relief through action — and through drinking. For those who crave oblivion, alcohol's the drug of choice.

Around 1972, when he was contemplating a radical shift in image to attract young country-music fans, Willie began a third and final incredibly rich writing phase.

Songs copywritten during this time include many of the songs that showed up two years later on the masterpiece album, "Phases and Stages": "Phases and Stages, Circles and Cycles," "No Love Around," "Pretend I Never Happened."

Around 1973, he wrote a moving tribute to the

crowded-out cowboy, "Slow-Moving Outlaw" and a second tribute to Paul, longstanding companion in his own footloose outlawry, "Devil in a Sleeping Bag."

Toward 1974 he wrote "It's Not Supposed To Be That Way," plus "Heaven and Hell" and "Pick Up the Tempo."

These last two songs depict the two-sided swords that action and movement become. As Willie anguishes, "sometimes it's heaven, sometimes it's hell, sometimes I don't even know." Life is action, but action can bring grief, which can only be accepted and resolved through more action, which can bring more grief—phases and stages, circles and cycles, scenes that we've all seen before.

But this endless cycle is positive, for as Gibran taught, to realize a dream is to lose it. The value comes in the process of attaining it. Once when a close associate commented that Willie and the family had finally made it to the top, Willie sharply contradicted him. "Don't ever say that," he warned, "because once you get to the top, there's no way to go but down."

Keep on keeping on. Survive.

Well, there's a lot of undefined space between the "Star-Spangled Banner" and the blues.

After 1974, Willie mainly wrote in response to the pressure of events. Although penetratingly conceived, "Red-Headed Stranger" contained very little new material by Willie, mainly just the transitions that pulled the album together.

He wrote the song, "Sound in Your Mind," for the album of the same name in 1976. For the next couple of years he wrote little at all. Just a few light, scattered pieces like "A Lear and a Limo Will Do" with Mickey

Raphael and "I Get Off on You" with Waylon.

"I used to write all the time when I had a lot of things to say," Willie commented. "Now, unless it's an idea that knocks me to my knees, I'll put it off until I need some songs."

Then, in 1979, under increasing criticism from the press about his lack of writing, he found a need for some songs. Obligated by a songwriting contract for the movie "Honeysuckle Rose," he wrote seven new songs, including Grammy award winner "On the Road Again," and the stunning "Angel Flying Too Close to the Ground."

Are Willie's songs about specific episodes in which he has actually been involved? "I am afraid the answer is yes," he sighs.

But, largely, Willie, the individual man, hides behind his songs. Willie shows us Willie, the everyman; the Willie who is both Willie and us.

"You know, people think they know Will," commented a longtime friend, "but it's Will who knows *them.*"

Willie, the psychologist who uncovers for us what we really feel.

As Patrick Carr once wrote, Willie's songs are "the work of the most profoundly realistic American songwriter currently addressing himself to the subject of the American ego talking to itself in the midst of a chaotic world."

Willie talking to himself, but we all hear—and understand.

So where does this place Willie on the songwriting heap of time? Perhaps it is up to one of his fellow songwriters to tell us.

Bill Littleton, writer emeritus among Nashville journalists, interviewed Tom T. Hall in 1968. "I read somewhere, sometime back," Littleton said, "that if William Shakespeare were alive today, he'd be writing for television. I tend to believe, however, that if he were alive today, he'd be writing country music. How do you feel about that, Tom?"

"Well," Hall paused, "there are a lot of people—and I'm one of them—who think Shakespeare *is* alive today." He paused again, and then firmly pronounced, "Only we know him as Willie Nelson."

THE TROUBLEMAKING KIND
(And His Motley Group of Friends)

True-blue, old-fashioned friendship of the biblical David and Jonathan variety, is one of Willie's most admirable traits. In a life woven of threads incessantly crisscrossing America, Willie's friends are the continuous threads that run so true.

Paul English has been Willie's friend, musical soulmate, business manager, bus driver, and all-around compadre for nearly thirty years—longer than some of the other members of the band have been alive.

"Paul's main job is to be my friend," Willie once said, "and that isn't always easy."

In the script of Willie's life, Paul seems to play a role somewhat analogous to that of the hooker with a heart of gold—a worldly man with a seedy background, who would probably slit his wrists, or take up arms, on behalf of Willie Nelson.

"I can't really say why we've been such good friends for so long, we're really not much alike," Paul has admitted. "But I love Willie, because he's taught me tolerance. I've learned a lot of patience from him—and I used to have a terrible temper.

"The only time I get impatient is when somebody takes advantage of him or says something unfair. Like when there was a rumor he was packing a gun, that got me mad. Everybody knows I'm the one with the pistol around here.

"But I don't know," Paul muses, "what he's learned from me."

Whatever Willie has learned, struck deep. The proof is that Willie put their friendship, as he has all his other deep feelings, in song. "The Devil in a Sleepin' Bag" and the almost legendary "Me and Paul," written at the lowest point of their years of struggling together, are Willie's expression of what Paul means to his life.

Paul's wife, Carlene, was a deep friend of Willie's also; someone he "knew and loved," until she tragically committed suicide. Willie dedicated his gospel album, "The Troublemaker," to her, and spilled out his troubled feelings about her death in the achingly elegant song of longing and loss, "I Still Can't Believe That You're Gone." Willie didn't play that song for a year after writing it, and then only when Paul said it was O.K.

Don Bowman, Hank Cochran, Larry Trader, Ray Price, Darrell Royal, Gene McCoslin—all are current friends in the twenty-year range. Paul Buskirk, featured on the album "Over the Rainbow," was Willie's boss at the guitar school way back in Houston.

Darrell Royal befriended Willie when Royal held the world on the tip of a longhorn's horn, and Willie wasn't even making footprints in Texas cow patties. Gene McCoslin, a rough-and-tumble Dallas promoter, gave up a good-paying job to promote Willie Nelson the night he heard a skinny little guy playing the Sportatorium in 1964.

When Willie returned to Austin in 1972, Royal gladly inducted Willie into his world of wealthy, politically well-placed friends. At the Back Door, a favorite hangout for Darrell and Willie, located behind Cisco's Mexican Bakery in the only slum Austin can dredge up, Royal threw a little soiree for a selected group of business associates.

The purpose of the evening was to expose them to Willie, just sitting on a stool playing his guitar and singing his own songs. Price to hear Willie Nelson: twenty-five dollars per couple.

"I was doing them a favor," Royal firmly asserts adding, "I don't think Willie had ever played before without people dancing."

Avid golf buddies, Royal and Willie share several personality traits. They both believe in holding fast to your friends and your roots, to "dancin' with the one what brung us" (as Darrell's gold album from Willie is inscribed).

Royal has a boxing pal named Louie who's always quibbling with him over whether it's better to be on the offensive or the defensive. "I say," Royal announces vigorously, "whatever it takes to win." Willie, as he's proven, agrees.

What is the foundation of their friendship? Royal hesitates, is a bit taken aback. "Well," he says tentatively, "I've never really thought about it. What do you think, Edith?" he asks, turning the question over to his delightful, vivacious wife. She ponders. "Willie doesn't demand anything of his friends," she finally says. "He just let's Darrell be himself."

On January 2, 1972, Willie hand-wrote this poem and gave it to Royal:

First and Goal
He was born to the game
Call it football by name
Or call it life, call it love
Call it soul
And he came here to win
He's done it time and again
Cause every morning it's first and goals.
— To "the Coach Royal"/Willie Nelson

But Willie's friendship is not based on mere sentiment. He sticks with his buddies through thick and thin, and comes through for his friends, even when it's not to his own best advantage.

Don Bowman is a longtime country comedian who frequently opens Willie's shows today. Bowman had his first hit on RCA with a novelty record, "Chet Atkins Make Me a Star" and, in the three years from 1966 to 1969, won the *Billboard Magazine*, *Record World Magazine*, and Country Music Association's awards for comedian of the year.

He has opened shows for Willie, on and off, for twenty years. "We'd tour out of a camper with Paul," Bowman recalls, "and I can remember the days when the three of us wouldn't have enough money between us for cigarettes."

Bowman still opens for Willie, but sadly, much of his comedy—although considered risqué and pacesetting when he developed it back in the '60s—is dated today. He is routinely panned by critics.

"A singing comedian told corny jokes and sang a song about a stereotypical homosexual that had the older members of the audience chuckling. The younger fans looked bored," wrote a Baltimore paper. "Kristofferson was followed by a ten-gallon-hatted moron who made jaded dope jokes and sang two songs: one about getting your girl to do anything you want by feeding her Quaaludes, and the other a nasty bit of homosexual baiting. Shame on Willie for sheltering this jerk in his entourage," wrote another.

Maybe Willie thinks Bowman is still funny—after all, he's approaching the age of the "older members of the audience." Or maybe he simply likes Bowman and appreciates his role as a convention-shattering comedian of a past decade. When Willie started his Lone Star Records in 1978, one of the first releases was Bowman's album, "Still Fighting Mental Health."

Johnny Bush became a well-known artist in his own right largely because of Willie. After quitting the job Willie had gotten him with Ray Price, he went to work for Willie as a drummer; he also fronted The Record Men, which gave him a chance to sing and build up a following.

Bush was dying to be a recording artist, but was turned down by every label in town. Seeing his own frustrations mirrored in those of his friend, Willie bankrolled a recording session for Bush. The session was leased to Stop Records, and Bush quickly hit with a Willie-penned song, "You Ought To Hear Me Cry."

Bush's success was still continuing in 1973 when he wrote "Whiskey River," the drinking classic Willie uses to open his shows.

"Willie Nelson is the greatest friend I have, and he is responsible for my career, because he believed in me," Bush said in 1969.

"I guess I did two things for Johnny," Willie once conceded. "I talked him into recording. Before that, he just took his band and traveled. Then I encouraged him to adopt the Ray Price format. Ray had changed styles by then, leaving a vacancy in that 'shuffle beat' sound."

Actually, there's another rather bizarre favor Bush claims Willie did for him—one in a series of odd incidents that pop to the surface every now and then. In 1969, Bush said, Willie cured him of a chronic illness.

"I wear a chain around my neck that was given to Willie Nelson by a priest," Bush told a reporter. "Willie gave the chain to me when I lost my voice once, and told me as long as I wore it, I would never lose my voice again. I never take it off, even though it has tarnished—and I haven't lost my voice since then."

Unfortunately, Bush's vocal spasms in the throat returned in 1973. It's not known whether he was still wearing the chain or not.

The career of Hank Cochran, one of Willie's very closest friends, still suffers from the chronic illness that dogged Willie's for so long. Although at the top as a songwriter, Cochran has never been able to really break through as a singer.

The author of "I Fall to Pieces," "Make the World Go Away," "She's Got You," "A Little Bitty Tear," "Funny Way of Laughing"—recipient of twenty songwriting awards and more—Cochran gave up his first recording contract when he urged Liberty to sign

Willie instead.

"Sincerity shows in everything Hank does," Willie wrote on the liner notes of a Cochran album in 1965; "it pours from his original songs, and it stand out above all else in his singing."

But after an initial hit, Cochran gradually evaporated as an artist. Addicted to boats, for years he mostly hung out on his beloved yacht, sailing the seas from east to west.

A few years back, encouraged by Willie, Hank put together a band and started opening for Willie on tour. Then Willie put him on a very successful "Austin City Limits" television special, and, shortly thereafter, featured Hank and his wife, Jeanne Seeley, another good friend, on the soundtrack of "Honeysuckle Rose." As a result, Cochran was signed to Elektra Records, and in 1980 released an album, "Make the World Go Away."

Larry Trader, the former roadie who now manages various Willie enterprises, says, "Willie and I have never had one argument in the twenty-two years I have known him. Not one. We are always able to talk things out and come to an understanding.

"I know I can always count on Will for a sincere and honest answer. I always know Willie will be honest with me. Brothers?" he says. "We're more than brothers—you can't always get that from a brother."

Perhaps Willie's admirably strong sense of friendship is rooted in a lifelong lack of continuity, that sense of being different, parentless, a musician, somehow set apart. Whatever the basis, friendship is the cement—the thing next to blood—that holds the family together.

"Someone once said that if you want to have friends, you have to be a friend," Willie explained. "I subscribe to that theory. Friends are very important to me, and I'll never do anything to drive them away.

"That's been one of the main blessings of this business," he affirmed, "that of making friends. Friends are a lot more important to me than any award I'll ever win.

"I don't apologize or defend anything I do to help a friend."

WALTZ ACROSS TEXAS

1972 — Loretta Lynn wins Entertainer of the Year
1972 — Opryland, USA opens
1972 — California pardons Merle Haggard

When Willie flipped a coin to decide whether to move back into sunny San Antonio, or head ninety miles north up the interstate to Austin; he hit the first heads-up in a lucky streak whose payoff would be the realization of his dreams.

Population about 300,000 when Willie arrived, ten percent black, twelve percent Mexican, thirteen percent college students, Austin — where Bobbie lived at the time — was a temperate jewel glimmering warmly in the midst of geological extremes.

To the west toward El Paso, to the southwest toward Mexico, to the northwest toward Abilene stretches relentless, dry-mouthed desert. Whispering hillocks of pines stroll and gossip to the east toward Alabama, murky pockets of swampland grumble along state roads southeast into voodoo Louisiana, as Interstate 35 sings slickly due north into the mahogany-paneled board rooms of Dallas.

A geological quirk called the Balcones Fault blocks

the eastern pines from pushing onto the blackland prairie that leads to the desert, and right on that gorgeous, peaceful interlude, the citizens of Austin reside, launching their sailboats from the banks of the Colorado River.

But just as a visitor settles down for a long, lazy snooze on the riverbank, the bravado of Texas leaps, tail flashing, from the surface, spraying water everywhere.

Capital of Texas, smallish Austin sports a state senate chamber modeled after the one owned by the United States—only nine feet taller. Corral for the University of Texas, Austin is beneficiary of the biggest university in the south (fourth in the nation). The University of Texas flashes an endowment second only to that of Harvard; fanatic alumni, who bequeath little tokens of school spirit such as oil wells, keep the amount growing.

During football season (a mental state which persists year 'round), packs of hot-blooded fans in burntorange shirts rush into the colossal stadium to bellow "The Eyes of Texas Are Upon You" (tune: "I've Been Working on the Railroad") while jabbing their arms into the air, fingers locked in the two-pronged "hook 'em horns" sign. With each collectively ego-swelling victory, faces of jock and scholar, Anglo and Hispanic, legislator and alumnus, glow with pride as the beloved university tower glows misty orange.

A forty-one-million-dollar performing arts center showcases music, drama, and dance; and the award-winning university newspaper, *The Daily Texan* publishes daily news of the college community, 40,000 strong, itself approximating a small town.

235

Political infighting is fierce, but rarely serious. During the radical '60s the SDS was viewed more as a local curiosity than a political force, and nowadays Austin has managed to osmose the monolithic, marble Lyndon Baines Johnson Presidential Library, into its delicately balanced persona.

Perched somewhere between the rugged western ways of the cowboy and the sugared-grits gentility of the South, an "aw shucks" city in a braggadocio state, Austin rarely takes sides amongst its willful bands of citizenry, but like a clucking mother, metes out equal allowances to each of her highly singular brood, hoping that all will grow up without major mishap, find their place in the world, and be happy.

With a surging student population and herds of big-expense-account legislators out for a high-rolling time, Austin has, since the mid-'60s, been a dream world for musicians.

Dozens of clubs offer free beer and/or varying quantities of bucks to singer/songwriters, folkies, and bands for a night's worth of playing. In a city of low taxes and low rent, a would-be singer could eke out a living in an incense-filled apartment on the edge of campus in a most congenial atmosphere.

If Darrell Royal presides over the whole of Texas through the monarchy of football, then Townsend Miller . . . well, doesn't really preside over, just coincides with, the musical world of Austin. For Townsend Miller is just as unassuming, genuine, indeterminate, and eccentric as the music scene of Austin itself.

Descending the elevator of the Merrill Lynch offices in his three-piece suit at five, the elegantly tall and gray-haired Miller heads home—not to a little spot of

236

cocktails with fellow stockbrokers and their well-mani-
cured wives; not to a well-informed evening in front of
the TV news, poring over commodity reports—but to
a nap.

Arising refreshed from his after-dinner snooze, say
around ten P.M., Townsend dons a cotton shirt and
jeans, sticks a white plastic bottle of TTT ("Townsend's Treacherous Treat") in his hip pocket, grabs up
a soft pack of regular Camels, hops in his little
foreign-made car, and zips out into the night life of
Austin.

Hovering at some ambiguous Peter Panian age between fifty and seventy, Townsend is greeted with
warm hugs, wide grins, enthusiastic hellos from musicians and club owners, ten, twenty, thirty, maybe
forty years younger than himself in the live-music
clubs all over Austin.

Townsend, you see, is their friend and their companion. For nearly a decade he has chronicled the ups
and downs of the most obscure and the most famous
in his twice-weekly column in the *Austin American-
Statesman.*

He volunteered for the job, and is not paid for his
labor of love to this day. A fan of country music since
boyhood, a journalism graduate of Rice University in
Houston, Townsend was forced to abandon those twin
addictions, and enter the economic mainstream when
four children popped up along the way. (One
daughter, who used to work for Waylon Jennings, is
now plying her way in Hollywood, and Townsend,
knowledgeable about this fickle business, sighs over
her fate.)

His columns constitute a detailed diary of the performing life of one of America's most intriguing and vibrant musical cities. It was Townsend who first noticed in print that remarkable migration, about 1972, of a highly talented collection of country-oriented former folkies into Austin: Jerry Jeff Walker, Michael Murphy, Steve Fromholtz, Doug Sahm, Townes Van Zandt, and numerous others.

Thus, it was with extreme interest that Townsend reported in his column of August 12, 1972 that: "Willie Nelson has moved to Austin. For the past week he has been busy getting his furniture and his family and his band members transported from Nashville.

"And he didn't waste any time contributing to civic endeavors," Townsend applauded. "He provided a big punch to the Aqua Festival (annual city music festival) country-western night by singing a few songs with Freda and the Firedogs."

Actually, however, his lead item on the same day was far more important than that newsy note. "Ole down-home country boy Willie Nelson on a psychedelic poster?" Townsend marveled. "Sure nuff! The posters were scattered around town this week to advertise Willie's appearance tonight at swingin' Armadillo World Headquarters."

Those psychedelic posters heralded the first step for Willie, now sporting a beard and long hair, and his "little plan."

That plan was built on Willie's keen-eyed observations a few months earlier at Dripping Springs—the sight of college kids turning out right along with fans the age of their parents (sometimes their actual parents!) to hear country music.

The first signs of a fusion of country music with

rock, in a way that appealed to college students, was pioneered on a national level by a self-destructive visionary named Gram Parsons, soulmate of the then-unknown Emmylou Harris.

In 1967, working with a group called the International Submarine Band, Parsons put out an album, "Safe at Home," described by one critic as a mixture of "Merle Haggard and Arthur Cruddup." In 1968, he joined the Byrds with Roger McGuinn and Chris Hillman to record the ground-breaking, country-influenced album, "Sweetheart of the Rodeo." In 1970, with the tentative, experimental Flying Burrito Brothers, he worked on nine tracks of their country-oriented, "Sleepless Nights."

His final album was released in 1973, before his virtually self-inflicted death. "Grievous Angel" included Emmylou and Elvis Presley's old band.

Simultaneously, Bob Dylan and bands like the Nitty Gritty Dirt Band and the Grateful Dead were showing college kids you could mix rock culture and country music and come up with terrific music. At one of the famous "Day on the Green" concerts in the Oakland Coliseum, the Grateful Dead introduced one of their own heroes: Waylon Jennings.

Then, in 1973, Jerry Jeff Walker released his landmark folk/country/rock, flat-out Texas "Viva Terlingua" album (cut in Luckenback, Texas) at precisely the ideal moment to give a huge boost to Willie's plans.

"It was really 'Viva Terlingua,' " says Kirby Warnock, editor of the Texas-based *Buddy Magazine*, "that showed everybody you could dress like a cowboy and smoke dope. The whole thing was just plain fun!

With Jerry Jeff and Michael Murphy you knew there'd be big crowds, lots of women, lots of drink. You could get drunk, really relax, not worry about how you looked."

Acts like Jerry Jeff and Michael Murphy contributed enormously through their hits and their image to the momentum of "progressive country music" that exploded out of Austin. But these artists actually had a strong folk base, as seen in the poetic, not-so-commercial lyrics of their music—a format typical of folk.

It was probably a wild-haired bunch called Freda and the Firedogs, under the gentle ministrations of a man named Kenneth Threadgill, who started the true blending of country and rock in the city of Austin.

Threadgill, in 1933 the recipient of the first beer license issued in Austin, had met Jimmie Rodgers in the early '30s and became one of America's few authentic interpreters of Rodgers' music.

For over forty years Threadgill entertained students and legislators at his combination gas station and beer joint near the university (gas up your car and gas up yourself).

Never known as anything more than just the Gas Station, although it quit selling petrol in 1948, this was a place for student radicals, conservative legislators, labor leaders, and just plain folks to sit at long tables and listen to Threadgill belt out old tunes, backed by his band, The Velvet Cowpasture.

In the late '60s, while a seedy, drafty, converted furniture store called the Vulcan Gas Company served as a hangout for Austin's freaked-out, psychedelic set, Freda, with her long, swinging brown hair (now known under her real name, Marcia Ball), would be

240

over at the Gas Station belting out "Stand By Your Man."

"It was all very tentative," says keen-eared Austin journalist Joe Nick Patoski, "but it showed kids it could be fun to drink beer and smoke dope, both."

"Jerry Jeff and those guys had more of a folk base," he adds. "In fact, a lot of the Austin scene was really a folk-music base. But pretty soon, you had all those stool sitters putting on cowboy hats and growing beards."

After springboarding Johnny Winters, the pilot light went out at the Vulcan Gas Company. In its place rose up a gentler but equally weird music hall housed in an old National Guard Armory, just a few yards from the Colorado River downtown. It was named the Armadillo World Headquarters.

With a craft shop and practice room for musicians, the Armadillo started out serving fruit juice and banana bread to laid-back dopers lounging around on blankets and low benches.

Soon, one of the owners, Eddie Wilson, a former public-relations man for the United States Brewer's Association, realized the club would—and only could—turn a profit, if they started serving liquor, i.e., beer. And beer equals country music. So the club began showcasing the country-oriented bands around Austin made up of college-age musicians.

"We would have stayed in debt forever 'til we stumbled onto the beer equation," Wilson once said; "country music and beer saved us."

The country music, however, was mostly of the folky, university-flavored variety. Bill Monroe played there, obviously much ill-at-ease, until a scrawny, long-haired kid jumped up and started buck-dancing to the music, whereupon the taciturn Monroe gave a tight-lipped grin, relaxed, and got with it. Later the rock-credentialed Flying Burrito Brothers came in with great success.

However, the Austin music scene was divided by a hog trough considerably wider than the Colorado River: Country-type music for college hippies, who smoked dope, bought cowboy hats with big feathers, read Furry Freak Brothers comics, and drank nothing but long-neck Lone Star; or honky-tonking music for farm boys and ranchers who drove mud-splattered pickups, who wanted new CBs and Cadillacs, who took out girl friends with teased-up, black-dyed hair, and who drank any kind of beer because it got them drunk enough to listen to "Okie from Muskogee" on the jukebox so they could feel like ol' Merle was finally gettin' America back on the track. Now these were different audiences entirely.

Those two bunches didn't think much of one another—at all.

"In 1972, no country musician would even go on stage with a beard," Townsend Miller declares flatly. "All the country acts played the Broken Spoke (bumper sticker: 'I dance country at the Broken Spoke') or Big G's up in Round Rock. No long-haired male dared go in a country honky-tonk," he asserts. "In fact, James White, who owned the Broken Spoke, wouldn't even let a hippie in his place."

Well, Big G's and the Broken Spoke were exactly the places Willie Nelson played when he came through Austin in the '60s and early '70s. Willie's fans were the farmboys, the shit-kickers, "mostly people my age who had been following me for the last ten years," Willie says. "They were thirty or forty years old."

"(College) people were afraid to go to a place like Big G's," Willie explains, "because long hair wasn't that acceptable back then. Some drunk cowboy would trip 'em on the way to the bathroom."

Then Eddie Wilson got the idea that he could turn an even tidier profit, and maybe help out the community spirit a little, if he could get all those redneck shit-kickers who poured into the Broken Spoke every Friday and Saturday night over at the Armadillo drinking beer.

"We thought if we could sell Willie Nelson to our audience, and bring in his old audience," Mike Tolleson, another Armadillo owner, explained, "we would cross sectors and integrate these scenes culturally. There had been a real sense of segregation in Austin, a pretty strong feeling of antagonism."

When Wilson suggested that Willie play the Armadillo, Townsend reported, "it took Willie Nelson exactly one split second to grasp the idea and accept the invitation," because, he added, "Willie is as closely attuned to the young as any country performer."

Tickled by the psychedelic Willie Nelson posters nailed up on light posts all around the university, Townsend gleefully noted that "those posters are possibly a first for a nationally ranked traditional country-music star."

"Willie has a huge following of fans in this area," he noted, "but most of them are pure country traditionalists."

Willie's appearance at the Armadillo, on the other hand, Townsend wrote, "boggles the mind" since the

Armadillo was "the gathering place for that vast, fast-growing army of long-haired young men and blue-jeaned gals who have discovered the joys of country music. Some are university students, some are 'street people,' some are simply local sons and daughters."

But nowhere, he added, "will you find country-music fans who are more dedicated or enthusiastic."

Townsend was pretty charged up when he wrote his column for the *American Statesman*. He could hardly wait to take a few slurps of TTT (2/3 vodka and 1/3 white crème de menthe, for mystery's sake), and go see what was gonna happen.

On the evening of August 12, Willie, who still called his band the old, kind of corny name, The Record Men, alternated sets with a young country music band named Greezy Wheels.

It was, as they say, a night to remember. The kids loved, adored, freaked out over Willie.

According to writer Jay Milner, Willie had put a new wrinkle in his live performing sound around 1971, about three months after Mickey Raphael joined the band. One night they were playing Gene McCoslin's Western Place in Dallas; Sammi Smith had dropped by and was singing a duet with Willie.

Suddenly, right after the bridge, Willie abruptly stopped singing and commanded, "Let's do that bridge again." The band turned right back around into a rollicking, bass-thumping groove. Milner and McCoslin, who apparently owns a tape of that night's show, feel this was the beginning of what Willie would later call a "little more beat" in the rhythm section of the progressive country sound.

Willie had also changed his looks to suit his (hoped

for) new audience's taste. "I knew that if I was going to do anything from that point on in my life, I was going to have to draw some attention to myself," Willie admits.

"The surest way to get someone to listen to you back then was to grow your hair down to your shoulders, put on an earring, let your beard grow 'till it's shaggy, and then get up on stage. They were *gonna* listen," he laughs, "but you damn well better have something to say."

Willie had started his hair growing around 1970, when he was still playing country bars all the time, and "I'll be honest with you," Willie once told Milner; "I was a little bit uneasy going into some of them goddamn joints I'd been working for twenty years. You know, with all them big old cowboys that love to beat up hippies, or at least always talked like they did."

"But they never said anything out of the way to me," Willie added. "The only people that said anything back then at first were the old women drunks."

However, in addition to growing his hair long "to attract attention," Willie threw off some sparks of "natural Nelson" when he added to Roy Blount, "Plus, I like to piss people off. I'd go around to truck stops hoping people would say something to me about my hair," he paused, "back before I was trying to take care of myself."

Although Joe Nick Patoski recalls there was a bit of a clash at the Armadillo between Willie's "used-car-salesmen types who toted a pistol" and the Armadillo's typical peacenik crowd, the music prevailed.

The next step was to bring ol' Waylon out to the

Armadillo. "He gave me a call one day," Waylon re-members, "and said, 'Hey, come on down here. I got-ta show you something.' "

Stepping on stage at the Armadillo, "I looked out at 2,000 long-haired people," Waylon says, "and I thought, 'oh, my God, what's he got me into?' "

Recalling that "the long-haired guys looked all right, except long-haired guys didn't like our music," Waylon sent as SOS offstage to Willie.

Willie walked over. "Just trust me," he told Waylon. "If they don't go for it, you're going down with me."

"But anyway," marvels Waylon, "I saw them, like, an ocean of kids, man, who freaked out over our music, and I couldn't believe it."

Afterward, Willie enthused to Waylon, "I think we have found something. I think we found people who understand us and who believe in what we're doing, who like us and take us like we are, as people, and can relate to our music."

"And," Waylon adds, "I think he was right."

SHOTGUN WILLIE

1973—Chet Atkins elected to Country Music
    Hall of Fame

By the end of 1972, country music was just a train
steaming toward a holdup—by Willie Nelson.

Much to his surprise, on the heels of the Armadillo
success, Willie suddenly found himself in demand on
the college circuit. "It really came as quite a shock
when all of a sudden we were asked to do college
dates," Willie said in October of 1972. "Kids all over
really dig country now, which is a great break for us
country boys. The college kids know our music," he
added, "and usually shout requests."

This was doubly surprising to a guy still mostly playing car dealership openings, lounges, parties around
oilmen's swimming pools, and firefighter's balls.

By 1972 Willie and The Record Men had logged
160,000 highway miles, and by 1973 had played every
state in the nation.

In 1975, they remodeled the Grumann mobile home
with eighty yards of red velvet inside and a sundeck on
top. They'd also bought a Greyhound Scenicruiser,

which had already been driven 200,000 miles. Paul's son, Darreyl Wayne, was taught to drive it; then they kept rolling in an endless round of dance halls, county fairs, and honky-tonks. They'd play the rough-riding Texas Prison Rodeo one month, the easygoing Kerrville Folk Festival a few months later.

In Austin, Royal would invite them to play for the football team in the comfortable letterman's lounge, and days later they'd be over at a country-music-loving car dealer's lot entertaining during the unveiling of the 1974 Fords and Mercurys.

Even as late as the latter part of 1974, with the second Fourth of July picnic and two critically praised Atlantic albums under his belt, Willie was still playing to crowds of fifty at L.A.'s Palomino Club.

Although the band constantly drained his finances, Willie almost never refused to do a benefit. To this day he still spends thousands of dollars of his own money, time, and fees doing benefits.

In March of 1974, they did a show to raise money for a college sophomore who needed brain surgery, then benefits for the Austin symphony, the Dallas symphony, for son Billy's school, for Indians, for political candidates, for cerebral palsy; the list goes on and on.

Generous and soft-hearted to the core, Willie just can't—or won't—say no. The "yes" comes not so much for who it's for, status-wise, but for what the personal relationship is. "We don't believe in causes," Paul once said; "we believe in people."

Despite the new wave of college dates, for the band there was only "a gradual acceptance," Paul explained, "more gradual than most people think, over the years. From two hundred and fifty dollars a week to five hundred dollars or whatever—we didn't really turn the corner as a band until 1975."

Willie, however, no longer dwelt on depressing details. One day they topped a hill in the lumbering old bus, and as they started down the incline, the clutch suddenly went out. They started careening down the road, bouncing from shoulder to shoulder.

A roadie, riding shotgun, dashed to the back of the bus where Willie and several guys were intently hunched over a poker hand. "The bus!" he frantically yelled. "The clutch's gone out!"

Willie didn't even look up. "Don't tell me about it," he snapped. "Can't you see I'm losing this game? Now, *deal.*"

Nonetheless, time was continuing its inexorable march toward destiny.

In mid-'72, Willie made friends with a musician who already carried enormous credibility on the college circuit—a piano player with both Frank Sinatra and the Rolling Stones, record producer for both Gary Lewis and Bob Dylan—who else, but Leon Russell.

Willie became a fan of Leon's one day when his daughter was listening to Joe Cocker's "Mad Dogs and Englishmen," which Russell produced. "I heard that being played downstairs in my daughter's room, so I went down to see who it was," Willie says. "I liked it so well, that I went to see him in Houston, and then I went to see him again in Albuquerque, and I made it a point to go up and introduce myself."

As it turns out, they had already met. Leon had played on Willie's first album out in Hollywood way back in Liberty Records days. "Half of that album I did in Nashville, and the other half I did in Holly-wood," Willie explains. "The half I did in California, there was a little skinny guy with real short hair, and no whiskers at all, playing the piano." Then, on the second album, Leon was called in to play on "Half a Man."

Willie didn't remember Leon out of the influx of strangers he had met in Hollywood, and the sessions were many notes ago to Leon, who got to listening to Willie's old albums and recognized his own playing.

Immediately on remeeting, they wanted to do some recording together; in fact, Leon invited Willie to sign up with his own label, Shelter Records.

But Willie was already in hot and heavy negotia-tions with Jerry Wexler, now putting together the first country division in the history of his venerable R&B company. On November 11, 1972 Townsend Miller reported Willie was on the way to New York to sign with Atlantic. Although it is sometimes said Willie was Atlantic's first country artist, Miller reported Atlantic was "the same label Austin's Freda and the Firedogs signed with recently."

"I've always loved good country music," Wexler ex-plained at the time. "Good, genuine country music is the blues, and I think the blues is the best music there is. There isn't a note Willie plays, not a note he sings, that isn't rich with the blues."

Shortly thereafter, Willie flew back to New York, loaded down with a stack of about two hundred songs he had written over the years, to record both a gospel album and a country album for Atlantic.

Wexler invited him to bring anybody he wanted to play on the session. Naturally, Willie jumped at the chance to test out his theories about recording with his own band—Bobbie, Bee, Paul, and Jimmy Day on steel.

Rumor had it that Russell, Bob Dylan, George Jones, and Kris were all going to show up. None of them made it, but Larry Gatlin, Dave Bromberg, Doug Sahm, Waylon, Jessi Colter, Red Lane, the Memphis Horns, and Bob Wills's fabulous fiddle player, Johnny Gimble, all made it (if not to New York) onto the album, which was recorded in parts in New York, Nashville, and Memphis. One of the string arrangements was even done by R&B great, Donny Hathaway.

They recorded the gospel album in two days. (It was later released as "The Troublemaker" on MCA's Songbird label.)

Then Willie got stumped. Surrounded by celebrities, and basking in freedom, Willie couldn't think of anything he wanted to say to the world.

"I was up in New York," he says, "and I had run out of songs to do. I was sitting around thinking about what a drag it was to have to go in and record when you didn't have anything to record, to try to make music when you didn't really have anything to say."

Sitting around in his underwear in his room at the Holiday Inn, gnawing on his brain and commiserating with himself, he suddenly grabbed a piece of toilet paper out of the bathroom and started writing. "Now, where Shotgun Willie came from, I don't know," he admits; "just off the top of my head."

A fun tribute to old John T. Floore, who used to market tailored sheets to the Ku Klux Klan for sixteen dollars (and net twelve dollars profit), "Shotgun

Willie" was the perfect lead song for an album debuting Willie's new bass-heavy, live band sound.

At one point, he got up, left the studio, fetched a cold beer, came back in, and unexpectedly launched into Bush's "Whiskey River." They worked twelve hours a day for five days, and ended up cutting an incredible thirty-three songs in five days.

Arif Mardin, masterful pop/R&B producer and head of Atlantic Records, was ecstatic. (Willie always seemed to have a way of nabbing the best producers in the business.)

Breaking out a fresh bottle of wine (1970 Château Bonnet entre deux mers), he poured out champagne glassfuls, and wearing Gucci shoes and jeans, toasted, "It's a record, even for Atlantic. *Thirty-three* cuts in one week!"

Despite Mardin's pleasure, the massive number of "Shotgun Willie" cuts may have been due more to Willie's uncertainty than musical dexterity. Possibly he was intimidated by the new freedom and environment (*the big chance*—oh, please, God, don't let me blow it!).

Songs on the album include two written way back in 1965 ("So Much To Do" and "She's Not for You"), one penned about 1969 ("Local Memory"), pal Bush's "Whiskey River," two Bob Wills tunes ("Stay All Night" and "Bubbles in My Beer"), and two Leon Russell songs ("You Look Like the Devil" and "A Song for You").

Willie debuted "Sad Songs and Waltzes," a music-wise song written in 1964 at Ridgetop as a tribute to his long history of being slightly out of synch; "Devil in a Sleepin' Bag," which backhands the more bleary side of life on the road; and "Slow Down Old World," beautiful with strings.

However raggedly it came together, "Shotgun Willie" was the ideal Willie Nelson sampler for the waiting legion of new, young fans. A little country rock, a little western swing, some blues, Willie's own band, vintage tunes from the '60s, some outlaw-tinged numbers, a dose of strings, and the sterling gem, Willie singing Leon's "A Song for You," with just voice and guitar. It doesn't get any better than that.

In April, 1973, Willie threw a special coming out party for the album, and also celebrated his fortieth birthday, at the Armadillo World Headquarters.

Three short months later, he staged the first annual Fourth of July Picnic on Burt Hulbert's ranch at Dripping Springs. It was the birth of 30,000 "hipbillies," as the picnickers were dubbed.

"Y'know, if there was just one thing that really *did* it," Willie said two years later, when he had a number-one single reverberating across the nation, "that first picnic was *it.*"

Conscious that the Dripping Springs festival was held when it was too cold and rainy, Willie moved his picnic to brain-numbing, searing hot, Fourth of July.

"The sun," Willie once noted, "is a great controller. Between the sun and the booze and the marijuana, folks don't have much inclination for trouble."

Reminiscent of the days with Crash Stewart when he put together a bunch of stars bigger than himself and called the package The Willie Nelson Show, Willie now invited the cream of the emerging country and rock set to "Willie Nelson's Fourth of July Picnic":

Waylon Jennings, Kris Kristofferson, Leon Russell, Tom T. Hall, Rita Coolidge, Billy Joe Shaver, Sammi Smith, Charlie Rich, Doug Sahm, and John Prine, plus some local bands like his Armadillo compadres, Greezy Wheels.

All promised to play without any guarantee, and if they made money, they'd split it.

It was a semislapdash affair, that Willie once claimed was organized in twenty-one days. They printed up a batch of hip-art posters showing an armadillo sneaking out from under an American flag with a Lone Star flag in its snout, and Eddie Wilson of the Armadillo and promoting buddy Gene McCoslin helped out.

Willie got himself tonsorially prepared for the mind-boggling heat by shaving off his beard, cutting his hair down to a business-respectable length, and donning designer sunglasses and a straw cowboy hat. Waylon, hair long and lank, was beardless, too.

On picnic eve, Willie and Leon and friends caroused all night out at Willie's ranch near the picnic site, while Darrell Royal hosted a little star-studded jam in the Governor's Suite in the Sheraton downtown for Kris and Rita, Billy Joe, Tom and Dixie Hall, Charlie Rich, John Prine, and a mess of Nashville songwriters.

"Why don't you do something?" Billy Joe urged Kris, who mumbled an O.K. and set off into an up-beat country melody, singing: "Well, I dig Bobby Dylan/and I love old Johnnh Cash/and I think Waylon Jennings/ is a table-thumping smash/And if you don't like Hank Williams/ you can kiss my ***."

When the laughter died down, Kris turned to Rich:

"Don't be offended," he grinned, "the only thing that rhymes with Rich is 'bitch,' and I wouldn't want to be calling you *that*, now would I?"

As the stars partied through the night, the crowds, 30,000 strong, were already gathering. In vans, pickups, and Cadillacs, they started pulling into tiny Dripping Springs in the stuffy, suffocating twilight.

Since the crowd was not allowed access to the well-prepared grounds and huge parking area inside the site until morning, they parked along the road in Dripping Springs, and slept the night.

When new crowds poured in the following morning, they saw cars parked along the road, and assumed they'd come as close as they could get. Stopping, they parked their cars, and headed out, walking in ninety-degree heat to the picnic, which they thought was just a few turns down a gravel road. They were ten miles away.

Even Billy Joe Shaver got caught in the havoc. Parking his car, he raced ahead on foot, leaving wife and mother-in-law behind, sure he was going to be late for his set.

Miles down the road, he finally hitched a ride with a reveler in a Volkswagen with a sun roof. Hopping in, Billy Joe stuck his body out the top into the cooling breeze, only to turn sideways, and to his surprise, see the driver standing beside him. The kid was driving with his toes!

Making it to the picnic too late to set up his band, he played solo and finished in time to greet his wife and mother-in-law, both seriously overexposed to the sun, and with big blood blisters on their feet.

The Hulburt ranch was far back in the hills down

rough, rocky, rain-gulched, white-stone calash roads. As the afternoon wore on, traffic set up clouds of choking white dust so thick drivers were forced to turn on their headlights and windshield wipers just to see through the eerie tornado swirling under the blazing sun.

But no catastrophe seemed able to undercut the epic-making nature of the day.

"It sure is a lot better than last year," Eddie Wilson observed, jerking a finger toward gun-toting cowboys and sheriffs patroling the crowd on horses. "Last year they were ridin' the fences with shotguns, scaring the hippies off."

Things got so together that Paul even married his new-found love, Diane Huddleston, on stage. Wearing his black Dracula cape, Paul chose Waylon as best man, while Sammi Smith was best woman. As they completed the nuptial kiss, a huge roar of approval rose up from the heat-fried crowd.

After a forty-minute power failure, and forty zillion joints smoked and beers guzzled, around four A.M., the party was over.

Thirty thousand (reports said 20,000 tickets were sold and 50,000 showed up) sun-baked, booze-soaked, grass-smoked, ecstatic zombies began choking the rough calash trail and the two-lane highway back into Austin.

"That picnic," Chet Flippo wrote in *Rolling Stone* in 1978, "was the first time I had witnessed the uncanny ability of 'Fast Eddie' to appear—or disappear—at exactly the right time.

"When the picnic ended . . . I decided to find a way back. I took off driving across flat ranchland and, finally, miles away, found an alternate highway. But between me and that highway was a locked cattle gate. I was just revving up my Chevy to ram the gate when, from out of the ghostly blackness, a Mercedes came roaring up beside me. Willie got out, nodded hello, and held up a key. He unlocked the gate, smiled good-by, and drove off."

The next morning, right on the front page of the *American Statesman* was a huge photo of Willie, Leon, and then UT football coach Darrell Royal. "In my mind," Willie said, "it brought it all together."

When the kids finally staggered home, with the enthusiasm of newborn Christians, they evangelistically pasted "Honk if you love Willie" bumper stickers next to the peace decals on the backs of their vans, and fervently pulled on T-shirts that rejoiced: "Matthew, Mark, Luke, and Willie."

In the minds of the media something clicked. That amorphous musical movement that seemed to emerge with the release of Jerry Jeff's "Viva Terlingua" earlier the same year, that was hinted in Willie and Waylon's public palling around together, now became startlingly clear.

The New York Times, the *Los Angeles Free Press*, *Rolling Stone*, *Newsweek* magazine, all concluded that there was a *new* country music afoot down in Texas, and that the center and heart of it all was a short, red-headed singer who had grown a beard, shaved his beard, moved out of Texas, moved to Nashville, moved out of Nashville, moved to Texas, somehow defied the powers that be, and gotten the kids interested in country music.

For his part, Willie told the *Houston Chronicle* that

he was planning to go to Hawaii with Connie—his first real vacation since he started playing in bands twenty years ago.

PHASE ONE AND ONLY ONE

1974—First number-one country song for
Waylon: "This Time"
1974—First book on Austin music scene: *The
Improbable Rise of Redneck Rock*

"No one had any idea there was that kind of market
out there," Willie explained to the press. "That's what
happens when you sit behind a desk a lot. Those guys
just didn't know that audience was there."

In October of 1972, Willie joined Waylon in
Nashville during the annual disc jockey convention,
and they staged an "appreciation concert" for their
fans at a downtown auditorium, distinctly separate
from the convention's official activities. This personally produced sideshow was less than appreciated by
some, and it set Nashville ears buzzing and tongues
wagging.

In November, the Nashville Songwriters Association
responded to the buzz, and inducted Willie into their
elite corps along with two of his best Nashville friends
of the '60s, Harlan Howard and Roger Miller.

Soon, everywhere you went in Nashville, you were

hearing Willie's name—linked with Waylon's, and Tompall's and Kinky Friedman's and Billy Joe Shaver's.

"On a trip through nighttime Music City, you just might run into all of them," wrote *Country Music Magazine* editor Peter McCabe, "in the 'Burger Boy' or 'Linebaugh's' or 'Tiny Tim's' or, for that matter, anywhere that might have a pinball machine; or else they could be propping up Tompall Glaser's Lincoln Mark IV in any one of the parking lots of the afore-mentioned establishments, passing around a bottle of Jack Daniel's. . . .

"Their noon is everybody's else's midnight; raising hell is a way of life rather than an occasional pastime. . . .

"They've been calling themselves 'the clique' for some time now, and certainly most of Nashville recog-nizes they're a little apart from the mainstream. They are frowned on in some quarters, tolerated in others; you might say they are the outlaws of country music."

And so they were born: the outlaws.

Even amongst the outlaws, Waylon and Willie, now both managed by hard-nosed negotiator Neil Reshen, who had structured Willie's contract with Atlantic and demanded for Waylon the right to produce his own records on RCA, were fast becoming identified as two of a kind—the troublemaking kind.

"I know that Tom T. and several of those people from Nashville are being pressured by a lot of dif-ferent people not to have anything to do with us," Willie told *Picking Up the Tempo* in 1975. "I think we've been designated as anti-Nashville. That's the image that has come down, which is not really true," he insisted, "but whenever our names come up, we are considered anti-Nashville."

What anti-Nashville meant was that Willie and Waylon were becoming famous, but (although Waylon lived in Nashville) they were doing it 2,000 miles away from Music City, USA; they weren't totally under Nashville's political control and weren't toeing the mark of polite behavior; they were making country sound more like rock and, in the process, scaring some people who had been around a long time and pretty much had their ducks in line and well under thumb. They were making some folks uneasy.

Like the time the Country Music Association tried to honor Austin by holding one of their quarterly board meetings there, and Doug Sahm, during the civilized question-and-answer period concerning the nature of the organization, so charmingly inquired: "What can we do to keep out your type?"

Willie and Waylon were fast becoming running buddies. "I was scheduled to perform in Madison Square Garden," Willie explained of a canceled date in 1974, "but I got tangled up with Waylon for about a week in Vegas, and was unable to get out of bed one morning. I had to give up a week's work in order to recuperate from that one party with Waylon, but it was worth it."

When Willie wrote "Pick Up the Tempo" and put it on his "Phases and Stages" album, Waylon said, "I think Willie wrote that more or less about me and him and our struggles along the way with our music.

"We're close, you know; we're like brothers. And we are brothers in a lot of ways. Closer than most brothers can get in some things. In our personal lives, and our life styles, you know, and our mistakes and our music."

At first, the "Shotgun Willie" album had gotten off to an ominously rocky start. The single, "Shotgun Willie," released around the time of the first Fourth of July picnic only made it to a low number sixty on the country charts. But "Stay All Night," released shortly after the picnic, zipped up to number twenty-two, Willie's highest charting record in five years. In quick order, the album picked up steam and, in six months, sold more than all his other previous albums combined.

Toward the end of 1973, Jerry Wexler urged Willie to record in Muscle Shoals, Alabama. He had a rhythm section down there he used on a lot of his big R&B hits—four guys cutting in a funky little studio, formerly a casket factory, in a backwater burg on the Tennessee River.

Until this year, Muscle Shoals was dry and had no clubs unless you headed thirty miles up to the Tennessee state line to drink beer at a honky-tonk—so visiting artists and the area's brilliant musicians had little to do except concentrate on music. Whatever the reasons, so many monster pop and country hits are cut there that the area's eight studios brazenly label their hometown, "The Hit Recording Capitol of the World."

"Jerry Wexler had a brainstorm that he wanted me to go to Muscle Shoals," Willie says. "Since he'd let me do the first one my way, I decided to let him do the second one his way, because he usually knows what he's talking about."

Wexler did. Although "Shotgun Willie" was popular with the public, "Phases and Stages" won Willie the hearts and pens of the powerful music critics on the coasts.

Lorraine Alterman of *The New York Times* described the Willie of "Phases and Stages" as "making country music that can even move those of us who think we despise it."

Robert Hilburn of the *Los Angeles Times* hailed it as "an important breakthrough," citing the rarity of concept albums in country music, and the care and taste with which the album was assembled.

It was compared to rock's "Tommy" and "Sgt. Pepper's Lonely Hearts Club Band" as an outstanding example of the concept album genre.

"Phases and Stages" is a magnetic album. On the lyrical level it affords a hypnotic view into Willie's ideas about men and women, love and sex. On the musical level, it makes a very clear point. It shows how Willie's music, through fifteen years of ups and downs, when put in the right hands and properly produced, retains a consistent, compelling personality.

Thanks to the outlaw and progressive music hype, a Fort Worth disc jockey had to suffer—in one of the more unhappy moments in live radio history—through the revelation of how little Willie's music, in essence, has changed.

At Christmas time in 1974, veteran disc jockey Lew Staples was interviewing Willie by phone in New York, where Willie had taken Connie and Paula to see the Christmas lights.

As the program progressed, Staples frequently announced his plans to play a record from Willie's early career and contrast it with a cut off "Phases and

Stages" to show how Willie's new outlaw sound was different from the overproduced Nashville days.

A naïve, sweet-voiced coed phoned in: "I'm a Yankee from Chicago," she cooed, "and I'm going to school here at SMU, and I was just introduced to Mr. Nelson's music, this morning, more or less. I was wondering what he feels distinguishes it from other country and western music?"

Naturally, Staples, (a fine D.J. and Willie fan) felt this was the ideal moment for the dramatic demonstration: he would now play two recordings—"Hello Walls" off Willie's first album on Liberty and "Pick Up the Tempo" off "Phases and Stages."

"What should we be listening for to hear the difference?" Staples eagerly asked Willie, the moment of truth at hand.

"Well, uh, I think, uh," Willie stumbled, "uh, it's going to be a little difficult to hear the difference between those two songs." He verified which cut of "Hello Walls" Staples planned to play, and repeated, "Oh, I see, well, it's going to be fairly similar to 'Pick Up the Tempo.' "

"Well, maybe I did a poor job, not being a musicologist," the D.J. semidesperately offered, "but, they're both waltzes and they sound different to me."

So they played the two recordings, made almost twelve years apart, one cut in Hollywood or Nashville with the Anita Kerr Singers oohing and aahing in the background; one cut in funky Muscle Shoals, Alabama.

When the music finished, Staples fumbled a bit more, obviously hoping against hope that Willie, to the expectantly waiting world, would mention some small difference in the two seemingly rather different records.

Willie, however, was simply totally silent.

MALE AND FEMALE, CREATED HE THEM

"It was a long time before I ran into any positive relationships between males and females," Willie once said, discussing the happiness he found with Connie as he neared middle age. Male-female relationships "have been a problem all my life," he confessed, adding, "Among a lot of people, it's been the number one problem in the world."

"Phases and Stages" is Willie's story of a marriage gone bad. The first half of the record speaks from the wife's point of view, the second half looks through the husband's eyes.

"I decided to write from both sides, just for the challenge," Willie says. "The man's side is autobiographical, of course. The woman's side? Well, they told me I hit it pretty close," he admits with satisfaction. "I might have been a girl in a previous life."

How incredibly closely Willie hits the way many women might feel in a loveless marriage, makes the album startling and the story come full circle.

The album is bound together with the "Phases and Stages" theme, which declares that life is just a universal stage on which "scenes that we've all seen before" are acted out over and over in the lives of millions of men and women—including ourselves.

As the album begins, the wife is at home, washing the dishes, thinking that here she is in the kitchen again, performing thankless menial tasks for a man who doesn't really care anymore. "Learning to hate" all "she once loved to do" for him, she sees that the marriage is emotionally dead. "Manfully," one might say, she decides simply to leave. "Walking is better than running away," she determines, "and crawling is no good at all."

"Pretend I Never Happened," she flings over her departing shoulder at the mental image of her absent husband. "Put me out of your mind," she advises, while admitting to herself she has become cold and sterile, just sleepwalking through the motions of married life.

Although horrified over the breakup of her daughter's marriage, mother welcomes her home and lets her sleep all day long to escape her problems. Finally beginning to shake off her depression, middle-aged "sister" ventures out into the corner beer joints, able to have a good time, but seeing she's not a girl anymore, that her jeans are a bit tighter these days.

Bruised and feeling her age, she poignantly asks, "How Will I Know I'm Falling in Love Again?" ("If I win or lose, how will I know?")

Her husband wakes up to a "Bloody-Mary Morning," discovering his wife has abruptly left. Distraught, he boards a plane from L.A. to Houston, "forgetting her the nature of my flight."

He heads downtown, only to find there's no love—no real feeling and companionship—to be had.

Depressed, he starts drinking.

The next morning, he experiences "the very first day since you left me." Struggling to put his thoughts in a song, he is mystified by what went wrong, still unable to believe that she'd go, that she would really leave him. Although he has neglected her and stepped out on her, like many a typical husband, he still can't see "what I did that was so wrong."

The multilayers of meaning in Willie's writing are vivid here. A beautiful, elegant love song, "I Still Can't Believe That You're Gone," originally written to express Willie's feelings over the suicide of Carlene English, becomes, in this new context, the statement of a bewildered man who has taken his wife for granted.

"It's Not Supposed To Be That Way," he moans. Despite all I do to you, he arrogantly asserts, you should know that I love you. But, he knows he hasn't been home to hold her, to comfort her. It doesn't really mean much, he admits, to say I love you, if "I can't be there to console you."

Just be careful, he warns her, if you become involved with another man after living so long in a cold relationship, sustained only by romantic fantasies. She may be burned by the "real fire" of love.

Sometimes life's heaven, sometimes it's hell, sometimes he can't even tell the difference, the husband wearily admits. The only thing he's sure of is the here and now, the physical; that heaven is "laying in my sweet baby's arms" and hell is "when baby's not there."

The resolution for the husband is not romantic doubt, but action—he needs to "Pick Up the Tempo," to keep moving on.

Although Willie is often described as the timeless voice of everyman, without race, creed, social status, or sex; "Phases and Stages" reeks with sexual identity.

The wife's actions have dignity, but are stereotypically feminine—she despairs over the loss of romance, retreats to her mother's home, worries about falling in love again. The man, however, takes definite, masculine action—flying all the way across the country to Houston, only to end up deciding more action is the answer.

Well, maybe Willie *was* once a woman in another life. In country music it is usually the woman, waiting patiently at home, who is abandoned and left behind. And throughout most of the '60s, this is the position Willie held in his songs—the one abandoned and left behind.

But now, in the '70s, in his writing period which emphasizes movement and action, he lets the woman leave. For once, the woman leaves. But she leaves just like a woman. She goes home to mamma.

In *this* life, Willie has been accused of being a male chauvinist. Certainly "Phases and Stages" portrays the actions many men and women are likely to take—more than it does the actions feminists would like for them to take.

And certainly Willie relishes the pose of the arrogant male. Like the night he commanded Connie be brought to him like some delicious morsel out of the sultan's harem. Or, consider this exchange:

Penthouse: "Then let's talk about women."

Willie: "Great, I'm for 'em."

Penthouse: "Any special kinds?"

Willie: "All of the above. Especially, young pretty ones."

Any man who wears pigtails below his shoulders and who plays the love scenes in his movies with his own hair flowing over the pillow longer than the heroine's, has got to have a strong sense of self.

Which Willie does—and it shows. To many women Willie projects an aura so confidently masculine, he doesn't even need to act macho. But as one of his masculine perogatives, Willie expects his heterosexual desirability to be properly appreciated.

Once while talking to a reporter with his daughter Lana, Lana mentioned that Willie had been referred to in one article as the father of progressive country music, and in another as the grandfather of the same.

"They said country granddad?" the writer chortled.

"Chunky granddad of progressive country," Lana reiterated.

Willie snapped to attention. "Is that a man or a woman that said that?"

"A man," Lana replied.

"That's all right, then," Willie conceded, "as long as it ain't a woman."

Well, appreciate they do. "Any woman who gets near Willie picks up on his masculinity right away," says the costume designer on *Honeysuckle Rose*. "It's not a barroom swagger, not a Marlboro man kind of macho, but something more subtle—gentility and warmth." (It's Connie who recalls the "warm, neat feeling" Willie's first smile gave her.)

"I remember," the designer continued, "Dyan Cannon saying how she wasn't sure, at first, what to think about the bandanna and braids. But you get close to him and look into those brown eyes, he's so sexy it can give you the shivers."

Or, as one female member of Willie's entourage puts it, Willie is "irresistible to women—so sensitive along with being so masculine—like Shane."

And just like Shane, Willie is the kind of man infuriating to women—just out of reach, out of control; the man who seems to love his own calling more than he loves his lovers.

Willie holds the cards in a relationship, because ultimately he is going to do just what he wants to do. If a woman doesn't like it, he's got his music; a far more powerful competitor than another woman.

In "Honeysuckle Rose," when Buck's wife walks out on stage to announce to the audience that she is divorcing him, there were widely differing ideas on the set about what ought to happen next. The director thought Buck's show ought to stop right there, as he rushed off the stage after her.

"But that didn't seem right to me," Willie says. "That's why we ended up doing 'Under the Double Eagle' and had me leave the stage during that. I was thinking, 'How would 8,000 or 10,000 people react to a concert being stopped, just because some dizzy blonde comes out on stage? It didn't seem to me like a professional would let something like that stop the show."

Work before relationships; self-fullfillment before compromise—song, then wine, then the woman.

This has been the problem in all three of Willie's marriages. Willie and Willie's music, not the wife, come first.

For musicians, life is often a marriage-go-round. It

was Jeannie Seeley, fourth wife of Hank Cochran, who took a good-natured swipe at the whole situation in her song, "We're Still Hangin' in There, Ain't We Jessi?" Jessi, of course, being none other than Waylon's wife, Jessi Colter, who, as Jeannie pointed out in song, is "Mrs. Jennings No. Three."

Marriage is especially difficult when the work is live music, which can easily keep country performers on the road more than two hundred days—and nights—a year.

"It sometimes takes more than a woman can contend with to be married to a guy who's gone all the time," says the man married to "Mrs. Nelson number three." "Of course, it always looks great in the beginnin' when you get to travel with your husband and everything. But then, when you have kids and have to stay home, it gets to be a drag.

"The old sayin' about absence making the heart grow fonder isn't necessarily true. When I met each of my wives, I was on the road—goin' up and down the highway to play music," he says with two broken marriages underfoot, "and that's what I'm still doing."

Are there temptations on the road? Willie was asked. "Sure there are," he honestly replied. "You get an audience of eight hundred people, half of them are pretty girls, and there are temptations."

In fact, Willie admitted to *Penthouse* that groupies (whom he suggested be given the more "dignified" monicker "star-fuckers") are "what keep a lot of us on the road so many years."

Now that he's moved into the movie-star stratosphere, the temptations are on an even more tantalizing plane of appetite. After spending an evening with women like Candice Bergen and Jane Fonda, Willie once moaned, "one is never the same again."

"I remember he came to New York when I was doing 'Starting Over,' " Burt Reynolds told *Country Music Magazine,* "and Candy Bergen had never heard of Willie. So he brought his guitar over and he sat down in the middle of the floor and started singing his songs. She would have followed him to Afghanistan."

His marriage to Connie (whom Willie favorably compared to Candice), however, seems to have a positive, permanent feeling the first two lacked. "Now that I'm married for keeps, with two kids," Willie once noticed, "my self-control seems to have improved somewhat."

"If I'm happy anytime at all," he disclosed, "it's gonna be when I'm happily married. The last several years I have been."

Willie, the emotionally buffeted boy, seems to desperately *need* to be married—not want, but need.

Each of his first two marriages was scarcely over (if legally at all) before he was seriously entangled with his next upcoming bride.

"I always feel like I need a home base," Willie confided to *Penthouse.* "There's something in me that makes me want to know that wherever I am, and whatever I'm doing, I can always go home to someone, someplace. Truthfully," he added, "it's not so much that I enjoy being there. Usually, when I do go home, after two or three days, I'm ready to go back on the road."

"We see him when we can," Connie once said bravely. "We miss him real bad, but we know that's what he wants to do. It wouldn't be right for him to stay home all the time—it would change him.

"Waiting for him is what we do best," she said. "We are content to wait for Will. It's worth it."

Sometimes Connie takes Paula Carlene, twelve, and Amy Lee, nine, on tour with Willie, where he proudly invites them to come up on stage and sing with him. But "if we go traveling with him," Connie says, "it's just a week here and a week there. I can take the kids, but they get tired after a week."

When asked if little Paula and Amy enjoy the fact that their daddy is a star, Willie replied, "Well, I think they'd rather me be at home."

Willie once noted that his matrimonial permanency stretches to about ten years, then fizzles. "This marriage," he recently said of his third, "has been going about ten years. It's at a critical stage. It's going to go one way or the other."

The making of *Honeysuckle Rose* apparently tilted the balance toward the other for a while.

Honeysuckle Rose is about country-music singer, Buck Bonham, and his band, perpetually "on the road again." The wife stays home with the kid, the husband runs around with a pretty, young female musician in his band, and the marriage nearly breaks up.

"The script was just like thirty days out of my life," Willie spilled the beans. "I can sympathize with Buck," he bluntly admitted. "He's a married guy who succumbs to temptations on a potholed highway. I've been that route myself." Even the triangle, he conceded was "real close. . . . I've been involved in those."

During the filming of *Honeysuckle Rose* rumors

started cropping up about Willie and Amy Irving, the glowing young actress who had her ankle grabbed at the end of *Carrie*, and who had landed the part of Buck's lover in the movie. (Before filming began, Irving had been dating Stephen Spielberg, director of *Close Encounters*.)

"The open romance between aging Willie and his lovely co-star is an amazing real-life enactment of the movie's script," the gossip columns buzzed.

Or an another writer offered after watching Willie wrap a bandanna around Amy's pretty forehead, the two seemed "extremely *simpatico*."

Willie refused to give the gossip columnists anything solid to sink their teeth into. "The script called for some good old-fashioned romancin'," he gamely claimed, "and I never thought it was illegal for people to enjoy workin' together.

"Those newspapers are just looking for something to write about," he protested weakly. "Amy and I, we became good friends during the movie.

"We had a good time," he said with finality.

But it was not only in far-off Hollywood, but right in Austin, where much of the movie was filmed, that people couldn't avoid what seemed to be happening before their eyes. "It was . . . well, sickening," said one person. "You know what finally ended it? Christmas. Christmas came and that kept Connie and Willie together for another year."

When asked how his family liked "Honeysuckle Rose," Willie observed that their reaction was "well, mixed."

"Connie," he told Jack Hurst, "saw it, and . . . she likes it," he said. "She likes the way the guy came home to his wife in the end. She liked that part, I'm sure."

It would be sad if Connie and Willie don't stick it out. Connie is a beautiful woman physically, and everyone who knows her says she has a beautiful spirit as well.

"She's an exceptional lady," Willie says. "She has been behind me . . . even before we met. She was a fan. I don't know, if she'll be able to put up with this life.

"My wife Connie helps me a lot mainly just by being a good critic," Willie once told national country-music writer, Bob Allen on the road in the Everglades. Allen noticed he glanced around the interior of the bus before continuing. "She'll give me good honest opinions—which are sometimes very hard to find."

It was Connie and Willie, driving through the night, who put together the "Red-Headed Stranger" album that finally broke Willie through to the top. In addition to sharing ideas, they share close friendships with Darrell and Edith Royal, and, before that split, with Kris Kristofferson and Rita Coolidge.

"Connie's a wonderful person," says Edith Royal, "very sweet and attentive to Willie."

"But," Connie once admitted to *People,* "I sometimes feel that he doesn't need me. He's got the road, and he's got his life. It's really easy to feel pushed aside."

Isn't the risk of his marriage breaking up greater, as he keeps complicating his schedule with more records, concerts, movies? he was asked. "Yeah, that's what Connie says, too," he conceded with a perplexed smile. "But—"

"But, what?" the writer asked.

"I like to keep busy."

So, who suffers most? "All my life I've missed my kids, because I've been on the road," Willie answers. "It's the biggest price I've had to pay for my success. And, sure, I feel guilty.

"I have grown kids and grandkids, and the older ones are not bitter at me; they understand. But my younger ones . . . It remains to be seen how they grow up."

With so many demands, often self-generated, with kids rarely seen, why does he keeping marrying and re-marrying and remarrying? Why doesn't he just live with somebody who will travel with him, and maintain a nice nest for them to return to?

"Whenever I was looking for companionship, it was usually there," Willie told *Playboy*. "I didn't have to go looking for it.

"But there was a period of time," he said, "when I wasn't playing music somewhere, and then it wasn't that easy to go out and score a girl. So," (like both the man and woman in "Phases and Stages"), "you find yourself going out and sitting in joints around town.

"Of course, there's a lot of people who like it that way," he adds, "Just one-night stands is all they're looking for. Most musicians who travel around from town to town and country to country will do that. They enjoy that type of relationship, as opposed to any long-term relationships, which they've always had bad experiences with.

"So, what happens is, a guy turns sixty, and he's had a wild, hot life. But all of a sudden, there's nobody around anymore. That's one of the problems."

Another problem with keeping a marriage going, once you've got one, Willie believes, is that people want sex, but disguise their desire as love. "There's this guy running off with this guy's girlfriend or this guy's wife, or something. There's a lot of that," he says knowledgeably, "so that's ninety percent sex I'd say. They try hard to make it love, but it's ninety percent sex."

Sex . . . male . . . female . . . me Tarzan, you Jane . . . we're down to the basics. So, how far apart are the players on this volatile stage?

Despite his all-male style, despite the forms society may create, "Women and men are almost identical to me," Willie told *Penthouse*.

"Their thoughts are not that much different," he has observed. "For one example, some people say that women change faster or behave more unpredictably than men. I don't believe that," he flatly asserts. "I think that men may just be more deceitful about their changing ideas. Women may make their feelings more obvious, and thus seem more flighty or unpredictable.

"But the thoughts and reactions of men and women are similar," he analyzes. "It's just that men are basically more shy about expressing themselves—except when they're drunk."

The *Penthouse* interviewer countered that a lot of modern psychologists might dispute that theory.

"Well, this isn't exactly deep psychology," Willie replied, "but I believe that, basically, when a man's looking at a woman and thinking, 'Boy, I'd like to fuck you,' she's probably at least considering the same possibility.

"Whether they do it or not doesn't depend on the difference between them. It depends on the circumstances or the morals involved."

But despite this rather liberated viewpoint, Willie falls back on the old saw that women just maybe don't realize how good they've got it. Harking back to the Indians, he points out how the braves got to go out and hunt all day while the women had to stay home in the tepee. "But if you'd ever been up in the mountains on horseback," Willie proposed, again from experience, "killed a three-hundred-pound deer, then carried it back down and dressed the son of a bitch . . . well, maybe it wasn't so bad to be sitting home all the time, making sure the water's hot."

Willie also subscribes to the southern belle-ish notion that women control men through subtle manipulation. "Over the centuries the fact that women have been physically weaker," he propounds, "has caused them to become shrewder and mentally stronger. Compensation.

"So, I think that anyone who underestimates a woman now," he concluded to *Penthouse*, "is making a mistake. I don't underestimate a woman one bit. I don't think she needs anything from me, except what I can give her during a show—or maybe afterward."

Well, women of the world need not underestimate Willie, either. Asked how he likes his women, Willie pondered a split second: "You mean do I like fat ones or skinny ones or tall ones or short ones or young ones or older ones? Yeah, I do."

PICK UP THE TEMPO, JUST A LITTLE

In 1974, the *San Antonio Light* declared Willie to be at "the peak of his popularity."

Glorying in his new-found success, Willie continued to pursue life with a vengeance. For starters, he got his driver's license revoked.

A notorious car pilot, addicted to floorboarding the powerful, purring engine of his blue Mercedes, Willie had developed the habit of carrying copies of his albums in the trunk of his car just to placate irate traffic cops.

This stratagem worked perfectly one late night in Odessa, Texas. "I was going back to the motel," Willie tells, "and I must have really been going fast. The next thing I know, I was pulled over and there were four squad cars around. I give them all albums, and it turns out they know me, so everything is cool in Odessa."

"They should have taken me to jail," he concedes uprightly, "because I was really drunk."

In Dallas, however, he was apprehended by an officer who "never heard of Willie Nelson and didn't want to know the son of a bitch," he grins. That one, he sighs, hauled him off to jail.

First, he was about to lose his license, then they took it, then he got it back, then they took it away again. Finally, Fast Eddie and the authorities worked out a little compromise. He could hold an "occupational license" which permitted him to drive between four P.M. and two A.M.—presumably, the hours he plied his occupation.

"I have to be pulled over and stopped by two A.M.," Willie deadpanned in 1975, "so if anybody finds me on the side of the road stopped, well, that's the reason. I'm waitin' til four P.M., so I can get out again."

Doubtless to protect himself in these late-night vigils, Willie also owned a Colt .357 for a while, that Gene McCoslin gave him. He'd had a gun before, but it was in the custody of the Dallas Police Department. "They kept saying they would give it back, if I would come up there," Willie noted, "but I said, 'oh, y'all can keep it.' "

As for the .357, he bought himself a box of shells, and "the first time I tried to shoot it—I had never shot a .357 before, and I saw them on TV using both hands—I didn't know they were putting that left hand through the trigger guard.

"I did it like I used to do my old .22, like a rifle, and I grabbed the barrel of that son of a bitch, and shot it, and sound waves went up both arms."

Willie didn't much fool around with the .357 after that. "If I put myself in the right mood, I can still hear the ringing in my ears," he once grimaced.

When Willie wasn't playing roulette with his right to drive, he and Connie were living on their forty-four-acre ranch on Fitzhugh Road near Dripping Springs. It was a Texas-style Ridgetop. Willie was always dropping in and out of the local feed store to pick up feed for his plowhorses and peacocks and laying hens.

But poor Willie just always seemed to have some varmit after his hens. This time it was a ring-tailed weasel who nailed ten out of twelve chickens.

"Me and Bee set some traps out there," Willie related glumly. "But nothing happened. I started to just poison the two hens that were left and kill him that way—when he ate the poisoned chicken, he'd die.

"Then I figured that the dirty son of a bitch would probably go down and crawl in my well to die, and I'd have to drink water off him for a year. So I decided that I would just leave him alone, or give him the other two chickens and move.

"I'm glad he don't eat horses," he added with a grin.

If he went into town, it was mostly to play golf and eat Mexican food with Darrell Royal. When he hit the road, it was often to play old stomping grounds, like Panther Hall in Fort Worth or the Longhorn Ballroom.

But now when he played those places, he was billed as a "progressive country artist." Despite Willie's satisfaction with the spate of new publicity, even bigger things were simmering.

Atlantic Records had decided to liquidate their fledgling country division, and as his recording contract faded out of existence, Willie was again plagued with record promotion problems. In spite of that, "Bloody Mary Morning," broke through the country top twenty to hit number seventeen in April, 1974. A few months later "After the Fire Is Gone," a duet with Tracy Nelson (no kin) also went to number seventeen.

Testing his new, youth-oriented drawing power at the rock listening room, The Troubadour in West Hollywood, he drew near-capacity crowds all week. Much to the approving delight of the press, Bob Dylan, Paul McCartney, Robbie Robertson of The Band, as well as Kris and Roger Miller, all made the show.

Even out in the hustings, it was clear *something* was going on.

Down in Edenton, Florida, near St. Petersburg, there was a place called The Feed Store Music Hall, about the only club in the area where you could hear country music.

In '73 or '74, the owner had arranged for Tompall Glaser to come down for two Saturday-night shows. Soon after, Tompall's manager called. He had this guy named Willie Nelson, down in Texas, who was wanting to get around the country more. How about both men, two ninety-minute shows, for $7,500. The owner agreed.

Months later, after the release of "Phases and Stages," the phone rang again. Bad news: the Nelson guy's price had gone up. Now it was $12,500 for him alone for two thirty-minute shows. Glaser's price had gone up, too.

Baffled, the owner calculated he would have to charge one hundred dollars a person to break even. He hired Little Jimmy Dickens instead.

"I had no idea I would ever be so 'famous' five years ago," Willie mused in 1979. In 1974 he was convinced he "was already famous. Shows you how dumb I was. I was doing O.K. Anything beyond that was gravy."

AND TAKE IT ON HOME

1975 — Emmylou Harris debuts on the country
        charts
1975 — Bob Wills dies

For over twenty years Willie had loved the saga of
the thunder-eyed, red-headed stranger from Blue
Rock Montana, mounted on a "raging black stallion,"
roaming the West grieving for "his little lost darlin'."

"Don't cross him, don't boss him," he would sing to
the kids in their beds at night, "he's wild in his sorrow,
ridin' and hidin' the pain." But he had never recorded
the song, because it had "too many verses."

Then, one long night, driving from Colorado to
Austin, Connie suggested that he design a whole
album around the ballad. "We were in Steamboat
Springs when we started," Willie says, "and by the
time we got to Denver, I had most of the album in my
head. We already had 'Blue Eyes Crying in the Rain,'
and I'd written 'Time of the Preacher.' "

As soon as they got home, Willie sat down with his
guitar and put down a rough version of the whole
album on tape.

As he was piecing the album together, he realized that the story would make a fantastic cowboy movie. "If you look at the back cover," Willie says, "you'll see the drawings and how I was visualizing a movie. I kind of had visions of *'Rocky.'* I thought about writing the movie, acting in it, and all that."

For nearly a year Willie had been negotiating with CBS Records, as his manager held out for big money and creative control—the right for Willie to produce his own records. They had won this important concession, and now everything was ready to go. He started looking around for a place to record.

"We'd been hearing through the grapevine," says recording engineer Phil York, "that Willie didn't want to record in Nashville because of the feeling and attitude there. He wanted to do his thing, his way—and he wanted to do a concept album."

York was chief engineer at a little studio just outside Dallas in Garland, Texas called Autumn Sound, mostly a place where ad agencies cut commercials.

In 1975, the owners had been upgrading the studio under the hand of York, who had engineered the hit "No Man Is an Island" for the VanDykes back in the '60s, and who had worked on parts of Helen Reddy's "I Am Woman."

A tall, thin, friendly young man with an engagingly soft voice and big wide smile, York was friends at the time with Mickey Raphael, and had been helping Mickey break into studio work.

"Mickey would bring his box of harmonicas over to the studio and sit out in the lobby," York recalls. "Clients would come out of the studio and he'd be sitting there playing the most marvelous harmonica.

Two times out of four, the client would say, 'Who's that? That's great! Let's put it on the record.' "

York called Mickey and told him Autumn Sound had just installed the first twenty-four-track studio in the area.

In December of 1974, right around Christmas, Willie came over to the studio and cut "Bonaparte's Retreat" and a few other tunes as a test session.

"They packed up their instruments and said, 'Well, mail us a copy,' " York remembers. "I said, 'You're not going to hang around for the mix?'

"Willie said, 'Mix? No just send us a tape.' "

So York mixed up a storm, and mailed Willie the tape.

To understand the significance of what happened in the little Garland studio, it is necessary to have a rudimentary idea of how a record is made.

The record producer is the person ultimately responsible for putting the whole recording session together. He selects the songs, hires the musicians, hires the recording engineer, and, in the studio, tells everyone, including the singer, what to do. Willie was now the producer of his own records for the first time.

The music is usually recorded on twenty-four-track tape which is two inches wide to accommodate all twenty-four of the tracks. Each track (a magnetic "line" on the two-inch-wide tape) is separate from the others.

You can record one or more instruments on each track. Usually, you record one instrument per track. (The "Red-Headed Stranger" album had so few instruments they only used ten or twelve of the twenty-four tracks.)

Each instrument is recorded on its track while the band is playing together in the studio. Each instrument (or singer) is isolated for sound. This prevents the sound of one instrument from "leaking" onto the track of another instrument, by being picked up in error on the microphone of the other instrument.

For example, the drummer will be playing the drums in a soundproof booth, and the guitar player will be sitting behind soundproof room dividers.

Generally, the singer does his or her part last, after the musical tracks are recorded. Standing in a sound-proof booth, he listens to the already recorded tracks on headphones and sings along. His voice goes on its own separate track. Just getting the vocal totally perfect may take the producer one or two days.

As the music and the singing are recorded, the sound goes through microphones into a large tape recorder and onto the two-inch tape. Between the microphones and the tape recorder is a complex mixing board.

This mixing board allows the recording engineer to make many adjustments to the sound—raise or lower the volume, add highs (treble) or lows (bass), echo, and other special effects.

The miracle is that you can do this independently to each separate track, and then mix them together in any combination you want.

For example, you might put some echo on the voice and nothing else. Then you might raise the volume of the bass guitar and lower the volume of the rhythm guitar, thus emphasizing the bass sound on the record. These adjustments can be done both during the original recording, and also later in what is called the "remixing" stage.

What is done in the remix is often just as important as what is done during the recording, because there are so many possible ways to change and alter the sound. Remixing might be compared to editing a book.

On a big pop album it is not unusual to spend one hundred fifty to two hundred hours in the studio, recording the music, recording the main vocal and the background voices, and remixing the sound. Pop album budgets commonly run $100,000, often going into the $200,000 range, occasionally even costing over one million dollars.

"Red-Headed Stranger" which Phil York estimates took about thirty-five studio hours and cost about $20,000 to record, may be the cheapest platinum record cut in recent history.

And little did York know what unorthodox approaches he would encounter working in the studio with Willie.

In the first place Willie didn't want to sing in a soundproof isolation booth, and he didn't want to wait until after the musical tracks were cut to do his singing. He wanted to sit right out there on the studio floor with the musicians, and sing while they played. He thought this would give the record a better, more natural feeling.

With the musicians grouped around him, and not well isolated for sound, this meant his voice could leak over onto all of the other tracks. Later, if you wanted to raise the volume of the bass, for example, you'd have a little bit of Willie's voice going up in volume right along with it.

"I pulled my hair out a whole lot," York grins ruefully. "Willie just said, 'I've gotta be out here in the middle of it; if there's any leak, there will have to be leak.' He said he wouldn't have the right contact, visually and otherwise."

The drum sound leaked onto the acoustic guitar track, and Willie's voice leaked into everything.

What York did was put Willie on a highly directional microphone (one that picks up sound from only one direction), and "I got him to work it right on his face. I mean right up against it, the whole way," York emphasizes.

Willie arrived at the studio with a cassette tape of the album in the rough. He played the tape all the way through for the band, then he would play each section at a time, and they would learn it.

"Willie's demanding in the studio, in a quiet way," says York, who later also engineered the "The Sound in Your Mind" and "Family Bible" albums. "For example, there might be two or three lead guitars. I've seen cases where there were two drummers, two bass players, wild stuff. A couple of guys playing totally unrelated stuff.

"On 'Red-Headed Stranger,' " he says, "they were all just blowing their best licks all at once. It was chaos. It was totally unorthodox.

"But! Willie has a quiet way of handling and controlling, such that you don't feel controlled. He's really marvelous at handling his people, and especially his own band," York reveals.

"For example, if there's two or three people just blowing really hot licks—like 'Blue Eyes Crying in the Rain.' He'd say, 'O.K., lay down your instruments everybody; just listen for a minute.' The drummer laid down his drumsticks, the bass player put his bass down.

"He said, 'Now, listen,' and just voice and guitar, he sang the whole song from beginning to end. 'Now,' he said, 'let's put with that what it really needs.' A couple of guys got up and left, said, 'Well, you don't really need me.'

"Now, he could have told that guy to leave. But they honestly listened and left. What was left was guitar, bass, harmonica, and I believe that's all there is on the whole record."

The days of recording developed their own rhythm. The band would sleep late, get up late, come over to the studio between two and four in the afternoon. They'd bring a snack and some beer, sit down and get revved up. Around six or seven or eight P.M., they'd start to record, and go until around midnight or one A.M.

"One funny thing about Willie's session," York laughs, just remembering, "I think it was Paul English who called and said, 'Phil, we'd like a really closed session—button it down all the way.'

"So, I put a different name on the schedule book," York says. "I didn't even tell my very own mother he was going to be in the studio, not a *soul* did I tell.

"Session time rolls around, band shows up, and about an hour later Willie shows up, and by that evening the whole countryside is in that studio from people that Willie and the band had invited! People were lined up like sardines in the hallway. It was really funny."

When the last song was done, Willie set down his guitar and walked into the control room. "Well, what do we do now?" the new producer asked York. "Well, we've got some time scheduled for mixing," York replied.

"Well, uh, when, uh," Willie searched, "how do you do that?"

"It dawned on me what he really meant," York says, still a trace of amazement in his voice. "I said, 'Wait a minute, have you ever sat in on your own mixes before?'

" 'Hell, no,' Willie replied, 'when I get done recording up there in Nashville, they tell me to take my guitar and go home. Next time I hear it, it's on the radio.'

"Well, bring up a chair and sit yourself down." York grinned. "I'm going to show you a thing or two."

"I didn't have to show him anything—he knew instinctively what to do," York adds, "but he had never had the privilege of sitting in on the mixing part of a session. That's what he said. It astounded me."

Willie, now holding what the music industry calls "creative control," insisted on almost no echo on the whole album (giving it a real, upfront, gritty sound). And he wouldn't let York limit his voice much, giving it a full, natural sound. Bobbie was playing the studio's new Dusendorfer, a $40,000-dollar piano which, York rhapsodizes, is "so majestic, it thunders."

"I really like the album personally," York says, "but

I thought it was different enough it couldn't possibly do anything in the world of formulated country.

"I didn't think it was the monumental stepping stone for Willie Nelson it turned out to be." York shakes his head. "I don't Willie realized it, either."

Executives at CBS Records certainly didn't realize it. In fact, they panicked.

Here was a newly signed artist, who hadn't had a real hit for fifteen years, to whom they had just committed who knows how many dollars, bringing in this self-produced, sparsely cut, mystical-sounding cowboy album, cut in a jingle studio in some town nobody ever heard of.

What does it take to make a star, Willie was once asked. "Well, one thing for sure," he replied; "one good way is to get a record label to invest so much money in you, cash up front, they have to make a star out of you to get their money back."

In Nashville, Waylon and Neil Reshen (who had negotiated Willie's CBS deal, and was still managing both Willie and Waylon), played the tape for a CBS executive. Well, it was a terrific little practice tape, the executive generously allowed, but probably not fit for public release.

Waylon was furious. "Let's go," he said to Reshen, and they stormed out. "This is why people drive ninety miles in the sun to hear Willie," he fumed.

Why didn't Willie put some strings on the thing? CBS executives frantically suggested. Although Willie admits, "I didn't know if it would sell myself, because I didn't exactly have a proven track record," he stuck to his guns for his first self-produced album to be released exactly as he had produced it.

"In the past," Willie says, "everything seemed to be watered down by a producer or record company or head of sales."

The first single released from the album, "Blue Eyes Crying in the Rain," shot to number one on July 19, 1975. At age forty-three, Willie finally had his first number-one country record.

Ironically, he didn't write the song. "Blue Eyes Crying in the Rain" was written by Fred Rose, mentor to Hank Williams who had encouraged Chet Atkins to give Nashville another try.

The "Red-Headed Stranger" album is, simply, a masterpiece. A cowboy tale of forsaken love, murder, revenge, horse thievery, and new-found romance, it is a mesmerizing saga. But far more than a mere story, the album unfolds a mystical allegory of sin and salvation—a reworking of the theme of "Yesterday's Wine," in the form of a parable of the old West. Charming on the surface, enormously deep and complex, "Red-Headed Stranger" is an album each person must listen to and interpret individually.

"What is different about this album from those you've done in the past?" *Picking Up the Tempo* asked Willie, shortly after the album's release.

"Nothing," he replied.

TIME OF THE PREACHER

Willie Nelson's career was never the same again. He now crossed over the boundary between star and Superstar, on the way to become, as Lefty Frizzell once ruefully sang, "a legend in my time."

"Willie Nelson has recently recorded an album so remarkable that it calls for a redefinition of the term, country music," Chet Flippo wrote. John Rockwell of *The New York Times* titled Willie the "acknowledged leader to country music's 'left wing' . . . working to cleanse Nashville of stale excesses by bringing it up to the present and back to its own folkish roots."

Official Nashville was in a quandary. Here it was July, and Willie had a nationally acclaimed, number-one record. October, when the Country Music Association awards would be given, was fast approaching. But the ballots had been mailed months before "Blue Eyes Crying in the Rain" was a hit. So Willie, talk of the nation, didn't even have a chance to win an award.

Not only did Nashville have to deal with that little pressure, but Waylon was acting up again. Waylon had been nominated not only for the prestigious Male Vocalist of the Year, but for that prize of all prizes: Entertainer of the Year. And nobody knew if he was going to even show up for the telecast.

What if he won, and wasn't there to get his award? Good grief, there would be Waylon snubbing Nashville, and Nashville acting like Willie Nelson didn't even exist. It would be *awful*.

Waylon was beyond control. Even at five P.M. on the day of the awards show, Waylon's own office staff didn't know if he was going to attend.

But they could invite Willie to make a cameo appearance on the program in honor of his accomplishments.

Much to everyone's relief, Willie seemed happy to be invited back—providing, of course, he could play with his own band.

Actually, Willie had been observing Nashville recently from afar, enjoying a belly laugh over a fight between country stars Ray Stevens and Webb Pierce.

Ever-enterprising, promoting Pierce had built a flashy guitar-shaped swimming pool in his backyard. Stevens lived across the street in the ritzy suburban neighborhood.

"Stevens," Willie gleefully related to a fellow Texan, "was going around with a petition, because the Grand Ole Opry has about eighty busloads of tourists that come by the stars' houses every week, and about ninety people fall out of a bus with Brownies and Kodaks.

"They come by Webb's to look at the guitar swimming pool. Busloads of them. Of course, Webb is out there selling them binoculars and his kids have set up a lemonade stand, and Ray Stevens didn't dig it. So he was out with a petition.

"And they asked Webb what he thought about it, and he said, 'Well, shit, Stevens shouldn't have moved across the street from a star.'

"So, they are having a lot of fun in Nashville," Willie noted fondly. "I really hate to be missing out on that."

When Willie arrived in Nashville to do the CMA awards show, he reassured the *Nashville Tennessean:* "There's no bitterness at all as far as me and Nashville are concerned. Now, there *might* be one or two guys walking around on the street that I'm not too happy with, but I'd never say I disliked the town as a whole."

It was a totally triumphal reentry. During every hour of the star-studded week, Willie was the man of the hour. The press, the industry watched every move he made. Willie was *it*—the prodigal son returned home.

"This year it should have been called 'Willie Nelson Week,' " wrote Townsend Miller, who had ventured out of mellow Austin for the big-time event. ("The trip was fun," Townsend reported when he got back, "but I haven't changed my mind about Nashville's music scene. It's insane! Just one endless madness of everyone trying to outdress and outhustle everyone else. It was great to return to Austin," he concluded with satisfaction.)

As for Willie, he couldn't seem to get enough of it—the waves of praise washing over him—he was *everywhere:* at the BMI awards dinner to honor top songwriters and music publishers of the year, at the Columbia Records artist showcase, at the private parties, at the hospitality suites, and—sentimentally—at Ernest Tubb's famous "Midnight Jamboree," broadcast nationally after the "Grand Ole Opry" sign-off, from a ramshackle old record store near Tootsie's—a store that stocked virtually every country record known to man.

Around midday, rumors started heating up that Willie was going to be at Ernest Tubb's at midnight. By nightfall, speculation was rife, and the store, which had a stage at the back, started filling up with the regular hard-country, lower-Broadway crowd, plus some irregulars: long-haired boys in prefaded jeans and brand-new cowboy boots.

Well-known country music journalist Michael Bane recorded the scene for the *Austin American-Statesman:* "In the middle of the crowd," he observed, "a tow-headed boy cranes his neck to see what's happening. He is wearing a Future Farmers of America jacket over his coveralls. . . .

"He starts to laugh. 'Mamma, Mamma,' he cries in an accent thick enough to cover biscuits; 'Mamma, lookit them hippies!' . . . The hippies in question are acting like they own the place, pushing through the crowd toward the stage. . . . But when the hippies climb up on stage, the boy's glee turns to bewilderment. . . . The Future Farmer's bewilderment gives way to genuine joy as it dawns on him. 'Gol-*darn*, Mamma, that's ol' Willie!' "

For the rest of the night, Bane reported, "dividing lines and labels of all kinds go out the window. To half the audience the word 'progressive' means 'Progressive Farmer'; to the other half the word 'farmer' means a character in a traveling-salesman joke. But all of them know Willie Nelson, and all of them have been through the experiences which are Willie's material."

A week after the awards show, Willie was still in Nashville. One morning, he got up about noon, had a breakfast of eggs, ham, and cantaloupe while the FM radio in the motel room played some soft dinner music. He then stood up to leave. He was going over to the RCA studio to record some stuff with Waylon.

WANTED: THE OUTLAWS

They were constantly linked together in the press—"Willon and Waylie," Don Bowman called them.

Waylon "the body" and Willie "the soul" of country music. Real men. Anti-Nashville. Doing their own thing. Brothers. Co-carousers. Texans (I presume). ("When are you going back to Nashville next?" a reporter asked Waylon. "Well, I live there," he replied.)

They were adored not only for their alikeness, but for their intriguing difference.

Short, red-headed Willie: eyes sparkling, smiling that warm benevolent smile, open to the world, thriving on his fans, handling the adoring crowds and clamoring press with such shrewd country-boy ease, always able to say the right things without even seeming to try, very together, in control, commander in chief of a loyal clan.

Tall, dark, lank-haired Waylon: leather-vested, prowling, brooding, reclusive, at once so macho and so vulnerable; harassed by adulation, shy even on stage, afraid to give interviews, too gentle for the dog-eat-dog entertainment machine, always teetering on the edge of some deep, dark chasm of defeat—his drug problems simmering beneath the surface.

"While Waylon is a cross between Billy the Kid and the clinical definition of insecurity," wrote Patrick Carr, "Willie plays the Guru with a Will of Iron."

It was an absolutely irresistible combination of oil and water, suspended in a solution of shared independence, wry humor, musical principles, free-wheeling life styles, and sheer camaraderie.

Since 1972, both Waylon and Willie had been striding toward musical control of their records. Winning it, both proved their musical instincts were on target.

While Willie was recording "Shotgun Willie," "Phases and Stages," and "Red-Headed Stranger," Waylon was turning out "Ladies Love Outlaws," "Lonesome, On'ry and Mean," "Honky-Tonk Heroes" ("the first album I had control over," he says), and "Dreaming My Dreams."

Their musical collaboration started in 1974 when Waylon and Willie together produced Waylon's "The Time" album, featuring his first number-one country single and four songs off Willie's "Phases and Stages" album.

None of this was going unnoticed by the astute marketing executive who had taken Chet Atkins' position as head of RCA's Nashville division: Jerry Bradley.

"The entire thing was really Jerry Bradley's idea," Waylon says of the marketing scheme that would become the epic-making "Wanted: The Outlaws" album.

What brewed in Bradley's brain was a stroke of promotional genius. He knew that both Willie and Waylon's wife, Jessi Colter, topping the country charts with the hit "I'm Not Lisa," had at one time both been signed to RCA Records. This meant that RCA had old recordings by the artists lying around in their vaults, collecting dust.

Bradley figured he could dig out the old recordings, let Waylon work them over in the studio to update the sound, add some current records by Waylon, group the whole thing together under a catchy title like "The Outlaws," and see what would happen. Who knows? It might sell 200,000 copies.

"I took 'em in and remixed 'em and added some things and sang harmony with Willie and what have you," Waylon said, "which is kind of hard to do. He back-phrases so far, you know, I told him, 'Hoss, you were laid back when they used to call it lazy.'

"And he said, 'Waylon, you were macho before anybody knew what it meant.'

"Willie's one of my best friends," Waylon concluded.

So was Tompall Glaser, at the time Waylon's business partner to boot. Waylon urged Bradley to put Tompall on the album; which he did.

With gritty, brown-tone photos of the fearsome four grouped on what looked like a wanted poster out of Gunsmoke, RCA released the album in 1976 under the title "Wanted: The Outlaws."

"Wanted: The Outlaws" became the first album

released out of Nashville to ever go platinum. By 1978, it had sold one and a half million copies. It shot to top-ten pop—not country—*pop*, the charts where Olivia Newton John and the Eagles and those types hung their hats. Nashville was blown out of the saddle—but, thank God, by one of their own finest sons: Jerry Bradley. Now the outlaws had a camp in Nashville, too.

In March, 1976, the single "Good-Hearted Woman," a Waylon and Willie duet (actually recorded by Waylon a year earlier at the Texas Opry House with Willie's voice added for the album) jumped up to number twenty-five on the pop (not country) charts. Number twenty-five on the hot one hundred most popular records of all music listeners in the entire nation.

Willie had also added his voice to Waylon's recording of "Heaven and Hell" to make another duet. Willie's two solo performances on the album were both taken off RCA's "Yesterday's Wine" album, now five years old.

Two years later when the "Waylon and Willie" album was released, Willie said, "I think this sounds more like the way we sound than the Outlaw album did. I think some of the songs in there were dated, or the sounds dated."

Nonetheless, "Wanted: The Outlaws" was a smash, and introduced the rough-and-ready outlaw ethos to the mainstream of American music listeners—who loved the whole shit-kicking idea.

All of a sudden, America's musical masses were dying to know every rowdy detail of the lives of these rip-roaring, cowboy heroes—right down to what brand of toothpaste they brushed with (if outlaws did that at all).

Ecstatic, RCA threw a big, fancy party in Nashville to celebrate the new sales sensations. Tompall was late. "Well, what'd ya expect," he growled, "an outlaw to be on time?"

That spring Willie received a Grammy nomination for "Blue Eyes Crying in the Rain."

Early on, Willie mentioned he felt "a little weird" about competing for the honor of Male Vocalist with friends: Waylon, Ray Stevens, Freddy Fender, Glen Campbell, and John Denver. But, "I guess we'll all go out there, sit in the audience, and chew our fingers with everybody else," he sighed.

On the glittering evening the Grammy Awards Show was aired on national TV, Willie's name was called out as winner of the Country Male Vocalist award. But the tennis-shoed outlaw wasn't there.

The press was astonished. Was it because he would have had to wear a tuxedo? "Well, I just didn't feel like going," said Willie, who watched it at home on TV, "and I really didn't think I would win. It's just one of those things, I guess."

With fall, the Country Music Association (CMA) awards rolled around again. Willie had never received a final nomination in any category of the CMA awards before, but this year, with plenty of time to vote, the prestigious members nominated him for five awards, including Male Vocalist and the top-of-the-heap biggie, Entertainer of the Year. "Good-Hearted Woman" was nominated for single of the year, "Wanted: The

Outlaws" for album of the year, and Willie and Waylon, to everyone's surprise and amusement, for vocal duo of the year (a prize always won by a male/female duo).

Waylon was nominated in competition with Willie for Male Vocalist, but that didn't matter, because Waylon wasn't going to the show anyway. Last year he'd only gone because Jessi finally talked him into it, and this year he wasn't going, period.

Willie, however, must have figured he was gonna win this one. Diplomatically explaining that he'd "never fallen out" with the pickers in town, Willie showed up.

Three times he was called to the front, where he flashed a mesmerizing smile and accepted with exquisitely restrained triumph "on behalf of me and ol' Waylon." The outlaws made off with album of the year, single of the year, and (to chuckles) vocal duo of the year.

Waylon-and-Willie partisans could hardly contain their glee. Standing there with Ronnie Milsap, Mel Tillis, the Statler Brothers—right between Kitty Wells and Dolly Parton—was "ol' Willie," dressed in his best formal bandanna, work shirt, jeans, and sneakers.

With that coup, Willie, 43, and Waylon, 39, just four years apart in age, became publicly indulged as the Tom Sawyer and Huck Finn of country music. On the one hand, they could do no wrong; on the other hand, whatever they did, everybody wanted to know about it.

They recorded each other's songs, sang on each other's albums, showed up at each other's shows, got in bad boyish trouble together, jibbed each other as only fast friends and blood brothers can.

"Is it true that all you people in Austin think that when you die, you're gonna go to Willie's house?" Waylon asked the audience on his "Waylon Live" LP. When the crowd roared their approval, Waylon laughed and shot back, "Well, you ain't."

"It don't matter who's in Austin. Bob Wills is still the king," Waylon brassily sang on "Dreaming My Dreams." "I wrote that to needle Willie," he joked later. "We were fighting at the time."

Waylon divulged that his favorite song of Willie's was "And So Will You, My Love," its title taken from a line by Elizabeth Taylor in the movie, *The Sandpiper*. But, together, they spoofed each other in song: "I'll Sing You in My Song, If You'll Sing Me in Yours" and "All This Good Ol' Waylon is Giving Me the Willies."

Willie proclaimed the friendship genuine, not just cooked up to sell records. He'd mention a concert in Louisville in '76, when the two men romped and laughed like soldier buddies reunited after a war, when Waylon showed up unexpectedly at the show.

Both publicly commiserated over their woman problems, although Willie loyally defused rumors of a Waylon/Jessi split. "They're back together in Nashville," he reassured the world. "They fight like cats and dogs, but we all have the same problems."

About a week before Waylon's arrest in August, 1977, on what he would insist was a cocaine setup, Willie and Waylon's bus was stopped and detained for several hours in DeKalb, Texas. They were fined two hundred dollars when local sheriffs found them carrying four cans of beer in a dry country. "The only good thing about it," Willie pointed out, "is we had forty cases in the luggage compartment, they *didn't* find."

That year Waylon released "Ol' Waylon," showcasing the Willie-Waylon duet, "Luckenbach, Texas." Willie was lounging around in the studio with Waylon when they got the idea for him to sing on the last verse, and since he didn't get any royalties or credit on the record, Willie allowed as how he was "just a nice guy, I guess," when it came to his pal, Waylon.

"I guess me and Waylon's as close as anybody could be," he told the Louisville paper. "We're both on the road goin' different places, but we still like to get together and have a good time."

In 1977, Willie was riding three number-one albums, including "The Sound in Your Mind," voted Country Album of the Year by *Billboard* magazine. Waylon was voted Number-One Country Artist of the Year by *Rolling Stone* and had stashed away three gold albums himself. "Luckenbach, Texas" catapulted onto the country charts at the highest position ever known for any country single.

That year Waylon swept the CMA balloting with five nominations. Willie got one—for singing on the last verse of "Luckenbach." Immediately both asked to have their names removed from the ballots, stating their relationship was a "warm and close one," and they disliked competing against each other.

(Manager Reshen, however, also revealed that they had some problems with "the way the show was structured," the fact that performers weren't allowed to sing with their own bands, the short time each act had to perform, and the way the winners were chosen.)

The CMA refused on the basis that they could not tamper with the members' selections, and the members, possibly feeling the boys were getting a bit big for their britches, honored the duo with zero awards.

Never one to let minor spats get in the way of big bucks, however, Jerry Bradley had donned his thinking cap again.

He got an artist to paint a portrait of Waylon and Willie, cheek to cheek, and discreetly propped it up behind his desk. When Waylon wandered into the office one day, there it was. And Waylon liked it.

Well, Bradley proposed, how about a Waylon and Willie album? Waylon was open to the idea. They discussed reworking more old tracks, but both Willie and Waylon decided they wanted to cut some new songs, more in line with their current rock-influenced sound.

"Waylon picked most of the songs," Willie announced in a joint interview. "I liked his choice. He played those two songs by Kris, for instance, and I said, 'I think they're great. Let's do them.'"

Whereupon Waylon looked astonished: "I was just playing 'em for you," he protested. "I hadn't picked them to record. I was surprised when you picked that 'Year 2003 Minus 25.'"

Whereupon Willie confessed: "We didn't do that much research on this album."

To eagerly waiting Americans, many of whom had scarcely ever heard of Waylon Jennings and Willie

Nelson before, "Wanted: The Outlaws" crossed pop; "Waylon and Willie" was the second terrific release by a brand-new team.

The album upended the country music industry by debuting at number one on the charts. It went platinum faster than any country album ever, selling half a million copies in two weeks.

But to country connoisseurs, who had been following Waylon and Willie for a long time, the outlaw bit was indeed getting a little out of hand, if not to say cutesy and uncreative. One writer noted that the "Waylon and Willie" album jacket was a "dead ringer for a Breck shampoo ad."

"What are Jennings, one of the greatest singers alive, and Nelson, one of the greatest writers alive, doing stringing daisies in the Luckenbach afternoon," tartly demanded critic-at-large Nick Tosches. " 'Mamas, Don't Let Your Babies Grow Up To Be Outlaws,' " he complained "is no less silly than 'Mamas, Don't Let Your Babies Grow Up To Be CPAs.' "

Or as Ed Ward put it, "I'd rather they drop this whole pose and go back to being Waylon and Willie."

But these were just the voices of country-music critics crying in the wilderness, for the big-time celebrity circuit was getting its hooks into the boys now.

"Mamas, Don't Let Your Babies Grow Up To Be Outlaws" topped out at number one on the country charts in January of 1978, then leaped across to the pop charts. Just a month earlier, Waylon and Willie had set out on a joint sixty-five-day tour. By March they were outgrossing any other act touring the United States except Sha Na Na.

"Man, I've been to some of those concerts that Willie and Waylon have done," said old songwriting pal Harlan Howard. "Oh God, it's just like going to a rock concert, except there's better songs, and you can hear the words."

Willie, who thrives on the road, was in his element. "I think it's important to play all kinds of places," he enthused. "I enjoy them for what they are. Halls, lounges, clubs. I even enjoy working motel rooms," he truthfully joked.

Edgy Waylon, however, tends to get worn down by crowds and strung out on the road. "It's like, it's boring," he once revealed. "Like you see what I mean right here in this room. You know, this is not the most inspiring. The green-and-yellow sign of the Holiday Inn ain't the most beautiful thing around here.

"And fatigue? It's easy, like I say, to start looking for something to get what we call 'get up!'," he confessed. "You have to get up for the shows, basically, mentally, you have to get yourself geared to it. It's hard to do that. Just to keep doing it year after year and day after day."

RCA was so "up," they couldn't seem to get enough of a good thing. The company threw a hugh bash for their pet duo at the Rainbow Room, the posh night club atop Rockefeller Center in New York City. The celebrity blowout turned into an unmitigated disaster for Waylon, who felt wary and trapped, which, in turn, made it into a stupid fiasco for an enraged Willie.

Writer Patrick Carr surrealistically described the event as being like a "thank-you party for successful young garment salesmen and their dates." On display like freaks at a sideshow, Waylon and Willie were seated on a raised dais in full view of the gawking press. "Which one's Waylon and which one's Willie?" New York PR-types eagerly inquired. "Where's the free albums?" squeaked long, lacquer-nailed secretaries.

As the carnival wore on and the duck à l'orange and cold salmon wore out, Waylon, known by friends as a shy, gentle, virtually paranoid man, edged farther and farther back into a dark corner, speaking only when spoken to, fidgeting, cutting his eyes to possible escape routes. "Oh, baby," he moaned to a friend, "I feel like I'm all tied up."

Willie, sitting beside him, shielding him against the crowd, was only partially successful in diverting the onslaught. "It's a very bad and very public situation," one onlooker grimaced. After the party Willie had planned to join Tracy Nelson on stage over at the Lone Star Café for a duet. Instead, he was up in his room, alone, fuming over "managerial mismanagement."

But a couple of months later, Willie, Waylon, and Jessi were back in New York for a second hyperactive media event. This one, staged by CBS Records at the Lone Star Café in Willie's honor, Willie seemed to enjoy to the hilt.

Movie star James Caan arrived in pointy-toed cowboy boots announcing that he was Willie's "biggest fan." Actor Jan Michael Vincent was there. John

311

Belushi, Jane Curtain, and Bill Murray from "Saturday Night Live" all showed up. Professional scene maker Andy Warhol was supposed to put in an appearance.

Willie played for three hours that night, without a break, ranging over every musical category known to western man. Pop maestro James Taylor, in jeans and tweed jacket, climbed on stage, hugged Willie, and they segued into a slow blues number. When the marathon ended with "Goodnight, Irene," Willie was in tears.

The night before, Waylon and Willie had played the Capital Centre in Washington, and presidential press secretary Jody Powell showed up backstage during intermission bearing an invitation from President Jimmy Carter for lunch the following day at the White House.

It was all pretty tony, high-powered stuff for two country boys used to kicking up sawdust in honky-tonks.

Riding the bubble upward, Willie and Waylon had been talking about returning to Austin and building a million-dollar studio, complete with golf course and Olympic-size swimming pool, overlooking Lake Travis. And they wanted to co-produce a concept album written by Willie called "The Convict and the Rose," based on the idea of reincarnation.

But toward the end of 1978, stories started appearing in newspapers across the country stating that the IRS had filed a lien against some property Willie owned in Evergreen, Colorado—an $185,000 home on eighteen acres, plus three other parcels of land he had bought in 1977. The IRS claimed he owed $71,991 in back taxes.

Rumor had it that Willie was extremely upset over the tax problem and blamed it on his and Waylon's co-manager Neil Reshen. But Waylon had taken Reshen's side. Now there was talk of a split between the two.

Willie denied it. "Waylon and I will always disagree on practically everything," he allowed with a grin, "but it has nothing to do with our friendship. I think that's why we'll always be friends—I don't try to tell him what to do, and he don't try to tell me what to do."

Enough said. Except Willie, who soon had a new manager, was heading nothing but up, whereas Waylon was headed for darkly troubled waters.

In early 1979, Waylon announced he was going to appear in a movie with John Travolta—a featured role in "Urban Cowboy," to be exact. "I'm sure folks out in Arizona where I was once a lowly paid D.J. will be surprised to see ol' Waylon doing so good," he joshed mildly.

The reporter mentioned Willie was getting ready to do "Honeysuckle Rose."

"Surely Willie isn't going to play the title role," Waylon jibbed. "Willie hasn't said anything to me about being in the movie," he mentioned, then added optimistically, "I don't think the project is far enough along to know who is going to be in the cast."

When "Honeysuckle Rose" was released, among the slew of Willie's friends featured in the movie and on the soundtrack album, the name of Waylon Jennings was not to be found.

For three defensive years, Willie and Waylon denied they had bad problems between them, but it was obvious they were going separate ways.

Then, in 1981, Willie suffered a collapsed lung in Hawaii and doubtless got to thinking mortal thoughts and mulling over the important things in life. Waylon queasily discovered he had been savagely ripped off by men he believed his closest friends, and in the resulting void, had time to ponder the fact that Willie was not among the traitors.

Suddenly, the duo appeared in the news.

During the 1981 Disc Jockey Convention in Nashville, Willie and Waylon startled everyone by showing up, with Merle Haggard, at the Nashville Songwriter's Association banquet.

Both were mum to questions from reporters, but word leaked out that they had been in the studio cutting a joint album for Willie's newly reactivated Lone Star Records. Naturally, this was totally unprovided for either in Willie's contract with CBS Records, or in Waylon's with RCA.

That little bit of contractual nonchalance caught even Jerry Bradley off guard. "I just heard about it last night," Bradley ventured reservedly. "It's hardly normal for two artists to cut a record for another label, but maybe something could be worked out."

Spotting Bradley's statement in the AP news stories across America, outlaw fans, deprived of Willon-and-Waylie music for three years, gratefully popped open a Lone Star beer, took a cool, deep swig, and belched with satisfaction. Their boys were back to "hardly normal."

I DIDN'T KNOW GOD MADE
HONKY-TONK HEROES

In the wee hours of the morning after a concert, Willie, some of his crew, a few guys in the band, and a couple of girls were sitting in Willie's motel room watching a silent movie on TV. Beast, the band's chow master, arrived to place five sandwiches, a bunch of bananas, a half-gallon of milk, and two bags of cookies at Willie's side.

As Willie's son Billy filled Beast in on the movie's plot, Willie poured a glass of milk and picked up a cookie.

He studied the glass of milk in one hand, looked at the cookie in the other. "Do you think," he asked, "this will blow the outlaw image?"

Well, all you deputies, what's an outlaw, anyhow? To paraphrase a Willie tune, sometimes they're good guys and sometimes they're bad guys, and sometimes you don't even know.

As far as the label "outlaw" goes, it's one that neither Waylon or Willie likes. In fact, they don't like any kind of labels much.

"I don't like labels," Willie made plain. "What I do is Willie Nelson music; what Leon does is Leon Russell music; what Waylon does is Waylon music. My definition of music is what my grandmother taught me—and that's whatever is pleasing to the ear. If rolling a peanut across the floor with your nose is pleasing to you, that's good music!

"I don't consider myself an outlaw," Willie says flatly. "I never robbed a bank."

Good point. 'Cause as writer Lester Bangs once pointed out, where he comes from, they shoot outlaws.

Willie thinks the first time he heard the word "outlaw" in connection with country music was in Lee Clayton's song, "Ladies Love Outlaws," recorded by Waylon in 1972.

Writer Peter McCabe used in 1973 to describe a Nashville gang—Waylon, Tompall, Billy Joe Shaver, and sometimes, Willie—who hung out together raising hell till dawn.

Whatever else, the "outlaws" are, they are musicians who want to record with their own bands instead of studio musicians; who demand the right to produce their own records; who hang around with rock musicians every now and then; who don't wear suits and ties (anymore) or dress up, no matter what the occasion; who wholeheartedly identify with college kids; and who let the world know they use drugs of all descriptions.

But it was up to Jerry Bradley, the straightest of all straight, hard-headed, business-sharp executives on Music Row, to link the word "outlaws" with Waylon and Willie in the minds of record buyers. And the duo went along with it, because it was a good publicity gimmick and it sold a lot of records.

As Waylon said, "Titles are made to merchandise and distribute. I don't really like the term "outlaws." I always thought it was corny."

"I think it's all rather colorful myself," Willie said of the outlaw movement. "It didn't hurt at all."

As for vocabulary, Willie prefers words like "non-conformist" or "antiestablishment." "Among those of us who've been called outlaws," he says, "I know we don't think of ourselves as being strongly against the law in a real-life sense. I think of an outlaw as a rebel, someone who knows what he wants, and isn't going to go along with everybody else's program.

"I don't think I should have to change the way I think or believe for anyone," he insists emphatically. "So far, I've managed to keep from doing it most of the time."

"If we fought for anything," Waylon says, "it was for the right to be ourselves, not to be typecast. I don't even want to be where Willie's at, except as a friend."

Being called an outlaw, of course, typecasts and stereotypes a musician in and of itself. While this outlaw bit's been getting out of hand, a lot of people have been getting the wrong idea about Willie Nelson's music.

Those who have heard nothing but "Wanted: The Outlaws" and "Waylon and Willie" have very stunted ideas of Willie's music, and the wide-ranging musical roots on which it's based.

After the two RCA outlaw albums hit, CBS wanted

Willie to release a record that would keep up the out-law image. Instead, he released "The Sound in Your Mind," a musical potpourri with the live feel of "Shotgun Willie": a sort of tribute to Willie's musical background, including "Lucky Old Sun," Lefty Frizzell's classic hit; "If You've Got the Money, I've Got the Time;" and a gospel song that goes with the ages, "Amazing Grace."

Next he came up with an entire album dedicated to Lefty Frizzell, titled simply "To Lefty from Willie." Although not outlaw in content, this gave Willie a chance to show some of his "nonconformist" attitude to CBS, which wasn't impressed with the project.

"We had a little difference of opinion on the album," Willie says. 'They weren't sure what I was trying to do, and obviously, they weren't that familiar with Lefty Frizzell. But I felt that all ten of the songs on the album could be number-one songs, because they all were at one time."

"Then," he continues, "we had a slight argument over the title of the album. I wanted to call it what it is — 'To Lefty from Willie' — with no pictures, no flair."

Ironically, "To Lefty from Willie" was released the week Lefty Frizzell, one of the greatest stylists in the history of country music, died. CBS producer Billy Sherrill, who has a rather wry sense of humor, suggested that the only other appropriate choice for the title was "Ten Songs That Killed Lefty Frizzell."

But to Willie it was serious business for Columbia to let him put out the album exactly the way he wanted. "I felt the same way about Lefty's music that you say some people feel about our music," he told a Florida reporter. "In other words, it was a religious experience for me to hear Lefty Frizzell sing, 'If You've Got the Money, I've Got the Time.'"

His next CBS album, of course, was the blockbuster "Stardust," about as "outlaw" as two little old ladies drinking tea—and about as "nonconformist" as they come.

Mike Reynolds of *Crawdaddy* has suggested that the best word to describe Willie is "maverick," after Samuel Maverick (1803-70), a rancher who refused to brand his stock. The word means, "a person who takes an independent stand, refusing to conform to that of his party or group."

Well, that's Willie all right—in fact, Willie usually isn't in any "party or group" unless it's one he started himself.

But whether he's a "maverick," an "outlaw," or a "nonconformist," Willie says they didn't invent the category when he and Waylon were born.

"The outlaw term could have been used a long time before Waylon and I got to Nashville," he declares. "It could have been used for Hank Williams, Hank Thompson, Bob Wills, Leon Payne, and Floyd Tillman.

"All those guys," he says, "saw fit to stay where they were and do their music in their own areas without operating exclusively out of Nashville—guys who weren't afraid to go ahead and do it the way they thought it ought to be."

Then, in Memphis, the day after Elvis died, Willie vowed Elvis "was the guy who really had it rough starting out. . . . Jerry Lee and Elvis were the first real outlaws, not me and Waylon."

If he deserves to be called an outlaw, Willie once asserted, it is simply because he's "cantankerous at times."

"Usually I don't consider myself an outlaw any more than Hank Williams was," he said. "He might be pretty hard to get along with."

One image Willie likes to promote is the cowboy image. He doesn't mind believing he's got some of the traits of his boyhood screen heroes. "Cowboys give off the freedom aura more than anybody I know—except Indians," he grins.

"I think the cowboy is a good, positive image. He may not always be on the side of the law, but he's on the *right* side."

In that case, in Willie's view, if Hopalong Cassidy were around today, he'd probably smoke a joint right along with his glass of buttermilk. Using illicit drugs is against the law, and open association with drugs is a prime way Willie and Waylon earned the "outlaw" image. But Willie thinks some drug laws are bad laws.

Willie draws clear lines between the danger of different drugs, as he sees it. He comes down hard on cocaine, but views marijuana as a "mild tranquilizer," comparable to Valium.

As for grass, "I've been smoking it since I was a boy," Willie told Roy Blount in *Esquire*. "Mexicans across the street from where we lived in Abbot grew it in their yard. In Abbott, Texas, nobody cared. And Abbott is probably one of the quietest, sanest places in the world.

"Some of the best marijuana I ever got," he added,

"came from narcotics agents. They'll bust somebody and come by and share it. Law officers knew before the rest of the public did, that it was harmless."

In fact, Willie attributes a lot of the uproar over marijuana to what he describes as "complete ignorance of the drug scene."

Willie, who admits he's tried about every form of drug in existence ("pills, acid, mescaline, cocaine, and a lot of whiskey") says, "There are still a lot of people around who aren't aware of the difference between cocaine and marijuana, even. So long as people are that ignorant, how can you expect them to know anything about the real drug problem?"

Willie does view cocaine use as a real drug problem. Seeing some members of his own band drifting over into serious cocaine abuse, Willie instituted a band rule: "If you're wired, you're fired."

"I felt the band's cocaine use was getting out of hand," Willie openly told *Penthouse*. "Some of the guys were spending too much money. It was also affecting their health. When you're wired, you stay up and party that much longer. Eventually, it can even affect your music.

"Marijuana has no aftereffects," he asserts. "You get a nice little buzz, and you don't pay for it later. Cocaine is a different story. You pay like hell for it when you get it, and you pay for weeks and months and maybe years after you use it."

As for himself, Willie told *Penthouse:* "It's a tossup which is worse: me high on cocaine or drunk on tequila. When I'm drunk, at least I'm funny. If you're not funny, why do any of that stuff?"

These days Willie has cut down on drinking and smoking (cigarettes), jogs daily, has gotten himself in good physical shape, although he's "by no means a puritan."

"I will smoke a joint of marijuana," he admits of the stuff he's reputed to pay $3,500 a pound for. "I don't like cocaine. Don't need pills. But that's just about the size of it. I smoke a joint every now and then, and I will take a drink of tequila with you."

As most any grass smoker will tell you, Willie finds pot enhances listening to music ("whiskey makes you want to fight, and marijuana makes you want to listen to music—and marijuana and beer together is probably the greatest truth serum ever"), but he says he can't write while smoking pot.

"Naw, I can't write when I'm high," he told Jack Hurst. "I've gotten drunk and tried to write, and I've gotten high and tried to write, but the best stuff I write is when I'm straight."

He also points out that, although people naturally assume he writes a lot about drug use, "I never made a lot of money singing about dope." It comes up in the line "Take back the weed, take back the cocaine, baby," but, he says that's "more or less an antidope song." And even where alcohol's concerned he wrote, "I gotta get drunk, and I sure do dread it."

"I write about all kinds of people and things," he observes mildly.

Willie's candid discussion of drug use has made him a hero with the drug set. The October, 1980, issue of *High Times*, a slick doper rag, had a split cover with Willie on one side and Johnny Rotten of the Sex

Pistols on the others. Caption: "This cover ain't big enuff for the both of us."

His drug use also caught the attention of a Dallas federal grand jury investigating narcotics trafficking across the United States in May of 1976. (It's worth noting this happened shortly after Willie won the Grammy for "Blue Eyes Crying in the Rain," and grand juries have been known to enjoy a little publicity themselves.)

Subpoenas were issued for Willie and Ray Price along with eighteen other people on May 26. At that point, the investigation into what newspapers said were international shipments of heroin and cocaine worth millions of dollars, had been under way for over two years.

When Willie emerged from the jury chambers on June 10, wearing jeans, tennis shoes, and a cowboy hat, and accompanied by two attorneys and Paul English, he declined to comment on his testimony.

On June 27, he told the *Austin American-Statesman*, "I don't know what they're doing. Trying to catch some dope dealers, I guess. But if they're as good investigators as I hope they are, they'll know I don't have anything to tell 'em."

Willie, as virtually every person who knows him tells story after story to testify, is an exceptionally kind, generous and warm-hearted man. One of the most contradictory puzzles about Willie is why he has, since the early days of his career, been surrounded by some very rough types.

It is men he has befriended, far more than Willie himself, who have built a hard-core, law-breaking, genuine outlaw/thug image for certain elements of his entourage.

As a result, Willie was once called "the most respected and the most feared man in Texas." It's a potent, sometimes scary combination.

On the one hand, you've got a man who can't seem to exhaust himself in doing good for other people. For example, Dr. and Mrs. Ben Parker, who own KBOP where Willie first worked as a D.J. down in Pleasanton, Texas, were recently trying to raise money for their Longhorn Museum, dedicated to the history of the cattle industry in that area.

Friends urged the Parkers to contact Willie about doing a benefit. It had been so many years. . . . "We thought a lot of Willie," Mrs. Parker says, "but we didn't think he thought about us at all." But Willie immediately agreed to do the benefit in April of 1981.

Due to changes in his schedule, Willie ended up having to charter two planes to fly his band from Reno to Texas, and paid over $6,000 out of his own pocket for an elaborate PA system. He played the show wearing his old KBOP lapel pin, sentimentally saved for over twenty-five years. "We have nothing but good to say about Willie Nelson," vows a still-astonished Mrs. Parker.

Then there was Gina, mentally retarded since birth who also contracted encephalitis, which threw her into a deep coma. For two months in 1978 she remained in unreachable sleep as hundreds of people tried to awaken her through therapy, constant motion, radio, television — anything.

Then one day music from a nearby concert filtered

through the window into her hospital room. It was Willie playing an outdoor concert and singing "Georgia on My Mind." Gina's eyes flickered, then opened. She looked around and smiled.

Her ecstatic parents began playing Willie Nelson records for her constantly, and when Willie heard what was happening, he began showering Gina with gifts—a new stereo, records, posters, a picture of himself carefully signed "To Gina, with love."

How does such soft-hearted beneficence fit with a man who seems to always have a dose of tough, ugly ex-cons and minor thugs in his circle? Who's been adopted by the Hell's Angels as one of their own? Who did a concert promoted by two Hell's Angels during which he dedicated a song to their chief, Sonny Barger, out on bail after thirteen months in jail?

Paul English says his background helps draw this element. Numerous publications have reported that Willie's band was trailed by the FBI for over a year in hopes that a notorious character and former friend of Paul's named Jimmy Renton might turn up along the way.

In 1978 the taint of underworld connection was intensified when it surfaced that Willie had loaned $5,000 to Travis Schnautz, who used the money to open the D. W. Rubb Massage Parlor in Austin. Schnautz was later killed by a shotgun blast, allegedly administered by contract killers.

Many well-known writers have reported eyewitness accounts of men associated with Willie toting guns, beating up people, and generally engaging in lowlife hoodlum behavior. This has occurred even at Willie's own picnics, presumably under his control, where, in fact, some of those seemingly in charge are reported as the ones exacerbating a violent atmosphere.

Jan Reid, who wrote the book, *The Improbable Rise of Redneck Rock*, the first book delving into the new Austin-based country music, later wrote an article in *Texas Monthly*, "Who Killed Redneck Rock?" in which he denounced the existence of a slew of nasty, violence-prone persons around Willie.

According to Bob Allen, in his book *Waylon & Willie*, sometime thereafter trouble developed when two members of Willie's "family" mistook a guitar player in an Austin night club, named John Reed, for Reid, cornered him, and threatened him with bodily harm.

In fact, the author of this book received repeated warnings from a knowledgeable person (*not* a member of Willie's business organization or "family") that unless the book had the official sanction of Willie's organization, she should not write the book at all. "You don't realize the kind of people you are dealing with," she was told. "There's a guy in Willie's bunch who can shoot the ears off a gnat at forty paces."

Waylon once told Chet Atkins, "Hell, Willie doesn't fight the establishment. He thinks fightin' the establishment is double parking on Music Row."

But fuel is added to the flame by other close associates like writer Bud Shrake who told Pete Axthelm in the August 14, 1978 issue of *Newsweek*, "The mistake some people make about the outlaws is thinking they're outlaws because they refused to play chords the way the Nashville establishment wanted them. To really appreciate these guys, you have to understand that they are genuinely interested in the commission of misdemeanors, if not felonies."

Willie, who told one reporter, "I never had any more trouble with the law than you have probably," takes the recurring hood association with an equanimity that is hard to accept—mainly because it contradicts so many positive traits of his character.

Maybe it grows out of his ideas about friendship and loyalty. Maybe it is the result of his extremely nonjudgmental attitude ("I'm not against anything in moderation"). Maybe, paradoxically, it is the product of his soft-hearted nature. "When these out of work ex-cons and small-time promoters come along needing a job, Willie just can't say no," defends one Austin journalist. "He doesn't even know some of the people who work for him."

"I have no idea who may walk down the hall next," Willie told Mike Reynolds of *Crawdaddy* in October, 1978. "It could be a politician, it could be a Hell's Angel. I have friends everywhere." Willie lit a joint and continued, "I'm not ashamed of the people that I'm around. Even though some of them are probably what some people would call, uh, disreputable characters."

After delving into the seedier side of Willie's environment in some detail, Reynolds concluded that, "The outlaw style has a double edge . . . the other blade carved a chic violent posture bolstered with the glories of a .44, petty larceny, and an ugly whiff of bigotry. To the less subtle mind, it condoned a romanticism of literal brutality and moral failing. In short, it attracted lowlifers who took the music's hype to be a style of mayhem and stupidity."

All this came to a head at the fourth Willie Nelson Fourth of July picnic in Gonzales, Texas in 1976.

In 1972, the second annual picnic, a three-day event held at Bryan, Texas, smack out in the middle of a sun-parched, dusty, treeless speedway, was pretty much of a disaster.

Wolfman Jack and the "Midnight Special" crew showed up to tape the whole program (adding the glamour of rock and roll), and Willie later deplored the taping as "just terrible. You could go from the front to the back and cut it up, and there wasn't a good point in there that I saw." Except for the quality of the talent, you could say the same for the whole Bryan picnic. (Willie went straight to Hawaii for two weeks with Connie the instant the fiasco was over.)

Things looked up, though, next year at Liberty Hill. (When asked at Bryan if he would ever hold another picnic, Willie laughed and replied, "Hell, I guess so. I'd hate to throw 4,000 thieves out of work.")

At Liberty Hill, Willie ran the whole thing himself, without partners, letting Gene McCoslin handle the promotion. "I think there's been more good than bad out of them," Willie explained on the eve of Liberty Hill, "and that's the reason we are having one this year."

They rented a lovely five hundred-acre site, bisected by the San Gabriel River, thirty miles northwest of Austin, with plenty of parking and trees for shade. Although the organization was ragged and the local deputy sheriff claimed, "If we had arrested all the naked and drunk people I saw, we'd have filled all the jails from here to Dallas," Willie proclaimed it a success of unexpected proportions.

"It was just mainly people sitting out there in the heat and drinking that old Lone Star beer," one official mildly commented. Or as another observer put it, the picnic was "re-humanized."

But in 1976 at Gonzales, the event sickeningly spun back around in an ugly direction. Although no one was murdered, the Gonzales picnic was compared in the press to the vicious rock festival, Altamount.

Every year the picnics had been getting bigger and bigger; now they were out of hand. Tens of thousands of nonpaying gate crashers tore down $40,000 worth of fence, McCoslin told the *Dallas Morning News*. Fifteen stabbings, seven rapes, and eight overdoses were reported, although not confirmed by the sheriff's department. A boy drowned in a stock tank.

Fist fights, urinating by passers-by on drunks lying on the ground, and overt sexual behavior was rife. A Baytown, Texas, man whose clothes caught fire during the picnic sued Willie for $150,000, claiming officials had failed to provide adequate emergency medical care.

Willie himself was criticized for not performing a full set with his band. But all in all, newspapers said, Willie felt terrible about the whole thing. Reportedly, he had $200,000 of his own money tied up in the half-million-dollar money-losing event.

Willie himself, who *Rolling Stone* said left for Hawaii *during* the picnic this time, seemed somewhat bewildered: "I've always been big for picnics and for a place where folks could hear live music. Picnics bring folks together."

Gonzales, the drug scene, the Hell's Angels, thugs, hoodlums—they were images that, fairly or unfairly, would dog him for years to come.

In 1980 Willie canceled an appearance at the Great Eastern Music Festival in Callaway, Virginia, where general hysteria was fueled by the local sheriff who emptied area jails and ordered up two helicopters, a pair of K-9 dogs, an armored car, twenty-five state Alcohol Beverage Control officers, fifty state troopers, and an entire wrecker service in preparation for the event.

"We're going to protect our churches from being pilfered, our homes from being vandalized, our daughters from being raped," ranted one local minister. Willie withdrew on the grounds that he feared for the safety of his fans.

"It really hurt him," Pop Nelson said in 1976 of the grand jury probe in Dallas. "That's why he had all this trouble with these folks down here" (residents of Gonzales opposed to the picnic). "It's because of all this bad publicity. I'd like to see some of the good stuff come out—like about the money he gives away."

In the midst of it all stands quiet, reserved, unassuming Willie, who usually carries his own luggage and who will stop and talk to the most humble of fans, asserting that he's just a guy—like the cowboys in white hats—who likes to do things his own way, the right way.

Good or bad, good *and* bad, Willie, one supposes, sees it all as just an up and down cycle of phases and stages.

For sure, whatever the origin of the term "outlaw," he's pleased to see the phase of the maverick given its moment of history. "I am glad to see the day of the outlaw coming in," he declared in 1976. We nonconformists are entitled to it, I think."

THE RED-HEADED STRANGER

The Red-Headed Stranger is riding and hiding . . . something. Not a fact, not an event . . . there is an ultimately impenetrable atom at the center of Willie Nelson's being.

The man is a mass of contradictions, all coalescing in a jumble once described as his "sweet wildness."

Not that he consciously tries to conceal anything much.

A writer once suggested there were questions Willie would doubtless prefer to not have asked. "You should have made it a point to ask those questions first," Willie replied, slightly offended. "I'd like to know what I don't want to talk about. I really can't think of anything I wouldn't talk about, because I don't have any secrets."

As Willie himself once offered: each person is actually three people—first, who you think you are; second, who someone else thinks you are; third, who you really are.

Men who have been close to "Will" (as he is called by those who know him well) for twenty or even thirty years, fall into baffled bemusement just trying to put him into words.

"I don't know how to explain it, he's just a different kind of guy," says Darrell Royal, searching for the right description.

One afternoon Willie and Darrell were walking back to the bus after a celebrity golf tournament—Willie was right behind Darrell. When he got to the door of the bus, Darrell turned around, and Willie had vanished.

Searching the crowd, he spotted Willie's white golf hat wandering off in the opposite direction down a neighborhood street. Some strangers in the crowd had invited Willie to their house for a drink, and he'd said O.K., and just meandered off with them. If it hadn't been for that white hat, Darrell would never have figured out what happened to him.

"He always does what he's supposed to do," Royal stresses. "He never makes excuses; I've never heard him plead sinus or laryngitis. He's very responsible, and always meets his commitments. But," he adds with perplexed fondness, "beyond that, he's very unpredictable."

Short and slim, dressed in scruffy jeans, imitation Adidas jogging shoes, some kind of bandanna twisted around his graying red hair, Willie hardly looks like a man who could command awe on sight.

It's when Willie looks out through those deep, penetrating, steely eyes that people first become unnerved, or bewitched. Even on the movie screen, filtered through cameras and film, their magnetism is startling. Little bolts of intensity springing out of spider webs of wrinkles under shaggy red eyebrows. And beneath the laser rays spreads the wide, cushioning, beatific smile. Soothing and accepting, inviting you to open the door and walk in.

Then the smile subsides, the eyes become remote, detached, observing you with a kind of speculative wonder—like a deer startled in the forest—and you realize Willie's stepped back inside and you are standing there, a stranger before the Red-Headed Stranger.

Whatever the outlaw image is, Willie's done his part to keep it undefined. He's always growing his beard, shaving off his beard, letting his hair go long, cutting it off, plaiting it in braids, tying it back in a ponytail, showing up in every kind of hat and shirt under creation. About the only sartorial items that stay the same are the jeans (which generally look like a Salvation Army notion of chic) and some variety of off-brand jogging shoes.

Hats, Willie maintains, are "real important." He's shown up topped by everything from a straw cowboy hat to a hound's-tooth-checked hunting cap, to a frizzy blue western hat with a long, swooping ostrich plume. "Hats and boots are an American tradition," he affirms. "It was O.K. for John Wayne, and O.K. for Geronimo, so it's got to be O.K. for anybody," he laughs in that soft, low $50,000 engine purr. "Nobody gives a damn if you wear a cowboy hat."

Billy Joe Shaver, who wrote the classic "Willie the Wandering Gypsy and Me" recalls the first time he met wandering Will: "I'd heard his records, of course, and he'd been a sort of a hero of mine for a long time. Then, I went to this party one night at Bobby Bare's or somebody's and Willie was there, wearing Bermuda shorts, cowboy boots, a football shirt, a cowboy hat, and one earring, and I said to myself: 'There he is. Willie the wandering gypsy.' "

Although Ray Price used to make his Cherokee Cowboys dress out in flashy, sequined outfits, on his own, Willie never adopted the Porter Wagoner, rhinestone-studded-wagon-wheel look. He wasn't alone in his restraint. Lots of artists preferred to follow the latest trends in middle American fashion, and Willie pretty much went along with that crowd.

So when he decided to adopt hippie/college-age outfits to attract attention to himself, he came in for a few surprises. "I think that anybody that has ever had long hair and a beard and went into a truck stop," Willie says flatly, "knows how it feels to be a nigger."

What about your pigtails? he was once asked. "What about them?" he retorted steely eyed. "It's my hair, and I'll wear it like I darn please." Then his eyes softened and he grinned. "Besides," he added, "there's nothing wrong with pigtails. Even little girls wear them."

He simply demands to be accepted—as is. "As is" has been described as "part Buddah and part Gabby Hayes," or as "a hippie Santa Claus," or as a Beverly Hills bartender put it, "He's the most interesting thing I've seen out here since the right turn on red."

This odd grab bag of traits has somehow amalgamated itself into an image that is, at the same time, sexy and awe-inspiring. To those who see it or feel it, it hits hard. To others, it's downright perplexing.

Doubtless, the sex-object claim is both the most fun

to talk about and the hardest to get your hands on (or, one should perhaps say, your thoughts organized about).

Willie is almost fifty and looks at least five or ten years older. It's easy to think of him as a grandfather. "He looks like a dirty old man, and when he sings, 'All of me, why not take all of me,'' I want to puke,' observed a teen-age girl in El Paso.

On the other hand, other teen-age girls, plus numerous big-city women, gaze into his dark, moist, continuously sparkling eyes, and are mesmerized.

Burt Reynolds, himself a certified sex object as well as Willie pal, doesn't exactly get it. "He has an enormous sex appeal, which I haven't figured out yet, but it must be true, because I keep hearing it from an awful lot of people," Burt says. "I think part of it stems from the fact that you just sort of have to accept who he is. There's something very sexy about that.

"Also," Burt generously allows, "there's nothing sexier than a man doing what he does best. And that's what he does best. He just does it, and is totally unashamed about it—in a taxicab, on a corner, on the top of a roof, on a boat—"

Willie's even been named in *Playgirl* magazine's poll as one of the ten sexiest men in the nation. Are you fixing to become an international sex symbol like Kris Kristofferson? Wille was asked. "Well," he softly drawled, and squinted his deeply lined eyes, "I don't guess there's any way I can avoid it, is there?"

Willie projects the air of a man that psychologists might call "fully realized." Willie is a man who has done what he set out to do, who is living his dream.

"I can't think of anything I want to do that I'm not doing," he once replied to a question. "That sounds like a powerful statement, but it's really true."

Well, does he worry about the problems that come with making it big? "No," Willie answered, "I don't."

Willie is extremely adept—and has been from boyhood—at selling himself (along with songs, encyclopedias, Fourth of July picnics, and so forth). He knows how to make people like him—or, you might say, he knows how to display his genuinely likable traits to best advantage.

Within the family, Willie's psychological mystery, his riveting eyes and sanctified smile, his facial expressions and body language that, at one and the same time, invite intimacy and yet ward off overfamiliarity—this close, but not too close, seductive persona breeds a virtually religious reverence or awe.

"Willie's the *godfather,*" a drunk band member told writer Bob Allen one night on a tour bus, speaking in hushed tones as he gingerly stepped over a couple of passed-out comrades in the aisle. "He's a good man. He's got an aura. He's got somethin' to say."

Even among his closest cronies, he's in the crowd, but not of the crowd. Except to his three wives, perhaps, he seems to exist in an eerie bubble of adulation. Band members speak of him like fanatic fans. His friends look to him for direction. He's constantly referred to as the "guru" or "minister" of his flock. An article in *Playboy,* emphasizing his beatific smile and calm presence, was even titled "Saint Willie."

Sometimes it seems like Willie's treated more like the pope than a person.

Willie was once told that people thought of him as "very mystical," that being in his presence was "spooky." What did he think of that description? "Well no," he replied, "at least not to myself. I don't seem that way to me."

To try to understand the contradictory traits of Willie, a person might want to consider the fact that at some point around the late '60s, early '70s, Willie changed his point of view.

The early Willie of Texas and Nashville was a highly erratic, hot-tempered, negative thinker, dominated by hair-trigger emotions, who could drag the worst out of any situation, who constantly flagellated himself with guilt and self-pity, who quit jobs without notice, lost guitars on moving trains, and sold songs for a song.

Then Willie got into reading some positive-type writers and decided to turn his mental life around. Smoking a lot of grass, which leveled off his super-hyper temperament, he started letting his brain have a little more influence over his feelings. He mentally transformed years of chaos and negative experiences from defeat into wisdom.

In short, he became a person who inspired confidence, who viewed life's ups and downs philosophically, to whom you could turn for advice.

In addition to golf and music, "I guess my other pastime is thinking," Willie once revealed. "I think a lot."

A writer once told Willie how the writer didn't like to do psychedelic drugs anymore, because it had got him thinking he had to go out into the mountains and face the devil. The whole thing just got too heavy. "You found out who it was," Willie commented of the man's fear of facing the devil. "It wasn't him, it was you."

Through the writings of Kahlil Gibran, Edgar and Hugh Cayce, the Rosicrucians, and others who espouse theories of reincarnation, Willie has looked closely at himself, his own life, and humanity at large. Although he sometimes seems to suffer from Christian guilt, he no longer claims to have deep Christian beliefs. But he does say he believes strongly in positive thinking.

He relates positive thinking to reincarnation in the sense that nothing—no matter how bad—is definite or permanent. Rather, all life is just moving in a circle or cyle that returns to the one master mind, only to reappear in a better form. Negativity has no permanence, and Willie abhors it.

"I just can't be around anything or anybody negative," he says. He compares himself to an ex-alcoholic, who can't afford to take even one drink for fear of slipping. "It's an amazing thing," he adds, "it snowballs. Just like one negative thought will snowball into a whole big bunch of 'em, a positive thought will do the same thing. It helps me continually."

He often sits and ponders reincarnation and "karma," which he simply expresses as "what goes around, comes around."

"Karma," he says, "is simple truth. You reap what you sow."

"We're taught to believe that all men are created equal," he quietly told Chet Flippo, "and yet we know that one guy is born without eyes and one guy is born with eyes. So that's not equal. They had to be born together in the beginning. At one time, we were all born at the same time.

"God imagines everyone, so we're all images of him—in the beginning. He made us all in the beginning, and since then, we've been coming back and forth. First time we came in, we knew a lot, and we've lost it along the way.

"Being down here is kinda like goin' through the university: you go through one grade at a time, and if you fail, you gotta go back and take those tests again."

Willie had a life reading done a few years ago. "It said I'd done something good in my last life, and that I was up for a reward in this one," he revealed, then added with a twist, "so you see, I figure I'm just getting what I deserve."

If he's getting the riches he deserves, Willie makes a point of passing them on to others. The one trait absolutely no one disagrees about is Willie's generosity.

His altruistic spirit is a combination of principles and a naturally warm-hearted, giving nature. "He's got a heart bigger than a watermelon," his father once said. "He sees somebody that needs something, and he reaches in his pocket. Whatever bill he gets hold of first, he gives away."

"He just can't say no to anybody," Connie agrees. "I've seen Will so tired he can't go any further. Then someone will ask one more thing from him, and he'll do it."

Those who don't understand that Willie's generosity springs in part from conviction, sometimes see it as a personality defect. "Willie's biggest flaw," one longtime acquaintance said, "is that he just can't say no. He's a notorious easy touch for people needing money, and people who need favors. He gets into trouble sometimes, because he overextends himself."

Willie admits that at one time, he got tired of people always asking him for favors. "It used to bother me," he says, "but now I realize I'm fortunate enough to be in a position to help others, so I do it."

Every Christmas Willie and the band used to play the holiday party at the Austin pool hall Willie had given Pop and Mom Nelson to run. Willie was walking up to the door one wintry night near Christmas, and a man walked up with a tray of belt buckles and asked Willie to buy one.

"How many have you got?" Willie asked. "Fifteen," the man replied. "I'll take 'em all," Willie responded, to the man's profuse thanks.

Walking into the festive pool hall, Willie started handing out the belt buckles, a warm "Merry Christmas" with each one. "Man, that was beautiful," said one of his band members. "You made that guy happy and gave him some Christmas money."

"No," Willie replied, "I made seventeen people happy. I made him happy, I made me happy, and I made fifteen people happy by giving them belt buckles. That's what it's all about."

It is parables of thought and action such as this that have made Willie the spiritual leader of the family.

"Someone once asked me," Willie recalls, "if I thought I had more insight into life than the next fellow. I didn't know how to answer," he says. "I still don't—except that maybe you can get an education

341

from loving and being loved, from hurting and being hurt. And if that's the case, I guess my education is pretty broad."

A life of ups and downs, highs and lows, has given him a calm that is almost eerily unflappable. Hyperalert, and always acutely aware of what's going on around him, at the same time Willie projects a mysterious aura of total calm and control. ("What people don't know," Willie once grinned, "is that I'm completely ripped.")

Don Bowman says the only person he knows who comes close to being as unflappable and laid back as Willie is Bobby Bare. "He just doesn't get upset," he says of Willie. "I mean, if he really wanted to get into it, he could drive himself crazy in twenty minutes! But all he wants is that guitar tuned and waitin' for him when he hits the stage every night."

Once Willie and several associates were flying to concert promoter Happy Shahan's ranch in Bracket-ville, Texas. When the plane came in to land, something quirked and the small private plane flipped over.

Hearing that Willie Nelson was in the crash, reporters flocked to the scene. Nobody was hurt, and as Willie stood quietly by the wreckage, a reporter asked what had gone through his mind. "Anytime you can walk away from a landing," he mildly replied, "it's perfect."

"There's a certain peacefulness in his eyes," says actor Jan Michael Vincent. Vincent went to visit Willie one day and ended up staying a week. "He's the guru," Vincent explained, "if not the chaplain."

"Willie's like a lighthouse, like a preacher," says Gary Busey, who played the lead in *The Buddy Holly Story*. "Every time I find myself in an emotional pressure situation, the first thought in my mind is, what would Willie do? 'Cause nothing seems to rattle him. I've had some problems here lately with my mind," he said in 1981. "Oh gosh, everything's moving so fast, what gear should I be in? And he'll tell me."

"A lot of people are watching me," Willie realizes. "Waiting to see what I'll do. I'm supposed to be old enough to know what I'm doing. A lot of people ask me for advice.

"I don't know if I've ever helped anyone," he modestly demurs, "but I enjoy being asked advice, giving my opinion.

"I always have an opinion on everything," he happily concedes. "I probably think I know everything—it gets me in trouble daily."

Well, as Kirby Warnock once said, Willie can't make up his mind if he wants to be in the pulpit or the honky-tonks. As he chaplains his flock, the irrepressible emergence of his wild side also gets him in trouble—occasionally.

Willie's driving, of course, is now legendary. He tears up the countryside piloting a silver-blue Mercedes 450 SEL.

"When the big money started rolling in, everybody told me I had to go right out and buy a Mercedes," Willie grins. "The only Mercedes I'd ever known was a girl I took out a long time ago in Mexico; though, come to think of it, she was pretty hot stuff."

His driver's license coming and going due to

"habitual" traffic offenses, Willie, who once said he likes to drive on tequila, reports that "at about one hundred forty-five miles per hour . . . she begins to lift off."

But in 1979 all his road renegadery was forgiven. The Texas Department of Public Safety starred Willie in a series of TV spots urging Texans to stick to the fifty-five-mile-an-hour speed limit: "Shotgun Willie likes to save gas and stay alive. Shotgun Willie likes to drive laid back at fifty-five."

In January of 1980, Willie was trapped and ticketed for driving laid back at eighty-five. He was late for a concert in Abilene, explained backsliding Willie, later seen sporting a burnt-orange T-shirt with the number eighty-five on the back and "laid back Willie" on the front.

Honeysuckle Rose was an autobiographical bad boy's confession for Willie. "I guess I've done all those things at one time or another," he said of Buck Bonham's antics in the movies, 'and more—too many to get in a movie."

As director Jerry Schatzberg commented, Willie was "very natural" in the love scenes. "The man's been married three times. . . . He's had a lot of experience there."

Willie, who sometimes calls blacks "niggers" and women "broads" or "chicks," has been hung with a few epithets himself. Asked if he was a "male chauvinist," he hesitated, then replied, "Uh, I probably am. I see all these terms and I say, 'Well, I guess I'm one of them—redneck and hippie and chauvinist."

344

It's safe to say Willie is a rural southerner, and a Texan on top of that, and attitudes typical of his up-bringing still enhance his personality.

He's never been one to shy away from the sight of a gun, for example. In 1975, *Picking Up the Tempo* editor Nelson Allen reminded him that in certain places "up north," they put people in jail for shooting a burglar breaking into their home.

"That's why we've got to be careful that we don't get into any of that shit down here in Texas," Willie warned. "I don't think we will. They can pass all the laws they want, but they're not going to disarm anybody who wants to be armed."

Although no real gun-totin', pistol-wavin' type, Willie will take up arms to settle a minor domestic spat. Once, when Lana left her husband and came to stay with Willie (inspiring the song "Sister's Comin' Home"), the irate husband charged over to take pos-session of their baby daughter. Willie and Paul English repelled him with a light spattering of gun-shots. "Daddy and Paul were taking up positions in the trees," Lana reported proudly.

Although reserved, Willie is not passive and not shy. "No, I don't think I'm shy," Willie opines. "I'm quiet, there's a difference. I don't think you can be shy and go on stage."

By nature, despite the mental control he practices, Willie's a person who can get uptight easily, and who, at one point in his life, tended to make snap decisions.

Although Crash Stewart contended that never in their five-year partnership did he and Willie have a cross word, he added, in the *San Antonio Light* that

345

"I learned in my early days with Willie that he was very intelligent and could make a proper decision, but I also learned not to trust Willie with a snap decision or allow him to make a decision when he was tired or upset.

"If I saw that a snap judgment from Willie wasn't the correct decision, I would suggest that he think it over, and in about twenty-four hours, the phone would ring and Willie would give me a decision which was, in my opinion, the right decision."

These days Willie lets the decision-making process ferment even longer than twenty-four hours. "One thing we've all learned from Willie," says his roadie T. Snake, "is that very few decisions have to be made immediately. If you just let things slide, they'll usually sort themselves out."

When he goes too long between tokes, Willie admits he gets "hyper." "Most people smoke to get high," *People* quoted a Willie pal, "Willie smokes to get normal."

The famous "natural Nelson" can flair at the slightest irritation. Willie has been known to rip insistently ringing telephones off walls, and to kick down a special peeve—closed doors. "I can't tell you how many doors he has kicked down," Connie laughed. "Sometimes he even has the key in his pocket."

The reason he likes grass, says Willie (who enjoys watching Sesame Street, most especially when stoned), is that "when I smoke a half-joint or joint, I don't get uptight about little things that go wrong."

He also uses jogging, an integral part of his new, positive life style, to keep his temper in line. "He has a temper," once wrote a close friend, "but he has learned to control it. I've seen times he's been real upset at someone goofing off, but he's been able to keep his composure.

"Before he says anything to him," the friend had observed, "he'll try to do some jogging to work off his steam. Then he has a clear head and can talk objectively with the person."

These days, rising above it all with a detachment that implies wisdom, Willie wrote Jack Hurst, "is a distinctive mixture of warm politeness and quiet reserve."

But Willie the roughneck constantly bubbles under. "His manner is so gentlemanly during an interview," Hurst continued, "that when four-letter words fall out of his beard, as they occasionally do, they are shocking."

"I'm a philosopher," Willie once announced to a newspaper reporter, taking a drag off a joint, and chasing it down with a swig of Perrier. He belched.

"I get off on belching," he grinned, Cheshire cat-style.

Although he's developed a well-informed business sense, Willie is still frequently oblivious to everyday methods of organization—like time.

Darrell Royal recalls that one day while playing golf, a fellow golfer asked Willie what time it was. "Willie looked at his watch. "Ten after," he promptly replied. "Ten after what?" the man asked. "I dunno," Willie said. "I ain't got no little hand on this thing."

Shrewd and intelligent, Willie's been rediscovering in recent years the traits that once made him consider becoming a lawyer. The owner of numerous real-estate holdings and business enterprises, Willie is an out-and-out workaholic, who's always got a dozen money-making projects going at once. "When things start settling down, I know it's time to start something new," he says.

Daily newspaper in hand, he's an island of calm in a sea of frantic associates, running off in all directions at once, openly admitting that they don't really know what they're doing, but since it's for Willie, it's bound to turn out all right.

He scans the newspapers "to try to figure out whether we're going to end up in a depression, whether we're going to get gasoline. I'm interested in all that," he announces engagingly. "Aren't you?"

He works hard "simply because I enjoy working," and unlike the days with the Cherokee Cowboys, once he gets paid for working, he doesn't like to throw it away. Does he gamble in Vegas? "I don't really do that much gambling," Willie replies. "I like to play nickel slots machines and a little blackjack. Not anything heavy."

Willie has an amazing ability to cultivate the friendship of people in high places. In addition to frequently being involved in some event with high-level Texas politicians, Willie was, during the Carter regime, first pal of the President of the United States.

Willie was constantly dropping in and out of the White House for lunch or soirees for stock-car racers. Carter was constantly dropping in on Willie's concerts (to sing "Amazing Grace" on stage, even). Rosalyn complained that the President played "Red-Headed

Stranger" too loud at night and kept her awake.

Thanks to knowing the prez, Willie found socialites turning up at his shows. "I've always liked country music," confided horse-set hostess Anita Madden, famous for her Kentucky Derby galas, "but I didn't tell anyone. It's more chic to like it now."

Willie even got blamed for Carter's losing the election. Pointing out that Willie botched singing the "Star-Spangled Banner" at the Democratic National Convention, Walter Richter wryly observed: "Consider the words that Willie just flat omitted, namely: 'and the rockets' red glare, the bombs bursting in air' . . . this was the first real indication that the Democrats were soft on defense."

In his own defense, Willie just puts it all down to friendship. "I used to be one of the first to criticize people who would use their position to influence people to vote in a certain way," Willie granted in 1980, but as for Carter, "The guy's just a friend of mine. If you were running for President, and you and I were friends, I'd be down here playing for you."

Darrell Royal, no slouch in the fame department himself, backs Willie up: "I've seen him turn off to powerful people who could help him, and turn down good money for gigs he didn't like."

Connie says Willie doesn't "ever want anybody to think that success has changed him."

He calls the flashy diamond horseshoe-shaped ring he wears (a gift from Paul who acquired it from a friend turned fence), his "one vulgar display of wealth." He's plenty wealthy, but he tries not to be ostentatious. He doesn't care much for pomp and circumstance.

When presented the key to a good-sized southern city, he later passed it on—with equal formality—to the nine-year-old sister of one of his sidemen.

"Willie's appeal is that he never plays the part of the high-rolling star," says Paul English. "They get the feeling from him that he's a real, normal person up there, not trying to put on a show."

Although he's got his thinking cap on firm, Willie the poet and songwriter still, in the end, navigates by feeling. "Everything I do," he claims, "is by feel. I may have a master plan in the back of my shoe, but I make my important decisions based on one hundred percent feel."

A man who thinks hard and feels deep is a powerful combination. Hank Williams felt deep. As Chet Atkins says, "The normal things just didn't excite Hank." Willie, however, is a man of exceeding balance. For every wasted night, there's a productive day (or vice versa).

Artistically conceding that expiring legendarily like Hank Williams, Billy Holiday, and Bessie Smith is "the way you ought to go," Willie also admitted to Roy Blount, "I guess I'm just too chicken shit ever to entirely self-destruct."

"In fact," Willie once concluded while nibbling fruit cocktail in a luxurious hotel room, "I think people just identify with me emotionally as a survivor."

What we finally know about Willie is that, like his characters in song, he just keeps on keeping on. The atom of unknowability that bonds his mass of human contradictions together, will, probably, never be penetrated.

Reporters sometimes try. But Willie has his methods. He'll divert an uncomfortable question sideways, or throw it off balance with humor. He doesn't mind distributing a few good-natured boners, either, such as the fact that he's been married "four or five times."

Reporters who arrive with penetrating lists of inquiries are often greeted by members of the band who present them with a joint of that $3,500-a-pound grass, or who introduce them to the joys of the "pillowcase bong," after which the writer finds his questions somehow exceedingly unimportant.

"I don't know," puzzled one excellent journalist. "Doing an interview with Willie is like being in a presence. It's tough to ask the hard questions."

Writer Roy Blount "Wrasslin' with This Thing Called Willie Nelson," as he titled his *Esquire* article, finally just walked out Willie's door, gloomily concluding that "It's disturbing to sit around too long with a country singer whom you feel more forlorn than."

"I can't think of anything I wouldn't want to talk about," Willie repeats, egging on the writers, "because I don't have any secrets."

Maybe he doesn't have any secrets—but is there really anybody who doesn't have any secrets? Even secrets from themselves?

Well, to not get so deep in the forest we fail to see the trees, it probably makes sense to just take Pop Nelson's word at face value.

"Willie always says," his dad once declared with a smile, "there are three things important to him: that Mercedes Benz, his beat-up guitar, and the ones who love him."

ON THE ROAD AGAIN . . . AND AGAIN . . .
AND . . .

Fast Eddie and the Electric Japs make their permanent address, as harmonica player Mickey Raphael puts it, on "Show Bus Number One."

Fast Eddie a/k/a Willie Hugh Nelson got his nickname for the speed with which he could dodge a bar fight. The Electric Japs got their nickname because the whole crew's just getting too famous to register as Willie Nelson and Family anymore.

In 1978 Willie both dumfounded and dazzled the nation by releasing the precedent-shattering "Stardust," a collection of ten favorite golden oldies culled from the pop hits of his boyhood days. As far from an outlaw's beard and bandanna as lavender and old lace, it was a smash.

Now a whole new audience of middle-aged fans, many of whom had never even heard his name before, jumped on the Willie wagon. In short order he was dubbed the "Platinum Outlaw" as "Stardust" became his first certified million seller.

"Maybe for someone that was in the position I was

in, it sounded a bit strange to do 'Stardust,' " Willie concedes, "but if you had followed me from the beginning up to where I was at that point, it wasn't strange at all."

The Willie Nelson phenomenon was becoming like an uncontrolled nuclear reaction—it just kept exploding, mushrooming bigger and bigger. As "Stardust" twinkled at the top of the charts, "Red-Headed Stranger," now over three years old, still rode a firm spot in the country top forty.

That same year saw Willie put two more Grammys on his mantel: Best Country Vocal Performance/Male for "Georgia on My Mind" and Best Country Vocal Performance/Duo for "Mamas, Don't Let Your Babies Grow Up To Be Cowboys."

The Country Music Hall of Fame in Nashville, shrine to country music's greatest, invited him to make a contribution. Willie sent a pair of sneakers and a headband.

Then in 1979, Willie Nelson, certified megastar and movie star, was nominated for the Country Music Association's most prestigious honor: Entertainer of the Year. He was up against Kenny Rogers.

Willie hadn't even attended a CMA awards show since 1976. But this year, there were two carrots: he would get to perform with Leon Russell, his co-everything on their recently released "One for the Road," plus he thought he would get to perform with one of his biggest heroes: Ernest Tubb. (That one didn't work out, though. Tubb, indeed one of the original outlaws, declined to perform without his own band.)

Also, Willie noted, the CMA, afraid of being stood

up again, "sent a jet after me, and I couldn't disappoint them."

If he won, his name would join one of the most distinguished lists in country music: Eddie Arnold, Glen Campbell, Johnny Cash, Merle Haggard, Charley Pride, Loretta Lynn, Roy Clark, Charlie Rich, John Denver, Mel Tillis, Ronnie Milsap, and Dolly Parton.

That night at the show, as he lost all the awards leading up to the biggest, Willie's hopes faded. "I thought for a while that Kenny Rogers was going to sweep all the awards," Willie admitted, "and I was probably the most shocked person in the building when my name was called."

Entertainer of the Year: Willie Nelson. The only winner to rouse a standing ovation from the formally attired audience, Willie stepped to the stage in a cowboy shirt and blue jeans, hair immaculately plaited in braids.

Accepting, he mentioned three men; all entertainers even more than mere singers in their heyday, all now eclipsed by the changing fortunes of time. "I'm reminded of Little Jimmy Dickens, Faron Young, Ferlin Husky," he quietly said to the national television audience in whom the names mostly elicited puzzled frowns. "I'd like to see those guys up here. They deserve it."

Although gracious and smiling, Willie was not overwhelmed. "Oh sure, it's a big thrill to win," he said later, "but I could have lived without it.

"It's music which keeps me going, not awards."

Despite being the holder of four Grammys, as well as the title Entertainer of the Year, Willie plays as many road dates as the lowliest star hustling the country trying to get his career off the ground.

Why?

Willie is a performing junkie. After cutting thirty-three sides in New York for his "Shotgun Willie" album, Willie dashed to the airport to catch a cab. "What's your hurry?" demanded a New York friend. "We gotta get back to Texas," Willie yelled as the cab pulled off. "We play in Round Rock tomorrow."

"I don't know what I'd do if I quit," Willie says simply. "I'd probably go crazy and get old and die in a couple of years, if I quit playing music. I don't think I could live without it."

To Willie, playing music is just plain fun. Performing takes place under the natural law as revealed by Saint Willie: "As long as it's fun we'll do it, and when it stops being fun, we won't do it."

Performing is not only fun, it's essential for his mental health. If he gets away from the stage too long, he gets to be a "disagreeable person."

"If I had my choice," Willie declares, "I'd play music four hours a night, seven days a week." Or, as they say in Texas, "as long as two or three are gathered in his name, Willie will pick and sing. . . ."

So, off they go, thirty motel rooms strong, via plane, auto, four buses, two tractor trailers . . . Fast Eddie and the Electric Japs . . . on the road again.

Showbus One, its destination sign predicting "Happy Tripping," is rolling home for Willie and the band. It's "like being on a ship or sailboat," he once said. "And you have to get your bus legs out here, just like you have to get your sea legs on a ship. Once you get them, you can dance up and down the aisle like every-body else."

A humongous animal of a man, nicknamed Beast, commands Le Café, an entire bus totally devoted to the pleasures of the stomach, i.e., food. Roadies, among the best in the business, cram a third bus: T. Snake, Poodie, B.C., Schroder, Kepkie, all with nick-names as colorful as their T-shirt slogans ("Love Your Enemies: Whiskey, Women, Tobacco").

Management types, the sound crew, equipment men, bus drivers, souvenir salesmen, a hairdresser (to plait Willie's red locks into braids), groupies, an ever-changing sea of assorted hangers-on sardine into the other bus. The tractor trailers transport sound and lighting gear.

Willie T-shirts, belt buckles, and souvenirs fill two additional vans. This sideshow is commandeered by Beau Franks, a Texan generally decked out in snake-skin boots and tons of gold, silver, and turquoise jewelry. He met Willie when he was an ad salesman at an Austin radio station. A week later, Willie saw him sitting in the front row of a concert, picked him out, and said, "Hi, Beau." He's been with Willie ever since.

Willie and the band once played on Bob Dylan's Rolling Thunder Revue, and "The Rolling Smoke Revue," as it's sometimes called, has the same atmo-sphere of a movable feast with a constantly changing human menu.

A hardcore of about twenty, including the band, has been handpicked by Willie over the years. Poodie, who grew up near Abbott, is Willie's road manager, running a crackerjack organization that only appears to thrive on confusion.

B.C. (Billy Cooper) is lieutenant road manager, security head, and, like others, an adept joint roller. T. (for "the," of course) Snake is general factotum. A lanky six-foot, ex-paratrooper, Snake, who spent a few days in the Bay of Pigs invasion, if asked his duties, will likely reply with a tight, thin-lipped grin, "Well, what do you want done?" But mostly Snake, who actually has a wide boyish smile, is registered as "confidant," assigned to Willie personally to make sure he "doesn't leave his shampoo in the tub."

The whole hybrid bunch, which often balloons up to as many as eighty on the road, are about as diverse as the audiences they draw: good ol' boys with big bellies and pointy-toed boots; good-looking, long-haired, bearded types who simulate college drop-ins or dropouts; heavies with ornate tattoos who look like charter members of the Bandidos, Texas' version of the Hell's Angels. The women, one writer noted, come in two kinds—real naked or real old-fashioned.

Riding the nation in silvery, shiny Showbus One with Willie are the guys in the band. Willie's band is a rather stable bunch in a business where most bands change personnel about as frequently as the guards at Buckingham Palace.

Paul, who these days carries a paunch over his silver-tooled belt, is a charter member—he's been with Willie twenty-seven years. Bee goes back to Ridgetop days. Bobbie, of course, plays piano—she's been with Willie since birth.

"Only band I know of that's played together

longer'n us was Elvis' band," Paul says proudly. "Rolling Stones, maybe, I ain't sure about them, but I'll bet we play more in one year than they do in three."

The basic lineup of the band is Willie on guitar and vocals; Jody Payne, guitar and vocals; Paul, drums; Bobbie, piano; Mickey Raphael, harmonica; Chris Etheridge, bass; Bee, bass; Grady Martin, guitar. Sometimes they also use Rex Ludwick on drums; Leon Russell frequently sits in for Bobbie; and Johnny Gimble tours frequently playing fiddle.

Mustachioed Jody Payne, with the gaunt, kindly face of a western marshal, used to be married to Sammi Smith. He turned up one day to play for Sammi on a bill along with Willie and just stayed.

Zany prankster Dan "Bee" Spears, came along when Jimmy Hardmen went into the army. He played bass with Willie on and off for ten years before leaving for "personal reasons" to join Waylon's band.

Bee was replaced by bearded, dark-haired Chris Etheridge, a hero among the country-rock set. Now in his early 30s, Chris has been on the road half his life, including stints with the Byrds, and then, in company with Gram Parsons, with the Flying Burrito Brothers.

One day around 1978, Willie heard a knock on the door, and there stood Bee, announcing he wanted to come back. "What took you so long?" Willie happily welcomed, and promptly had a band with *two* bass players.

Mickey Raphael, the lanky, sexy, brilliant harmonica player, blew tuba in his high-school marching band until graduating from a North Dallas prep school in 1969. He took up harmonica while flunking

358

out of junior college, played with Waylon for a while, then met Willie at a party after a Dallas football game hosted by Darrell Royal.

Willie noticed this guy "just playing fantastic," and when Mickey showed up with his harmonica at a benefit in Lancaster, Texas, a few weeks later, he just stayed, too. That was about ten years ago.

Sandy-haired, round-faced Rex got added sort of by accident, while they were trying to launch Jody on a solo career. Paul would come out to play behind Jody, and the crowd would go nuts thinking he was about to introduce Willie. Jody hardly had a chance in the ensuing uproar. So, they added Rex to introduce Jody and play drums behind him.

Then at the CMA awards, two drum sets were already on stage and Paul invited Rex to come on up and play. "Rex gives us more of a rock feel," Paul says of the band that now has *two* drummers. "I'm more country myself; I like playing with brushes. I use sticks only for dynamics."

Gray-haired, Buddha-esque, good ol' boy Grady, masks sizzling talent behind his easygoing ways. A relatively new addition, he's known Willie since Nashville days when he played on many of Willie's RCA records. In his own world, Grady is as much a legend as Willie is in his.

He played on Buddy Holly's very first record, picked on many of Elvis' records in the '60s, and added those hot licks to Brenda Lee's early hits. Grady "literally produced" the tons of hits he played on, Harlan Howard says. "If there was any sound come up on 'em, any unusual sound, he came up with it," Howard swears.

When it's Grady's turn for a long lead on stage, Willie often just stops dead in his tracks, turns, and watches—wrapped up in the wizardy of Grady's flowing fingers.

Spiffy, clean-cut Johnny Gimble fielding his all-American Will Rogers smile, is equally a legend in the annals of fiddling. Originally with Bob Wills, Gimble is surely the feelingest fiddle player in the world. When he smiles that big smile and cuts into the opening licks of "Faded Love," the universe just seems to wipe away a tear of joy.

At bedtime, when the rest of the guys are lounging around in grimy T-shirts and frayed cut-offs, neat-as-a-pin Johnny will pop to the front to bid all good night in his crisply pressed, blue cotton pajamas.

Shy, high-strung Bobbie, metabolism like a hummingbird, is idolized by her protective, admiring, all-male companions. "Her playing is so simple and to the point." So Chris Etheridge praises the woman the band refers to as "an angel flying too close to the ground" in their rough-and-rowdy world.

Bobbie says she doesn't think much about being the only female in the band, but she keeps pretty much to herself, spending the long hours on the road reading and missing her current husband, Jack, a successful stockbroker.

"You know," she told Joan Ackerman-Blount in her slow, wondering voice, "what I really miss on the road is a good cup of coffee. It just knocks me out when I get served coffee in a real china cup."

Around 1979, talk surfaced that Bobbie was thinking about retiring from the road, and, sure enough,

Leon Russell started sitting in in her place.

Russell, a vivid performer who hooted and hollered in the song choruses, talked to the audience, and was apt to jump up and do a jig on stage; added a whole new dimension to what was temporarily billed as the "Willie Nelson–Leon Russell Show."

"Leon is just a genius, that's all," Willie says.

The band is, and always has been, a labor of love for Willie. Till the early or mid-'70s, he consistently lost money just trying to keep the band together and on the road. These days, however, Willie's boys are some of the best paid in the business.

Talk has it that Paul made $150,000 in 1978 just as a drummer. Plus the guys get a $10,000-a-whack bonus every time Willie uses them on an album. That's over and above the regular union scale they earn in the studio; over and above the top-flight accommodations and tasty meals provided by Beast.

"I'd rather give it to the guys who are working for me than give it to the government," Willie once explained. "And once you get in a certain tax bracket, you're giving it away, anyway."

"Willie's got the highest paid staff in country music," Paul asserted to *Newsweek*, "but a lot of us have worked for nothing in the past, and we'd do it again for him, if we had to."

Money helps, but the cement that holds Willie's band together is a tight, double-bonding glue: friendship with each other and respect for Willie.

"The thing we've got going for us is that we like each other," Willie once said, "we sincerely like each other."

And one and all totally adores—if not worships—Willie. Even the guys in the band, who see him in his underwear, talk about Willie like the most far-removed, fantasizing fan.

"I don't think Willie has ever had a bad thought," Mickey Raphael once rather astonishingly offered.

"Seriously," Jody Payne told *Country Style*, "Willie Nelson is the greatest man I have ever met in my life. Who is your favorite music writer?" he interrogated the reporter. "Short story writer? Novelist? Mystery writer? What I'm trying to say," he explains, "is that if you were to ask me those questions, then Willie Nelson would get my personal vote for all categories."

"We have a simple understanding," Larry Trader wrote in the *San Antonio Light*. "Will tells me what he wants done, and I do it. I wake up every morning excited about doing things that'll make Will happy." Truly—the man means it.

It's Willie who calls the shots and Willie who's the focus of all attention. Poodie, B.C., Snake, and the others run an exceedingly tight ship, all targeted on seeing to the needs of Willie. "It's amazing," says one envious observer; "all Willie has to do is walk out on stage, pick up his guitar, and sing."

Willie, Darrell Royal says, has a wonderful, subtle way of dealing with the members of the family. "He never tells anybody to do this or do that," reveals Royal; "it's 'Would you?' or 'Why not try this?'" The thank you is equally subtle: "Just a smile from Willie can let you know that he really appreciates what you are doing," Royal says.

If he's freed from many details, it's still Willie who

carries the ultimate responsibility for the whole family, their musical direction, and their financial futures. This heavy mental load, plus the physical strain of two hundred and fifty nights a year on the road, caused Willie to collapse on a Dallas stage in 1976 after a strenuous round of concerts.

In August, 1981, after doing fifty-four shows in twenty-eight days, Willie was jogging in Hawaii, plunged into a pool for a swim, and suffered a collapsed lung.

Although he can certainly afford to fly to all his shows, Willie likes to ride the bus. That's where he can escape from it all, from the ringing phones, the continual demands of outsiders; where he can relax from it all—and keep moving.

"I haven't seen much of the country," he admits (as Loretta Lynn once did), "but I've been all over it a thousand times, just laying in the back with the blinds drawn. I guess it's the perpetual motion I like."

Willie's perpetual-motion machine is a cross-country Greyhound customized to the hilt.

The lounge area up front has a Betamax video player, two color televisions, and an audiophile-quality stereo system—all built in at ceiling height. Below are swivel easy chairs, a small restaurant-style booth and table, a built-in couch, and a boat-size galley with ice chest.

The middle section is lined with stacks of four sleeping bunks on each side of the aisle.

At the back, through a private door, is Willie's room: a bed, a couch, and a personal ice chest well supplied with beer.

One night when they were playing North Dakota, Frank Fools Crow, the eighty-nine-year old spiritual advisor for the Lakota Indian Nation, walked up on stage. He presented Willie with the hat he wears on the back of the "Stardust" album, and recited a prayer in his native tongue. Addressed to Grandfather God, he asked for mercy and relief from outsiders encroaching on the lands of his people. His grandson handed Willie a poster of the Four Winds Prayer in English.

The Four Winds Prayer, the only poster on the bus, hangs above Willie's customary seat in the lounge, flanked by furry puppets of Cookie Monster and Big Bird.

Most anything is liable to happen on the bus.

Fans keep the bus supplied with presents for Willie—a two-tiered cake topped with a tiny pair of icing tennis shoes, a near-real-sized, turkey-shaped bottle of 101 proof Wild Turkey whiskey. All offerings are gratefully wolfed down by the band to the last crumb or drop.

Comradeship is enhanced by glass gallon jars of moonshine (with dozens of corpselike cherries dead of an overdose on the bottom) and thick cigars of high-priced, high-powered grass. "One of the things I like about smoking," Willie says, "is that it's something like a ritual. You pass it around. It creates a sort of fellowship."

The real high, though, are the concerts—the massive doses of unqualified adoration dished out by cheering fans. It takes the band hours, winding into the wee ones of the morning, to pull down from these highs. Intense poker games lead the therapy, with Snake gleefully signaling to one and all what Bee is holding, while the trash cans pile up with barbecue chip bags, ripped-open Chips Ahoy sacks, squashed cigarette boxes, and empty beer cans.

Or Bee, fully endorsed by Willie as one of the craziest people he knows, may pull out the culmination of years of research: the notorious "pillowcase bong."

A device frequently road-tested on writers, this invention consists of a pillowcase with a small hole cut out of the stitched end. A long cardboard tube, like the ones in rolls of paper towels, is inserted partway through the hole. On the outside end of the tube is a second hole. A fat joint is pushed into this.

The subject puts his head inside the pillowcase. The researcher lights up the joint. The experiment consists of staying enpillowcased for the entire joint. Only the most stainless-steel-brained can count to five on emerging.

One night Bee decided to introduce a public relations man to the family spirit. Plowing through the jammed bus wearing a woman's slip, Bee crash-landed on the startled man's lap, pulling him, along with Willie, out into the aisle. "Now you can show everybody what this crowd's really like," Willie volunteered to the publicist's photographer, as he struggled to his knees.

By four A.M. everybody may be calm enough, or drunk enough, or high enough, to sleep—in a bunk, in the aisle, or snoozing in the booth, beer can still dangling in hand.

Over at Le Café, Beast greets the morning as commander of the pièce de résistance of the caravan—the former mobile dressing rooms of Porter Wagoner and Dolly Parton converted into a cream- and brown-striped chow bus, with complete kitchen and eight two-seater tables, at a cost of $56,000.

"Willie's a down-home person," Beast told the *American Statesman.* "He likes plain food that sticks to the ribs, like black-eyed peas and chicken-fried steak. Every once in a while he'll say, 'Let's have pinto beans, cornbread, and buttermilk with sliced onions.' "

Beast, in his middle 30s, started washing dishes at age thirteen in his hometown of Iowa City, Iowa. He used to cook for rock and roll groups like the Beach Boys, Kiss, and the Rolling Stones, but got tired of their idiosyncrasies—the Rolling Stones, for example, insisted on tea in their dressing room—in a sterling-silver tea service.

Willie likes to take his own cook along, because it helps everybody stay a little healthier, and it helps him keep his weight down. He doesn't eat many sweets or drink carbonated drinks and may just pour himself a bowl of cereal before a show. A dedicated jogger, he has dropped from one hundred eighty to one hundred fifty pounds, and even got gigantic, hairy Beast into jogging. At one point Beast lost seventy pounds—down to a svelte two hundred and forty.

Dinner is served promptly at six P.M., the chuck bus holds sixteen at a sitting, and some days Beast will cook for as many as sixty. When the mood strikes, he'll set up a concert of charcoal grills and treat one and all to spicy, Texas-style barbecue.

Although the band may play twenty straight one-night stands, despite little inconveniences along the way, "You more or less overcome them," Willie says, "when you feel like you're always moving on."

As wandering Willie and his band of gypsies ramble and roll o'er the face of our nation, is there any word he'd like to send to the friends and neighbors back home? Willie ponders that one a spell, then roguishly smiles: "Just tell 'em we're having a hell of a time out here."

WHERE'S THE SHOW?

During the first few months he worked with Willie, Mickey Raphael seriously considered quitting.

He just couldn't figure out where on earth Willie was coming from musically. Finally it dawned on Mickey that Willie was really more of a jazz artist than a country singer, in terms of the way he came across on stage.

Still, it took two or three months for Mickey, who had been playing with Waylon and B. W. Stevenson, to get comfortable and "competent" on shows with improvising Willie. "Waylon's music is more cut and dried, I guess you'd say," he told Jay Milner. "It took me maybe two or three days to learn to play with them. Waylon's band is tight. Rehearsed.

"Willie just flows the way he feels that night. You can't get it from his records."

"We don't never rehearse," Paul declares of Willie's bunch. With them the arrangements are loose, the phrasing varies, the feeling swoops and sways, rises and falls, depending on where Willie's head and mood are landing.

Every lick the band picks on stage is extemporized around Willie's guitar playing. All the other instruments zero in on Willie, and it's follow that guitar!

In the middle of a song Willie may roam to the front of the stage to put on a hat tossed at him by a fan, and Jody will pick up the lead without a missed beat. Sometimes Jody will do it twenty or thirty times a night—shift from rhythm to lead when Willie drops the lead.

"If you hear something twice in a row you follow it," Paul grins. "We're always workin' on the songs that-away. Willie calls it playin' with 'em instead of just playin' 'em."

A stunned local critic reported that Willie "kingpins probably the loosest show played in front of the loosest audiences in Nevada history" when, in 1978, Willie scored a major breakthrough by getting himself booked in plush Harrah's Hotel in Reno.

Agent Stew Carnall had to buy tickets for several Harrah's executives and fly them to one of Willie's concerts in the midwest just to convince them the idea could work. They flew home raving converts, testifying that Willie was electrifying audiences across the nation. Quickly, he was booked into Harrah's showroom.

Cowboys flew in from all over the country, and Harrah's ritzy gambling resort almost went into shock. "Last night's cocktail show was wild," panted one dazed waitress. "They were even standing on the tables."

"Experiencing a Nelson show is a primer on how-to-break-every-showbiz-taboo-and-still-succeed," continued the critic.

Willie's next Reno booking promised to be so big, it had to be moved to Harrah's Convention Center, where he sold out twelve straight shows.

In 1979, Caesar's Palace decided they had better get in on the act, and took a calculated gamble by booking Willie into their luxurious Circus Maximus showroom in Las Vegas.

Willie had been playing Vegas for twenty-five years, but while the big-time acts crooned "Funny How Time Slips Away" at fancy dinner shows on the Strip, Willie was playing across the tracks downtown at the Golden Nugget, known as the home of country-western entertainment in Vegas.

By the end of his first ninety-minute set in the Circus Maximus, good-timing gamblers were standing on top of the tables and chairs and screaming for more.

"I haven't seen a reaction like this since Elvis," said one incredulous veteran observer. "Who would have believed you would ever see that much excitement in a Las Vegas showroom? I thought Caesar's was crazy when they booked him."

"Harrah's, Panther Hall, the Sportatorium — they're all beer joints," Willie shrugged. "The upholstery's just a little better in some."

Willie's concerts are a blood-tingling half-breed of honky-tonk and hallelujah — the perfect schizophrenic presentation of a sinner who wants to save souls.

One of Willie's old pals, like Don Bowman or Hank Cochran, opens the night. The only hint of Willie is his guitar, sitting on stage, tuned and ready to go.

Willie is hanging around backstage or on the bus, just waiting for the signal from Snake. Snake will poke his head in the door: "You've got fifteen minutes." Willie will nod and light up another joint.

Then it's time. " 'Bye," says Willie, waving his horseshoe diamond big as the Ritz. "I gotta go pick."

He walks out on stage and the audience erupts. The Lone Star flag unfurls, and the crowd drops into Willie's unchanging hands. Willie's been doing virtually the exact same show for years, and nobody, but a few carping critics, seems to mind a bit.

He'll open with "Whiskey River" then segue into "Stay All Night." There'll be a bluesy medley of his biggest songwriting successes: "Funny How Time Slips Away," "Crazy," "Night Life." Then the ballads are jerked to their feet in an onslaught of hell-raising honky-tonk tunes that turn right around and bow their heads to a soul-saving string of old gospel standards.

As memorable as the music itself is the holy-rolling, shit-kicking mania it provokes. A Willie Nelson concert is, as they say, an . . . experience.

The kids are ready to boogie from Willie's first saintly smile. Their parents, hoping to hear "Moonlight in Vermont," stick plugs in their ears. Thus begins a nonstop orgy of the spirit and the flesh.

Although the crowd's geared up for the unsanctified side of the spiritual spectrum, many seem to come away from the shows carrying a mystical, almost religious feeling. As Willie bounces from "Whiskey River" to "Just As I Am," from "Picking Up the Tempo" to "Amazing Grace," the kids that came to get down and dirty, leave, somehow, cleansed.

To those who don't feel it, it's hard to intellectualize: "The music often seems strangely incongruous with the apparent mindlessness it prompts," one critic observed.

"As is often the case with Nelson's performances," which contain "miles and miles of soulful ballads," the songs did not always match the flow of the crowd's "dynamics," an Oakland, California reviewer complained.

The show is a paradox—a sentiment as opposed to common sense. It doesn't all hang together logically, but those who have the ears to hear will even claim to be "healed," to be "cured" by the performance.

Willie admits that he'd heard somewhere, or read somewhere that he was supposed to be able to heal people, "but I never did know that I really healed anybody." As for the story of a man jumping up in the front row, claiming to be cured of paralysis, "I think probably his downer wore off or something," Willie says.

But even a musical peer like Emmylou Harris senses something restorative in Willie's music. "There's a certain benevolence, you know, that goes along with being with Willie," she reveals. "It's a learning experience to see what he is to people, to see what he does to people, and how healing his music can be.

"There's no piousness to it at all. I mean that people can get out there and yell and holler and scream, and then he can silence them with those old hymns," she's observed. "He plays the kinds of music, and does things to people that they need. It almost takes the place of going to church, I think, for a lot of people."

Willie, with his compelling and kindly eyes, who

describes his shows as a "fellowship" or "ritual," has a charismatic way of making each individual listener in the audience feel he's singing for them alone.

As Willie picks and sings, fans begin to pass hats up to the stage—cowboy hats, knitted rooster hats, softball hats—sometimes Willie tries on as many as a dozen hats in a show. Along with the hats come flowers, bottles of Jack Daniel's, and love notes (which Willie will read to himself and stick in his back pocket with a nod of approval).

With Leon on stage looking like Methuselah in cowboy getup; Paul swirling around in his devilish cape; Bobbie, cool and detached in her black witchy woman hat; and forty or so onlookers hanging around on stage under the Lone Star flag; most anything can happen. One night Bee, in red flannel underwear with a pair of shorts à la Superman, walked out on stage with his bass and nobody even noticed.

Willie plays for hours, and hours, and hours, and . . . sometimes he does fifty songs a night. He'll end a set at 11:40 P.M., then announce, "Everybody count to three and get drunk! I don't know what time it is, and I don't care!" Then he'll turn right back around, strike up "Whiskey River" and head straight back into a whole new set.

Then he'll walk off stage, take a few tokes off a joint held by a waiting roadie, walk back on stage, strike up "Whiskey River"; this can go on for four or five hours as band boys meander out on stage to deliver glasses of tequila, vodka, bourbon, cans of cold beer.

Willie seems to have picked up several pointers from that best of bandleaders, Bob Wills. "Bob loved it on stage," Willie wrote in *Country Music Magazine*. "He never took an intermission in his shows. He'd start at eight and play straight through to midnight without a break, and the people would be dancing all the time."

Finally, somewhere between here and eternity, as the evening's perpetual picking peaks, everybody backstage and in the wings—even little Paula and Amy, if they're visiting with Connie—will gather on stage for a mass congregational singing of "Will the Circle Be Unbroken" or "Amazing Grace."

"There's a lot of people who I'm sure experience religious experiences during 'Amazing Grace,' and 'Will the Circle Be Unbroken' and 'Uncloudy Day,'" Willie explained to *Playboy*. "They receive religious experiences without even knowing it. But they're certainly acting like people we've all seen receiving them before."

And as he told Chet Flippo, "In their minds, they are relating the music to something else, and I appreciate that. There *are* answers in music."

The next day, of course, some local civic group, like the Lions Club, will ban "western dances" from their coliseum, because thirteen tables were broken (but paid for). At the Anaheim Stadium in California when Willie played with Merle Haggard, 30,000 fans got to clapping and dancing so boisterously the stadium swayed noticeably, causing alarmed officials to flash a warning on the message board: "For safety purposes, please do not dance on the club level."

Willie says it's just the way their grandmammas and granddaddys acted back at the Whitney Pavilion when he and his brother-in-law booked in Bob Wills in the '40s.

"A lot of beer drinkers who like to dance" he calls revelers of both generations. "It's amazing to have seen it then, and it's amazing to see it now," he rejoices; "to see the same music getting all these people stirred up and enjoying themselves the same way they were twenty-five or thirty years ago. The same songs, even."

Willie seems to truly love and enjoy his fans; to not feel harassed by and imposed on by fans, as many big stars do.

He'll give autograph after autograph, chat with folks, even stand in the pouring rain to talk softly with a bedazzled little girl hanging on crutches. For forty-five minutes, he'll stick around, patiently greeting each person—not like a fan, but like another human being.

Once a young would-be star named Billy sneaked into a posh postconcert reception for wealthy Carter contributors, and handed Willie a copy of his album featuring "A Song for Willie." Willie grinned, tore off the cellophane, and stuck out the album. "Billy," he asked, "will you sign this for me?"

Willie insists his fans be treated fairly. In 1981 it came out that twenty fair directors on a show in California had bought up all 1,400 reserved seats before they were offered to the public. Willie canceled, stating he was not interested in performing anywhere his fans couldn't buy tickets on an open basis.

Furthermore, as Willie has learned from experience, it pays to keep your ears to the ground—to stay aware of what the public's thinking and wanting to hear. "I like to see who's crazy enough to stay around," he explains of his after-show lingering. "I wonder who they are, what they're thinking. It keeps me in touch with who's out there listening."

But one-on-one contact with fans is getting harder for Willie these days. "Used to be Willie could come to a place, walk around before a show, and then go over to his hotel and check in under his real name," says a member of the sound crew. "But not no more. He has to stay in the bus. They'll swarm his ass!"

Despite these problems, Willie shuns the trappings of superstardom. He doesn't like security guards. "Look," he once told a protective associate who had hired six bodyguards to run interference, "it's easier to spot seven people walking through a stage door than it is to spot one man. I can get in and out a lot safer and quicker by myself."

"He doesn't want that bodyguard image," affirms Darrell Royal; "he just starts walking off that stage and never stops, so people just can't get to him."

Just starting and never stopping—that's Willie.

After every tour, Willie says he swears it will be his last. "But after I'm home for a couple of days, I'm ready to go back on the road."

For a man and his band, addicted to freedom, to moving on, the road life is the good life. And as Chris Etheridge pointed out, now that success rides shotgun with them, the deal is a good one.

"Sure we sound happy," Chris told Pete Axthelm in 1978. "Who could ask for a better deal than we've got? Hell, I've been with Willie less than a year, and I've already met my two idols, President Carter and George Jones."

"Stick with me kid," Willie replied, overhearing the remark, "and you'll be wearing horse turds big as diamonds."

IF YOU'VE GOT THE TIME, HONEY, I'VE GOT THE . . .

"As far as Willie goes," his dad told the *Dallas Times Herald* in 1976, "you can see that he turned out to be right about his music, and I was wrong. I had always preached to him that music wouldn't get him anywhere."

"Well," interrupted Mom Nelson, "he always was bullheaded."

But Pop wanted to finish. "You know," he continued, "one day after all of this had happened, he came up to me and said, 'Pop, you've been right ninety-nine times out of a hundred, but I just got lucky.' "

Today Willie owns in Austin: fourteen downtown acres including an eighty-unit apartment complex, the 1,700-seat Austin Opry House, and the Backstage Club, a listening room/bar; he owns just outside Austin: the seventy-five acre Pedernales Country Club and Recording Studio (with golf course, Olympic-size swimming pool, state-of-the-art recording studio, and several condominiums), plus a forty-four acre ranch equipped with a $750,000 limestone ranch house, barns, and horses.

In Colorado he owns: a three-story Swiss chalet on a mountaintop outside Denver and a one hundred-acre ranch west of Denver, site for a $185,000 four-bedroom house (1977 price).

In Nashville he owns: the two hundred and eighty-five-acre farm at Ridgetop with a cozy log house nestled in the hills.

In California he has: an apartment on the beach at Malibu (where Linda Ronstadt and others of such ilk reside).

Throughout the world he collects money from: Willie Nelson Music (containing most of his songs written since 1970), the writer royalties on all his other songs, his own record label called Lone Star Records, a recording contract with CBS (paying royalties on all the gold and platinum albums), royalties off Willie Jeans, live performing fees, and movie royalties.

Then there are the tour buses, tractor trailers, Lear jet, Mercedes, and various other little extras.

Well, as Willie says, "I have all the material things I need, and a couple I don't."

On the road these days life is high, wide, and handsome. When Willie played Harrah's in Reno, his suite, accentuated by a baby grand, had a picture window overlooking Nevada, and a bedroom, up a flight of stairs, overlooking California. Everything in the room, except six huge pillows, was done in beige and crystal—the sofa, the fireplace, the chairs, the thick carpet, the magazine rack, the bar, the stereo system. As Willie chatted with a man in a business suit down in the living area, a maid appeared from the kitchen-dining area in the loft of the split-level suite. "Dinner is served, Mr. Nelson," she announced.

Last year on a date in Florida, Willie mentioned he had spent the previous day playing golf. It only surfaced later that he had been playing in *Austin*, where he had been whisked in his Lear jet to relax from touring, putting around on his very own golf course. After appearing in Florida, Willie again boarded his private plane and jetted across country to Denver.

When Willie and Connie first moved to Austin from Ridgetop, they lived on the ranch outside town near Dripping Springs. Their big, white-stone ranch mansion has a large entranceway with tall wooden double doors graced with lovely glass panels. The house overlooks Barton Creek, and one wall of the living room is all windows looking out across the backyard to the wide, lazy creek.

In 1977 Willie made $100,000 worth of improvements on the house. In one room a bronze Texas armadillo spits a steady stream of water into a jacuzzi as stained-glass flamingos stand in a peaceful semicircle and watch. Pictures, paintings, posters are everywhere. Decorating highlights include a grand piano in the den, a three hundred and sixty-degree fireplace, a bar, a French-style phone, and a chair made out of polished steer horns.

A big barn sits close to the house and Willie, an avid horseman, keeps some horses on the ranch, but remarked a few years ago that he seldom rides them because "they're getting to be as old as I am, and they really don't like to be ridden."

As Williemania intensified through the mid-'70s, it became harder and harder for Connie to stay at the ranch while Willie was on the road. "Friends," would drop by and stay on for days. Fans would drive out and ogle the place.

In defense, Willie built an enormous security barrier around the property that gives it somewhat the look of a minimum-security work farm. A high stone fence with barbed wire strung along the top blocks the property from the road, and huge metal gates and a cow catcher stand guard over the drive. If you want in, you pull up next to a stone post with an all-weather speaker mounted in it, push a button, and announce yourself.

On her own, Willie constantly gone, Connie felt besieged and harassed, and in the summer of 1977, she and the girls moved to Colorado. There was an immediate uproar—Honk-if-you-love-Willie was deserting Austin.

Asked if he was abandoning Austin forever, Willie replied, "Why sure, there's just too many Mexicans down there for me." Then he chuckled, "Next thing, they'll be saying is we've gone and drained the lakes, too."

Complementing the three-story Swiss chalet outside Denver, the house in resortlike Evergreen is well situated for serene skiing and mountain jogging. That house has 5,000 square feet, two and three-quarter baths, and three moss rock fireplaces. The house was situated on twenty-five acres, and Willie also purchased an adjoining sixty-four and four tenths vacant acres.

The apartment in Malibu is in the same building where Booker T. Jones (of Booker T. and the MGs) and his wife (sister of Rita Coolidge) lived while he and Willie were working on the "Stardust" album.

Although Willie and Waylon first started talking in 1976 about jointly purchasing the abandoned Pedernales Country Club to house a luxurious recording studio outside Austin, in a series of on-and-off deals, Willie alone finally bought the almost totally dilapidated building and grounds for $300,000.

After holding two picnics on the site, and after deciding Colorado didn't suit him as much as Texas, Willie started fixing the place up in 1981 — to the tune of hundreds of thousands of dollars. The seventy-five-acre complex, opened in late 1981, is breathtaking.

The old country club restaurant, overlooking the swimming pool, has been converted into a recording studio. Still intact in the elegant studio are huge former dining-room windows, through which one looks across the swimming pool for miles into the distance, and which frame Lake Travis stretching eighty miles through the rolling hills.

The complex includes a golf course, the pool, a jogging track, a jacuzzi, tennis courts, and facilities for hang-gliding and trail bikes. Housing on the site includes condos for studio personnel and assorted members of the family, as well as a three-bedroom tract house for Willie, stuck right against a water hazard on the golf course.

Oh yes, the forty-four-acre ranch. Mom and Pop lived there for a while; Lana lives there on and off — just whoever needs it. Bobbie's son, Freddie Joe, lives in a little cottage at the entrance to the Ridgetop farm. The log house is reserved for Willie when he's in Nashville.

"Earning enough money these days so that I don't have to worry about the kids makes it a lot easier," Willie understates to the hilt as he buys new cars for all his kids and diversifies his investments at an exponential rate.

Under the new presidency of Chips Moman, a hit pop and country record producer (who designed the Pedernales Studio), Willie is even reviving his Lone Star Records label.

First started around 1975 as a subsidiary of CBS, who quickly became disenchanted, Lone Star Records moved to Mercury around 1978. "Willon and Waylee" by Don Bowman was the first release, and Willie also signed Larry G. Hudson, Steve Fromholtz (writer of "I'd Have To Be Crazy"), Cooder Browne, the Geezinslaw Brothers, and Ray Wylie Hubbard, all Austin acts.

Lone Star Records was an attempt to give these artists the total artistic freedom Willie had wanted so long for himself. But, in a replay of Willie's RCA career, Lone Star never got off the ground. Mercury, Willie said, in words sounding like a description of his own records, "wasn't sure what to do with the music or how to classify it." The label folded, but is back on the burner as a priority now.

Willie Jeans, on the other hand, took off like a horse on a fast track. Hitting the market in August, 1980, Willie Western Wear debuted jeans, announcing upcoming shirts and sweatshirts. (At one point,

Willie even endorsed sunglasses which he dispensed in great quantity from the back of his car.)

Willie Jeans, back pockets emblazoned with guitars, Texas maps, tennis shoes, double barrel shotguns, etc., sold 575,000 pairs the first three months alone. Willie's cut was fifty cents each.

But under heavy kidding and criticism as a designer outlaw, Willie became disenchanted with the under-thirty-dollar jeans. "I think they're made too cheap and cost too much money," he announced the following year. "They're going to have to upgrade the material a little bit, or I'm not going to lend my name to it anymore."

Then in 1980, he returned to his high-school days' passion—sports. But this time it was Willie handing out big bucks, not trying to win small-time scholarships.

Through friend and movie star James Garner, he acquired an interest in a Dallas NBA expansion team. One of the twenty-four unlimited partnerships was estimated to have cost Willie a cool $932,000.

Orchestrated by Willie's manager, all these business dealings are carried out by an army of specialized lawyers—one for movies, one for records, one for song publishing, and so forth.

Willie has made good money since the early '60s, when his songwriting royalties started rolling in, but back then he hardly thought once about slinging his money around. Now he's taking a look, and taking it twice.

"For forty years," Willie told *People* as early as 1976, "I was living on borrowed money, and I didn't care, because I couldn't come close to paying it all back. Now I'm getting to the position where I can pay it all off, and where I used to throw away hundred-dollar bills, now I'm bitching about nickels."

So, with his new-found sense of fiscal responsibility, does the old outlaw know how much money he's making these days?

"No," he replies.

Well, who does?

"The IRS," he grins. "That's what Tom T. Hall says. If you want to find out who the Entertainer of the Year is, check with the IRS."

SOMEWHERE OVER THE RAINBOW

By the time Willie was ready to shoot Honeysuckle Rose, a remake of the classic *Intermezzo*—the film of a star-crossed romance between an eminent older violinist and a young piano teacher that made Ingrid Berman a star—would-be actresses were clamoring for Bergman's role.

Gossip columnist Suzy's columns were twittering over the contenders. Linda Ronstadt was seriously considering the role for her movie debut. Tanya Tucker, Debra Allen, and Rita Coolidge were all dying to play the young musical protégé. Shirley MacClaine, Loretta Lynn, and Emmylou (until she got pregnant) were being considered for the wife's part.

Willie's career on the silver screen had certainly kicked off with considerably more luck than he had experienced on the electronic screen of TV. "I don't like myself on television so much," declared Willie who's never done well projecting himself on TV, except on the tastefully produced, artist-oriented "Austin City Limits" series.

"TV's just a bad picture as far as I'm concerned,"

Willie says, exposing the dislike many recording stars have, but never express, for television. "The speakers aren't big enough. The sound is bad. And the screen's too small, you can't see the whole band.

"You've got to stand right there, look at this camera, you're subject to too many producers and directors," and then, insult of insults, "people sit there in their living room and criticize you for free."

All that's enough to make a singing cowboy ride off into the sunset—and charge admission. Which is exactly what Willie had been dying to do ever since he was a boy sitting in a dark movie house rooting for Red Ryder, Whip Wilson, Lash LaRue, and all those guys.

Willie talked about making a movie as early as 1977 when he announced he would play a•bounty hunter with Kris Kristofferson and Glen Campbell in a film called *Gone to Texas.* Apparently that project went to Texas and didn't come back.

Then one night Willie was visiting at CBS producer Billy Sherrill's house in Nashville and met a good-looking blond—Robert Redford.

Redford was in town trying to round up some country singers to do a benefit for his environmentalist Citizens' Action Committee.

Bob and Will hit it off "pretty good," Willie said. In fact, they flew back to California together, and in fact, Redford asked Willie if he'd like to get into the movies. Willie said sure, and Redford just nodded.

In a few weeks Redford was on the phone offering Willie a part in *The Electric Horseman.* With Redford's credentials, Willie quickly accepted. "By the time I was asked to be in movies, I was over forty years old," Willie once explained, "and I knew if I was going to be in a movie now, it was going to be a good one. It was too late to start being in any bad movies."

But in his first screen role, Willie didn't get to play a singing cowboy. It was a straight part, a guy with a job something like Poodie's or B.C.'s or Snake's—making sure his boss, a retired rodeo cowboy who stayed drunk a lot, showed up for work on time.

But Willie did get credit for delivering the movie's most outrageous line. Asked by another character what his plans were for the evening, Willie ad-libbed: "I'm gonna get me a bottle of tequila, a Keno girl who can suck the chrome off a trailer hitch, and kinda kick back." The crew broke up laughing, and, to Willie's surprise, the line stayed in.

"I just play myself," Willie said of the part of Wendell. "I just do all the lines and the reactions the way I would do them normally."

As one critic put it, when Willie plays himself, he's totally convincing "in somewhat the same way Harold Russell (a handless amputee) was in his role as the handless amputee in *The Best Years of Our Lives.*"

Willie's fellow actors—real professionals—praised him for his realness in front of the camera. "He has a built-in sense of truth," the director said.

"Country-music people have a certain homeyness about them," Willie offered, "and that's what they told me it takes to make a good actor—honesty."

Although he didn't sing in the movie, Willie did sing on the soundtrack album, *The Electric Horseman*. It was his fifth album in 1979 and included fine versions of "Midnight Rider," "My Heroes Have Always Been Cowboys," and other saddling-up songs.

Actually, the hardest part of movie acting seemed to be not performing with the band for the ten or twelve weeks filming lasted. "I go crazy," he said about not getting to play, "making music is an exercise I need to stay healthy."

Following the release of *The Electric Horseman*, Willie was asked if he was on the way to becoming another Kristofferson — a big movie star who's not all that good an actor and who doesn't write songs anymore. Willie professed to not quite understand what the reviewer was getting at.

Actually, his notices were excellent, and suddenly country music's Entertainer of the Year was favorably linked with the heaviest of names in tinseltown.

A lot of talk cropped up about making a movie of Willie's life, or making a movie of "Red-Headed Stranger," either or both starring, of course, Robert Redford.

"He hasn't said no," Willie said of Redford playing the Red-Headed Stranger. "He's read the script and he likes it, and he wanted to read the second draft. Now he's read that, and I'm just waitin' to hear from him, yes or no."

Redford, yes or no, must have been busy with the Citizens' Action Committee, because the next thing that came along was Willie fixing to be his own star of his own movie, *Honeysuckle Rose* — not the story of his life, but close to it.

Originally titled *Sad Songs and Waltzes* after one of

389

Willie's finest songs, the starring prizes of *Honeysuckle Rose* went to Amy Irving, as the young musical protégé, and Dyan Cannon as the wife. Slim Pickens played Irving's father.

Willie played Willie (alias Buck Bonham). Heavily reworked to fit the musical life style of a country-music star on the rise, the script, Willie said, had something for everyone, "especially pickers."

How close was Buck to Willie? "Probably real close, to me and every musician," Willie granted.

Most of the filming was done around Austin, a good bit, in fact, right on Willie's ranch. A veteran Hollywood publicist pronounced the set "one of the loosest" he'd ever been on.

Extras would line up in Willie's front yard for their noontime box of Kentucky Fried Chicken, while Willie would sit in a trailer parked in the driveway studying the spectacle.

Everybody from Dyan Cannon on down to the lowliest Hollywood grip was trying to get into this Texas thing. As one onlooker put it, "all the crew people are trying real hard to look like Texans, and everybody else looks normal."

"I'd never heard of Willie Nelson before the movie," admitted Cannon. "Isn't that shocking? I had to go out and buy one of his albums to find out what he sounded like. But then, wham!"

Equipment trucks were festooned with "Honk If You Love Willie" bumper stickers. Director Jerry Schatzberg ("Seduction of Joe Tynan") was wearing a Willie Nelson hat and belt buckle. Amy Irving started playing a black Stratocaster, and Cannon started talking about making a country album. And the whole atmosphere on the set looked like Willie was doing Warner Bros. a favor by letting them throw a movie at his house.

As for Amy and Dyan, they spent a couple of weeks "working their asses off," Willie praised, "learning to do what we've done all our lives.

"Now," Willie said, "I've got to turn right around and do what they've been doing all their lives."

Carrying the lead role in a major film is a different can of worms than doing a bit part in the shadow of Robert Redford, but Willie seemed to slide in easy.

Willie mostly compared acting to singing. "There's a certain rhythm involved in delivering lines," he suggested, "whether you're singing 'em or speaking 'em."

"I always told myself," Slim Pickens cracked, "don't work with kids or animals. Now I'm going to add guitar players to that list. When that son of a gun says something, it sounds so natural, like he's the first one ever to use that particular phrase."

"Willie was much less insecure than a lot of people I've worked with," commented Schatzberg. "He is less temperamental and he *listens*. He may have been a little apprehensive during his first dramatic scenes, but once he started going, oh boy, he just took over!"

At one spot in the filming, things got very realistic. In the scene where Dyan Cannon comes on stage to announce she's divorcing Buck, the audience, many of whom knew Willie is married to a blonde, thought the scene was for real. They started booing Cannon off the stage—that stayed in the movie.

Honeysuckle Rose (the title crops up just once, on

the mailbox of Buck's ranch) was released to enormous hoopla, with premieres in both Austin and Hollywood.

Willie drove himself to the Austin premiere, but stepped out of the car sporting a new pair of Willie Jeans, a "Honeysuckle Rose" T-shirt, and a dark cowboy hat.

After the premiere, Willie, the walking billboard, and his classy limousine-borne guests repaired to the Willie-owned Austin Opry House for a spread of ham hocks, crowder peas, and cornbread chunks.

The West Coast premiere was staged at famous Mann's Chinese Theatre in Hollywood. Rita Coolidge, Arte Johnson, Emmylou, Rodney Crowell, and super car salesman Cal Worthington all arrived in limos. This time Willie showed up, just in time to take a seat, in genuine faded Levi's and an Adidas T-shirt.

The after-show bash was held on the western set of a movie lot in Burbank, where tuxedoed waiters served canapés along fake dirt streets and boardwalks. Commented one nostalgic Willie buddie: "I remember when they used to throw beer bottles at him at Gilley's when they liked him. Now Hollywood's throwing parties."

Willie was impervious to those who accused him of selling out. "Sounds like a lot of jealousy to me," he brushed questions off. "I don't think there's a guitar player in the country who wouldn't go to Hollywood and make a movie, if he were asked. If there is, I'd like to meet him. He's an idiot."

Despite the fanfare and millions poured into advertising, *Honeysuckle Rose* opened to lukewarm reviews and mediocre grosses. The script was poorly received, dubbed nothing more "than a Nelson concert held together by the skimpiest semblance of a plot," or scathingly put on a par with an episode of "Gilligan's Island."

Although Willie stated he had a lot of input into the movie, working closely with Texas friend and screenwriter Bill Witliff, Witliff later told *American Film* that "I sure don't want to take the blame for 'Honeysuckle Rose.' Jerry Schatzberg had preconceived ideas about what life on the road was like, and refused to see the reality of it."

Despite the film's floundering, advance orders for the soundtrack album exceeded advance orders for any Willie Nelson album.

The album also rescued Willie from critics who had been sniping at his failure to include any new self-penned songs on three previous years' worth of albums.

Willie admitted that "my songwriting has suffered a bit recently," and now that Hollywood had replaced hunger, "I really have to sit down and push myself to write. I go for months when I can't write my name," he quipped.

Harlan Howard explains the syndrome well. "The Frizzells, the Ernest Tubbses, all those people wrote their own early hits," he told writer/historian John Lomax. "Once they actually achieved stardom, very few of them managed to write class songs. The thing is that all are really good writers . . . but, you've only got one little brain, and once you get into show biz, a band, and a routine, tours, movies, and everything, why it certainly cuts into your creativity."

Willie contracted to write six or eight original songs for *Honeysuckle Rose*, and as filming neared, hadn't done a one.

One day, on a flight from an Atlanta concert to Austin, Schatzberg told Willie that unless he wrote some songs, the movie wasn't going to have a shot at an Academy Award.

In a few minutes, Willie pulled out his plane ticket and started scribbling on the back. The scribbling was the 1980 Grammy award winner for Best Country Song: "On the Road Again."

Despite the indifferent reaction to *Honeysuckle Rose*, Willie was hooked. He said he might even want to try some directing.

Pursuing further projects, he cemented forces with Witliff, a screenwriter whose Texas-soaked scripts tend to delve into the concept of the family.

Willie had first been impressed by Witliff's made-for-TV movie, *Thaddeus Rose and Eddie*, the story of two old Texas bachelors who avoid families and responsibilities by drinking and chasing women. Their moment of truth arrives when they finally realize they need the security of lasting relationships.

The Raggedy Man which Witliff wrote for Sissy Spacek deals with the strength of a young Texas mother abandoned by the elusive father of her two boys. Witliff originally conceived *Honeysuckle Rose* as the story of a man forced to choose between two families: an adolescent family (the band) with which he can escape responsibilities, and a real family which needs his attention and commitment.

A few months after starting *Honeysuckle*, Willie

asked Witliff, if he had any other scripts lying around. He did—his very first.

"Willie," Witliff recalls, "literally stuck his finger in the middle of the script, opened it, read two pages, closed it, and said, 'I want to be that guy.' "

The character was Barbarosa, based on an old Anglo, whose ears had been cut off as punishment for stealing cattle; Witliff's grandfather had met as a kid back in the 1890s.

In the film, Barbarosa desperately desires to be part of his Mexican wife's aristocratic family, but they shun him as the despised gringo who has corrupted the family blood. Three generations of the family try to kill Barbarosa, but all fail. Eventually, he becomes the yardstick by which the entire family measures itself—he's at once their quarry, pride, and purpose.

Willie stars as Barbarosa in the film and Gary Busey co-stars as the Anglo's pal.

Barbarosa is just one of a mass of celluloid projects. *The King of Texas* will dramatize the story of Willie's life. *The Songwriter*, which he plans to do with Kristofferson, is like *The Sting*, Nashville style.

Willie also made a cameo appearance in *The Thief* with James Caan in the fall of '81 and Witliff and Willie have repurchased the *Red-Headed Stranger* script from Universal Pictures.

"Universal thought Robert Redford had to be the red-headed stranger in order for a western to have a chance at the box office," Witliff said. "Willie and I bought it back, because we have a lot of faith in the story, even without a big star."

Willie still suffers from picking fever when he's

stuck on a set for months emoting in front of a movie camera, but he declares movie-making is nowhere as rough on the old body as twenty one-nighters strung out on 2,000 miles of highway. As he grinned after wrapping up *The Electric Horseman* — "bein' a movie star sure beats workin'."

THE JAZZ SINGER

It's seven o'clock on a July evening in Abbott, Texas. On the curving street that leads into town, grandmothers in calico sunbonnets are out in cool, green front yards watering the grass as the blazing red sun sinks to the horizon.

The mayor of Abbott, a short friendly man in a cowboy hat, remembers Bobbie and Willie Nelson were "nice kids," not shy just "country, you know." Bobbie, he says, used to play piano over at the school, but he's not sure whatever happened to her.

Mr. and Mrs. McKamie still live nearby. In the '40s Mr. McKamie was superintendent of schools in Abbott, and Mrs. McKamie taught Willie fifth grade. Mrs. McKamie burned the gravy on Thanksgiving Day a few years ago when she heard Willie on TV singing the national anthem.

Around a curve and across the railroad tracks, Main Street is totally deserted. The stores, the surrounding fields, the cotton gins are empty—not a soul in sight.

The barber shop is closed for the day. Inside the

dim windows everything looks about like it did the day it opened fifty years ago, just a few years before Myrle Nelson Harvey left town. Old U.S. maps are thumb-tacked to the walls. An open Bible lies atop a yellowed train schedule in reach of a now-antique barber chair. On a faded, chipped Coca-Cola sign, Zippy invites you to take "the pause that refreshes."

Abbott . . . so peaceful, so serene, so respectably shriveling into a smaller and smaller leaf . . . so easy to comprehend these sane small-town lives . . . until . . .

Here they come. Heading in from the opposite side of town, a dusty old clunker (like rich folks drove before gas went so high) is chugging this way. Muffler backfiring, it gradually rattles on by—a young black man driving, a raw-bone white woman snuggled at his side.

Suddenly, from an intersecting road, two well-worn sedans come swerving up Main Street. From down the tracks the fast-approaching roar of a freight train rises; the engine's whistle blasts. The black- and white-striped bars of the railroad crossing jerk down.

Bumper to bumper the cars screech on their brakes, cut sharp to the left, floorboard up on the tracks, cut sharp to the right, zig-zagging in dead pursuit through the closed barriers, a hair's breadth ahead of the onrushing train.

Abbott—now only three hundred and forty strong—still can't keep 'em down on the farm.

At this very moment their favorite son is luxuriously encamped in glittery Las Vegas, name up in lights at the Sahara Hotel.

398

It's not the Nite Owl, but it's the night life, and Willie Hugh Nelson is still up on stage . . . still improvising, still going with the feel, still playing it the way the moment moves, still in every way—the jazz singer.

Most of his dreams already dreamed, he's only got three tough questions these days (1) can he really act? (2) can he hold his third marriage together? (3) can he keep his health?

In the summer of 1981, in Hawaii, after jogging seven miles, Willie plunged into an icy swimming pool and suffered a collapsed lung. It was a frightening blow to a man who's been in better health in recent years than he was at thirty.

Darrell Royal once went and rented Willie a locker just to try to get him into running. "He couldn't even make it around the four-forty," Royal says.

For years Willie badly abused his body—heavy smoking, heavy drinking, drugs, too many one-nighters on the road—sometimes staying up for three days straight.

"I could see myself disintegrating before my eyes," Willie admits.

Now, down from a chubby one hundred eighty to a trim one hundred fifty, he relishes challenging fellow jogger Kris Kristofferson to marathon running duels on the slopes of Hawaii.

One vacation, Willie, Kris, and Willie's manager ran the seven-and-a-half-mile round trip from Waikiki to Diamond Head three times in one day. Kris didn't make the third loop. "He crapped out on the third," as Willie put it with competitive glee.

The day after those three successive circuits, Willie flew all night from Hawaii to Los Angeles, arrived at six P.M., got off the plane, and immediately started looking around for a likely place to run.

Running has cut down on Willie's smoking (regular cigarettes) and drinking. He's just lost the desire for it. "I found that when I started running I cut down on my drinking," he says. "And I don't go for nicotine anymore. One drug leads to another. I start drinking, and I want a cigarette. Food's the same," he's decided. "It's a drug. Coffee is the worst of all."

Occasionally, though, he'll still tie one on with tequila. "I don't know why I drink so much tequila," he asked one bleary-eyed morning. "It sure makes me drunk as hell. Come to think of it, that's why I drink it."

Part of Willie's running is meditation—arms flung out, controlled bursts of breathing—a regimen designed to cleanse body and soul.

But Willie's not solitary when he runs. He'll visit—with almost anybody who comes along. "If I feel like stopping and talking to people, I will," he told *Country Style*. "The other day a guy stopped me. I went in his house, drank a beer, smoked a joint, and took off!"

Long an outdoorsman, Willie still thoroughly enjoys swimming, skiing, horseback riding, and above all, golf. Willie, Royal says, is about an eighteen-handicap golfer.

For the past nine years they have hosted a celebrity golf tournament benefiting the Boy's Clubs. The last one was simply called the "Darrell/Willie."

400

These days Willie's about the biggest celebrity at his celebrity tournament, and frankly, he gets off on being a star. Do you like being recognized on the street? he was asked. "Yeah," he grinned. "I don't mind at all."

Willie's not only made it into the full-tilt Hollywood celebrity, gossip-column circuit, but he also exists in a perilous psychological atmosphere of unceasing adulation.

In addition to the reverence with which he is treated by members of the family, he's now showered with the hype awe of professional public relations types working his movies and records. "Willie is magic everywhere I go," gushed one in tones as golden as the salary he receives for uttering them.

But Willie tries to keep his boots on his roots, and his sights in line. "I'm not different from any of the other weekend cowboys," opined the wealthy outlaw in 1980. "It's just that what I do all the time, all of them can only do on weekends."

Willie's agenda, except for a brief rest following his collapsed lung, still goes full-tilt.

In 1979, the Mystic Moods Orchestra, Willie, and jazz vocalist Anita O'Day each released five albums, earning them the distinction of being the most recorded artists in their fields. (By then Willie was already sitting on four platinum albums: "The Red-Headed Stranger," "Wanted: The Outlaws," "Waylon and Willie," and "Stardust.")

Two of Willie's five were tributes to peers at the top of his list—Leon Russell and Kris Kristofferson.

In the fall of 1978 Willie and Leon took a mutual

vacation in Burbank, recorded six days and nights nonstop, and put down an incredible one hundred three songs. They released twenty on the double LP, "One for the Road" and had a number-one hit with "Heartbreak Hotel."

Citing Kris as a "poet" who is "virtually unknown these days as a songwriter," Willie recorded nine of the best known songs from Kris's catalog on "Willie Nelson sings Kristofferson." The single "Help Me Make It Through the Night" soared up to number four.

Both albums went gold, as did a two-record set recorded live at Harrah's, "Willie and Family Live," and a Christmas album titled "Pretty Paper," after his old Orbison smash.

Although *The Electric Horseman* got critics off his back about not writing songs, still, all the Stardust stuff, and duo albums, and tribute albums were beginning to make reviewers yawn.

"Will his future albums be nothing more than revivals of old favorites?" Mick Martin asked in 1979. "Are the rock hits of the '60s next?"

As Lester Bangs insists, classic country music skates along on an edge of danger "accruing from songs reflective of lives in some way lived close to the psychotic edge where every action is at once overwhelmingly profound and queasily absurd."

Living miles back from the psychotic edge, unmoved by the critics' despair over his lack of same, Willie moved next, not to the rock hits of the '60s, but to the country hits of the '50s.

1980 brought "San Antonio Rose," another duet

album, this time with his old boss Ray Price. Produced by Willie in Nashville, the album stayed on the charts for over a year, and the single, "Crazy Arms," climbed up to number sixteen.

Price, who Willie simply said is "one of the voices I think everybody has to hear," was ecstatic over his revived career, promptly bought two new Rolls-Royces, and reported he felt "like a bride on her wedding night."

Musically, 1980 and '81 seemed to be years for Willie to complete cycles bringing his past into his present. Later in 1980, he and Bobbie drove over to the little Garland studio, just the two of them, and recorded an album dedicated to Mama Nelson. Willie sang old gospel songs, Bobbie played piano, and they named it "Family Bible."

In '81 he harked back into Houston days and recorded an album with another old boss, Paul Buskirk. Cut in two nights at Mickey Gilley's studio in Houston, the album has no drums, just two rhythm guitars, bass, fiddle, and lead guitar.

A tribute to Django Reinhardt, "Somewhere Over the Rainbow," is a delightful LP, containing tunes like "Little Red Wagon," "I'm Gonna Sit Right Down and Write Myself a Letter," and even an instrumental of "Twinkle, Twinkle, Little Star."

Although critically well-received, the sparsely produced album didn't sell very well, and in late 1981 CBS rush-released "Willie Nelson's Greatest Hits."

That collection almost totally ignores the pop classics Willie has reintroduced to his public in recent years. Only "Georgia on My Mind" made it onto the greatest hits—everything else shrewdly goes back to the lucrative country-rock, outlaw sound.

The Fourth of July picnics aged with time and became yesterday's wine.

After pseudo picnics in 1977 and 1978 in Tulsa, Dallas, and Kansas City, Willie held the last two friendly affairs on the grounds of his own Pedernales Country Club outside Austin. The final picnic, featuring a large balloon emblazoned with "Honeysuckle Rose" coasted down to a public relations man's purr.

In 1981, Willie didn't have one. "It's just too much," he said with a shrug. "Takes six months before and six months after, before we're done." Just too many lawsuits, Willie added. Besides, he didn't want to keep inconveniencing his neighbors out at the country club.

His albums, his marriages, his fortunes do all truly seem to move in circles and cycles, and it often seems that nothing is permanently lost.

Willie keeps seeing his old RCA albums reissued and rereleased, hitting higher on the charts than they ever did during the days he was on the label. He and Martha are good friends. Shirley was last seen in Nashville bringing some new songs to the offices of Willie Nelson Music.

Even the tapes he believed burned in the fire at Ridgetop, turned up. Mom and Pop Nelson found them while sifting through ashes in the basement, and after doctoring up, they were released on the album "Face of a Fighter."

The family itself is in a perpetual process of reincarnation—new roots springing up as old deep-seated ones wither and die.

Showing where Willie inherits much of his vitality,

Mama Nelson lived to be ninety-five, before she passed away in a rest home in Fort Worth in 1980.

Pop Nelson, a fun-loving, unassuming man, who took great pride in Willie—and all his children—died in 1978, at age sixty-five, of bone cancer.

Willie's mother Myrle, now in her late 60s, apparently still lives around Yakima, Washington where she cherishes among her mementos a gold album of "The Red-Headed Stranger," given to her by Willie.

Myrle, evidently, sometimes regrets not having a larger role in her famous son's life. A few years ago a woman placed a long-distance call from Washington to the *Austin American-Statesman* announcing that she was Willie Nelson's genuine mother.

"I feel like the Mona Lisa," she complained spiritedly. "I'm Willie Nelson's mother, and that other woman is getting all the credit!"

That "other woman" and Pop Nelson ran Willie's Pool Hall in South Austin, until Pop's death. Although Mom protested she had never been in a pool hall in her life, they papered the walls with Willie photos, letters, posters, and mementos; put a horseshoe pit out back; started serving Mom's famous chicken and dumplings; and turned the place into a money-maker.

Still attractive and exotically dark-haired, Lorraine, who calls everybody "honey," lives in an apartment owned by Willie, with Doyle's son, Lonnie. The modern apartment is filled with Willie mementos, a large oil painting of Pop playing fiddle, and a huge trophy topped by a crown that reads "Queen of Willie's Pool Hall" in glitter.

All of Willie's children by Martha have grown up to

have dark-skinned, black-haired Indian good looks.

Lana, now about twenty-seven, has four children of her own, and helps Willie run the Pedernales Country Club. A couple of years ago, she spent a year and a half sorting through family photos late at night while her kids were asleep, putting together the *Willie Nelson Family Album* as a present to her dad for his birthday.

It's a lovely, moving tribute, laced together with songs that tell Willie's life. Paul English tooled the leather cover.

Susie's even closer to her dad since her husband was tragically killed in a car accident, and she frequently calls Willie on the road for advice, although she jokes "he's always out jogging when I call!"

Billie plays some guitar, writes songs, and travels on the road with Willie.

Paula and Amy go to school in Colorado where Willie boasts they are "real smart. Every home should have an Amy," says doting Willie, who likes to kid around with big sister, Paula.

Paula will wander in during an important interview. "Go away, I'm busy," Willie says.

"Why can't I stay?" she demands.

" 'Cause you're a little ol' girl," Willie replies.

"Well, help me carry something," Paula says, exploring a new tactic.

"I can't," Willie groans back. "My legs are broke."

The whole family, related and otherwise, gets together at least three times a year: twice a year when Willie plays Lake Tahoe, and on Christmas or New Year's Day when he plays the Summit in Houston.

But even these days wandering Willie doesn't always

make his shows in a Mercedes or jet. On the way to a press conference at the Superdome in New Orleans, Willie's bus broke down in Oklahoma. The bus couldn't be fixed, so he started hitchhiking. He got a ride with a truck driver, but the truck broke down, too. At press conference time, the National Guard and Oklahoma Highway Patrol were out looking for Willie.

As long as it's fun, Willie says, he'll keep going. His idea of the perfect life? "Do a tour with the band, then take a vacation, then do a movie, then take a vacation, then do another tour. That would be the ideal situation," he says, "especially if, during the movie, you could still do a few concerts."

Has he still got things he wants to do? "Oh, there's one Holiday Inn in Beaumont" he's never been to, he grins.

Actually, he might get the urge to go to Australia, or Japan, or Iran, he says. Then there's some more albums on the burner. Let's see . . . one with Ray Charles, and B.B. King, and Les Paul, and Rita Coolidge, and Carl Smith, and Hank Cochran, and Webb Pierce (no, take that back—he's just done it), and Dolly and Emmylou and Linda Ronstadt and Crystal Gayle and Mary Kay Place and . . . "I'd like to do a tour sometime with me and about thirty girl singers," Willie proclaims. "That way, when the night's over, all the girls won't be gone."

Willie's still looking ahead, still improvising, still navigating by feel, still mentally, spiritually, and musically—the jazz singer.

He doesn't repudiate his past feelings and instincts, says he really wouldn't do anything different, just maybe a little faster.

"I've seen lots of people, including friends," he reveals "who work all their life for something, and then blow it. Once they make it, they're afraid of losing it.

"One thing that has helped me is that I've had so many ups and downs in the last thirty years, that I've learned to live with both. I've come back from a lot of failures."

JUST AS I AM

The University Baptist Church in Austin is an affluent, respectable congregation, nestled close to the multimillion-dollar towers of the University of Texas. Here, comfortably set, heaven-bound Southern Baptists faithfully attend services and conscientiously fulfill their three-times-weekly obligation to God.

In 1975, the minister, about forty-two years old and a friend of Darrell Royal's, got the unorthodox idea of inviting Willie Nelson to participate in a Sunday-night church service.

Although he had darkened few church doors over the past twenty years, Willie was intrigued, and said O.K.

Arriving in tennis shoes and T-shirt, Willie sat up on the podium with the preacher. He brought his guitar, and Bobbie came, too, to play piano.

Willie was supposed to sing some songs, and the preacher, deeply elated over this public meeting—this reconciliation, he hoped—between organized religion and outlawry, had prepared some questions.

After cordial introductions, the service began.

"How did you envision Jesus as a boy?" the preacher first asked.

"Well," Willie remembered and smiled, "we had pictures of him."

"Where do you think you would find Jesus, if you were going to look in Austin for him today," the preacher continued.

Willie paused, observing the congregation sitting in stately pews below and in the big white balcony above. "I think you might find him at the Armadillo World Headquarters," he replied simply. "It would have been a good spot, and he would have enjoyed it."

No one gasped, but the reaction of the conservative Baptists was unclear. Then Willie sang. After his first song, the sedate congregation burst into loud applause—right in church. And each time Willie sang a familiar hymn like "Amazing Grace" or a song like "Family Bible," they would applaud. Willie was obviously elated—and moved by this unexpected acceptance.

"What do you think about God?" the preacher continued. "Well, he's somewhere up there above Jesus," Willie offered. "We are the image of God—or he's the image of us. I'm not sure which," he hesitantly added.

Then with obvious pleasure, he reminisced about his boyhood, about sitting on his front porch in Abbott listening to the Christians sing, about how he'd "been to church a lot of times" that way "without going."

"I live day to day, one day at a time," he explained of his nomadic ways to the stable, well-established Christians. "I've always moved around, because I like to move. The human race," he observed, "is a moving thing."

Well, the preacher gingerly proposed, hadn't Willie in his day been accused of being a bit "loose"?

"I've been accused of being a little loose," Willie frankly admitted, then added with conviction, "I believe in looseness, too."

In that case, the preacher wondered, what would Willie consider a sin? Willie responded vaguely.

What, in his mind, is wrong? the preacher more boldly probed. "A person can answer what is right or wrong for themselves," Willie finally assured the preacher with quiet confidence. "If they think long enough, they'll come up with the answer."

With each song that he sang, and each round of joyous applause from the congregation, Willie was obviously becoming more deeply moved and inspired by this reunion with the roots of his childhood.

He told of his confrontation with the Metropolitan Baptist Church in Fort Worth; remembered the days of his first hit, "Hello Walls"; and even regaled the assembly with the tale of Ray Price and the rooster. "I used to tell Ray Price I owed him a lot of money for an education," he joked. "I'd just look at him and do the exact opposite."

As the service neared its end, Willie, eyes heavenly bright with the memories and the moment, began softly singing with Bobbie playing gently behind.

"Just as I am . . . without one plea . . . but that thy blood . . ." The congregation spontaneously joined in, sweet and low, and Willie's voice faltered, ". . . was shed for me. . . . Upon thy promise I believe . . ." Willie choked out the words, "Oh, Lamb

411

of God, I come to thee, oh . . ." Willie was no longer singing. His guitar slid slackly into his lap, and tears streamed down his rough, bearded cheeks.

For years acutely tuned to her brother's most subtle emotional change on stage, Bobbie leaned into the keyboard and the beautiful, pleading strains of Mama Nelson's girl, playing "Just As I Am," backed by a whole congregation singing softly in unison from pews below and balcony above, filled the huge auditorium. In a time, Willie was able to pull his guitar to his chest and lead the final words, "Just as I am . . . I come to thee . . . Oh, Lamb of God, I come . . . I come."

There was no applause. But into the poised silence, the preacher introduced one more question.

How, he gently asked, would Willie want the world to remember Willie Nelson?

Willie, eyes glistening with tears, looked at his interrogator. The congregation sat, waiting, still as a band of angels paused in flight.

"Just tell them I meant well," he quietly answered.

•

THANKS . . .

To Tom Lindley, who shoulders the parts I find hardest, and lends me the strength to carry on;

To Chuck Schwartz, who anticipates what I need before I even know;

To Bill Littleton, a veritable encyclopedia and indubitable friend;

To Townsend Miller, Darrell and Edith Royal, Bob Allen, John Lomax, Kirby Warnock, Phil York, Martha Scott, Skip and Larry, Miriam DeMaro, Dr. Thomas S. Johnson, Chet Atkins, Biff Collie, Hank Riddle, Doyle Riddle, Eloise Riddle, Mrs. Ben Parker, Mrs. Ira Nelson, Joe Nick Patoski, Sam Borgerson and Jesse, who I hope to see one of these days.

To the fine folks around Abbott: Virginia Sullins, Greg Gant, Tom Fajkus, Frank Clements, and Agnes Marak.

To the excellent staff of the Country Music Foundation Library: Ronnie Pugh, Terry Gordon, Danny Hatcher, Bob Oermann, Kyle Young, Sharon Polling, and Missy Palmer.

To these writers whose writings shed great light on country music: Bill Malone (*The Smithsonian Collec-*

tion of Classic Country Music), **Doug Green** (*Country Roots*), and Paul Hemphill (*The Nashville Sound*).

To Willie for chronicling his life in song (many of the chapter headings in this book are derived from songs written or sung by Willie Nelson).

And to Terry Woodford, who has taught me many special things over the past four years, but most of all the meaning of that sign in the Willie Nelson General Store: MAN NEVER FAILS, HE ONLY QUITS TRYING.

.

YOU WILL ALSO WANT TO READ . . .

THE SANCTION (775, $2.95)
by William W. Johnstone
After thirteen years, the Army decided that it didn't need the use of Jim Prince's killer instincts anymore. Lost and alone, he searched for love. But the Army had made a decision about that as well. . . .

THE SIN (479, $2.25)
by Robert Vaughan
Leah's sensuality drove men wild: too wild. And she used it unmercifully on everyone—even after she was murdered!

ACT OF LOVE (735, $2.50)
by Joe Lansdale
They were crimes of lust, cold-blooded murders. And each time, it was an act of love. But this was something the victims would never know. . . .

LAST OF THE DOG TEAM (736, $2.50)
by William W. Johnstone
Kovak was the perfect patriotic killing machine—murdering on the government's command. But there was one command Kovak couldn't obey: the command to stop!

WITHOUT MERCY (847, $2.95)
by Leonard Jordan
Cynthia liked working in the flesh trade in New York's Times Square—until the night she left the Crown Club with the wrong man. . . .

Available wherever paperbacks are sold, or order direct from the Publisher. Send cover price plus 50¢ for mailing and handling to Zebra Books, 475 Park Avenue South, New York, N.Y. 10016. DO NOT SEND CASH.

FIRST-RATE ADVENTURES FOR MEN